MONSTER
HUNTER
MEMOIRS

SAINTS

BAEN BOOKS by LARRY CORREIA

THE MONSTER HUNTER INTERNATIONAL SERIES
Monster Hunter International
Monster Hunter Vendetta
Monster Hunter Alpha
The Monster Hunters (compilation)
Monster Hunter Legion
Monster Hunter Nemesis
Monster Hunter Siege
Monster Hunter Guardian (with Sarah A. Hoyt)
Monster Hunter Bloodlines
The Monster Hunter Files (anthology edited with Bryan Thomas Schmidt)
Monster Hunter Fantom (anthology edited by
Martin Fajkus and Jakub Mařík) forthcoming

MONSTER HUNTER MEMOIRS
Monster Hunter Memoirs: Grunge (with John Ringo)
Monster Hunter Memoirs: Sinners (with John Ringo)
Monster Hunter Memoirs: Saints (with John Ringo)
Monster Hunter Memoirs: Fever (with Jason Cordova)

THE SAGA OF THE FORGOTTEN WARRIOR
Son of the Black Sword • *House of Assassins*
Destroyer of Worlds • *Tower of Silence*
Graveyard of Demons

THE GRIMNOIR CHRONICLES
Hard Magic • *Spellbound* • *Warbound*

DEAD SIX (WITH MIKE KUPARI)
Dead Six • *Swords of Exodus* • *Alliance of Shadows*
Invisible Wars (omnibus)

NOIR ANTHOLOGIES (EDITED WITH KACEY EZELL)
Noir Fatale
No Game for Knights
Down These Mean Streets

Gun Runner (with John D. Brown)
Target Rich Environment (short story collection)
Target Rich Environment, Vol. 2 (short story collection)
Servants of War (with Steve Diamond)

To purchase any of these titles in e-book form, please go to www.baen.com.

MONSTER HUNTER
MEMOIRS

SAINTS

Larry Correia &
John Ringo

Monster Hunter Memoirs: Saints

A Baen Books Original

Baen Publishing Enterprises
P.O. Box 1403
Riverdale, NY 10471
www.baen.com

ISBN: 978-1-9821-9383-6

Cover art by Alan Pollack

First printing, July 2018
First mass market printing: July 2019
First trade paperback printing, December 2024

Distributed by Simon & Schuster
1230 Avenue of the Americas
New York, NY 10020

Library of Congress Control Number: 2018022289

Printed in the United States of America

10 9 8 7 6 5 4 3 2 1

As always

For Captain Tamara Long, USAF

Born: May 12, 1979

Died: March 23, 2003, Afghanistan

You fly with the angels now.

And

Sir Terence David John "Terry" Pratchett, Kt, OBE

April 28, 1948–March 12, 2015

I hope the Reaper liked his portrayal.

For what hope is there but the Care of the Reaper Man?

ACKNOWLEDGEMENTS

While I was writing these books, the great English fantasy author Terry Pratchett passed away.

There have been many great words spoken about Terry. I cannot really add to them. I can simply say that his passing was a great loss to the written word, to SF/F and even to SF/F fandom. For various reasons, my reading (as noted in a previous acknowledgement) has dropped off sharply since becoming a professional author. Pratchett was my comfort read. He was always there for me when I needed to escape both the mundane world and the worlds in my head. Because his worlds were even more rich and textured. And oh-my-God were they funnier!

If you have never read Pratchett, you're wrong. My suggestion is pick up a copy of *Guards! Guards!* and start there. There are some of his works that are lesser (I detest *Sourcery* personally) but the same can be said of any author. (Ahem. *Ghost.* Ahem.) However, do start with his earlier works. Learn the background of the Witches (*Equal Rites*) and the Guards (the previously noted *Guards! Guards!*) And Death. Oh, my, Death. Only Pratchett could have made Death himself an approachable and even humorous figure. One of the best novels I've ever read is *Reaper Man,* followed closely by *Hogfather.* I'm sure that when the Reaper came for one of modern English's greatest authors, he had a few words to say. Hopefully they were "liked your books."

If you have read Pratchett, I hope you like the occasional less-than-subtle homages in this book. I'm still trying to fit in the Librarian but I think that might be in a later book.

—John Ringo

We wrote about how the MHI Memoirs novels came about in the previous acknowledgements. It isn't often that you get surprised by a really successful author saying "Hey, I wrote a bunch of books in your universe, want them?"

The hard part for me was tweaking things to fit the rest of the Monster Hunter universe, while trying to not change John's vision or voice. Editing is tough. To me, writing is easy and fun while editing is hard work. So I just want to say I couldn't have done this project without the help of our excellent editor and publisher. So thank you, Toni Weisskopf, for putting up with us.

And again, I want to thank John for creating the memoirs.

I hope you guys enjoy this one.

—Larry Correia

MONSTER
HUNTER
MEMOIRS
SAINTS

PROLOGUE

You know that feeling when the worst is over? When you realize you might just live through this? For anyone who's reading this who isn't a Hunter (and how the hell did you get your hands on this book?), say you've just been in a car wreck. Everything stops crashing and you realize you're still alive. Uninjured even. Relief floods your body like a physical force.

That was what we were feeling right before a slime and tentacle covered Rottweiler literally came through the fucking wall and tore into one of the drillers. It kept shaking the guy even though he'd dropped stone dead as soon as it bit him.

I just opened up the spout on the fire hose and hit that Rottweiler bastard with a full-power blast of holy water. It began rolling around and shrieking.

"We're surrounded," Sam Haven said from behind me.

"Cut the water!" Milo yelled to Boss Shackleford as slime ghouls started piling through the nearest hole. "I need to go flame on!"

"Fuck this!" I shut off the valve and dropped the hose. "Flame on, go hot!"

I lifted my 203 and launched a grenade. The round hit a ghoul in the head and the explosion shredded the undead around him. But it wasn't stopping the tide. The dark god's tentacles picked them up like puppets on strings and put them right back in the fight.

I realized I was surrounded by a nimbus of light. Looking over my shoulder, I saw that Father Ferguson had his cross raised above

1

his head. The undead were quailing back from it, but they were still being driven forward. The Old One did not care about their pain.

"That's got them stalled," the boss said. "Let's rest in peace these sons of bitches!"

I just ignored the M-16 part of the 203 and started laying waste with the grenade launcher. Sam was right next to me hitting the masses of undead as fast as he could reload.

Then the light started to fail.

I looked over my shoulder and Father Ferguson was sweating like a pig. "Father?"

"It's fighting me. It's pushing back against the power of God. And it is quite powerful."

I recalled the fragmentary scroll I'd discovered, which had eventually led us to the truth about this monster, *Even the power of Buddha was insufficient against the monster of the deeps.* While Father Ferguson had a lot of faith, he wasn't more powerful than an Old One. Even a larval one.

"We've got to hold this rig 'til it's dead!" All I knew at that point was we had to keep killing as long as it took. As long as we lasted. "We can't give another inch!"

The undead were pressing forward, a solid wall of red eyes and grasping hands. When they got under the range we could fire grenades, we switched to kinetic but 5.56 barely pisses off wights. The vamps had their fangs out. I looked down and there was a fucking Siamese cat with enormously long incisors. It looked like a baby saber-tooth tiger. I think it might have been a fucking *cat* vampire. A vampire cat. Was that even possible? That was just too wrong to begin to describe. It was even sort of cool looking.

It was just at the edge of arming range for the 203 so I blew it away with a 40mm grenade.

They were getting down to hand-to-hand range and I drew my sword from the sheath. Maybe this was the battle for which the Lord had returned me to this vale of tears. At least it would be a battle to tell Saint Pete about.

As the undead closed in, I started servicing hands and arms first. Keep them from grabbing me, keep them from grabbing the Padre. Whenever I could, I slashed through the slimy cords tethered to their backs. Once severed from the Old One, the undead were quickly destroyed by the ward stone.

But there were just too damned many of them.

"We're about to be overrun," Boss Shackleford said, pulling out a grenade. "Seems like now's a good time to see the other side."

As he said that, there was a sound like thunder. A low, deep, rumbling followed by the blast of a horn. It wasn't your normal horn. It was a terrifying sound that struck right into the bowels and said, *This is evil. Run.*

A massive gate opened in the floor of the warehouse and with a crackle of Fey energy, a Wild Hunt erupted in all its eldritch horror.

How bad of a day are you having when a Wild Hunt showing up is a *good* thing?

You might be wondering how I got myself into this predicament.

I blame, well, myself. Fully. This was unquestionably entirely my fault.

My name is Oliver Chadwick Gardenier. Call me Chad.

This is my job. I'm a Monster Hunter.

Note:

This is the last of the three memoirs Albert found in the archives. They'd been in the section damaged during the Christmas Party incident of 1995, and lost ever since. I hadn't even known these things existed until Al brought them to me. Heck, I was surprised Chad had ever written anything other than stuffy academic papers for Oxford or strongly worded letters to congressmen.

What you are holding in your hands is the complete manuscript. The version we'll eventually put in the library—that any regular newbie could just wander in and read—is going to have a few bits redacted for obvious reasons. Like secret identities, or any parts where the company might have kind of sort of accidentally broken the law and worked with PUFF-applicable entities, that sort of thing.

Chad wrote these so that future Hunters could learn from those who came before. Except obviously he couldn't tell the story to the end. I started writing an afterword myself, but I just couldn't do it. It brought back too many memories and I ended up standing in front of the memorial wall for a long time, reading names. I'm going to show these memoirs to Earl Harbinger. He and Chad didn't always get along, but I think he needs to be the one to finish the story. People need to know how it ended. Iron Hand deserves that.

Milo Ivan Anderson
Monster Hunter International
Cazador, Alabama

BOOK ONE

Embrace the Suck

CHAPTER 1

In primus, I quit.

Ray III had called. Happy Face was inbound. It was two days after Mardi Gras and I was finally going to get some reinforcements. I told them I'd be in the office and the door was open.

I was in Trevor's office behind the desk, pushing all the paperwork involved in a Class Four event, when Earl walked in with a really closed expression. Sometimes you gotta do another contract even when you know the shit was probably going to hit the fan. Right? MCB's Special Response Team was in town. How bad could it be?

I was the only survivor of Team Hoodoo. Every other member had died on Fat Tuesday, along with all the regular field agents of MCB, New Orleans, and most of the Sheriff's Special Investigations Unit. *That's* how bad.

Team Happy Face, Earl's team, heavy hitters for Monster Hunter International, the MHI elite, our designated SWAT, had been chasing down a pishtaco in Peru while the rest of my team had their skulls cracked and their brains sucked out. When New Orleans was already out of control and it was Mardi Gras, they'd taken a contract out of the country and left us hanging. Earl should have known. He should have been there.

I'd told Agent Myers, regarding the incident that caused him to leave MHI, "Sometimes, shit happens in this business. Get over it."

Those words burned now. Shit had happened. Generally, I got over it. I'd blown my best friend's head off to save him a long, lingering, death. New Orleans had seen a bunch of Hunters come and go, most of them dead. I was at the point of not bothering to learn their names.

But Fat Tuesday had been a bit much. I was done. With some help, a lot of help really, I'd handled all the arrangements. Remi, my "gentleman's gentleman," had handled shipping the urns of the recently deceased to their families—those that had them. Trevor's and Fred's were sitting up on a shelf in the team shack. Madam Courtney had arranged the funeral procession. Most of the time I'd been writing reports and filling out PUFF paperwork.

Then there was the government. The Monster Control Bureau agents I'd worked with for a year were dead. We'd fought together, worked together, partied together in a way that was unique for both MHI and MCB. I understood why they did what they did. I didn't like it. They didn't like it. Nobody liked it. It was brutal and awful...and it was necessary. New Orleans was the test case for when the First Reason no longer worked.

I'd had one meeting with the incoming MCB replacements. That hadn't gone well.

I'd had to go back to the site of the incident. Most of the bodies had been cleared up thanks to the efforts of the Louisiana National Guard, but we were still finding the fluorescent mantis shrimp when they started to smell. Most of the waterfront in the French Quarter was closed off. Tourists were still in town and trying to find out what was happening.

I was talking to a National Guard lieutenant, thanking him for ensuring Shelbye's gear got returned, when Captain Rivette walked up with a couple of MCB agents.

Rivette was the head of the NOLA Sheriff's Special Investigations Unit, SIU. Heavy-set, balding blond hair, fifties, watery blue eyes. He spent as much time in his office as possible and never, personally, got anywhere near hoodoo if he could avoid it.

"Iron Hand. This is Special Agent Phillip Campbell and Agent Jack Robinson from MCB. Special Agent Campbell, Agent Oliver Chadwick Gardenier."

"Call me Chad," I said, holding out my hand. It was covered in some shrimp goo.

"Mr. Gardenier." Campbell was medium height, black hair, sharp eyes, real slick. He looked at the hand then back up but didn't extend his. "Quite a mess you made here. This is going to be hell to cover up."

"Okay." I dropped my hand. "You want to play it that way, that's fine. We kept a Class Four from turning into a Class Five when it hit the parade live on national television. But if you want to blame the heroes instead of, you know, whoever raised these things, you can feel free. Dealt with that sort of shit from MCB most of my career. Also seen your kind come and go from New Orleans when you fucking *crack*."

"I am not going to crack, as you say," Campbell snarled. "I also am not going to allow the sort of unprofessional behavior that Castro considered normal. Be clear on that. We are going to shut down supernatural outbreaks in this town. New Orleans *is* going to be brought to heel. And so are you."

"Good luck on that," I said, nodding. "Be glad to see it. The town brought to heel. Especially given that I've already had to bury a bunch of my people and still have more to take care of. Cutting down on our casualty rate would be nice. Like to know how you're going to do that in this town, but if you do, more power to you."

"For one thing, no more out of control response. No more use of explosives when something less obvious can do. And no—let me repeat, *no*—use of light antitank weapons! I cannot believe you weren't charged for that in the first place!"

"Yeah." I shook my head. "Not going to listen to you on that one. Especially given how many we've lost even *with* 'out of control response.' And before you bow up and explain all the hell and damnation you can bring down on my head, be aware that I'm better friends with the people who pay your salary than *you* are. And if it takes taking a trip to DC to explain why you have to use a LAW on something two stories tall that regenerates, I'll take that trip. Or a Barrett on a giant, regenerating superfrog. Or C4. Or claymores, 'cause *I'm tired of burying people, you useless fuck!*"

That initial exchange would determine the future course of my working relationship with Special Agent Campbell. It didn't go well.

"You use language like that with me again and I'll have you charged!"

"Then fucking *charge me*, Boy Scout." I walked away. "This is *your* problem not mine."

So that's why when Earl Harbinger walked in, I just stood up and waved at the desk.

"All yours," I said. "I quit."

"Chad," Ray Shackleford had followed Earl into the office.

"Don't." I walked around the desk and to the door. Ray was blocking it. "If you don't mind?"

"Let him go," Earl said. "It's okay. Where you going? We're going to have to send you the check."

"I've still got the house. Send it there. Now if you'll excuse me?"

As I walked by the team room, Milo was there. Milo Anderson was one of my best friends. Probably my best living friend.

"Chad..." Milo looked pained.

"Nice knowing you, Milo." I walked out.

Remi had already made the arrangements. I had two weeks scheduled at a Sandals Resort in Jamaica. I'd asked Points, Cheryl Collins, if she wanted to go. I knew it was a mistake. She'd take it as a sign I wanted to expand and improve on the relationship. I didn't really care.

I have a really firm belief, reinforced by Ash Wednesday when I'd cremated all my brothers- and sisters-in-arms, that nobody in this business should have close attachments. No kids. No spouses. Not even serious relationships. I was to the point of not even wanting to have *friends*. Because about the time I got to liking somebody, they up and died.

Plenty of people disagreed. Susan Shackleford, Ray IV's wife, was not only beautiful but a fairly serious breeder with three kids so far. The fact that a little later on she died in her thirties, still beautiful, and leaving behind those three kids and her grieving husband sort of makes my case.

I'd met Points, so called for "points all her own, sitting way up high," not long after I'd gotten to New Orleans. She was a waitress and aerobics instructor by actual profession but "professional cheerleader" by avocation. Brunette, slender, brown eyes, great legs and very nice chest. Incredible ass. We'd been an off-again, on-again thing ever since. But I'd always been real clear about not having any serious relationship. And when she hadn't believed me I'd slept with her best friend to make the point.

Was that a nice thing to do? No. Was it better than leaving behind a grieving widow and orphans? Yes, in my opinion.

So I'd always kept it light. I was good in bed; she generally had a good time. I was even up for the occasional shoulder to cry on and the one time she'd gotten into a really bad relationship with a seriously fucked-up stalker, I'd convinced him he needed to find someone else to stalk.

Dangling upside down in a tree with a bunch of shamblers under you all night will do that.

But she was going to see going away for two weeks as an upgrade in the relationship. I knew that. What I wasn't sure, at that point, was if it was or not. Because I really had quit. And if I wasn't a Monster Hunter anymore, things like real relationships were a possibility.

Two weeks at Sandals sort of cured me of a lot of illusions.

First of all, any idea how *boring* a place like that is?

There are any number of fun activities at a Sandals Resort! Just ask their promoters!

1. Sit on a beach getting sun! Ever woken up on a beach, sunburned, screaming about giant spiders? People look at you funny.

2. Go swimming! Ever fought a luska? I hadn't but I'd heard about them. Every time I looked at the water, I wanted to have my guns with me. People look at you funny when you go swimming with an Uzi on your back. Not that I *had* my Uzi. I didn't have *any* weapons except a little pocket knife. It was terrifying. For three years I'd been heavily armed at *all* times.

The time I killed a loup-garou while out *jogging* had convinced me that the *real* reason for the Second Amendment was the Founding Fathers knew damned well there was supernatural and wanted their citizenry prepared. I'm surprised it didn't read "For the purposes of a well regulated militia, the right to keep and bear arms, especially loaded with silver, shall not be infringed."

3. Go shopping. Cheryl certainly loved that aspect. I was so full of PUFF money I could probably support her shopping habits for some time. But not indefinitely.

4. Party all night long! There was dancing! Calypso bands! Let your hair down! That I sort of got into. Drink enough you can sort of forget black shadows in a cemetery tearing you apart while zombies closed in. Or fluorescent mantis shrimp flying through the air to crack your skull open. Spiders bigger than a

mammoth. But they always came back when you were dealing with the hangover.

5. Screwing. They don't specifically mention that in the brochure but it's implied. Did a lot of that. But no matter how hard I screwed, I could not get the image of fluorescent shrimp pouring up the side of a bell tower to take out Shelbye.

6. Talking. Again, not specifically mentioned in the brochure. It was, however, the last point that made it clear Points and I weren't suited for anything longer than, say, a few hours now and again. We had exactly nothing to talk about.

Look, I am, God help me, an intellectual. I may have hated that fact growing up and fought against it but it is nonetheless true. I have a doctorate from Oxford in linguistics. I wrote the first definitive work on North American Yeti (Sasquatch, Bigfoot). I wrote the dictionary and linguistics text on their language. I wrote the dictionary and linguistics text on North American Gnoll as well as an analysis of their social structure here versus that of Europe and England. Ditto Swamp-Ape, Florida and Louisiana tribes, and Laurentian yeti. I do third-order polynomials in my head.

Assuming I was going to quit and get a real job—what *is* a real job?—and settle down behind a white picket fence, it would have to be with someone I could carry on an adult conversation. That wasn't Points.

There were other guys there. From time to time we'd all cluster up to get away from our airhead girlfriends, fiancées, wives (some of them were on honeymoons) to have *guy conversations.*

I can talk about football. It's not my favorite topic but I sort of keep up when I can. Hell, I've got fifty-yard-line season tickets for every Saints game. Not that I used them personally. Who had time? I traded them for favors. I can talk about stocks and bonds. Commodities is something of a specialty when I have the time to focus. I can talk about portfolios; I have one and keep up with it. I can definitely talk about girls and screwing the couple of times we went out deep sea fishing. I've got a million stories along those lines though I had to sort of dance around the subject of trailer park elf girls. I can play poker. Hell, I could be a professional poker player. It's a matter of being able to do the odds in your head and knowing when to fold.

The problem I kept running into was...Let me do this properly.

"Hey, Tom," Keith said. "This is Chad."

Keith Brown was one of those guys that instantly knows everyone and does all the introductions. He worked in Corporate Relations, which he'd had to explain to me. Basically, it was schmoozing bigwigs from other corporations to smooth out deals. Corporation A, his, wants to get Corporation B to go in on buying a big piece of property. Could be another company, could be real estate, whatever. Keith's job was to know everything possible about the likes and dislikes of Corporation B's movers and shakers and make sure they had a good time while the negotiations were going on. Something like that.

He could simply not get out of mode at Sandals. So he instantly introduced himself and in three minutes knew everything about you. Well, except me. I was sort of an enigma on some stuff.

"Tom," I said, shaking "Tom's" hand.

"Tom's a broker with Morgan Stanley in the City. Chad is a former Marine and . . ." Keith paused and frowned.

"I do classified security work. As in violence security, not 'securities.' Mostly associated with federal and local governments. Some corporate."

I've got a hooking scar on the left side of my face courtesy of a loup-garou. My nose has a cut through it, right on the bone, from a shotgun pellet. The side of my neck is stitched like Frankenstein from another pellet that's still lodged against my esophagus. You wear shorts and short-sleeved shirts at Sandals. Mine was a Team Hoodoo polo. I'd had to have it made, they weren't issue. Embroidered MHI on the chest with a shrunken head. So all the scars on my arms and legs were exposed. Between the bombing and my job, I'm a baby-faced, blond, short, muscular Frankenstein.

"Looks like you've seen a lot of action," Tom said, shaking my hand back. He was a pretty big guy, iron pumper, crusher grip.

I crushed back harder. He winced. I had much the smaller hands and they sort of look fine. They're not. He probably should have noticed the Popeye forearms.

"Beirut bombing among others," I said, finally letting him go.

At which point, we would talk about Tom's job. Because . . . classified.

Or I'm pigging out on shrimp.

"You really seem to like the shrimp, Chad!" Keith would say.

"Just trying to get the little bastards back," I said, popping another one in my face.

Yeah. Only Points got that and she sort of flinched. She knew outside of New Orleans you didn't talk about hoodoo. She hadn't been there, thank God. She'd been uptown partying with some linemen from the New Orleans Saints. But she knew what had happened. It wasn't like you could keep a secret in New Orleans.

Do I pick up a finance degree, put on a suit and go get a job in the City? I'm one of those guys who with a couple week's study could pass any bar you'd care to name. I've got beaucoup contacts. I could get any job I'd want to do. Be a Monster Hunter lobbyist in DC and run with the big dogs?

I missed killing monsters.

There is a feeling you get. There are no words to express the real meaning of *victory*. English lacks the verbs and adjectives for the emotions. There is no cool deal, no great win in court, no power play that would ever equal standing on the carcass of some powerful dead thing you'd just defeated.

What are the joys of a man? A strong sword in the hand. Check. A field of victory. Check.

To see the bodies of his enemies slain. Oh, yeah.

I was ragingly pissed off at MHI. I felt like they'd left us to hang.

But it was like I told Myers when he was getting all billy-bad cop. Shit happens in this business. Getting pissy 'cause something went wrong meant you needed to go find another line of work. Go live behind a picket fence and think that will protect you from the things that go bump in the night.

There's a saying, don't remember who said it: I have loved the stars too fondly to ever fear the night. I have loved the night too fondly to ever fear the stars. And the night I loved the most fondly was the night where bad things were creeping through it and I was the thin line between light and darkness, between life and death, where I was the baddest motherfucker in that dark valley.

I was a Monster Hunter. I was a stone killer who missed the rush like a heroin addict misses horse. Once an addict, always an addict. I could get a job in the City. I could pretend it wasn't real.

But I would always be an addict. It was all I would ever be, could ever be. Maybe, someday, I'd retire. Maybe, someday, I'd find some young thing who wasn't a steel-bellied airhead and settle down. Buy a castle, stock it with heavy weapons and raise some seriously fucked-up kids who were just as stone killers and would probably rebel by becoming monster advocates.

Someday. But not today.

Remi met us at the airport. I dropped Points at her apartment with the promise I'd call her. Which I did. A couple of weeks later.

Then I had Remi drive to the office.

"Hey, Milo," I said, walking past the team room again.

"Chad?" Milo said, getting up. He was in armor and on call.

I just waved and walked to the office. Earl was in there, smoking like a chimney, clearly furious about the paperwork.

"I refuse to be the team lead," I said without preamble.

"Got it." Earl didn't really show any reaction. "Franklin's already taken over as team lead so no problem. Milo, leave us alone. And close the door . . . Sit down, Hand."

"I'm just a Hunter. All I'm ever going to be."

"I wasn't going to ask you to be team lead anyway. Shut up and sit down." Earl opened a drawer and pulled out a bottle. He poured some for me into a coffee cup and shoved it toward me. "Drink and listen."

I'd drink. Don't know if I'd listen.

"I'm going to say this once. I know you're mad. You feel abandoned. Only we all thought things were getting back to normal, or as normal as this town can get. You had a full team, and the Feds' best elite strike force camped next door. Yes, if I'd known what would happen, I would've been here. Only I've got a few hundred other Hunters scattered across the world to worry about, and sorry, I ain't got a magic crystal ball predicting the future to tell me which ones are in the most danger. You want to hold a grudge, fine. Just don't let it get in the way of your job. So either get over it, or get the fuck out."

"Fine."

"When can you be back on?"

"Tomorrow," I said. "I've got to get my gear back in operation."

"See you tomorrow at nine," Earl said, nodding.

"Just in time for the full moon. When are you leaving?"

"I'll be in town but unavailable."

"I still say we put a radio tranq collar on you and it would work. Let you out of your cage to handle shambler hordes. Tranq you when you're done. Reload it. Put you back in the cage. Lather, rinse, repeat."

"Because I know why you're pissed, I'll let you say that once," Earl said.

"You don't realize how serious I am. I already made the collar."

CHAPTER 2

I was back on duty. Same team room. Different team. I was just getting to know most of them. A couple of faces were familiar.

Franklin Moore had been on the MHI team that responded to a zombie outbreak in Elkins, West Virginia, only to find it had been cleared by a recently discharged Marine named, well, me. Five-eight, brawny, black and unflappable. That covered Franklin. He'd taken over as head of Team Hoodoo and kept the name.

David King, aka Decay, had helped me out about a year before with some vampires. He'd joined MHI after he finished recovering from a torn-up forearm, gone through training and spent the next six months working with our New York team. He wasn't a New Orleans native but knew the town from a couple of years working as security in clubs, mostly Goth/punk. Six-four, blond but shaved scalp, which was normal in Team Hoodoo, solidly built.

The Happy Face team would remain in town to backfill us until Team Hoodoo was back up to speed...supposedly, unless Earl felt like screwing me over again on a whim. Most of them I knew, especially Ray IV and Milo.

As I walked in and sat down, Milo waved.

"Chad. Earl said you'd be back. Glad to see he was right."

"Glad he's such a fucking clairvoyant," I said.

Milo looked hurt. Earl had saved his life and avenged his family. Earl was like a dad to him. Milo was just too damned nice for his own good. Hurting Milo's feelings always felt like kicking puppies.

"I'm back. That's all there is to it. Shit happened. Time to get my game face on."

"So," Ray said. "Subject change. Susan wanted me to say thanks for Julie's birthday gift, Chad."

He didn't sound like he actually meant thanks. Sounded more like Susan had said other words.

"Did Julie like it?" I perked up. The Shackleford kids were adorable.

"Right up until we had to explain it was going to have to go to a nice farm upstate to live with all the other baby kaiju."

"Why?" I asked. "Those things take like a hundred years to grow to any size."

"Whass a kaiju?" Norbert LeClerc asked.

Norbert was another recruit from New Orleans. About a year before, we'd started to recruit through the *New Orleans Truth Teller*, the paper the MCB published that covered local hoodoo. The MCB worked very hard to cover up the existence of the supernatural. In the case of the *Truth Teller*, it was a matter of lying by telling the truth badly. The *Truth Teller* was full of misspellings, bad grammar, and things that had clearly never happened. It looked like it was published by a psycho. But embedded in it were many true stories of supernatural outbreaks. That way, if some true story filtered out of New Orleans, somebody else could "disprove" it by pointing to the *Truth Teller*.

I'd heard already that the New Breed of MCB in New Orleans had put a stop to it. But a year or so ago we'd used it to do a full-scale recruiting drive. LeClerc was one of the returnees from that campaign.

Young, black, skinny, but more muscular wiry than when I'd first met him, he was functionally illiterate and as purely street as you were going to get. But he'd done pretty well for six months on my old team in Seattle and, again, knew the town, so that was a bonus.

"Godzilla," Decay said. "Baby godzilla."

"Did you know the juveniles climb trees?" Ray said.

"Duh. It keeps them away from the cannibal adolescents."

"Have you ever tried to get a baby kaiju out of a live oak?" Ray asked.

"No. Was it funny? Did you get a home movie?"

"Oh, yeah it was funny as heck," Milo said, grinning. "We've got about two hours of video of Ray cussing up a storm trying to catch that thing. They're fast!"

"And they start breathing fire really young," Ray added, holding up his arm. "Which is where the fresh burn scars come from. Oh, and Susan wanted me to add that you owe us a new refrigerator."

"Why refrigerator?"

"It figured out where they were keeping the fish!" Milo said, howling. "And it burned a little circular hole in the bottom of the door! Climbed right in and ate everything in the fridge!"

"I'll cut you a check."

"Where'd you score a baby kaiju?" Decay asked.

"I've got friends in low places. And I didn't score a baby kaiju. I scored a kaiju egg. And painted it up to look like an Easter egg."

"We've learned to *carefully* examine *all* of Chad's gifts," Ray said darkly. "He got that one by us."

"Ray and Susan's kids say Uncle Chad always gets them the best gifts." Milo giggled. "Like those flash-bangs you gave Nate."

"You gave a kid a *flash-bang*?" Jon Glenn said.

Jon Glenn was another *Truth Teller* returnee. Heavy-set, bearded and still wearing that stupid beret. At least he'd gotten rid of the SAS badge. Seriously obnoxious, obsessive, libertarian, paranoid schizo. His abilities were proven in earning nearly three hundred grand in PUFF money before he even found out about PUFF. I'd put up with the constant diatribes about the evils of government, special interests and iron triangles for the headbanger hoodoo-killer mentality. He still was annoying.

"No," I said innocently. "Julie had mentioned that what Nate really needed for Christmas was a lump of coal. So I sent him some."

"Which turned out to be, essentially, very powerful fireworks *disguised* as lumps of coal," Ray said drily.

"I did warn you on that one. Nate's little. I didn't want him to get hurt."

"You mentioned that for coal it was, and I quote, a *little energetic*," Ray said. "You didn't say *it fucking explodes with tremendously loud bangs*."

"That is the chemical definition of energetic. You should have remembered my sole high school A was in chemistry."

"Which was, to be clear, one hell of a surprise," Ray said. "Especially in our fireplace."

"That was the point," I said.

"That's evil," Decay said. "I like it."

"I will never have kids of my own and the only nieces and nephews I might ever have are from my brother who I avoid like the plague. And assuming he ever spawns, they will be—let me make this clear—spawn. So all I've got to spoil is Ray and Susan's kids. I put a lot of thought and energy into spoiling them."

"The kaiju burned a stack of Julie's favorite copies of *Guns & Ammo*," Ray said.

"Replaceable," I said. "And I'm sure it gave her useful experience in the operation of a fire extinguisher. Besides, baby kaiju are cute."

"It was cute," Milo said. "Julie was heartbroken when Ray and Susan took it away."

"Making us the bad guys," Ray said.

"That's what parents are for. Parents are meanies. Uncles are fun. That's why I don't intend to be a parent and love being an uncle. I hope you didn't actually kill it. Not only are those things endangered, they're expensive as hell."

"We didn't. You're not the only one with contacts. We got it shipped to a kaiju island."

"There are kaiju *islands*?" Decay asked.

"Where do you think they come from?" Milo said.

"The life cycle of kaiju is breed in water, lay eggs on land," I explained. "Something like turtles. But instead of returning to the water, the young spend their first century on land. They are omnivorous and cannibalistic, which is why the very young climb trees. To get away from their older siblings. They're also hunted by various other critters. Seagulls will eat a baby kaiju. Very high death rate and the mature adults are rare and breed very rarely. Only about one kaiju in ten thousand makes it to adulthood."

"Then they eat Tokyo," Milo said.

"Only found on certain islands near the Japanese coast," Ray added. "The Japanese consider them something like gods and protect the islands where they grow. Couple of them aren't even on maps. When they're about two centuries old they go back to the water, where they are still preyed upon by bigger kaiju, great whites and giant squid. Until they get big enough to eat back. When they get *really* big…"

"They eat Tokyo," Milo repeated.

"They eat Tokyo," Ray agreed. "Almost always those are females looking for a good place to lay eggs. Tokyo Bay used to be one of their main laying grounds and the Japanese islands used to be a primary growth area. So the Japanese hunters try to drive them back into the water rather than kill them."

"And sometimes they lay eggs while stomping all over power lines. Which are worth a pretty penny on the black market."

"Which are strictly forbidden for trade by the Japanese government," Ray said darkly. "As we were reminded."

"Which are why they're worth a pretty penny." I shrugged.

"The little ones are really pretty just before they, you know, blast plasma," Milo said. "They get all glowy in blue and red..."

"Which gives you *just* enough time to jump off a branch that's twenty feet up in the air," Ray said, "and sprain your ankle."

"Big guys," I said, shrugging again. "No agility."

Earl entered the room. "We got a call."

"Oh, thank God," Ray replied.

"Shamblers in a cemetery."

"I've got it." I stood up. "You'd think this town would eventually run out of bodies..."

I was up on the wall of the cemetery, coaching Norbert in the finer arts of killing shamblers while avoiding being bit, when MCB showed up.

Be aware, before the Revenge of the Crawfish, MCB rarely, if ever, showed up for an incident. Trying to keep a lid on knowledge of hoodoo in New Orleans was like trying to deny the existence of rain in Seattle. But the new crop of agents were serious players from DC. They were going to shut down any reference to hoodoo in New Orleans and *get this town under control!*

Yeah. Right.

"What the hell do you think you're doing up there?" Agent Larry Rivera yelled.

There was a Special Agent in Charge and two Senior Agents assigned to New Orleans. In addition, they generally had a junior agent shadowing each as well as a cast of I wasn't sure how many working in the office doing background cover-up. Rivera was the new second Senior Agent along with Jack Robinson who I'd met briefly before my *vacation*. Serious player with time in the SRT and that bulky spec-ops look. He knew his job and wasn't taking any shit from hunters, by God.

"I'm shooting zombies." I personally felt that was fairly obvious. You could see the arms waving through the wrought-iron gate.

"Right up there in front of *everybody*?" he practically screamed. "You're right off I-10! There are hundreds of people just *passing through New Orleans* watching you right now! This would be a Class One event if it wasn't for your grandstanding! Now it's at least a Class Three!"

"Aware that the answer is yes, would you prefer we get down on the ground and get bit? From up here we're out of reach and—"

"*I don't care what your excuse is!*" the agent screamed. "*Don't do this in plain sight!*"

"Or what?" I asked, leaning over and shooting another shambler.

"Or I'll place you under arrest!"

So now I was in the back of a squad car, minding my own business. Great first day back at work.

Earl paid my bail for discharge of a weapon in the city limits. Remi picked me up, bland faced. I thought about the issue the whole way home.

"Remi," I said as we walked in the door, "could you be so kind as to call Congressman Terry and begin planning a dinner party for . . . ten guests? Nice one. Four days after the full moon has passed."

"The guest list, sir?" Remi asked.

"Myself, hostess. I'll need an appropriate hostess. Miss Collins won't do for this. Please enquire with Madam Courtney on that subject. Ask her to ask the loas. Congressman Randolph and whichever wife he's on. Madam Courtney and gentleman. Councilman Delon plus one . . ."

"The councilman, sir . . ." Remi said uncomfortably.

"Councilman Delon and Madam Courtney are not friends." My real estate lady was also a powerful hoodoo practitioner, White side. "I am aware. Last, Supervisory Special Agent Campbell plus one."

"Again, sir . . ."

"You doubt Special Agent Campbell will attend? That is why I need Mr. Terry."

✧   ✧   ✧

"Hey, Gary," I said.

Garrett Terry and I had known each other for a while. Two years before while handling a zombie outbreak in a small town in Washington, who should show up but the local congressman. He was from a neighboring town, had gone to school in the town zombies had just wiped out, was just read in on the existence of the supernatural, and was that pissed about everything hoodoo and how it was handled by the government.

That was when I'd gotten involved in politics. Not doing politics, working background. I raised campaign finance funds from Hunters and funneled them, via the congressman and his senior aide, Bert Kemper, to other congresscritters. I'd even testified before the Select Committee on Unearthly Forces a time or two.

Surprisingly enough, Hunters prior to my involvement had very little voice in the whole thing. I hadn't changed that entirely but I'd gotten the voice out there. There was still more money going to monster advocacy groups than Hunters, even with PUFF bonuses, but we at least had a voice and some representatives that were on our side for more reasons than the ongoing campaign money. Our lobbyist regularly pointed out that one of the reasons monster advocates were always around to schmooze was that they weren't, you know, out there fighting monsters and saving people.

"Hey, Chad," Gary said. "You never call, you never write..."

"Katie didn't get the babushka doll?" I asked, referring to the congressman's daughter.

"You got any idea how hard it is to convince a six-year-old not to talk about a magic babushka doll?"

"She can talk about it all she wants. Nobody's going to believe her."

"She wanted to take it to school for show and tell."

"That might cause issues," I replied.

"Where in the hell did you *get* that thing?"

A babushka doll is one of those Russian dolls where you open up the outer doll and there's another smaller one inside. Open that up and there's another. Mostly there's generally six. Really good ones are up to ten or twelve. The magic babushka had about sixty. All the same size instead of increasingly smaller. But in addition, all you had to do was say a magic word and they started bouncing around and singing a Ukrainian nursery rhyme about Baba Yaga. Very cool. Much better than a Teddy Ruxpin.

"I have contacts. Like one of the senior aides on the SCUF committee."

"So you must want something," Gary said.

"I need an arm twisted. I'm planning a small get-together after the next full moon. Some friends and acquaintances. Congressman Arnold..."

"Seriously?"

"You know I've made contributions."

"The guy makes Huey Long look honest," Gary said.

"Which is part of the point. I'll get him for the party. That's not the issue. He'll show up just to keep the money flowing and 'cause I set a good table. With whatever bimbo he's currently married to or shagging. Problem is Campbell."

"Name doesn't ring a bell."

"Supervisory Special Agent Campbell. MCB's finest. New boss here in NOLA."

"Problems?" Gary asked.

"I just got released from NOLA PD custody. For discharge of a firearm in city limits."

"Isn't that sort of your job?" the congressman asked, confused.

"The actual reason was I was standing on a wall potting zombies, and I quote, 'in full view of everyone.' 'Cause I didn't want to get down on the ground and get bit. Which annoyed one of the new guys from MCB here in town. When I refused to comply with his directives to put myself and my newbie partner in harm's way, he placed me under arrest."

"Oh."

"So I'd like to invite Agent Campbell to a friendly party. With a corrupt congressman who is, also, one of the senior Democrat members of the SCUF committee, which decides not only how much funding MCB gets but who gets promoted and who doesn't, a houdoun White priestess with more contacts than God, and a NOLA city council member who's a known Dark hoodoo dabbler, who is one of the congressman's main supporters."

"Chad, do you *like* playing with fire?" I could hear the unstated groan. And I was pretty sure he'd start stress eating right after this call. He never ate anything but salads when we'd eaten out but he kept a drawer full of Moon Pies in his desk.

"It's going to be a few days after the full moon. We've partially gotten the loup-garou infestation under control." And by we I meant Earl. "But the full moon, still, is a major issue every month. I think he'll be sufficiently beaten up by that he might see some sense. If not, I'll have to up the ante. 'Cause I'm not going to be told to take chances by MCB with *our* casualty rate. Not going to happen. Are we making lots of money in this town? Yep. Tons. Is it worth the casualty rate? We're on the edge of saying no, Gary. And if MHI isn't here, who's going to control the hoodoo? Some other company? Nobody is as good as we are and everyone knows it. Look at what happened in Portland. If we can't do it, who can? SIU has already been hammered. You going to permanently install an SRT? Or you just going to let the hoodoo flow and let local MCB try to handle it?"

"I understand," Gary said.

"I don't think you do. I don't think *anyone* does. 'Cause there's no one left who has the experience of *fighting this shit* in this damned city day in and day out. I know damned good and well Campbell doesn't. We damned near had a Class Five at Mardi Gras. We came within a big pile of *our* bodies of having mantis shrimp cracking Brent Musburger's skull right in front of God and everybody!"

"Yeah, I got the briefing on that. I'm sorry about your friends."

"That wasn't our fault, but the first thing Campbell did when he came to town was chew *my* ass for it. The sole fucking survivor, Garrett. That's who got his ass chewed. The guy who'd held the fucking line and saved not only hundreds of lives but kept it from turning up on live television! Because I was the only one *left* to chew their ass! Everyone else, Garrett, was fucking *dead* with their *brains scooped out*. So, I'll be *God-damned* if I'm going to take shit from some no-account, no-experience, no-guts MCB agent who thinks his only job is intimidating people! I fucking quit, Garrett. I quit Monster Hunting! For two weeks I was *done*! And if this is what we're going to be dealing with, I'm damned well not going to be fighting hoodoo *and* MCB. And neither will MHI."

"I'd heard you took a vacation. I hadn't gotten the rest of that."

"So pull whatever strings you need to pull. Twist whatever arms you need to twist, but Campbell is *going* to accept an invitation to a dinner party. And by then maybe he'll be amenable to reason. Maybe he'll realize that this isn't DC, this isn't St. Louis. This is the City of the Dead and life is short and cheap in this fucking town. Assuming you don't spend eternity as an animated corpse."

"Listen ... There's other things going on. Can you take a few days?" Garrett asked.

I thought about that for a few seconds. "As long as I'm back for the full moon. Why?"

"Seriously need a sit down. Something's come up." That sounded ominous.

"I'll call Earl and catch a flight," I said.

CHAPTER 3

I'd arranged with Earl for a couple more days, told him why, and hit the first flight to DC. Something was rotten in Sodom on Potomac. But that was usually the case.

A car met me at the Dulles and headed south into Prince William County.

"You sure we're going the right way?" I asked. I hadn't made hotel arrangements since I could do that in DC just as easy. But I generally stayed in town.

"The address I was given is in Manassas, sir," the driver said.

"Odd," I replied. "But let's see where it leads."

I'd picked up my checked guns and moved them to more appropriate places in a restroom in the airport. I didn't believe that Garrett Terry would set me up. But that didn't mean someone hadn't. If I was deep in the shit with MCB, strange things might happen.

The two-story house in Manassas was in a plain suburb. Nothing to distinguish it from a million more in the area.

The congressman's aide, Bert Kemper, was outside before the driver could get out to get my bags.

"We need to get inside," he said, looking around nervously.

"You seriously need to get your game on. We weren't followed. Unless there's a tracer."

"We just need to get inside," Bert said. "You do. Quick."

Congressman Garrett Terry, aka Gary, representative of and for the Fourth District, Washington State, was waiting in the house.

"Gary." I shook his hand.

The congressman was tall and rangy with weathered features from growing up a cowboy. He'd passed the bar and later run for Congress, but he still had that cowboy look.

"Chad," Gary said. "Come on in and get situated. We need a talk."

"Sounds like I've been called into the principal's office."

"More like we both have," Gary said, sitting down on the couch. He had a highball of scotch and it didn't look like his first.

"What's MCB doing now?" I asked.

"Not even sure it's MCB," Gary said as Bert came in and perched on a chair. "You're under investigation. We got that third-hand. Because due to my close relationship with you, so am I."

"Congressional Ethics panel?"

"Criminal," Bert said. "But we don't even know what charge."

"Oh, it's MCB. That has their fingerprints all over it. As long as it's an ongoing investigation they can keep up the smear campaign indefinitely. They don't have to charge me with anything. In fact, no charges are better than definite information. People can make up whatever charges they want in their heads. The scarier the better."

"That's what we've been saying," Bert said. "Everyone inside knows MCB is our professional weasels. This has weasel written all over it."

"We've been hitting all our usual contacts but we're not getting many results," Gary said. "There've been a lot of investigations lately and a lot of careers destroyed."

"Iran-Contra, the stuff with Good Time Charlie. Got it." I thought about it for a few seconds. "That phone work?" Gary nodded. "I take it this is a clean safe house? I'm going to have to make a lot of phone calls. Long distance."

"Should be clean enough," Bert said. "Who are you going to call?"

"Everybody. You don't charge straight at MCB and you don't shout and whine and complain. What you do is start a reverse fire. What is MCB hiding that they're trying to shut me down? What do they know that you don't know? Who's really pulling the strings? MCB's been acting even squirrelier than normal lately. I'm surprised, given all their resources, that they haven't been able to find this ring that's kidnapping and selling virgins.

Since I've been coming up with most of the leads, it's funny that they're suddenly smearing *me*. Why would they be doing that?

"I'll show them how popular they actually are. I'll start with Van Helsing. They have a great rapport with MI4. I'll get them asking those questions across the pond. I'll call everyone who MCB might have asked questions about me and see what questions they're asking. And I'll brainstorm with all of them, to let them ask the questions and get it planted in their minds. Before long, MCB will be answering so many queries about what's going on that they'll have better things to do than fuck with Chadwick Gardenier. Or his friendly congressman."

"You're evil," Gary said, shaking his head. "I like it."

"I grew up with the sort of people who do this like breathing," I said, shrugging. "Alinsky. Vilify, demonize, destroy. It's what they're trying with me. Then, Congressman, *you* get to start asking *them* hard questions. Like why haven't they found that ring? Like why monster attacks are on an uptick everywhere and they can't seem to get a root cause? Like are they really worth the money we're spending on them, since they don't really seem to be protecting the world at all? They seem to be mostly playing politics. 'Perhaps, Director, if you paid a little more attention to your job, we wouldn't be having these problems.'"

"MCB is a tough nut to crack. They've got a lot of clout in this town," Gary warned. "They've ruined congressmen before."

"That's why we start the counterfire first. Asking them now would seem to be trying to clear your name."

"And if there's a point?" Bert said. "I mean, Chad, we trust you, but what if there's a basis to the investigation?"

"Are there things to investigate about me? Sure. I work in New Orleans. The whole place is corrupt as hell. You don't get anything done there without paying people off."

"I don't think so. I looked into that," Gary said, shaking his head. "I did get it's not a corruption thing. It's a mystical thing. Supernatural. As in, you're playing the other side."

"Hmmm..." I said, frowning. "I made a deal with a Fey queen once." I thought about it for a few seconds again. "I've got contacts that are PUFF-applicable. My house was found through a houdoun priestess, but she's White side. I'm not seeing anything, honestly. But when I ask the questions, I'll see what they're asking about."

"We need to go," Bert said. "And Gary was not here."

"I've played this game a bit. Got it."

First thing in the morning, predawn, I called the Van Helsing Institute.

VHI was similar in some respects to MHI and very different in others. It was a group of paid Monster Hunters, like MHI. Differences branched out from there. For one thing, it also had a nonprofit supernatural research side associated with the Royal Society for the Study of the Supernatural. It shared its extensive collection of supernatural research, including memoirs like this one, with Oxford and the BSS. It also tended more towards, hem, "smart" Hunters versus the MHI approach of "if you don't have tattoos, you're probably not worth hiring!"

Fortunately, Dr. Rigby was available to take my call.

Dr. Rigby was a character. Crazy eyebrows, crazy hair, crazy English academic one each. Looked like Einstein crossed with Gene Wilder. More on the Einstein brains. He'd dropped out of Reading to join the Royal Navy right after Dunkirk. After getting a destroyer blown out from under him in the North Atlantic, a major came to visit him in the hospital and asked a lot of questions. Tests of memory, tested his knowledge of French. Then asked him if he'd like to do something more dangerous than guarding convoys but also a bit more interesting.

Which was how he ended up first in the Royal Marine Commandos doing cross-channel raids into occupied France, then on to working with the Resistance in France and Germany. It was during the latter period he'd started working on the supernatural side. After the war, he completed his degree at Reading and went straight into hunting.

At one point in Seattle, while recovering from major surgery, I'd gone over to England to see how Van Helsing operated and we'd clicked. Once a Marine, always a Marine or something. Also something about being able to communicate at a level above farts and grunts.

"Chad, boy, how are you doing?" Rigby asked.

"Surprisingly enough, not in recovery," I said. "We had a bit of an event at Mardi Gras. But it was one of those you either survived uninjured or you didn't survive at all. I was uninjured."

"I heard that the rest of your team was lost. My condolences."

"They fought the good fight. New business and old business. Choose."

"Old business," Rigby replied. "We have found several possible references to your mysterious burrower. Alas, the only one that we found that quite fits the description is limited in detail."

A while ago I had asked for Rigby's help to try and identify an unknown type of monster that had snatched several people from their homes in New Orleans. It tunneled through their floors and left behind few clues. We had started calling it the basement boogie, which was a stupid name, but it worked.

"Limited is more than we have. Details such as they are?"

"An ethnologist, Thomas Bowditch, studying witch doctors in the lands of the Ashanti, came upon a curious ritual. A powerful witch doctor would sacrifice slaves to what he described as a massive amorphous wormlike creature. The witch doctor professed that the emanations from the worm were the source of his great power, notably the power to raise the dead. The slaves would be chained near a 'great turmoil of earth,' then the witch doctor would chant prayers and cast herbs upon a symbol laid into the ground. The symbol appeared to be some sort of fungus rather than something inscribed. After the proper ritual was complete, the witch doctor would run away quickly. Then the worm would erupt.

"His description becomes somewhat erratic at that point. He has a clear drawing of the symbol but the drawing of the worm is mostly eyes and teeth. Were it not for his description of it as 'a loathsome white foul thing, unclean and evil,' I would say shoggoth. But white mitigates against it. The writings were first to be published in his seminal work, *Mission from Cape Coast Castle to Ashanti*, but British Supernatural Service became aware of his writings on witch doctors and forced a selective edit. We managed to find a copy of the edited portions at Oxford."

"Thank you, Doctor. That's an interesting possibility."

"I'd suggest checking for the symbol near the eruptions," Dr. Rigby said. "I'll fax you a copy of the symbol."

"Please. To my home, preferably. I'm currently out of town but I'll pick it up when I get back. And, again, thank you."

"I'd be curious to know if this is, in fact, what you are dealing with. If the witch doctor's statements are correct, that would explain the constant necromantic outbreaks in your area."

"Agreed," I said. "But that text describes a single eruption. We've had dozens."

"That's assuming this was the only such site," Dr. Rigby pointed out. "This was deepest, darkest Africa at the time. Admittedly, the Ashanti were fairly developed for the period. But it's possible there were other sites which were unknown to the traveler. He left Ashanti soon thereafter at least in part, I surmise, from horror. He's quite positive about most of the rest of the culture but not that part. So concludes old business. New business? Perhaps a bit of a tiff with the American Monster Control Bureau?"

"You've heard from them?"

"From MI4," Rigby said. "Asking various questions under the Official Secrets Act."

"About an ongoing investigation they cannot divulge."

"I suspected that was the new business. To the extent I may know, I cannot divulge the nature of the investigation. Official Secrets."

"I'm less clear on that act than similar ones in the United States. Can you divulge the nature of the questions? I am trying to determine if this investigation has some validity or if it is a fishing expedition as part of a smear campaign."

"I'll have to think about that," Rigby said. "But is there a reason for such a smear campaign?"

"I'm unsure. I have to wonder why this has come up now? If it is a deliberate smear campaign, to what end? I have been active in politics for nearly three years. They don't like that I'm it but you'd think they'd gotten past that by now. Has something happened recently? Some shift in the political winds? The only real change was the loss of most of MCB New Orleans and the replacement office head."

"Perhaps, but have there been any recent cases where your name would have come up?"

"Well . . ." I had to think it over for a moment. "There is one. We've had a systematic series of raids on homes primarily in search of virgins, where they were sold for supernatural purposes."

"The Seattle Lich," Rigby said. "We heard about that."

"I worked with the FBI a bit, which has the primary duty of investigating the nonsupernatural aspect of the case. They're stymied. Very little evidence to go on. But what puzzles me, in terms of the MCB, is that this is a *major* case. There have been over a hundred young women disappear who match the profile and those are just the *known* cases."

"In my experience, Chad, virgins are a valuable commodity among cultists. Especially those who worship the Great Old Ones. They are a vital component in many of their more powerful summoning rituals. Terrible business indeed. The MCB should be extremely concerned."

"Yet MCB seems either disinterested in pursuing it or... something. It seems...odd."

"Do you think MCB is..." Dr. Rigby paused. "You're not suggesting collusion, I hope."

"I'm simply puzzled. Maybe? They seem to be more and more hostile towards hunting. They seem to believe that if all the Hunters stopped hunting, monster problems would go away. That we are the provocateurs rather than defenders."

"That has always been an undercurrent of MCB and MI4, lad." Rigby chuckled. "If we weren't such a problem, the problem would go away. The undercurrent is that they feel are superior at Monster Hunting, even though that has repeatedly proven untrue."

"Monster events are on an uptick, so their hostility is on an uptick. I suppose the cause and effect could be there. They are more hostile because there is more work. I suppose that could be it."

"Or the hostility could be linked to the monster uptick?" Rigby said. "That, again, would assume collusion in their ranks."

"Which even I find hard to believe." I said. "Franks works there."

"Indeed." Rigby shuddered.

"So I guess the question is, returning to the main point, can you divulge the nature of their questions about me?"

"Very well. They were mostly about your relationship with your family. Specifically your mother and brother."

"Thornton?" I didn't think about my hated elder brother much. I wasn't even sure where he was living and what he had done with himself. "Mother I can understand. She's a monster advocate. A group I could see the MCB being less than thrilled about. But I have no idea why they'd be asking questions about Thornton. Did they specify?"

"Really can't say, lad. However...Your question about the virgins is interesting. That is really all I can say on the matter."

"Curiouser and curiouser."

✦   ✦   ✦

I had never realized just how many contacts I'd built up over the years.

Jesus, I had a lot of numbers.

Most of them said the same thing as Rigby. Not all of them were read in on Unearthly Forces. Those had been asked questions by mysterious men from the "FBI." My dad said there were particularly pointed questions about Thornton and our relationship. I found out from him that Thornton had joined some cult out in California called the Church of the Sepulcher. Which, come to think of it, didn't sound good at all. He also said that his answer about our relationship was a frank admission that Thornton had been a serial abuser and as far as I was concerned he could drop dead. I admitted that was pretty much the case.

Oshiro had not been contacted. The FBI did not just ask yakuza bosses questions. And our relationship had mostly been at arm's length. But they had questioned people in Saury who knew me and most of the questions related to anything they knew about my brother. Had I ever been seen in his company? Did they have times I was positively present in Seattle?

Given the number of receipts from Saury, the answer was if something was going on outside the Seattle area, I probably had an alibi. The Doctors Nelson had gotten similar inquiries. I'm sure that went over well. They purely hated the MCB.

Oshiro also said other contacts indicated that the investigators were asking about the virgin selling ring. I'd not only been on the lich case, where a previously known string of disappearances and serial killings had finally been linked to the supernatural, but also the zombie outbreak where I had met Congressman Terry. A necromancer had been collecting potential sacrifices there, and according to his last words, they were to be traded to some group called the Dark Masters. Oshiro had picked up from Tong contacts that something had the FBI ringing alarm bells about *me* and my involvement. Where they got the information, unknown and unconfirmed.

Special Agent Don Grant was the lead agent on the missing girls' case. He was in, and even took my call.

"So, I'm now a *suspect*? I suppose it wouldn't be the first time that someone who was helpful turned out to be involved. But that's also fairly rare."

"Not as rare as you might think," Grant said. "Anything else?"

"Am I a serious suspect?" I asked. "'Cause right now it looks as if MCB is using it as a smear campaign."

"That's where it's coming from is all I can say. Probably shouldn't even say that. But MCB said that you were now a suspect."

"I've got alibis out the wazoo. I don't think I was in the same *state* as most of those girls when they were kidnapped. And I was on call almost the whole time or working."

"I really can't discuss it, Mr. Gardenier."

We'd had a couple of dinners and drinks batting this case back and forth. He'd called me Chad. Now it was Mr. Gardenier. Which means he suspected I was involved somehow.

"Okay, Don. I'm not involved. Period. I'm busy as shit in New Orleans trying to keep a lid on this hellhole. MCB is crawling up my ass *and* running some secret-squirrel investigation. The job of the MCB is lying and smearing people. That's their entire job. So you can either take *my* word that I'm not a culprit or take the word of some supposedly sworn agent who spends his entire career wiping his ass with the Constitution. Just one question. What's it going to take for me to get this off my back?"

"I really can't say. Is there anything else?"

"Will solving it for you do it?" I said. "I've got shitloads of other things to do, but if that's what it takes, I'll just let the citizens of New Orleans *die* to hold your hand for you!"

"What part of 'I can't talk about this' is unclear?" Grant said. "You're a God-damned *suspect*, Chad!"

"How? Not. In. The. Same. State."

"MCB was clear. They have you pegged as part of the ring. I don't know where they got their information from."

"Well, then they are fucking *wrong*, okay?" I snarled. "Okay, fine. Get it. I'm a suspect. I am guilty until proven innocent. That's how the MCB works. Hell, that's how I work. Now I just have to find out why I'm a suspect so I can clear my name. Which is impossible if nobody will *tell* me why I'm a suspect! I get it, can't talk about it. Fine. I'll call you when you can talk to me again. Bye."

Except at some point during that he had hung up on me.

Oh, this was bad.

MCB had identified me as being part of a ring that kidnapped little girls to be used as human sacrifices. In most cases killing their entire families using necromancy and necromantic entities like wights and revenants.

There were two possibilities: Either MCB was doing this to deliberately smear me or they actually thought I was involved. Either way, my name was Mud. If it was a hit job, MCB could go right on saying they had evidence but it was part of an ongoing investigation.

MCB seriously needed an inspector general.

If they really thought I was involved, knew it for anywhere close to a fact, I'd already be in a basement somewhere either being put down, or undergoing "hostile interrogation." That didn't mean they didn't consider me a suspect. They could be letting me roam free to see where I led. Or they could not have *quite* enough proof. Or they were going to garrote me the minute I walked out the door.

Or they knew I wasn't involved and picked the worst possible case to smear me with.

Why me? More interestingly, why Thornton? Why ask people about my relationship to Thornton?

I had tried to forget I'd ever had a brother. Thornton was an unmitigated bully growing up. Seriously, horribly abusive. One of those guys who could get away with it from being just so pathological that nobody could see the evil. It was easier to never think about him.

But two... entities had mentioned him. One was when I was dead in heaven. Pete had said... What was it? It was years ago and while I was dead. "Your brother is headed in the direction of evil." Something like that. I wouldn't say "headed" so much as "got it down" based on growing up with him.

But Queen Shalana had mentioned him as well while I was taking the Harper's Challenge. "Your brother is of another faction."

The government grouped Unearthly Forces into different "factions." God was, from the POV of people like my mother, simply one faction of Outworld Entities. I doubted Thornton had found Jesus. Fey wasn't a possibility because the Queen had said "another" faction. The two cases where the Dark Masters came up both involved necromancy. Necromancy was Old Ones' magic. Not everyone dabbling in that worked directly for the Old Ones, but they went hand in hand.

So was Thornton involved in some necromantic cult?

A call to Ray confirmed that the Church of the Sepulcher had turned up on MHI's radar before. Only the full name was the Church of the Unholy Sepulcher. A sepulcher was a holding place for the sacramental items during the Easter celebration but it referred to the Old French and Latin for a tomb. So...Church of the Unholy Tomb. Satan worshippers? On the other hand, an unholy tomb was simply a tomb that contained something unholy. Or in which something unholy was trapped or buried.

Those are not dead which sleeping lie...

Assume the MCB are actually being heroes. I knew a lot of them, whatever their actions, were more duty-bound than I was. They felt like they were the only people holding the line against the End Times which would, yeah, be worse than New Orleans.

The MCB loathed magic, but I'd heard they kept "consultants" on tap for serious cases. Making a bunch of powerful sacrifices to Old Ones certainly qualified. They'd probably done some sort of reading or scrying. So why would they peg me, Chadwick Gardenier, as being involved in this ring? I wasn't, I knew that. So assuming this *wasn't* a smear campaign, how had they come up with me as a suspect? It had to be my blood relation to Thornton.

I would worry about how to deal with that later. Right now, I needed a plane. I had until sunset, Central time, to get back to work. It was full moon in New Orleans.

I made one last call.

"Remi," I said. "Have you sent out the dinner invitations yet?"

"No, sir," Remi said. "I was intending to in tomorrow's mail."

"Hold off," I said. "Something's come up."

CHAPTER 4

"God-dammit!" Agent Robinson swore. "Get these people *out* of here!"

It was just another case of New Orleans street theater. Shamblers had gotten out of Mount Olivet, because a gate had been left open, and trickled up Warrington Drive. As soon as Hoodoo Squad cleared the last of them, people started to flood out of their houses to see what was the matter. Normal primate curiosity.

Which was, apparently, illegal. At least according to MCB.

Agent Robinson was going nuts. He struck me as being the high-strung and emotional type anyway, and it didn't help there were some citizens out on their yards, or walking up and down the road, checking out the freshly rekilled zombies.

"Good shooting, sir," I said, examining the head shots.

One gentleman was Mr. Conrad Burrows of 310 Warrington Drive. Fifties, balding, he was carrying a Marlin lever action rifle, probably .30-30 by the looks of it, and wearing a bathrobe. He'd popped a couple shamblers before we had gotten here. The houses on Warrington were mostly solidly built ranch style from the 1960s. All of them had barred windows. It was apparent there'd been no additional casualties in this neighborhood.

"Thank you, son. High compliment coming from Hoodoo Squad," Mr. Burrows said.

"Will you turn off that stupid light!" Agent Robinson stormed over to me.

"Who's that asshole?" Mr. Burrows whispered.

"The government man," I warned.

"Damn it, Gardenier. what were you told about doing this in front of God and everybody?"

"You gotta go where the zombies are, Agent. When's coroner get here?"

"You'll be doing this the right way from now on! None of this getting receipts from the Coroner. Just collect tissue samples."

"One bag of ears, coming up," I said, pulling out a mesh bag.

"You should just collect brain samples," Robinson ordered.

"Not my first rodeo. Either one works as you can determine if they are all separate entities. And handing you a bag full of smelly zombie ears, which is perfectly legal and within PUFF requirements, is *so* much more fun. Care to give me the FINGr now?"

FINGr referred to the Federal Incident Number, General. We had to have that along with the Federal Unearthly Creature Code Number and Confirmation of Kill number to file for the Perpetual Unearthly Forces Funds bounty. You had to have the COK, the FINGr and the FUCCN to get PUFF'd. Look, I didn't make up these acronyms, I just had to use them on a daily basis.

"Just get the tissue samples," Robinson said, "and get your gear off. Incident is over. We don't want any questions."

"It's the full moon. I've already got another call," I said. "And you won't *have* any questions here. Maybe one or two new transplants in this neighborhood are unaware of the existence of hoodoo. The long-time locals won't say a word. Nice thing about New Orleans, most of the residents can answer your questions before you ask them and read their own riot act. Ask Mr. Burrows here if there are any new residents who have to get informed this isn't something you talk about. You're done."

"Do your job and let me do mine," Robinson growled. "If I had my way, you'd already be in one of those graves."

That sounded like he was personally offended...Robinson probably knew about the investigation. I took a shot in the dark. "Your scrying was misinterpreted."

That shot in the dark hit home.

"Who the hell have you been talking to?"

"Everyone," I said. "Including FBI. And the casting was a misinterpretation, bub."

"It's pretty hard to misinterpret that you started the ring, *bub*!" Robinson shouted. "If we had more than a reading on it, you'd be in the ground where you belong!"

"Whoa, whoa," Mr. Burrows said, holding up his unarmed hand. "What's this about?"

"Classified," Robinson snapped.

"I'm suspected of being seriously involved in a hoodoo ring," I said. "Other than that, classified. Problem being, I know I'm innocent. These guys clearly want to hang me. And they're basing my involvement on a bad spell casting."

"We don't have bad spellcasters," Robinson ground out.

"The FBI uses hoodoo?" Mr. Burrows said.

"Your wizards are for *shit*," I said, closing the trunk of my car. "There's twenty hoodoo men and women in this town would turn your wizards' hair white! Drawing a tarot card or casting the bones isn't the hard part." Now I knew what the investigation was based upon. The next thing would be finding out exactly what they'd done. "Anyone can cast dem bones, Agent. The hard part is *interpretation*. Which is *very* subject to influence. So if the person asking the questions *wants* a certain answer, like that I'm involved, they'll *get* that answer if it is even vaguely possible. I could be involved because I've had contact with the people involved. As in, *brushed elbows with them at the mall. That's all the contact necessary.* Which is why castings are *never* allowed for kill orders. *Smart* people in your chain of command *know* that. Even if you don't. Or as Abraham Lincoln once said, 'My distinguished colleague has his facts in order but his conclusions are in error.'"

Mr. Burrows let out a bray of laughter at that that had Robinson looking confused.

"Sir, you need to go back into your house," Robinson snapped, falling back on the MCB's default tactic of intimidation.

"Make me," Robinson said. "I got rights, son."

"They'll take them away," I warned. "Generally for good reason. Not in this case, but he'll spend taxpayer time ruining your life for petty revenge because he can."

"No," Robinson ground out. "No, I won't. Because that is not how I do this. But Mr...."

"Burrows."

"You're not contributing to this conversation," Robinson said.

"At least he recognized the joke. Look, Agent, I'm not the bad guy. The interpretation of the casting was wrong. If I'm involved it's because I took out a lich and one of their necromancers in Washington."

"Alpha and omega is pretty hard to misinterpret, asshole," Robinson said. "Beginner and ender. You've probably already packed it up when you found out we were onto you."

Alpha and omega? I was going to have to look into that.

"Robinson, how many more girls are going to have to get kidnapped, and how many more families are going to have to die before you quit looking in the wrong direction?"

"That's terrible," Burrows said.

"We're in a terrible business," I said.

"Gathered that," Mr. Burrows said. "This a sex thing?"

"Virgin sacrifices," I said.

"Okay, that's about enough!" Robinson snapped. "Sir, go back in your house or I'm going to arrest you as a material witness and hold you indefinitely, yes, just to be petty. And, yes, I can do it and get away with it. Gardenier, go collect your tissue samples and keep your damned mouth shut! I don't know who has been spilling their guts but I'm going to damned well find out!"

Look in a mirror, asshole, I thought.

The full moon had not been so bad. With the two loup-garou that had been turning unsuspecting people during the off-moon time gone, we'd only had about ten calls a day. Usual mess of little demons, homunculi, undead, what have you. The problem being, MCB thought this was normal and had been their usual dicks. With special emphasis in my case.

A few days later I'd sat down with Earl and Ray III and read them in. Earl was looking wasted as he usually did after the full moon. A few steaks would fix that right up.

"MCB has been asking everyone and their brother about my involvement in the virgin sacrifice ring. Part of that is they've got a casting that I'm involved. The 'alpha and omega.' I don't know why or exactly what the casting was, but that puts me squarely in their sights as a suspect. So all my usual political contacts are running for cover."

"Just like politicians to be useless when you need them," Earl said.

"Gary's doing his best but because we're closely connected he's in the crosshairs, too. The rest are, yeah, playing CYA. Problem being, MCB's going to be all over my ass until I prove my innocence. And probably even then 'cause you can't really disprove a negative. Part I don't get is my brother's name is involved as well. I haven't been able to get anything on why, there. But right now it's a whisper campaign and I'm losing. Any thoughts?"

"Pick a country without extradition."

"Not helping, Earl. Do you know what sort of casting it is based upon, Chad?" Ray asked.

"No. I tossed out a couple of possibles and nobody bit. I think if MCB was sure of my involvement, I'd be in the ground. I know Robinson wants to put me there."

"We can try to reverse engineer it," Ray said. "Figure out what they were casting for. Possibly use the 'alpha and omega' prophecy and see where it leads. We'd need a good caster."

"Magic always comes back to bite you in the ass," Earl replied.

"Sometimes you've got to fight fire with fire, Earl," Ray said, not sharing his superior's biases. "We'd need a good caster, somebody with legit skills."

"We're in New Orleans. Throw a rock. I know some good White casters," I said. "White as in faction, not race."

"You find someone strong enough, they'll be able to figure out how the MCB came to their conclusions, and then we can get ahead of them." Ray seemed to love the idea.

"I'm telling you, kids. Magic is a crutch. Hunters should only use it when there's no other choice. Trinkets and simple enchantments are bad enough, and even those let you down when you start to count on them. You've got it in your head that magic is an easy way out, but it's always got a cost," Earl said.

"*Magic* is just a terrible description for fundamental forces we simply don't understand well," Ray insisted. "It should just be another tool in our tool box. We use dangerous tools all the time—bombs, guns, no problem. The key is understanding how to use them safely. Magic is no different."

"Bullshit. Guns and bombs don't corrupt your soul and drive you insane."

"Earl, you're hung up on this superstitious, old-fashioned prejudice—" Ray said.

"Which I earned the hard way. There ain't no such thing as a free lunch."

It felt like they'd had this argument a few times already.

"Okay. Table that idea for now. Second point," I said. "Oxford and Rigby turned up a possible for our basement boogie."

"Which is?" Ray asked.

I brought out the papers Dr. Rigby had faxed to my house and laid them out. "There was an ethnologist in what is now Ghana who stumbled upon a powerful houdoun priest. The priest, whose primary power was over the undead, would sacrifice slaves to a large wormlike entity."

Ray was quickly scanning over the materials as Earl sort of leafed through them. "Sounds like a minion creation of the Old Ones."

"Shoggoth maybe?" Earl asked.

"White, gray, green," I said. "So, no. And appeared to continue underground. Wormlike."

"This is a new one to me," Ray said, frowning. "And I've never seen the symbol."

The symbol felt pretty blasphemous in itself. One of those things that even in a fax oozed evil. I wasn't looking forward to seeing the worm.

"They didn't write that either. Supposedly fungus grew in that shape. What isn't clear is how to get it to come out," I said. "There are no details on that."

"Holy water," Earl said.

"Why holy water?" Ray asked.

"Just a hunch based on that symbol," Earl said. "Assholes like to summon things like this: 'Please come forth, O Great Worm!' Then it comes out and eats the sacrifice and gives power. Pour some holy water on this and it'll come out ready to kill whatever just burned the hell out of its sign."

"I thought you'd never seen this," I said.

"Never seen this *in particular*. Worms and such coming out of the ground. But I've seen things *like* it. And if that don't work, try something else. The important thing is you offend it somehow."

"Gotta find the symbol first," Ray said.

"Got a dozen places to look," I replied.

4030 Eagle Street was the first place I'd run into the basement boogie. The house was a single-story ranch in Holly Grove near the New Orleans country club. Decent neighborhood but had the standard New Orleans locked-down-tight-with-bars thing going. Barred windows and doors in New Orleans were for more than keeping out burglars.

The friendly next-door neighbor I'd met on my first visit, with the late and very much missed Shelbye, didn't appear to be home. Which was a pity. His wife made great sweet tea.

Ray and I entered cautiously. Except for a buildup of mold in the corners, not much had changed. The place was still more or less identical. Given that the door was busted open, I'd expected New Orleans various "neighborhood association" members to have thoroughly looted it. But nothing had been touched.

Even the burglars in New Orleans didn't touch hoodoo houses.

"There's the hole," I said, pointing to the remnants of the exit point. The concrete slab had been busted wide open in a shower of concrete about a meter and a half wide. Dirt was piled up around it.

"Looks like the place has been ransacked," Ray said.

"I was thinking it hadn't changed. This is what it looked like when Shelbye and I checked it out nearly a year ago."

"And it's still closed?"

"Nobody would live here after that. Except maybe an idiot Yankee transplant."

"Well, let's see if we can find that symbol," Ray said, casting around.

"If it's under the slab, we'll have our work cut out for us. But if it's under the carpet..."

It was under the carpet. The hole was in the middle of the living room. In one corner we found the symbol under the carpet. Right next to a doll.

"Couple who lived here were older," I said, looking at the doll. "Their grandkids were visiting. Six people, four of them children, vanished without a trace."

"Eaten by this amorphous worm," Ray said, looking at the symbol. Sure enough, it was a slimy collection of spores. It was hard to tell if it had been drawn in something and then bloomed, or if it had just spontaneously grown that way. He glanced suspiciously at the hole. "I guess let's try the holy water thing and see what happens."

"Let me get the sprayer. That way we can shoot it from the door and run like hell."

We had filled a plastic weed sprayer with holy water on the way here. Most of the local churches knew Hoodoo Squad. I stood in the doorway and pumped the sprayer until it was pressurized.

"Ready when you are." Ray had taken up a position by one of the barred windows looking into the living room and drew his pistol. We weren't really sure what, if anything, was going to come out of the hole, but he was ready to put a bullet in it.

I squirted the holy water into the corner. I emptied the whole container. We had to wait a few minutes while the water ran down the cracks.

The floor began to rumble.

"Oh, it's a-comin'," I said, bounding away from the open door and over to where Ray was standing.

Bad move.

It was massive. All eyes and gray-green leprous skin and grinding teeth. "Amorphous worm" is the only reasonable description for that loathsome monstrosity that suddenly filled the living room with its foul bulk. Semitransparent, you could see alien and vile organs bulging and writhing beneath its pustulant membrane. Maggots crawling in eye sockets were reasonable and decent compared to that gelatinous unholy *thing* that erupted from the ground.

"Ugly," Ray said, trying for an Academy Award for Master of Understatement.

The blasphemous monster, denied any prey, seemed to sense us by the window. Or perhaps one of the thousands of mad, red winking eyes spotted us there. A bulging pseudopod squirted toward us.

"Run!"

The glass shattered out in a blast as we got out of the house fast. Ray hadn't even bothered to pull the trigger. It wouldn't have done any good. As we reached the dead front lawn its bulk pressed between the bars. They began to give way under its mass. The bars finally succumbed and burst forth along with its bloated flesh.

But as the wretched thing touched sunlight it quailed, roiling back and steaming under the direct light of God's sun. It could not withstand the light.

It shrunk back then with a disgusting liquescent sound and disappeared back into the tainted ground.

The street was quiet.

"Keep moving," Ray said. "It might not like sun but I don't want it coming up under us."

"I'm for that," I said, trying to stay calm. I'd seen some shit but that was fucking vile.

"Okay," Earl said after we'd finished our verbal report. "Sure sounds like some minion of the Old Ones."

I called Dr. Rigby and thank him for the tip. I was also able to give him some more details of the investigation and why I was a suspect. He was guarded in his reply but agreed to look into it. I said we'd contact him again when we had more information on this amorphous worm.

"But how do we kill it?" Ray asked.

"Them," I said. "We've had fourteen incidents of eruptions. So, how do we kill *them*."

"Assuming there's a different one at each hole, and not one big gummy worm blob thingy tunneling around town," Ray mused. He was handling this better than I was.

"Either way, my answer is Kill It With Fire!"

"Might work," Earl said, nodding. "But it would take a hell of a lot of fire. MCB will shit bricks if we burn down a neighborhood."

"Timer." Ray suggested. "We put something in there with a fuse on it, leave the offering, then get the hell out of the way."

"Pig," I said. "Put a gutted pig in the house. You can put a lot of thermite into the cavity of a pig, and I intend to pack the shit out of that sucker. Hook up a ten- or twenty-second delay on it. Hook the fuse igniter to a wire. Thing comes up, all angry again, sees the offering, swallows it. Goes back down. Fuse pulls."

"One problem," Ray said. "Assuming we kill it, we're going to need to file on it. The only previous reference to this thing is a single story from Ghana in the 1700s that might not even be the same thing. If this is a totally new entity, Treasury will have to make a ruling."

"Shit," Earl said. "We're gonna have to call the PUFF adjuster."

The PUFF adjuster's name was Harold P. Coslow, Junior. He had appeared out of nowhere when we were setting our worm trap. We'd chosen a different house in case the first worm had gotten wise. It was another ranch house, 1506 Andry Street, in the Lower Ninth Ward. The street was definitely ghetto but had the usual New Orleans crowd hanging around. Franklin had notified MCB, and they had insisted on a perimeter that held back the crowds this time.

The adjuster was shorter than me, so maybe five foot three. Hunched back. Bald head covered by an old-fashioned fedora. Shabby black wool overcoat, carefully cared for but ancient and used, which had to be stifling since it was about a hundred freaking degrees. If it bothered him it wasn't evident. Black eyes with a hound dog's expression. Worn, equally well-cared-for brown leather shoes I suspected had been rebuilt over and over again. You just knew he had a change purse in his shabby but well-cared-for pocket. He was carrying a brown briefcase that was as worn as the rest of his ensemble.

"Mr. Coslow," Earl said, nodding his head deferentially.

Earl wasn't deferential to anybody. I mean *anybody*! Who the hell *was* this guy?

Mr. Coslow looked at him for a moment and pulled a leather-bound journal from his overcoat pocket. He read it for a moment.

"Is it still Harbinger?" he asked.

"Yes, sir."

"It is difficult to keep up, you know," Mr. Coslow said, putting the book away. "Shackleford, Wolf, Harbinger—I do wish you would pick a name and stick to it. It complicates my paperwork."

"I apologize. I have to live out here. People ask questions."

"You suspect a kifo minyoo," Mr. Coslow said.

"Excuse me, sir?" I said carefully. If Earl was treating this guy with kid gloves, I was going to practically grovel. "You know what this is?"

"No. If it *is* a kifo minyoo, I will have to observe it with my own eyes. The secretions are similar enough to other entities they are hard to sort out. I rather doubt kifo minyoo, however. There has never been a recorded mava paṇauvaā in North America. They have only been found in West Africa, interior Indonesia and northwest Mongolia. Then there is the problem of finding the mava paṇauvaā. While individual pseudopods are PUFF-applicable, without removal of the mava paṇauvaā, destroying them is quite pointless."

"It *attacked* us with a worm," I said.

"The worm as you call it *is* the pseudopod, young man," Coslow snapped. "A kifo minyoo is a feasting entity of a mava paṇauvaā. It is estimated they can have up to sixty such protuberances, and the body could be one hundred and twenty meters in length. Previously recorded supernatural generation fields for an Old One servant entity of that size were approximately seventeen kilometers in radius as a red zone with a yellow zone out to fifty-six kilometers. Which would, admittedly, explain the high level of undead activity in this region. I still strongly doubt a kifo minyoo. Rare does not begin to describe them. Similar fungoid symbols can also be found with mara ugaulaka, dauoa gildru, lefu leraba and kurth vedekje, all of which have been found in North America. But we shall see."

I wanted to ask questions. Follow up. Was he saying there was some sort of massive entity under New Orleans and the giant shoggoth worms were just sprouts off of it? But I could tell that asking more questions was a way to really piss this guy off. I could only think of one thing useful to say.

"Fuuuuck," Earl said, taking the words right out of my mouth. "This is like a yemek daire. Shit."

"Yes. Related, or at least originating in the same reality. Assuming mava paṇauvaā, this could be significantly larger and more powerful," Coslow said, nodding at Earl as if he were a student who had managed to just miss putting on a dunce cap. "My time is valuable, Mr. . . . Harbinger."

"We're about ready," Earl said.

Ray and Decay were setting the trap. We'd gotten a pig from a slaughter house, complete except for being gutted, then packed it with thermite and an igniter.

"Done," Ray said, coming out of the house. "You do realize this is enough thermite to melt the turret of the USS *Iowa*?"

"This had better not cause a big incident," Special Agent Campbell said, striding over. "We've got enough questions about what's—" When he saw the PUFF adjuster, he stopped. "Oh . . . Sorry, sir. I didn't realize you were here."

Everybody was scared of Mr. Coslow. I was starting to like him.

"My time is, as I previously noted, valuable," Coslow said as he gave the agent a stern nod. "I don't have the patience for another First Reason argument now. May we begin? I should note that there may be a good bit of quite unwholesome smoke. Mortals should don breathing filters."

Mortals?

Earl just crossed his arms and sighed.

"Put on y'all's gas masks," he said.

We donned respirators as Ray started the pump.

We were well back from the house this time. There was the awful shaking of the ground then the eruption. As the house rattled, Coslow casually strolled up to the window and looked through. I could tell from the set of his shoulders it was professional curiosity. And he hadn't donned a gas mask. Neither had Earl.

The thing didn't try to get out of the house. Apparently, the pig was sufficient offering. There, with another blasphemous liquid sound, it was gone. I started to reach for my gas mask and Earl put his hand on my arm and shook his head.

Then there was another rumble, harder this time. It was like being in about a magnitude five earthquake based on my time in Seattle. Then gray-green smoke started pouring out the front door of the house.

Even with the gas mask it felt unclean. I wished I'd put on MOPP gear or a silver suit. I backed up as it poured out of the house in a wave of fumes and horror.

Eventually the smoke stopped gushing forth and Mr. Coslow walked over to the group. If the smoke had bothered the PUFF adjuster, it was not apparent. He brushed some dust from the arm of his old overcoat.

"I stand corrected. Kifo minyoo. Large. FUCCN 11189-3. A well developed mava paṇauvaā is now positively identified in North America. Mava paṇauvaā is FUCCN 11189-1. That is my official ruling. I will send the paperwork to the MCB. You gentlemen have quite a problem on your hands." He walked away without another word.

Then the arguments started.

"Sheeeit," Earl said, rubbing his fingers through his hair. I'd never seen him so upset. "Do we know *anything* about a . . ."

"Mava paṇauvaā," Ray and I both chimed in.

Campbell, with no PUFF adjuster to fear, had taken out his anger on us. We were bad boys for causing an incident, even though we'd done as instructed and given them plenty of advance warning. I suppose he'd prefer we just let the damned thing live and eat more people.

He wasn't interested in the fact that there appeared to be a massive entity hiding under New Orleans. Seemed to think that was none of our concern. We were ordered to leave the area while he "handled the incident we'd caused."

I was starting to get really tired of his crap. And even though we'd figured out how to kill the kifo minyoo, which was apparently just one of what was probably sixty-something giant blob snakes growing out of the giant mava paṇauvaā, which had probably been under this spot since before the dinosaurs.

"I'm saying it sounds Hindi," I said.

"Swahili," Ray suggested.

"Could be Minangkabau. He mentioned they're found in interior Indonesia."

"What the hell is...?" Earl said, then stopped and snarled. "I hate this kind of *shit*! Shit you don't know about and don't understand is the worst kind of shit in this business! PUFF adjusters never tell you shit either. They just pronounce and go. They're so top-secret tight-lipped you never know if they've got actual intel, or they're just pulling guesses out of their ass."

"Earl," Ray chimed. "Let me and Chad research it. We'll find something. We've got the names, now, at least. That's a start. I don't give a shit what this new MCB fella says, there's a PUFF on this thing which means we kill as many as we can find. Starting with all the incidents."

"We still don't know how much the PUFF is," Milo said.

"Susan's looking into it now that we have the FUCCN," Ray said. "Doesn't really matter. These things need to be dealt with."

"If we start killing them, will more erupt?" Milo asked, frowning. "These are part of one big thing, right? They're like its tongue. Tongues? Tentacle tongues? Whatever. We burn one, will it start making others? That weird Coslow guy said there could be a bunch more. That could be bad."

"How often do they erupt?" Earl asked.

"Random," I said. "But seems to be increasing."

"If they're increasing, we need to just kill them and hope for the best," Ray said. "And find out what we can about the mava paṇauvaā and how to kill it."

"Fire," Milo said. "Lots of fire."

"Action beats reaction, but if reaction is all we got, we take it," Earl said. "Until we know how to kill the body, we'll bait every previous attack spot, and when there's a new eruption, we'll hit that one too. Once we know how to kill the body, we'll take it out."

"We've got to find it first," I said. "A hundred meters sounds big. But we don't know how deep it is or where it is located, exactly. So we can't just drill down to it. Until we can find the central body, we're going to be killing these things forever."

"Then we keep killing them forever," Earl said. "Shake the trees. Ray..."

"I'll head back to Cazador and see what's in the archives," Ray said.

"Iron Hand, they like you at Oxford. Assuming the MCB hasn't blocked your passport..."

"I'll book a trip."

"Probably best to keep you out of MCB's eyesight for a while anyway. And we still need to get to the bottom of you being under investigation. I don't like it when they slander my people. I'll spread the word to be on the lookout for your idiot brother."

"Thank you." It was nice to have people at your back.

"Milo..."

"I'll handle the teams killing these things." He rubbed his hands together with glee. "Kill it with fire!" he added with a mad cackle.

"Coordinate with Franklin. Hoodoo Squad's busy enough as it is, so we'll work the bait traps in when it's best for them." Earl cleared his throat. "Now, I know everybody is excited, but you need to realize what we're up against here. I've fought creations of the Old Ones before. They're rare, and that's a blessing. I can't accentuate enough how serious this is. What the adjustor said about the radius? The more powerful servants of the Old Ones twist *reality* just by existing. The veil gets thin when they're around."

I had briefed everyone else on my encounter with the powerful—maybe even master—vampire during Mardi Gras. "This must be the outsider Jack warned me about."

"Yeah. This thing beneath us, it's why New Orleans is so fucked up, why every little wannabe chickenshit witch doctor can suddenly raise the dead and create giant monsters," Earl growled. "You've got your assignments. We're going to take our time, do this right, get our shit together, and kill this motherfucker dead. Get to work."

✧   ✧   ✧

I had to stick around for at least one kifo kill. It was my idea, after all. And it turned out the PUFF was pretty damned decent. Milo and the teams were about to make a pretty penny off of giant slug monster barbeque.

We carried the pig over in the team van. It was two hundred pounds dressed weight. Serious porker. This time we were going back to Eagle Street. MCB had reluctantly accepted our argument that if it had a PUFF, we were allowed to kill it. But they'd insisted on evacuating the neighborhood and coming up with some bullshit cover story. I think it had to do with methane gas or something.

The reason it was bullshit was New Orleans. Most here knew hoodoo was real and serious. All you had to do was walk along the street banging on doors and saying "Gonna be some serious hoodoo. Bars won't help. Best get out."

Of course, then there were the people who wanted to know what the gubmint going to do foh them? Where's we gonna stay? You gotta put us up a hotel! An' buy us a hot meal!

Despite the diction, these were not entirely or even primarily one race. Just as every politician and city worker in New Orleans had a hand out, every resident had one pointed straight at the government. Or so it generally seemed. Nobody seemed to want to take action for themselves. Mow a lawn? Somebody else's problem. Hoodoo crap on your driveway? What the gubmint gonna do 'bout that? I ain't cleanin' it up!

Hoodoo? Ain't my problem!

I'd met decent, hard-working, law-abiding people in New Orleans. I'd met people who were willing to stand up and fight the good fight. I knew they existed. But Diogenes would have his work cut out for him in this place. I was fairly certain one of these days God would get so fed up with the hellhole He'd go all Old Testament and bring down full-on Biblical Wrath.

Back to killing things.

We'd waited to pack and rig the pig until we had it in the building. Why? Two hundred pounds dressed weight and another hundred pounds of thermite—that's why.

And since we were all "boots and suspenders" types when it came to explosions and arson, we didn't stop with just thermite and a fuse igniter. In the pig, along with all the thermite, were three detonation sequences, one electrical, two mechanical.

"Oh, come on," I said. "I want to bring the worm up! I'm on a flight to England tonight! These things are super rare! This might be the only chance I'll get!"

"Fine, fine." Milo handed over the sprayer. "You can tickle its funny bone or whatever."

"More like whatever." I put on my respirator. "Fire in the hole!"

This time I was going to watch what happened through a window. Milo waited outside with me.

Up came the blasphemous kifo minyoo. It was still hard to look at but I hung in there. It raged a bit until an edge of its loathsome body touched the pig. Then in an instant the porker was gone. It was hard to even see what happened but it seemed to have just slid over it and engulfed the massive hog. The thing lumped around for a bit, looking for more snacks, then slid down into the hole apparently satisfied with its offering. I could see one of the wires tighten then slack, indicating it had pulled the appropriate pin. The wire with the electrical detonation sequence was spooling out like we'd caught a world-class marlin.

Then the ground started to shake and smoke began gushing out of the hole.

"Oh, yeah!" I pumped my fist up and down. "Crispy kifo!"

And then the worm, mortally wounded, came gushing back out of the hole.

I thought it was ugly before. Now it was ugly and on fire. And very very pissed.

"Time to leave," I said, skipping away. "Tell me we have fire trucks standing by!"

"Look, it's dead," I said to Agent Robinson, standing by the smoldering and thoroughly destroyed house. "That's *our* job. Cleanup is *yours*."

I was getting really tired of handcuffs...

CHAPTER 5

"Dr. Rigby." I shook his hand when I arrived at the Institute.

I knew I wasn't safe there from pursuit by the MCB. But there was a certain weight taken off my shoulders.

"Chad." Rigby waved me to one of the wing-backed chairs in his office.

The primary Institute offices were in a large Georgian mansion in Midsomer. Convenient to Oxford and a bit less convenient to London, the estate was a useful place to train incoming Monster Hunters as well as kick back and relax when things got a bit on the tough side. The grounds were pleasant and heavily warded, the local pub was good and many of the locals had been read in on supernatural at one time or another.

Rigby's office had large windows letting in pleasant English spring sunshine. I definitely was starting to feel my shoulders unwind.

"Have you found anything more about the entity?" Tea had been laid out. English high tea was another thing I'd missed. Only the English could do scones.

"Nothing beyond the Ashanti reference," Rigby said, taking a bite of scone. "We've scoured our archives and have a team looking at Oxford."

"The PUFF adjuster said that they were only known in West Africa, northwestern Mongolia and interior Indonesia. The only area that's been extensively studied by English ethnologists, of those three, is Africa."

"A point we're discovering," Rigby said. "But there has been very little formal research into Mongolia or Indonesia. At least the interior. The Dutch did some work on coastal areas. You should look into pre-Enlightenment archives from those areas. I believe Oxford has many from the Chinese as well as extensive records from the Indians. Alas, mostly untranslated from a variety of different languages and dialects, many of which are lost."

"Fortunately, I'm good with languages." I shrugged. "I'm going to just do research for a while and hope that I can come up with something. The PUFF adjuster definitely knew more than he was telling."

"They always do," Rigby said with a sigh. "I've only dealt with the American adjusters three times in my entire career. They are the independent oversight over the PUFF program, I've been told. It is a very small, secretive, and select group which requires a certain kind of expertise."

"I didn't really get the feeling he was a saint." I shook my head. "But he certainly was odd."

"Which one was it?"

"Coslow."

"Ah, yes." Rigby winced. "Dealt with him when I was a junior operative. Taught me to mind my P's and Q's I'll say that. Do not waste his time. He becomes rather surly. However, enough about our mysterious worm for now. Since we are together and not speaking over a potentially wiretapped line, it is time to dwell on the MCB believing you are in league with a death cult."

"I'm not."

"If I thought for the briefest moment you were, we would not be having this meeting. The MCB's findings are rubbish. I spoke to some of my contacts at MI4 based on your information. They're not willing to get involved. Not worth their time. But they did confirm that the information came from a reading and that it indicated you were the alpha and omega of this sacrifice-selling ring."

"I certainly didn't start it but I'd be more than willing to end it. Did they vouchsafe the nature of the casting?"

"They did not." Rigby shrugged. "The one contact who was most open said he was unaware of the details. But he also said you and your brother were entwined in the matter supernaturally. 'Fated as Cain and Abel' was the exact quote he'd been given.

I pointed out that could have myriad interpretations. I think MI4 is humoring them, but since you were still allowed in the country, at this point I don't think anyone on this side of the pond thinks you're a culprit."

"I've got people asking around, trying to find my brother, but he's gone off the grid. Once he's found, we're going to have a little talk."

"Having a family member fall in with dark forces is a terrible thing. Are you prepared for the repercussions?"

I snorted.

Rigby nodded thoughtfully. "Very well then. Personal history aside, please refrain from jumping to conclusions. That would make you no different than the MCB. The meaning of this reading could be something a bit more complex."

"I hate the complicated hoodoo." I frowned. "I like the big stuff you can shoot."

"Don't we all, lad, don't we all. So, you are off to research your menacing kifo?"

"Definitely," I said. "I always feel like a salmon returning to its stream there."

"They go to those streams to mate and die, Chad."

"Ever seen the girls at Oxford, Doctor?" I asked, smiling. "I'll just have to avoid the die part!"

The main Oxford library was well known to visitors. They even had tours. Not at this point the largest library in the world, it was nonetheless extensive, and its rare books collection was one of the finest in the world. There were Marlowe manuscripts from the time of Shakespeare, original Dickens first drafts, and rare scrolls from the time of the library of Alexandria.

What was less well known to all but the most stringent researchers were the many supplementary libraries scattered around the town. Most of those were designated to specific areas, one was devoted solely to anthropology, another to linguistics, still others to math and sciences. Those held an enormous amount of information garnered over the centuries.

What a select few people knew about was tucked away in Summertown, mostly *under* an unpretentious and not particularly large manse, was the Library for the Study of the Supernatural and Occult, aka the Unseen Library.

On the surface it was, again, a very small place. The building was three stories and about ten thousand feet. In the various rooms were many general works of the occult. Books about the supernatural you could find, with some looking, in any standard library.

But take the side door into the basement. Show your ID to the nice librarian with the subgun behind the desk and you entered the *real* library.

It was an unknown number of stories deep. The deeper the level, the higher the clearance needed from the BSS to enter, and the guards here were polite, professional, and ready to kill anybody. As a visiting "scholar" I was only allowed access to the first two floors.

Supposedly there was a copy here of every book, manuscript, scroll, and tattooed flesh chunk with supernatural information on it, ever discovered by the British Empire. It was rumored that the lower levels had vaults containing the most powerful of grimoires, original copies of the *Necronomicon*, *Das Rad der Zeit*, the *Cluiche na gcathaoireacha* and other works so deep and evil I wasn't even sure of their names.

They kept the books in Oxford. They kept the artifacts in London. However, since there had been an incident involving a mummy and a rogue MI4 operative, that collection had been closed to scholars. Or at least that's what the VHI people told me over drinks.

I started in the Oriental sector and dove in. I was up on Hindi and sort of familiar with Cantonese. I quickly discovered that wasn't going to be enough. Most of the texts held there were not only in other languages, they were in obscure dialects thereof.

It was in a scroll written by a Gujarat yogi and traveler that I found the first reference to the mava paṇauvaā. The traveler, one Sundar Drupada, had studied the magic of the Hulontalangio. He described a similar sacrifice to the Ashanti as well as great power over the dead. However, the Hulontalangio wizards were more knowledgeable of the beast he called the mava paṇauvaā, which translated in Gujarati as "Mother Worm." They knew what they were sacrificing to was simply an extension of the Great Worm which lay below. But exactly where below was unclear. The text spoke in increasingly shrill tones of subterranean horrors that lingered beneath the earth, he listed dozens including the well-known shoggoth, grinders and something I'd never heard of called the *Āntarika-pavitra karatāṁ tuṁ-ghṛṇājanaka-ri'ēkśana-dharmāndha,* which he appeared to find the most horrible of all. The book eventually drifted off into mad ravings.

Even figuring out who the Hulontalangio were took a few days as there were no other references to them. I went back to the main library, then the ethnology library, and finally found a reference to a Dutch punitive expedition which had been sent into a department of the Indonesian territories to deal with a tribe that were slave traders, cannibals, and workers of black magic. They had "destroyed their unclean altars and their black deity" and returned to Jakarta with heavy losses. But nowhere in the libraries was there an original report from the expedition. Just a report of "heavy losses fighting the unclean forces of the dark god." And no description of how to destroy the dark god, presumably the mava paṇauvaā. Or it was possible they just destroyed the kifo pseudopods. In which case, the damned mava was still there.

I checked Oxford's references and if there was an extant original report, they couldn't find it. Not even through the Dutch. Stuff got lost over the years.

I did find one other item which was an early news report, in Dutch, that spoke of the walking dead attacking the expedition. Okay, so the local houdoun used shamblers. Good to know.

For West Africa there was only the Ashanti report. That was it for Indonesia. That only left Mongolia.

I searched for a week—during which there was no sign of my brother but Milo torched a few more kifos—before finding a reference in a decayed scroll seized from the Imperial Library in China during the Boxer Rebellion. According to the documents, the scroll and numerous others were taken as loot by a Hunter who was at the time a major in the British infantry. He had recognized the scrolls as containing supernatural information and, rather than have them be destroyed or end up in some other officer's library, had traded two Ming vases for them.

The very decayed scroll was in the dialect of the Eastern Jin Dynasty, dating it to between 317 A.D. and 420 A.D. It spoke of a punitive expedition against a mystical force which went deep into Hun territory north of the Great Wall. The expedition was ordered by the Light of Heaven for infractions against the

Order of the Heavens. This generally meant really black magic. The Huns were not the culprits. They were much more fearful of magic than the Chinese. The culprit was a foreign, did not say what nation, alchemist. He had raised a great dark god in the Hulun Buir region. This dark god was in turn bringing all manner of dead things back to life such that the alchemist had a vast army of the undead with which he planned to unseat the Son of Heaven from his throne and bring all of China into a long night of dark magics.

At least that was what I could get from the fragments of the scroll.

What happened was unclear. The scroll was very degraded. It looked as if, with the allowance and even support of the Huns, a General Kong Li Rong led a large expedition deep into the arid wastes of the Hulun Buir. Only a fragment of the force returned, bearing the beheaded body of their general. The great evil had been defeated and destroyed utterly by the alchemists of the emperor but none of them had survived either. The general had ordered that all the fallen were to be beheaded and in most case their bodies burned.

It was in pieces and I had to guess as to the meaning of some of the pictograms. Pictograms are always more of a by-guess-and-by-gosh thing but in this case it was worse. They were barely legible, most of them were half eaten away and a single pictogram of the period could have a dozen meanings. As an example, the pictogram for "water" could, depending on variables, mean water in general, rain, a spring, being transparent, being opaque, a lake, an ocean, a river, et cetera.

But the sole useful reference was to "mining/digging/boring/tunneling to the darkness/deeps/cavern/hole in the ground" and "bringing to the darkness/etcetera the powder/ash/sand/dust of the sun/fire/volcano."

The reason for the slash is that any of the above meanings would hold for what I was pretty sure were the pictograms. Ancient languages frankly suck.

What that probably meant was what made sense. Find the worm body, dig down to it and burn it with alchemical fire. The Chinese of that period knew not only the making of gunpowder but various other fast burning chemicals. I checked and they even knew how to make an early version of thermite.

However, the alchemical fire was of no use so they called upon a mystic to fight the beast. The pictogram for that could mean alchemist, wizard, sorcerer or certain categories of priests including Tibetan or Ainu shamans. They then attacked it with materials which were known only to them. That damaged the beast, possibly killed it.

Alas, the bit about what happened *after* that was the most degraded. The main noticeable bit was that the writing changed. The writing up to that point had been in one hand, then changed to a less capable hand. The scroll was marked with the chop of the scribe to General Kong Li Rong at the beginning. The latter chop was of a lesser scribe and it was in part his less capable writing as well as preparation of the inks that made the rest of the scroll pretty much useless. There was a list of casualties that appeared to be long to the extent it could be read. And the writing to that point was more or less a log by the general. After that it was by a Captain Tai Bo Li. But how the general had died and why a lesser captain was now in charge of the remnant force was missing or illegible.

The main battle seemed to have taken place *after* they got down to the mava paṇauvaā.

That was worthwhile to know.

As it turned out, it was pretty much the *most* important thing to know.

There also wasn't a single reference on how to *find* the damned thing.

I went searching for anything I could find about General Kong Li Rong or Captain Tai but there wasn't much. The problem was that every dynasty in the long history of China had at one point or another tried to erase prior history so as to make themselves look more important. Mao's destruction of religious texts and historical documents during his reign was simply a continuation of a very long process. Most Chinese history depended upon secondary sourcing and remembered details and was thus extremely suspect.

General Kong had had an illustrious career to that point and his death was noted in remnant Imperial archives. He was laid in state with great honors and guaranteed a position in heaven. Captain Tai was promoted to general for his exploits, unspecified in other documents, and also went on to great things. But there was no further information about the Lost Expedition. There were no references to which alchemists they had brought with them to fight the mava paṇauvaā nor what mystic "stuff" they used.

I talked to a professor who was a specialist in the period and he really had nothing to add. He'd never read that particular scroll and did find it fascinating. Since he wasn't read in on supernatural, he saw it as just another punitive expedition of an evil empire oppressing the poor herders and farmers of the region who, based upon the "great mother" being, were probably matriarchal and...

Could we get back to the point? Were there any extant writings by alchemists of the period?

There were. The particular emperor of that period was a proponent of Tibetan alchemists and had filled his court with useless soothsayers and shamans from Tibet instead of spending the money on the poor and downtrodden people of...

GAH! Not ancient Tibetan!

Ancient Tibetan is the worst ancient language *ever*. Except maybe Coptic. In both cases all the words are suppositional, meaning they are dependent upon other information in the text and outside of the text, and the Tibetans for religious reasons absolutely opposed direct description of anything abhorrent or unclean. They wouldn't even directly describe poisons.

To explain, when it came to anything "bad" or "unwholesome," the ancient Tibetans were more politically correct than a Harvard academic. They were so into euphemisms it was insane.

Example: The Tibetans wrote many books about medicine. Say that they are describing the symptoms of cyanide poisoning. They would describe the *symptoms*—bluing of the lips, fingertips and tongue—but when they got to the *cause*...

"The cause of this malady is that which is of the Fire of Deva, that which is of the Dust of Shetal, that which is of the Path of the Heron."

You would have to then go try to find something that explained what that meant. Problem being that it was invariably word of mouth and very closed even then. A junior doctor might look up the text and find that the malady was described but would have to go to a more senior lama or shaman to ask what the hell "that which is of the Fire of Deva" was. Because you didn't get to learn about poisons until you were a trusted fourth dong or something. And even then it was hierarchical. Sort of like MCB come to think of it. Everything unclean was classified.

Since most of the senior lamas and shamans (who knew what all the classified euphemisms meant) had been killed by the Chinese Communists in the takeover of Tibet, for being, you know, lamas and shamans and thus unclean in the eyes of Communists, most of the really hard information a Hunter needed had been lost.

Also, the way the writing is *laid out* has always made my brain ache. And I'm good with cuneiform and Sanskrit. Ancient Tibetan? Hate it.

I should probably add an explanation. As noted above, every time the Chinese went through a major civil war, which was frequent in their history, the winners would try to get rid of history and were in many cases very thorough about it. This isn't a purely Chinese thing. The Mayans and Byzantines did much the same thing. Try to find specific details about Jeshua, a carpenter of Nazareth, sometime. You'll find references to references; you can find his name in indexes of tax records, for example, but all the original references are missing. Why? Byzantines collected them all up and either hid or destroyed them.

The Tibetans never really had a civil war so their written knowledge had been preserved for thousands of years continuously. It was nearly impossible to decipher, but it had been preserved. That was until the fucking ChiComs came along and destroyed it. Fuckers. I might hate ancient Tibetan but I hate book-burners more.

I reminded myself that at least it wasn't Coptic and dug into the texts that were available from the period.

Oddly enough, most of those were in the regular Tibetan section. I'd used those libraries extensively when studying Yeti so they were familiar stomping grounds. It was well known that the supernatural didn't exist and all these references to demons, yeti and walking dead were just superstitious nonsense. And since the Tibetans were so oblique in everything they wrote it was nearly impossible to glean actual incantations, spells, demonic names, et cetera. All those details were handed down by word of mouth and unless the Dalai Lama knew them, they were lost to time. So the writings, unlike that of medieval alchemists, Islamic sufis, and Hindi yogis, were harmless enough. You had to really know your stuff to get anything out of them.

The other problem is that Tibetans had all sorts of references to call it "what lies beneath." In their mystical pantheon, Hell isn't that far down in the ground. Miners and farmers are tightly bound to the Wheel by the fact that both dig in the ground which is, in and of itself, unclean. And they firmly believed that there are monsters absolutely *riddling* the crust of the earth. Drop a shovel and you're going to hit some demon or other eldritch thing. They were especially scared shitless of some buried sleeping monster called "unbinder of the path and unmaker of all things."

So finding a reference to one *particular* monster in underground Mongolia was tough. They also had very little concept of geography outside of Tibet. The Chinese may be described as insular but it's *nothing* compared to classic Tibetans. If it wasn't in Tibet, it didn't really exist. And if it was in Tibet its location was described the same way a small-town resident would describe a location. "Up the valley where Tom used to live, take a left where his house used to be. Walk nineteen paces of the length of the Most Illustrious Lotus. Dig down about as tall as Adam who lives over in the next valley and you'll find the Eater of Air."

Never try to follow a Tibetan treasure map.

I finally found a third- or fourthhand story that seemed to match the data.

A major lama of great alchemical knowledge had been engaged by a "King of the Lower Lands" (to the Chinese "the Son of Heaven," to the Tibetans of the period nearly as important as a rich farmer) to accompany an expedition to fight a great evil. This evil, like most evils in Tibetan hoodoo, was found to exist at a great depth. The user thereof was a sorcerer of "lands to the West beyond the enlightenment of the Buddha," which could mean anything from the Persian Empire westward.

There were some problems getting to the location of the beast, battles didn't really matter to the Tibetans. But the lama had used the power of "the peace of Buddha" to put most of those to rest. Then he cast the "rune of Onesh" to determine the location of the "foul one." After it was positively located, "ones who plumb the depths for riches at loss to their soul upon the Wheel," miners in other words, were summoned to dig down to the depths and find this foul beast.

This took more than ten cycles of the moon, during which time the lama was also said to have cured many illnesses including

MONSTER HUNTER MEMOIRS: SAINTS

most notably blindness, brought people fully back from the dead and summoned a great chariot of fire from the sky to ride about doing good deeds.

Given my job, I wasn't sure which bits were entirely made up and which bits were pure history.

The mava was described in detail. I mean, really extreme detail. Went on for a page and a half. Problem being, it was all in nearly impenetrable euphemisms. The body was "of the crown/head/sun/light/helmet of the Most Enlightened." There were many "of that which is of the high/airy/well-loved/most holy places." However, the horror of the sight of the thing came through even with all the euphemisms and the ancient Tibetan.

Once the foul body of the beast was exposed, pathetic and useless alchemists of the Low Lands—Chinese in other words—tried various forms of their alchemy and magic to attack the beast to no avail. Many were lost in battling it. The lama was persuaded to take a hand and laid unguents upon it and certain rare alchemical materials.

This caused the beast great harm and it, in turn, reacted by summoning "its servants" from the "unclean earth." What the servants were was unclear. It was assumed you'd *know* what the servants of the beast were! So what were they? The kifo worm pseudopods? Shoggoths? Grinders? Homunculi? There were many of the "servants" described, but without that word-of-mouth knowledge you really got bupkes. Exact description was forbidden!

Damn ancient Tibetans!

The lama again brought "the peace of Buddha" to many of them but it was insufficient. The beast was pushing back and even the power of Buddha has limits. Many of the rest of the expedition fell and even became servants/sacrifices/monsters to/of the great beast. But in time they were defeated as was the foul beast. The lama perished in battle along with many lesser souls, you know those "bound upon the Wheel" lowlanders, i.e. Chinese, but the story was brought back by his apprentice and thus it is written. I shall bow to the four winds.

So...

You find this Great Worm Mother using the rune of Onesh. Dig down to it. We could probably drill these days. Lots of oil drilling in Louisiana. Hit it with some sort of mystic unguents. That may not kill it right away. Then it brings its "servants" to attack you. The servants were probably the kifo worms. Fire for those, bring flamethrowers. It looked as if the Chinese expedition had lost about five thousand people fighting this thing. They didn't have flamethrowers and good explosives, so I was pretty sure we could keep the casualties under five thousand.

The "rune of Onesh" was surprisingly easy to find. It had been written about any number of times. The rune was inscribed on a jade pendant which was then enchanted and it basically pointed towards certain types of evil—primarily undead, but it sounded like basically anything with the stink of the Old Ones on it. I hadn't been aware of the rune but it sounded useful as hell as long as it worked for someone other than a Buddhist lama. And if they were the only ones who could use it, I knew where to find dozens of lamas in the US. Some of them might even be able to translate the rare unguents and alchemical stuff.

On a tip from Rigby, I ran down to London and some of the alleyways behind Portobello Road and picked up an authentic rune of Onesh pretty quickly and surprisingly cheap. It appeared fairly old and I suspected it might have fallen into the shopkeeper's hands after falling out of the back of a truck. Given that whoever the previous owner was they probably had no clue of its use or its value, I could live with that.

I didn't bother to go to Chinatown to see what I could dig up about alchemical materials. The Chinese ones hadn't worked anyway and they'd ended up using fire. If this thing was as big as the PUFF adjuster suggested, we'd probably need quite a bit of thermite. Maybe magnesium would do it? Then the servants would attack and we'd defeat them, hopefully with fewer than five thousand casualties, then defeat the mava paṇauvaā and live happily ever after.

Sure. It was going to be eeeasy. But at least it was the beginning of a plan.

I had no clue what the PUFF was going to be on an entity that was supposed to be over a hundred meters long, but it was sure to be pretty decent. Depending on how many servants and what kind, I suspected we were all going to be able to retire.

Assuming we didn't take five thousand casualties when we only had a handful of people.

This was going to get interesting.

✧   ✧   ✧

When I returned to the library, the guards politely but sternly barred me from entrance. It turned out that when the MCB had realized I'd left the country, they'd asked their British counterparts to monitor my activity. Even though the MCB had a working relationship with MI4, it wasn't like secretive government bureaucracies communicated efficiently, so when MI4 *eventually* got around to processing their request weeks later, and it was discovered that a suspected cult member had been hanging out in the world's best collection of occult tomes delving into ancient mysteries, MI4 had shit a brick.

Having caused an international incident, it was time to go home.

CHAPTER 6

When I got to the offices after my trip, Milo, Ray and Earl were all there. I'd called and told them I'd found some information so they were waiting for the report.

"So," Earl growled. "You found something. Took you long enough."

"We lost Evans while you were gone," Ray said. "Bit by a shambler."

"Evans?" I asked.

"Tall guy?" Milo said. "Blond? Used to be with Miami?"

"Does not ring a bell... Oh, Colt Python guy?"

"Probably," Earl said. "They starting to blend?"

"Little bit." I laid out my notes. "You want some clue about how much fun I had finding all this stuff? Should I talk about my love of ancient Tibetan? And let me be clear that love is used in the most sarcastic of senses? Or how much fun it is trying to figure out *which* particular meaning of a pictogram is intended in Jin Dynastic Chinese? I'd say 'Mandarin' or 'Cantonese' but those are both the equivalent of modern English versus, say, *Latin*. Or that there are no modern extant copies of anything about this thing? That everything was on old scrolls so worm-eaten and faded, copied and recopied by hand that I was spending half my time just figuring out what the next letter *might* mean?"

"We get it," Earl said. "You're smart and it was tough. Nobody cares."

69

"The thing is definitely an entity created by the Great Old Ones, and it empowers necromancy."

"We already were pretty sure of that," Ray said.

"There are only three of them ever known to exist. As the PUFF adjuster mentioned. Africa, Indonesia and Mongolia. There's no record of the one in Africa being destroyed. Possible it was moved over here at some point. Or there might be a seed that came from there. Worth noting there may be another still there. The Indonesian one was killed by a Dutch expedition. Presumably. Very little extant information. Just a couple of survivors and I was unable to find the original report."

"Just a couple of survivors?" Earl said. "Out of how many?"

"Looks like a couple of companies of Dutch East India Marines and about a regiment of local sepoys."

"Jesus," Ray said. "What got them?"

"Again, very little information." I pushed the papers his way. Ray didn't have my gift for languages, but he was smart as I was. Using the translated notes he might come up with something I missed. "But here's everything I found."

"So, undead," Earl said, shrugging. "Which we already had. What else is going to try and murder us?"

"So I went looking for something in Mongolia. A Chinese expedition was sent up into the Hun lands to quote 'fight a great evil.' The expedition's size was the equivalent of two legions. About ten thousand troops. They got back with about three thousand."

"Okay, that's not good," Ray said.

"You think?" I said.

"What period," Ray asked. "Oh, Jin. Eastern or Western?"

"Eastern. Xiaowu period."

"Those were good troops," Ray said. "Highly disciplined, experienced and trained. Pretty serious warriors."

"Yep," I said. "The loss of most of the expedition I think contributed to the Xiaowu turning over power and the demise of the Eastern Jin. But I digress. The main source of information was a thirdhand story from the POV of an apprentice to a powerful Tibetan lama who accompanied the expedition."

"Fascinating," Ray said. Milo looked confused. Earl was annoyed.

"The expedition had to, again, fight local supporters and a wizard from somewhere to the West. Could have been from anywhere West. Tibetans weren't all up on geography. The lama found the body of the thing using the rune of Onesh when the supporters were cleared off. They got miners to dig down to it. The Chinese alchemists tried to burn it with fire but weren't able to do much damage. Sounds like they were using gunpowder. The lama hit it with some sort of mystic unguents and that apparently pissed it off. Unguents unclear. Then it raised its 'servants.' Servants also unclear. I'm thinking that's probably the kifo worm pseudopods. Basically it wasn't 'servants' but the worm itself apparently attacking through those. They can stretch out, obviously, for miles. But I could be wrong. It was the second battle that killed most of the expedition. The lama managed to kill it but he was killed as well. That part of the scroll was degraded badly. An apprentice survived and brought the story back to Tibet. And be aware, all of this is not nearly as clear in the writings. This is mostly interpretation and guesses. But that *seems* to be what happened."

"Holy shit. Enough already." Earl sighed, obviously impatient. "Did you get *anything* solid?"

"Earl, there is nothing *solid* about *any* of this ancient tomes shit, okay?" I snapped angrily. "And I'm getting to it! I worked on this shit for a solid month. Smoke another fucking cigarette and *wait*!"

Earl scowled. Ray and Milo exchanged a nervous glance.

"Chad..." Earl stubbed out the end of his cigarette in an ashtray, then set his hands flat on the desk, took a breath, and addressed me in a very calm manner. "I'm gonna state this in a way you can wrap your big old brain around. I know it's real important for you to feel like the smartest asshole in the room, but I've got work to do. So actionable intel now, history minutia trivia fun time later... *Get to the fucking point already*."

"They had to deal with the local tribe, fierce cannibals, and the necromancers who were using the entity for power. So what caused what casualties is unclear, but when we attack the body, all hell is going to break loose."

"Got it," Earl said, lighting another cigarette. Guy was a freaking chimney. "So find it, drill down, then hit the monster with some mystic crap we don't know, then fight its servants we don't know, but which were badass enough to wipe out an army. Anything else?"

"There's a large contingent of Tibetans out in Colorado. I could go see their shamans with my notes and see if they know what unguents to use."

"Do it. You may annoy the hell out of me sometimes, but you're good at that kind of thing."

"We're going to collect the PUFF on a hundred-plus-meter Old One–category entity that has been making it easy to raise the dead and attracting monsters to New Orleans for *centuries*," I said. "I'm thinking we're going to make bank on this. Assuming anyone survives."

"Assuming MCB doesn't say it's out of our league and take over from us," Ray said.

"Then we just don't tell them," I said. "Let *them* go sort through ancient scrolls."

"Speaking of MCB, you're still not in the clear, there."

"I got some thoughts on that in England. I'm going to go see a voodoo woman and try to replicate what MCB did to determine I was a suspect."

"You know my opinion on the matter."

"Well, you're not the one being hounded by the MCB, and nobody knows where my brother is to straighten this out the old-fashioned way. I'll leave it to the hoodoo lady to figure that out. Maybe I can get enough information from her to show MCB how their casting was misinterpreted. Or at least get that to the political side to start to pull some of the heat off."

"Never trust a politician or a wizard."

"There's two kinds of trust, Earl," I said, looking him in the eye. "One is honesty. The other is competence. There are very few people I trust on both. I can count on the thumbs of one hand the number I trust on both. And I'm including myself in that number."

"You don't trust me?" Milo said.

We were driving back from clearing some shamblers out of a cemetery. In deference to MCB's new policies we'd kept it discreet. Agent Robinson was easily excitable, and I was tired of getting arrested.

"If it came down to me or the Shacklefords, who would you choose?" I asked. "You don't have to answer but it's one of the bases. I love you like a brother, Milo—a real brother, not my shithead brother. But totally trust you? I don't actually totally trust me. Are you honest? Sure. As honest as anyone can be. But try to honestly answer the original question. Are you always competent? In ways that amaze even me. But I wouldn't want you to represent me in court. And there are emotional connections you have that are stronger than your connection to me. Would you do something for me, something very important, if you thought it violated your faith or your soul? I would hope not. If Earl was dead set against it? I think you'd tend to take Earl's side. I don't mind that. I don't like you less for it. But you can see where I don't trust you entirely thereby."

"I guess there's some logic," Milo said, frowning. "But it isn't about loyalty as much as it is about right and wrong. Mostly it sounds like you trying to justify being a butthead."

"Uncool, man. Now, I'm going to go do some stuff that will make you uncomfortable," I said, pulling up to the team shack. "So I'm going to go do it alone. Because I don't trust you not to say something that will cause an issue."

"What are you going to do?"

"I'm going to go see a voodoo lady. And get my future read in tea leaves and tarot cards and there might be a chicken sacrificed."

"Those people are..." Milo grimaced and started to get out. "Whatever."

"Milo." I held up my hand. "You really are the closest person I have to a brother. So please be aware, the reverse is *not* true. I'd literally give up my soul for yours."

"I...Don't," Milo said, then shrugged. "That isn't how souls work anyway."

"I doubt it will ever be an issue, but I got to go get my voodoo on. See yuh, brother."

I went to see my real estate agent.

Madam Courtney was a revered hoodoo lady but her hoodoo had always been of the "White." When I'd first met her, I had not realized just how respected she was in the hoodoo world. She made charms and healing potions, cast blessings and such. She'd never been known to lift a finger in harm against anyone. It should be noted that despite being houdoun, Madam Courtney attended Catholic mass every Sunday, without fail, as well as on major saints' days and at various other times. She had, in addition, attended Sunday school every week her entire life. Not "with few exceptions." She'd once attended Sunday school and church while suffering from raging pneumonia.

So I couldn't imagine a better hoodoo woman to see to determine what MCB had found out and possibly more. When I'd said there were twenty wizards in New Orleans better than MCB's, I was serious and was friends with one of the top three, and her office was conveniently located in Bayou St. John.

The place was covered in charms and hoodoo decorations. After her attractive young secretary led me back through the bead curtain, Madam Courtney came around her desk to give me a hug. As usual she was dressed in bright colors and wearing a bunch of jewelry and amulets. "Oliver Chadwick Gardenier, my favorite client. Sit. Sit! Now, what is the bother for you?"

"I need you to talk to your loas."

The first few times I had met her, Madam Courtney had constantly admonished me to *trust in the loas.* "It is serious then?" she asked as returned to her chair. Without asking if I wanted one or not, she poured two glasses from a bottle of dark rum.

"I have come under suspicion by the authorities of being involved in a very foul crime. They won't give me details but I've determined they were looking for those who are involved and did some sort of casting. I was found to be connected as was my brother. The problem being, I am not involved in any way that I am aware. I swear this to you, Madam Courtney."

"No need. I know you too well to believe such things."

"But the casting has me as being, according to them, 'the alpha and omega.' That I created it and that I can end it. I swear I did not create it though I would like to end it."

"What is this foul crime?" Madam Courtney asked.

"There is a group who are kidnapping girls to be used as virgin sacrifices, and selling them to those of the Dark and the Black who need such. They often kill whole families to get girls who are the right type. The only information I have is that they're called the Dark Masters."

"Ah."

"You've heard of them." I wasn't surprised. Madam Courtney knew *everybody.*

"Rumors only. They're not from around here. They work up north and out west, Yankees and scoundrels. So foul with the

Black that I'm surprised they can maintain the semblance of being human. They call themselves Dark Masters as they think they are more powerful than the loas. They revel in sin. Many in this town work with the Dark and the Black, but I would have no clue, though, why anyone would put you in their midst."

"That's the question I've been asking everyone. The only thing I can think is to... The term I'd use is 'reverse engineer' the casting. To try to do the casting that whoever the Feds hired did and see what comes of it."

"But you know not what casting," Madam Courtney said, frowning. "And it could be many. It depends on what they were looking for."

"Could there be a way to look for the girls instead? That may have been what they were doing. Could a federal hoodoo man have tried to find who took them, and somehow my name came up by mistake?"

"To find the girls, or them as took them, I'd need something of theirs. Not just something they touched, something that is of them. Hair, toenails. Do you have such?"

"Not currently. I can possibly find something, but that victim would probably already have passed on."

"Such a thing is vile," Madam Courtney said angrily. "*Find me* something of one of the girls who was took. We will trust the loas to show us the way!"

"Thank you, Madam Courtney. I truly appreciate the help." I got up, laid an envelope on the table, and let myself out. When it came to the hoodoo side of her business, you didn't ask Madam Courtney how much her help cost. It cost what you paid. If you had nothing, she would help you for free. If you were rich, you were expected to pay as much as was reasonable. The envelope contained ten thousand dollars. I was pretty sure she'd give most of it away to the needy anyway.

CHAPTER 7

Unfortunately, this necessitated another out-of-town trip.

Franklin was not happy to see me leaving town again, especially with being down a body again and me being the Hunter most familiar with New Orleans, but I had a job to do. I was going to get my name cleared one way or the other.

My files on the virgin kidnappings ring went back to when I was still in good graces with the FBI. MHI had gotten a few of the files on the remaining missing, after we rescued those girls from the Seattle Lich. It was virtually guaranteed all of those girls were already sacrificed, but it was the only thing I had to go on.

The nearest suspected victim where the family was still alive was in Arkansas. But there was an event in Pueblo that fit the MO, and while that wasn't *close* to Crestone—nothing was close to Crestone—it was closer than, say, Arkansas. And Crestone was the Tibetan town I needed to visit to see about what unguents you used to wipe out an Old One's entity. Also, I had an in in Pueblo.

It was good to be armed again. The one problem with visiting England was being continuously at the mercy of whatever evil thing might pop up at any time. They had arms at the Institute, but God help you if you were caught walking around Oxford with a 1911 in your waistband. English politicians were firm believers that everyone should be a victim and English constables looked at carrying a pistol as equivalent to a thermonuclear device.

I hired a plane. Less hassle that way. Not a jet, I wasn't going to spend that much. A twin-engine Beech. Faster than driving, and I could load up as many guns as I wanted. I told the pilot I was going big game hunting. Which was almost the truth.

First stop was Crestone. Going to Pueblo was going to dredge up old memories, victims', families', mine. Crestone was easier.

Crestone, Colorado, is even more the definition of middle of nowhere than Yuma, my late friend Jesse's hometown. It was damned near the center of Colorado but on the far side of the Front Range from Denver and most of the main areas of CO and in, if not Colorado's most arid region, then pretty darn close. Put it this way: the nearest major attraction was Great Sand Dunes National Park.

It was an old mining town that had just about dried up and drifted away with the sand dunes until the 1950s. Them damn Chi-Coms had taken over China then invaded Tibet. (Then promptly burned six thousand years of history.) There wasn't much the US government could do about China but they could try to start an armed rebellion in Tibet. Tibet had been independent for as long as anyone could remember. And they'd stayed that way by not only being hard to access but being good fighters. So, train up some Tibetans and send them back to train others. Set up an air-lift like they'd done for the Chinese in World War II. Made perfect sense.

Where to put these Tibetans where they'd be at home and keep their lungs ready for the heights while training?

When they activated the Army's 10th Mountain Division, nobody and I mean *nobody* could figure out why the *hell* they'd put it in New York when they had Colorado just sitting there. The answer, of course, was "there was this congressman."

The CIA black ops program put these Tibetans where it made most sense: Crestone. Tibet was mostly arid. Crestone was in an arid part of Colorado. Tibet was very high. Crestone was in a high part of Colorado. There were nearby mountains that were even higher. Best of all, Crestone was so far away from anything that nobody in 1958 was going to look there. Pretty much the same arguments as why they set up Oak Ridge in Appalachia.

So they took two hundred Tibetan "fighters" and some of their families out of refugee camps in India and Nepal and brought them to Crestone, Colorado, to start training to retake their homeland. Victory was assured!

Enter the Dalai Lama, who got wind of the program. The Dalai Lama was an absolute Buddhist pacifist and there's no group more pacifist than Buddhist pacifists. He also had been basically the king of Tibet and was, like the Japanese emperor, the highest moral authority. He put his sandaled foot down and forbade any of them from engaging in combat. To do so would damn them for eternity upon the Wheel.

So much for the armed Free Tibet program. And note to people who think my mother's approach is right: The nonviolent approach of Gandhi and Martin Luther King requires a government that is in some way Western, moral, and beholden to the will of the people. Fascist and Communist dictatorships don't give a shit. Anything but an armed Free Tibet program is flapping your gums to no avail. End international relations pro-tip.

So the Tibetans were told to not talk to anyone about the original plan, each given a small severance package and residency papers and the CIA walked away.

That left about five hundred Tibetans in the middle of bum-fuck *nowhere*. (Not to mention a bunch of CIA case officers who had to find a new career specialty. Fortunately, the Vietnam War was just heating up . . .) All the mines were closed and there were about no jobs.

Paradise! The land of opportunity! To Tibetans, Crestone looked like nirvana! There was so much water! (Remember the thing about the sand dunes.) There were electric lights! You didn't have to go collect sticks over miles of parched terrain to cook dinner and hold off the biting cold of a Tibetan summer!

To make a long story short, they settled in. They started businesses which covered the whole "no jobs" thing. They got irrigation credits and started farms. They walked the hills and found overlooked mineral deposits, found out who the local babu was that had to be paid off and started small mines. (Mining in Tibet had been even more tightly controlled than in the US and almost as corrupt.) They dug in and worked and not a few of them became rich.

The United States is a nation of immigrants. We need more like the Tibetans.

Some of them had eventually moved away. There was a large Tibetan population in Seattle for example. That was where I hooked up with them. The occasional times that I'd needed a charm in Seattle I'd used either Chinese or Tibetans. It always boggled them that a round-eye could speak their language and in many cases read the ancient tongues better than they could.

But the CIA hadn't only brought fighters. They'd also brought shamans because if you're going to move a group as tied in to the supernatural as the Tibetans, that's what you do. They won't move without having a lama or a shaman tell them which way is the correct way to place their foot. Because, let me make this clear, Tibet really *is* rife with hoodoo. Go up the wrong valley in Tibet and you're going to get your soul sucked out and your bones spit on the ground.

Some of those shamans were still around. Older now, creakier, more powerful, and a few of them very knowledgeable. When the shamans in Seattle had a question they couldn't answer, they'd take a pilgrimage to Crestone. And when it was really tough, they'd talk to Father Pema. Pema meant *Lotus* but it wasn't considered by the Tibetans to be a girly name. The lotus has a special meaning in Buddhism. And Father Lotus was the most powerful and knowledgeable Tibetan shaman in the New World.

Crestone still looked like an Old West mining town. Many of the downtown buildings were from the original boom period in the late 1800s. Single-story, clapboard siding, covered porches elevated to get away from the mud when it, rarely, rained. There were some newer houses, a few brick, mostly cheap vinyl siding and single-story. Cars were up on blocks in many yards and there were a few vegetable gardens here and there. Only the main drags, Colorado 71 and Country Road 5/10, were paved.

Father Pema's house was on Alder Street near North Crestone Creek. The house was old, clapboard, but was well cared for. Freshly painted with a straggling front lawn and a garden on the side that I suspected ran mostly to medicinal and magical herbs. Hopefully all of them were legal but some of Tibetan medicine used hemp extracts. I suspected those plants were somewhere up in the mountains, probably tended to by apprentices. And some Tibetan medicinal plants were more powerful than peyote, if not on the controlled substances list.

Father Pema was tricky. Sometimes he'd talk to a round-eye and sometimes not. Hell, sometimes he'd blow off other shamans. And he didn't have a phone: if you wanted to talk to him you had to come see him. Calling ahead wasn't preferred. You presented yourself at his house and he'd get to you at his convenience.

But if he had a weakness, it was the same as Madam Courtney's. And I had two bottles of a locally made, New Orleans, dark spiced rum with me.

It was late spring by then but there were still patches of snow in sheltered areas and coming from New Orleans it was cold as shit. I'd rented a car at the nearest airport. The heater didn't work. I was freezing my ass off. It felt wonderful.

I walked up on Father Pema's porch and knocked on the door. It was answered by a young male Tibetan who looked like one of the "round-eyes all need to be buried" types.

"I'm looking for Father Pema," I said in Tibetan. I held out the bottles still in a brown paper bag. "I bring gifts."

"Father Pema does not talk to barbarians," the kid said haughtily.

"He has spoken to me before. It regards certain writings of a lama from the first century."

I put this in correct Tibetan phraseology which was more or less: The words of a grand master of the eternal Wheel from the time of the King of the Eighteenth Lotus Petal Lying on the Waters of the Buddha.

Which clearly confused the hell out of Pema's new apprentice.

"The what?" he said in English.

"I've got some Tibetan writing from the first century A.D. I need his interpretation." I switched to English and tapped the satchel on my hip. "I also need him to figure out what material I need to destroy a major mava. And by major I mean the largest ever found in North America. I'm known to Father Lotus. Tell him it's Tiewan."

"I'll see if he's in." The kid took the bottles. He still looked puzzled.

I took a seat on one of the rockers on the porch and settled down to wait. It might be a few seconds, it might be days. That was the way Father Pema worked.

As it was, it was about two hours when the door opened and Father Pema walked out.

He was ancient. Exact ages, like real names, are something the Tibetans don't talk about. The birth date of a child has magic significance so they're cagey about their birthdays. But he had to be around ninety.

He was short—I've never seen a tall Tibetan—wiry, very muscular legs and a grip like an industrial press. "Iron Hand. What problems do you bring an old man this time?"

"We suspect there is a mava in New Orleans," I said in Tibetan, pulling out my notes from Oxford. "A great beast of the deep with many parts that extend long distances. The notes I have called it a 'mother of worms.'"

"There is a mother of worms in this land?" Pema exclaimed.

Tibetans don't show fear or surprise. He was afraid and surprised.

"So we suspect. I have the writings of the lama which defeated one to the north of Tibet in the first century."

"Where did you find the writings of the Most Perfect Lama Thubten?" Pema said eagerly.

"They are not the writings of the lama. They are words of one of his surviving apprentices. I found them in the library at Oxford. These are only notes."

"I would see even the notes of such." He held out his hand.

I sat down as the old shaman read through my notes. They were in Tibetan, or at least my version of it. Some of the notes were exact copying of the manuscripts. You couldn't photocopy something that old and fragile.

"I would love to see the original," Father Pema said when he was done reading.

It was after dark and the cold was starting to get to me. I was wearing a sweater and coat. Father Pema was in shorts and a short-sleeved shirt. I wasn't going to complain.

"I'll gladly pay your way to visit Oxford. The scholars there would love to have someone of your knowledge visit."

"That would involve traveling by aeroplane and ship, yes? I've done that before. I did not like it."

"Airplanes have gotten much better since the 1950s."

"I don't even like cars. I like my feet on the ground. What would you know?"

"What are the unguents and materials used by the Most Perfect Thubten to defeat the Great Worm Mother?"

"This is knowledge known only to the Most Perfect." Pema handed the notes back. "I am barely a scraper of the ground compared to the Most Perfect Lamas."

A "Most Perfect Lama" was the Tibetan equivalent of a cardinal. There were probably five left on earth and none of those would give me the time of day.

"Also," Pema said, "much of this knowledge was lost in the

Great Corruption." That was what they called the Chinese invasion. "I doubt that a Most Perfect Lama would give such information to you and I suspect that none know these arts in this time. They are lost forever."

"Were any of them ever written? Perhaps in tomes of medicine or healing? Would I be able to find any hint in such?"

"If there is a library that has this, such a library may have the original recipes. But..." He took a deep breath. "The mystic unguents of the Most Perfect would have been merely a carrier for the power of the Great Lotus. You simply need the power of strong healing and that which fights the corruption of the earth. It is any material which represents the blessed faith of the good. It need not be Tibetan."

"That sounds like..."

"I hate to say this," Pema said, getting up, "but you can probably drown it in a few thousand gallons of holy water. Best if it's blessed by a truly devoted priest, but that's much easier to get your hands on. Anything else?"

"No. That's it."

He walked into the house without saying goodbye.

I got back in my rattletrap rental and headed back to the airport. Maybe the heat in the fleabag motel would be working.

It wasn't.

Pueblo was in a region equally as arid as Crestone, but was a typical modern American town. This time I'd called ahead. Admittedly just from the airport. And there was, thank God, an Avis outlet so I had a decent car.

The door to the two-story home was opened by a teenage girl. I barely recognized her. The last time I'd seen her she'd been two years younger, filthy, covered in sores and terrified. Also strapped to an altar in the middle of a firefight.

"Chad!" she shouted, throwing her arms around me. "It's so good to see you!" That was also very loud.

Mandy Cummings would speak very loudly for the rest of her life. That was my fault. And Milo's. Explosions wreck your hearing. She also had fine scars on the right side of her face and some sight loss in the right eye. It was all collateral damage, but we had managed to save her life.

I hugged back. She'd gotten much more squeezable.

"You've grown."

"I have you guys to thank for it." Mandy grinned.

Her family was gathered in the hallway watching this with bemusement. I wasn't sure what they'd been told about Mandy's rescue and I'd have to deal with that carefully. Before MCB Seattle even got to the scene we'd told the girls they couldn't talk about what actually happened to them. The Doctors Nelson were psychologists by original trade and had helped the girls as best they could. Mandy seemed to have mostly recovered from the ordeal.

"I'm Chad Gardenier." I held my hand out to her father.

"We were sort of surprised when you called." Arthur Cummings was forties, balding but solid. From what I remembered he worked in construction.

The rescuees had been from all over the western United States so we hadn't ended up meeting any of the families. Some of the girls held in the container were from the Pueblo area. Others who had been captured in the area had been separated out, either not virgins or sold elsewhere. And that was why I was there. Mandy had been at a girls' night with friends when the ring had attacked the house. The ring had killed the rest of the family and taken all the girls. Two had been rescued by MHI, in Mandy's case by the thinnest of margins. My information on the cover story was that it was "a Satan-worshipping serial killer ring." Which was close to the truth.

"You're one of the men who rescued Mandy," the mother said. Clara Cummings was short, plump and blonde. Nice enough looking for being in her forties.

"Yes, ma'am."

"Where are my manners?" She gestured toward the living room. "Please come in."

"You're FBI?" Mr. Cummings said when we were situated. Mrs. Cummings had gone to get snacks.

"No, sir. My company is hired to handle certain types of cases by the government." I waved at the various scars on my face. "The types of cases where people end up like this. Sort of bounty hunters. Other than that, it's classified."

"Okay. Mandy's told us how she wasn't supposed to talk about certain things, but damn it, people have a right to know!"

"I agree, sir, and I disagree. *Why*, in both cases, is not only highly classified, it would take hours and hours to explain. And some of it, frankly, you probably wouldn't believe. So I'll leave it at that. Bottom line, I helped saved your daughter's life, but now I really need your help."

"You can pretty much ask for anything," he said, hugging Mandy to him. "You on the run?"

"No," I said, not adding *but it's getting close.* "It's about the people who took Mandy. I need to talk to the parents of girls who . . . didn't get them back."

"They hardly talk to us," Mandy said unhappily. And loudly. "They wanted to know what happened and I couldn't really talk about it. The Hamiltons . . . was where they took us. They're all . . . gone. The Morrisons and the Hawkins divorced. We really only ever see the Simpsons 'cause we still go to the same church. I have a hard time looking Mr. and Mrs. Simpson in the eye. We used to be friends."

"Grief changes things. But I really need to talk to as many of the families as I can. I need something from them as well. But I'll talk to them."

"We can tell you where they live," Mr. Cummings said, shrugging. "Give you some numbers. But like Mandy said, they don't really talk to us anymore."

"That'll be fine."

They might not talk to the Cummings anymore, but say "it's about your missing daughter" and grieving parents will tell you *anything.*

The Simpsons' house was practically identical to the Cummings. US suburb, one each. It was also right around the corner.

Irene and Warren Simpson had four children. Their middle daughter, Marcella, had gone over to a friend's one night and never returned. The Hamilton house had been burned to the ground. At first they'd thought their daughter had died in a fire. Then came the word that none of the bodies of the girls had been found. Then it was suspected one of the girls had started the fire. Then the FBI showed up and they found out it matched a string of disappearances.

They'd called their local police department for information. They'd called the FBI. They'd put up fliers. They'd gone on local television. But their daughter had disappeared into the night. They were willing to talk to anyone who might give them some closure. They just wanted to know if she was alive or dead. Anything.

I knew there would never be closure. Their daughter was positively identified as having been sacrificed by the Seattle Lich. And the way the lich got rid of the bodies was to feed them, bones and all, to his pet ghouls. There wasn't so much as a scrap of hair left of their daughter. Since MCB wasn't about to let that out, the parents would die waiting for word of their daughter's fate.

Frankly, I wasn't going to tell them that, even if it wouldn't put me in more trouble with the MCB. I wasn't going to look them in the eye and say "Your daughter's soul was torn out with her heart and used to power an undead being, one that is still on the loose, so until it's killed, her soul is trapped between worlds, and her body was eaten by ghouls. Sorry."

Yeah. Wasn't going there.

"I was one of the people who rescued Mandy Cummings," was what I said to the two parents. "My company is also involved in looking for news of other victims, including your daughter, Marcella."

"Is there anything you can tell us?" Mr. Simpson asked, holding his wife's hand.

"Not really. You got word that this was a ring, right?"

"Yes," Mrs. Simpson said. "Satan worshippers! How in God's name can something like that go on in this day and age?"

"Not in God's name, ma'am, that I can tell you for sure. I won't tell you that we're going to get your daughter back like we did Mandy. I tell you that as sort of an expert in this area, she's most certainly gone. You understand that?"

"Yes." Mrs. Simpson teared up. There was a box of Kleenex on the table and I pulled one out and handed it to her. They were used to these sorts of conversations and prepared.

"There is a new scientific way to identify remains," I said carefully. "I don't know if you know this, but bodies are found all over the US all the time. What we're trying to do is sort out some of those unidentified remains, Jane Does, ones that match the general description of your daughter and other potential victims."

"Why are they unidentifiable?" her sister Robyn asked.

"I'd really rather not get into that, just...when some hunters find a body in the woods that's been there for...a while. Sometimes they don't even realize it's a human body."

"Oh." Robyn got pale.

"Wasn't there *any* word on Marcella when you found Mandy and Risa?" Mr. Simpson asked.

"Not that I can get into. This is an ongoing investigation. I know you want some information—anything. But if the people who took your daughter, who are continuing to take other people's daughters, get word of details of the investigation, it can make them change their patterns, making it harder to find them. And it's hard enough as it is. Also, if any information leaks out from the investigation, it can compromise the trial. I'm pretty sure you don't want your daughter's kidnappers released on a technicality. That's why the FBI is so close to the vest with information and I have to be as well. What I need, though, is fairly simple. I just need a few hairs."

"Hairs?" Mrs. Simpson demanded. "You're not one of those damned *psychics* are you?"

"No," I said, not adding: *But I know a few.* "The reason is the identification method. You've heard of DNA? It's found in every living cell. It's what's passed down from you to your children, and it's as unique as a fingerprint for an individual. We'll take the hairs and run what's called a DNA profile. Then compare it to potential... remains that might be Marcella. At the very least, it may give you some closure if we can find her body."

"I guess that makes sense," Mr. Simpson said.

"Do you have her hairbrush? One that *only* she used?"

"We do," Mrs. Simpson said, tearing up again.

I handed her more tissues.

I'd wanted to kill these assholes before, but now this was feeling really personal.

Dealing with all the families was painful. It was one of the reasons I never could have been a cop. I preferred killing monsters to handing over tissues. It wasn't that I was bad at detective work. Being a detective was about figuring out patterns, and I was really good at pattern recognition. But crying families was not my thing.

I also had to track down the Morrisons and then the Hawkins. The mothers had kept mementos of their daughters. In both cases the girls were their only children and between the grief, the silences, the wondering, the couples had divorced.

It turned out all the families had kept keepsakes. I had four hair samples from the victims for Madam Courtney to use.

I was glad as hell to head back to New Orleans, heat and all. I was ready to kill me some monsters. Preferably the monsters who were taking these girls but anything would do.

CHAPTER 8

I really should get back to monster killing but this is a memoir about the job. And part of the job, when you get past dumb-grunt me monster killer, is finding out about the monsters. Tracking them down. Figuring out how to kill them. So you're going to have to bear with me.

When I got back to New Orleans nothing much had changed. MCB was still riding our asses. We'd gotten in a replacement for Evans and with the loup-garou infestation under control, New Orleans was only mildly impossible to manage. My first week back, besides the meeting with Madam Courtney and trying to track the mava paṇauvaā, we had some calls, but it was all the usual shit. Nothing terribly interesting.

Milo was a bomb-in-pig-stuffing, kifo-killing machine. He'd baited every single eruption site and gotten another hit. There hadn't been any more new attacks since we'd gone on the offensive.

So the second day I was back I took the hair samples to Madam Courtney's residence. Despite the fact that I knew the door was probably unlocked, you don't barge into a hoodoo woman's house. So I waited for her to let me in. Strangely enough, her house wasn't nearly as decorated with charms and trinkets as her office, so a lot of those were probably just for show.

"Them the girls?" she asked as I pulled out the baggies with hair samples.

Pro-tip: Carry rubber gloves and ziploc bags with you at all times. There are things you don't want to touch with your hands and you have to take tissue samples for Confirmation of Kill.

In this case I had four plastic baggies with the names written on them. Tracey Morrison, Meghan Hawkins, Marcella Simpson, and Sherri Harvey. Two blondes, a strawberry blonde, and a bottle blonde with brown roots. Those and memories were about all that remained of those four girls. Morrison, Hawkins and Simpson were all positively identified as being sacrificed. Harvey had been separated off from the other girls and presumably sold to some other bastard who wanted a virgin sacrifice.

"Yes, ma'am." I handed over the baggies.

We'd moved to the small kitchen table in the room for this and she pulled out each one carefully and laid them out on a white cloth. Then she closed her eyes and appeared to go to sleep with her hands held out over the hairs. She stayed like that, head down for a bit, then her eyes flashed open.

"This one is alive," she said, holding up the strands of bottle-blonde hair from Sherri Harvey. "The loas can't find her, she's warded, but she still lives. The rest is gone. Two is in heaven. One, this one," she said, holding up Marcella Simpson's hairs, "her soul be held in a vessel of the unclean. But this one be alive here to earth."

"That's . . . odd. Given what this ring does I'd have thought she'd be heart-ripped by now."

"The loas say she wasn't totally without sin." Madam Courtney ran the hairs through her hands, eyes closed. "She was a wild one, this one. Hard life. Sad. But still alive. Worse, now. She's gone *evil*, this one."

"Joined the group?"

"Can't rightly tell. But she gone to the Black, can tell that. The loas see a darkness clinging to her. Now to try and figure out why the G-man thinks you have something to do with it."

She started by casting the bones, looking for more informa-tion on the girls or those who had held them. On the ones who were dead, there was little information. But when she cast upon Sherri Harvey, the one still alive, she got more and asked for one of my hairs. I was shaved bald so I had to clip a fingernail. Then she cast them together, holding the strands of hair and a fingernail in her hands, eyes closed.

"It is true," she said in a deep voice, eyes now open and

unseeing. "You are the alpha and omega of this taking. You were the one who started this. And you shall be the one to finish it."

"Madam Courtney, that makes no sense!"

"You are bound to your brother. Cain and Abel. Yin and yang. You brought this to the world through that binding. You are the source of this taking. You shall be its end." Her eyes closed and she shuddered and lay back in the wooden chair, exhausted.

"Are you okay?"

"I'm fine. The White loas are angry. Fearsome anger! But not at you. You may have somehow caused this, but not maliciously. You are not the true culprit. That I'm sure of now. The loas are not mad at you, but they're angry as hell at your brother, though."

I didn't know how it made me feel to have it confirmed that Thornton was behind this. Certainly not surprised.

"He is an instrument of evil as sure as you were chosen for good." Madam Courtney paused to take a big gulp of rum. "You're the beginning and end but he's the whole middle. These sins are his doing. The loas was clear on that."

"Then I get the Cain and Abel reference, because the minute I find him I'm going to go full-on Cain."

"That would appear to be your calling." My real estate lady heartily agreed with my murder plans.

"Can you find him?"

"Doubt it. Even with a hair or such. Sure he's warded as well. What I might be able to find is this one," she added, picking up Marcella Simpson's hair. "This one is the power for an unclean vessel. I can feel the vessel. Ain't far off. Not New Orleans near, but it moves."

"Moves?"

"I can feel it moving now," she said, her voice deepening again. "Traveling. Feeding. Defiling. The monstrous vessel is warded. The soul, though, the soul of the innocent cries out for release. For heaven. For peace. It is tormented within that vessel. It longs for heaven, for a rescuer. This soul I can find, Mr. Gardenier. This soul *you* can find."

She opened her eyes and shook herself again.

"Them loas be all *over* this. *Angry* loas. I can *see* them warrior loas. They be shakin' out their wings, shakin' off the dust of centuries, ready to *fly* they so angry! Find these and you may have no job to do! The loas will rip their black hearts out with fiery hands! Come back in three days. I'll have something you can track this soul down with."

The sooner the better to track down my stupid brother, but I could make use of those days. "Good. I have to see a woman about a horse."

This time I wasn't meeting in an out-of-the-way house. This time I strode through the halls of power unafraid. This time I was meeting power players right in the open. Because this time in DC, I going to bring a smack-down to MCB.

Convincing Garrett to arrange the meeting with the senior member of the Republican side of the aisle, a senator from Oklahoma, as well as the chairwoman, a Democrat congresswoman from California, had been tough. My point was that it was do or die. Trying to duck and cover on slander like this only worked so long.

"We're nearly late," Bert said, looking at his watch.

"Nearly is not the same as late," I said. "I have no intention of turning up forty minutes early."

"You'd better have something concrete," the congressman's aide said.

"MCB doesn't have anything concrete. I'm going to give the committee the same thing the MCB's been peddling but with the details left in. And a week from now I'm going to hammer it home with a stake."

"Honorable Chairwoman," I said, shaking her hand.

I cordially detested Congresswoman Jeanette O'Brien (D, CA) and the same could be said in reverse. She was a huge proponent of my mother's side of the argument, "give monsters a chance." Mostly, I was sure, because of round-robin funding. Give the monster advocates grants and they sent money back to fund the congresswoman's campaigns. Then there was the fact that, like most members of the Select Committee on Unearthly Forces, she had never personally dealt with the aftermath of a group of vampires.

When I'd started doing the same round robin with PUFF money, it had upset the apple cart. But since my funding had been "cross-aisle"—not one dime of monster-lover grant money *ever* went to Republicans—she had to give at least lip service to paying attention lest she lose support from the Democrat side.

That was the only reason she was giving me the time of day. I had been allotted ten minutes in front of the Select Committee to make my case.

"Mr. Gardenier," she said, shaking my hand then taking a seat behind her big desk along with the rest of the politicians. "You begged for this meeting. Make it quick."

"As I'm sure you all know, I've recently been slandered by the MCB. I would like to point out that slander is their stock in trade. Often necessarily, but anyone associated with this committee should recognize that when someone uses slander on a daily basis for their job, using it for politics becomes second nature."

"Uh-huh . . . And you expect me to believe the MCB has been feeding us maliciously motivated lies?"

"Far from it. It's incompetence, which given that our country depends on the MCB for protection from the most heinous of all enemies, is far far worse. It was slander *based upon* incompetence and for purely political ends."

"You've lost me." Senator Vaughn was one of the slower committee members. "Which was it?"

"Both. I did the same thing MCB did. I went to a spellcaster and had a reading done on the location and status of some of the victims. I obtained hair samples from some of the victims' families and took them to a very powerful White voodoo woman in New Orleans. She confirmed most of what the MCB said."

"Then MCB's investigation could hardly be called slander," the chairwoman said. "The only reason you haven't been arrested is that Gary stuck his neck out for you. He's rapidly run out of favors. This meeting is his last one."

Garret Terry didn't look very happy when she put that out there so brazenly.

"I said *most*. The alpha and omega part, yes, but that basic information, Madam Chairwoman, is useless without good analysis. Which MCB screwed up entirely. I'm sure they got a very strong reading that I was involved, but that is because spirits were practically screaming that I needed to be involved in the case. I'm the one who is supposed to end it. *Get* me involved. Make me a *part* of it!"

She actually laughed out loud. "When hell freezes over."

"So you're saying you're not involved in the ring?" another congressman asked.

"Do you seriously think I've got *time* to kidnap children?" I snapped. "No, I am not. But what the casting actually meant was that to stop the ring I had to *become* involved—in the investigation. I am the omega. He who shall end it. The only one who can end it for whatever reason."

"How?" Senator Vaughn asked.

"I'll do what MCB should have done two years ago. I'll track the souls of the victims. Because *I* am not incompetent."

"You strolled in here thinking that we're just going to take you at your word, just because some two-bit New Orleans parlor witch you dredged up contradicts the report provided by the multibillion-dollar federal agency." The chairwoman snorted. "That's pretty incompetent."

"Give me a week and I'll find and shut this kidnapping ring down myself. I'll do in two weeks what the MCB hasn't been able to do in two years." I sure hoped I wouldn't come to regret that promise.

"Ahem, Chad, I should probably point out that if you do so, the MCB will simply say that you were involved all along, and are now just covering your tracks," Congressman Terry said.

"I'm sure they will. Which illustrates the real problem here. Anything can be considered 'being involved,' actual intent and actions be damned. Madam Chairwoman, all the illustrious members of the committee, are you aware that you are fundamentally in the same position as Congressman Terry?"

"Excuse me?" she asked.

"You take money from people who are involved in necromancy. You have close supporters who are potentially PUFF-applicable."

"How *dare* you say that!" the congresswoman shouted.

"Because it is true? So does Congressman Bouvrier, Senator Coshan, Senator Vaughn—I can continue listing members of the committee, Republican and Democrat. And each and every one of you, daily, have interaction with those who work with the supernatural, just from MCB agents alone. They, in turn, have contact with necromancers. A casting about any one of you, even those who consider themselves sacrosanct, would probably turn up similar connections."

"It certainly isn't on purpose, but I can guaran-damn-tee that all of us have gotten donations from some slimy individuals," Congressman Terry said.

There was some muttering, nodding, and shrugs. Most of the committee didn't care about me one way or the other, but they didn't like the idea that the MCB could hit them with the same hammer.

"All and *equally*. Which brings up the real problem. MCB used a poorly done, badly analyzed casting to attack a member of your committee. Congressmen Terry has done no wrong, except associate with a falsely accused man. As MCB can do at any time they choose to any one of you they want."

"The MCB wouldn't do that to one of us," insisted Vaughn.

"They just did. Are you going to allow MCB to jerk your leash? The way it's set up, isn't the leash supposed to be on them? Are you willing to relinquish that power and let MCB decide, through slander and lies which are their stock in trade, who is and who is not to be on *your* committee? Because the second you let MCB have that power, they will take it from you, and never give it back."

"Boy has a point," Senator Bouvrier said thoughtfully.

"That is a very serious accusation," a congresswoman snapped.

"I'm not making an *accusation*. I'm making an *observation*. I don't care. This is politics. You choose your bedfellows; the congressmen and senators choose theirs. That's how it works. MCB should not be deciding who is and is not acceptable on this committee based on that. If they made it on the basis of who has the worst contacts, many of your supporters could not pass that test. Nor could you. So are you going to let them decide through whisper campaigns?"

About half the committee seemed thoughtful about the idea of an out-of-control MCB. The other half wanted me to get cancer and die. That was a better ratio than I'd hoped for.

"Your time is up," the chairwoman said. "We'll look into this."

"Please do," I said, standing up. "In the meantime, I have a case to solve."

I picked up the soul tracker from Madam Courtney after getting back from DC. Now I just had to make good on my promise to track them down. For which I would need help.

"You want to take somebody *else*?" Franklin said.

New Orleans seemed to be heating up again. The full moon was on the way and we didn't need more people missing, but this was something that had to be done now.

"I kind of told the Select Committee that I'd have the case solved by the end of the week."

Franklin groaned.

"Which means tracking down and terminating a kidnapping ring that uses at least two wights that we know of. Can I take two wights? Sure. Can I take two wights, some armed humans and probably some other undead at the same time? Not so sure. I need backup."

Franklin groaned again, louder this time. This was why I didn't ever want to be a team lead. "Damn it, Chad."

"Come on, Franklin. Just one good guy."

"Got a new guy arriving today." Franklin sighed. "Fresh out of training. I need him here but maybe this will give him some more experience before the full moon."

"I know beggars can't be choosers, but a newbie? I don't have time to babysit a newbie. I promised *Congress*."

"He's good. Or should be. Former SEAL chief."

"Great," I said, grimacing. "A fuckin' *squid*. What's his name?"

"Sam Haven."

CHAPTER 9

Of course I got a *fuckin'* cowboy.

Don't get me wrong, Sam Haven turned out to be a great guy, but it took a while for us to click. I'm sort of an intellectual though I can play the dumb game. I like the finer things in life. I'm seriously into martial arts and bushido. Sam was then and is now all about being the "rangy tough guy." Born in Montana, raised on rodeo and pitching hay bales. If you'd tried to tell me that in a couple years he would be considered one of the best Hunters in the company, I wouldn't have believed you. I felt like Franklin had stuck me with some tobacco-spitting, cowboy-hat-and-boots-wearing ex-squid who clearly thought his shit don't stink.

"So, let me get this straight," Sam drawled, spitting into his disgusting cup. It was a coffee mug with his SEAL team logo on it. "Some group has been abducting girls for the last few years and killing their families and the FBI and MCB can't solve shit, but we've got only a few days to track the kidnapping cocksuckers down using bullshit hocus-pocus?"

We were driving up I-10 towards 49. The tracker, a simple crystal pendant with Marcella Simpson's hair wrapped around it, was swinging in a generally northwesterly direction. I'd just hooked it to my rearview mirror and off we went.

"It's not hocus-pocus. It's hoodoo," I said. "Magic. It'll work."

"You say so, pal."

Sam's SEAL team had been on a training mission when a nearby cruise liner had been attacked. They'd inserted by helicopter, only to discover that the ship had been swarmed by Deep Ones—monsters which were a "save the last bullet for yourself" type. Especially when they were breeding, which they were in this case.

Sam's team had mostly been wiped out. Only two of the SEALs had survived: the lieutenant by hiding in a locker, Sam by running around killing everything that wasn't human. Total hero stuff from what Franklin had told me.

Problem being, MCB, when they'd arrived, had just gone and killed everyone who was implanted and anyone who *might* be implanted. Was it overkill? Wasn't there. Keeping Deep Ones down was a major concern. Probably something less drastic they could have done but MCB tends to work on scorched earth. Often it's all they have *time* to do.

Sam had complained about the murdered civilians, loudly and as officially as he was allowed. Which meant MCB had to take care of the problem child. My guess was SEAL high command went all weenie when they offered to off him. Instead, Sam's career was trashed and the coward lieutenant was suddenly a hero. Sam quit in disgust. The lieutenant, unsurprisingly, joined MCB. He'd fit right in. Probably make director some day.

Or maybe not. I'd met good MCB agents. I missed Higgins and Castro nearly as much as I missed Trevor and Shelbye. But I wasn't going to poke that bull with Haven. And a good bit of the question would be based on who was on the committee and whether the chairwoman would allow it to be gelded or not.

"Magic crystals...What kind of chickenshit mission have I signed up for?" Sam muttered as he looked at the charm. "If it's so easy, how come the MCB never hired a magician to build them one of these?"

"MCB's got magic," I said. "What they don't have is Madam Courtney."

"Who's Madam Courtney?"

"One powerful-as-shit voodoo woman. White voodoo. If you're going to be working in New Orleans you really should get to know her. She's also one hell of a real estate lady. You should see the house she found for me...But I don't think the loas—think of them as angels—would show just anybody the way. I'm supposed to be the one who ends this," I said, nodding at the hair. "One of the cult's undead is powered by the soul of that girl. Where it is, there will be its master."

"Uh-huh..."

"Marcella's soul is sort of bound in a tiny slice of hell, and she's screaming to be rescued. Like I said, powerful-as-shit White voodoo. Madam Courtney says the loas are all over this and angry. That 'magic crystal' you're sneering at represents a little girl who was murdered to power a strong undead, who is screaming for us to come kill it and let her poor tortured soul go to heaven. It'll work because angels want me to find her."

"This job is fucking weird."

"You think *this* is weird? You might want to find another profession."

"Nah, I'm good. Let's go rescue some damsels from the nefarious assholes of evil."

"Don't get too wrapped up on that one. Most of the girls we save, they're so mentally messed up you don't want to get involved. On the other hand, Hoodoo Squad is pretty popular in New Orleans. Finding girls is not an issue."

"That wasn't the direction I was thinking...but I've heard New Orleans knows how to party. The girls nice here?"

"Who wants nice girls? Nothing better than a slutty elf chick."

"Elf? Now you're just fucking with me."

"You've got to be shitting me," Sam said, laughing.

"I'd suggest you check the scars on my ass but I don't let swabbies that near my butt," I said.

"Oh, you did not go there, jarhead!"

"That story is *totally* made up," I said, shaking my head. "I've been to Rota! There is no way that is true! Bangkok, maybe. Not Rota."

"God is my witness." Sam held up one hand and put the other over his heart. "And you're one to talk. Next thing you're going to tell me you rescued some princess from a tower..."

"Oh!" Sam said. "That is totally grody! Jesus! Did I just say 'grody'?"

"I *told* you. Even at this range Fey magic is like totally

pernicious and infective. You need to keep careful watch on that sort of thing in this job."

"So you play the *violin*?"

"Got a *problem* with that, pinniped boy?"

"Nah," Sam said. "I play the banjo, *sinker* boy."

"Sinker boy?" I'd never heard that one.

"One of our missions is to recover Marines killed in amphibious operations. Was. Whatever. SEAL mission. Amphib sinks, Marines are weighed down with all their gear. You know, sinkers. Great spots for a little spear fishing I might add. Fish just flock to a good jarhead sinker."

"That is so sick it might even be true," I said.

"Don't get me started on newbie pilots in P'cola..."

I-49 sort of peters out in Texarkana where we stayed overnight in a fleabag motel. We had to unload Honeybear's trunk 'cause I wasn't going to leave all the dangerous shit in the parking lot to get stolen.

"You carry LAWs?" Sam said.

"That an issue?"

"Naw. I love 'em."

"Stick those in the golf bag with the guns. I'd rather people not see them around here. There might be talk."

"Ya think?" Then he got towards the bottom. "That case is mil-spec. And it's still sealed. Why's it painted brown?"

"So people won't notice what it says is inside," I said, pulling out another couple of ammo cans. "You going to tote or ask questions?"

"What *would* it say was inside?" Sam asked as he carried the case toward the room. "If it wasn't badly spray-painted brown, that is. Because from the size, weight and shape, it's a case of claymores."

"Okay," I said, putting my hands on my hips. "Are you accusing me of being *stupid enough* to carry claymores in my trunk?"

"That's what I thought," Sam said, grinning ear to ear. "We gonna get to use 'em?"

"Depends on what we find when we get to the end of the rainbow. I only brought ten of them."

We took I-30 out of Texarkana the next day and shortly afterwards found ourselves on God-help-me US 82, the Northeast Texas Trail as it proudly proclaimed.

Two-lane blacktop and fuck all. And I do mean, *fuck all*. There were trees and some houses and stuff at least. But it was just...Holy crap. Fuck. All.

Fortunately, Sam had a lot of stories. So did I. And while he had a sorely awful taste in music—Conway Twitty? Seriously?—it was my car and I was driving and he didn't actually hate hard rock and what metal we could find, so we got along that way. Because if it had been the other way around, he'd have lost his head to Mo No Ken.

He hadn't really asked about the sword but when I'd been working on it I could tell he was looking at it sort of like "who is this fucker with his samurai bullshit?" He had a CAR-15, a SIG P220, and a big-ass bowie knife on his belt to compliment the general cowboy attitude and attire.

We stopped at a roadhouse for lunch and he fit right in. Me, not so much. I was wearing a tailored MHI polo shirt and khakis. What? I like to look good. Sue me.

We stayed on 82 for a few hours then started to get more of a movement north from the pendant. So we turned north towards Denison on 69. Up through Durant, Oklahoma, then west again to Madill through more fuck-all and two-lane roads. Fortunately there was light traffic and anything moving slow I could pass with Honeybear, my 1976 Cutlass Supreme. I was totally ignoring the double nickel. If I got stopped, I had half a dozen get-out-of-jail-free cards to call in.

We did get stopped once, just short of the Oklahoma border, by a Texas Ranger. I was blowing along a back road doing somewhere around a hundred and twenty. He came around a corner in the other direction, slowed, turned on the blue lights and turned around. I just slowed down and pulled over when I saw him slowing.

He was like some sort of a stereotype. Six foot nine thousand. Blond from what I could see as he got out of his car. He did the get-out-real-slow unfolding thing. Set his hat on his head, and walked up real slow, pulling out his ticket book.

"You gentlemen in a hurry to get somewhere?" he asked politely.

I knew the Rangers handled a good bit of their own hoodoo. So I just handed over an MHI card.

"What's the incident?" All of a sudden the Ranger was real serious like.

"We're tracking a group of kidnappers." I gestured at the pendant, which was clearly not plumb. "Looks like they've headed into Oklahoma. Use of supernatural entities, necromancy, kidnapping for use in the supernatural and, oh yeah, serial first-degree murder."

"Keep it between the lines." He handed me back the card. "I'll call a couple of buddies up Durant way, case you get stopped up there."

"Thank you, Ranger. Keep it. You never know when you're gonna need it."

"Will do." He tucked it into a pocket.

I sped off and was over eighty before he was out of sight.

"I thought all this stuff was OPSEC?" Sam said.

"Some groups are read in, others aren't. You'll learn who is and isn't wherever you're working. Rangers are all read in before they hit the road their first day. They've got such large patrol areas, they have to be fully in the know. And generally they take care of most of Texas' hoodoo. Or as they like to put it, one Ranger, one revenant."

"I thought it was one Ranger, one riot."

"Yeah. Sure." I chuckled. "And Sam Houston never killed any vampires."

It was late night as we rolled through a tiny little unnamed hamlet near Madill, Oklahoma. The pendant's swings had become more pronounced every time we made a turn. It was clear we were getting close. It currently pointed straight ahead and well off plumb.

"This fits the target type." I stopped Honeybear on a deserted side road. "Out of the way area, Bible Belt, sort of place you might actually find some virgins. The only reason I can think they'd be out in an area like this is to make a raid. A house somewhere nearby is going to burn tonight unless we stop it."

"Frago?" Sam said.

Fortunately I spoke semifluent pinniped. He was asking for a "fragmentary order" or in other words "what's the plan?"

"Rig, find, terminate."

"Romeo, Foxtrot, Tango, it is." Sam got out of the car.

I'd had to pull a lot of stuff out of Honeybear's trunk to accommodate Sam's gear. The Barrett probably wasn't going to be used, so there went the need for all the .50 cal. I hadn't been sure if it would be open country or closed so I had my M-14 and the Uzi. Despite the fact that this was pure open country, I went with the Uzi. We'd probably find them around houses.

I threw my vest on over my armor, zipped it up, then attached the Uzi to it. Sam was rocking the CAR-15 on a single-point sling. Last, I retrieved Mo No Ken.

"I gotta ask..."

"Don't," I said. "Just watch. Your job, if it comes to close action, is to shoot things to slow them down and let *me* handle it. Try for head shots if you can make them."

Sam just shook his head like I'd said something stupid. "I'll try and manage."

"Especially the wights. If they've got revenants, same thing. Wights are stronger, savage, and can paralyze you with a touch. Revenants are going to look more like people, and can use weapons, but their movements are jerky. They're like automated flesh robots."

Whenever possible before an op I stretch. Seems silly. It's like the pissing thing. I'm one of those guys who fights three-dimensionally. Up, down, sideways, around. I didn't stretch long but it was long enough to get out the road kinks. And I'd stretched that morning and after each meal, so I was pretty limber. Sam simply grabbed some extra mags and stuck fresh dip in his lip.

Then we loaded back up. After taking a piss. Sam already knew about that one.

By the time we were rolling, the pendant was moving. So was our target.

I kept the lights off and drove by the moonlight. I had NVGs if I needed them but the rubber straps were a bitch to put on. Sam had his stupid cowboy hat on and was holding his NVGs up taking a look around from time to time.

We found the target on the outskirts of Madill. There was a white panel van parked outside the house and the front door was already busted open. We could hear the screaming from inside through the open windows.

Someone came out the front door, holding a shotgun. Possibly human, possibly a revenant.

"Target!" I said, driving Honeybear right into the yard. "Front d—"

Before I'd finished my warning, Sam stuck the CAR out his window and fired.

From a moving car, in the dark, nearly a hundred yards away, Sam dropped him with a head shot. Yeah. The newbie would "manage."

We stopped and bailed out of the car. The body was already trying to get up, leaking brains be damned.

"Revenant. Mine." I swept my sword from the sheath.

"I'm going in," Sam said.

This revenant was new. Fast and strong but not real agile and not particularly bright. It was reaching for its dropped shotgun. Blood sprayed in the moonlight as I ran past swinging Mo No Ken. Then I followed Sam through the door.

My partner was already shooting. A CAR is really loud inside a small living room.

A wight was dragging a brown-haired girl by her hair towards the door through the living room as I entered. Sam had knocked one of its eyes out and half its skull off. I didn't even slow down. One slash down and the hand holding the girl's hair was still clutching it but on the floor. Slash and one leg was gone. Slash and the head was flying.

We swept through the house. A human male had been pouring kerosene on the kitchen floor. He dropped his can and went for a pistol stuffed in his waistband. Sam shifted over and put two in his heart. Since cultists had a tendency to rise from the dead, I moved up and slashed as he fell. Blood and kerosene mingled on the floor from the spilled containers.

Another wight was in the upstairs hallway. It was just leaving one of the bedrooms. From the screaming, I had expected it to be covered in blood, but neither seemed to have killed anyone yet.

We didn't wait for it to change its mind. Sam riddled it with bullets. The wight slammed into the wall, but it was damned near impossible to finish one of these off with a gun. "Hold on!" I moved past Sam. As the wight charged I turned to saber stance, slashed both its wrists and drove the point of Mo No Ken through its eye socket. That didn't kill it, but it sure as hell slowed it down. It gave me enough time to pull my sword out and do a quick and tight slash.

Off with their heads. Also doesn't kill them. You have to burn them to be sure. But as long as you keep the head and body separated, they're pretty much useless.

So I punted the head down the stairs as Sam cleared the

rooms. Sort of tingles your foot when you kick a wight but doesn't paralyze. Pro-tip.

The family was alive. They were all paralyzed from the wights. The fuckers were going to burn them alive in their own beds.

"Clear!" Sam looked out the bedroom window. "The van's gone." The rest of the kidnappers had bailed while we'd been fighting their wights. "These folks gonna be okay?"

"The paralysis will wear off." I ran for the stairs. "We have to catch that van."

Sam was right behind me. "You're not half good with that sword, are you?"

"Bit," I said. "We can't let them get too far ahead."

"We've still got the tracker."

"Odds are one of these was the vessel," I said.

"Shit."

When we got downstairs, I paused to kick the wight's head again into the front hallway. Then found the other one and rolled it towards the front door. Then both of them got kicked out the front door. Did I ever mention I used to play soccer? Both heads soared into the neighboring yards. Let them try to join up with the bodies now. I added the revenant's head for good measure. Made it across the road with that one.

"Which way did they go?" I asked as we got back in the car.

"That way," Sam said, pointing behind us.

I spun Honeybear around in a doughnut and handed him my sword.

"Wipe and sheathe that, would you? Watch your fingers."

"Check it out. Tracker's still working."

Sure enough, Madam Courtney's little amulet was still swaying.

We pounded up Main Street in a cloud of dust and a hail of gravel. And Sam had to start singing.

"*Dirt road main street.*" He sang, lustily and badly. "*She walked off in baaare feet!*"

"I've got perfect pitch, you fucker," I said.

"Think they're singing the same song?" Sam asked.

There were taillights way ahead of us.

"They are not getting away."

They had a big head start, but there was no way a Chevy van was going to outrun Honeybear. I took the turn left onto Highway 70 in a spray of gravel. This time of night there was virtually no traffic. I put my foot down. The road was more or less straight and I watched it, the van, and my compression meter until I got to the right poundage. Then I hit the big red button.

"You got nitrous in this thing?" Sam bellowed in delight.

"Fuck yeah, I got nitrous."

"I'm going to pass them." I was gaining on the van and still accelerating. "Then get past them. Then you lean out and hit them with that LAW in the back seat. Right in the engine block."

"Might not be many people to question."

"MCB can hire a necromancer to question them after they're dead, but they are *not* getting away."

"Except we don't know if they got any hostages out of that house before we got there," Sam pointed out.

He was right. "Shit."

"Just stick on them."

The van suddenly slowed, braked and turned onto a side road.

"And now we're losing them again," Sam said.

"Hang on."

I turned off the nitrous, hit the parking brake and did a moonshiner's turn. Then we were headed back their way again.

The side road was dirt again and went straight on to nowhere. The washboard effect was rattling the hell out of Honeybear. I wasn't sure what they were thinking of doing but I doubted it was good.

"Get ready for a furball when we get up to them," I said. "This is probably going to involve gunplay. So you'll be more at home than I."

"Gunfights I can handle," Sam said. "You can leave the High-lander katana in the car."

"You watched that movie?"

"I fucking love that movie," Sam said. *"There can be only one!"*

Ahead of the van I spotted the lights of an oil rig. There was a tractor trailer parked there, and a bunch of figures milling around.

"Looks like our kidnappers weren't traveling alone."

The van slammed on the brakes, the doors flew open, and several people jumped out. From the way they were greeted, the people waiting with the semi were definitely their allies. The bodies passing in front of the headlights were moving in a jerky, twitchy manner.

"Revenants," I said.

"Needing decapitation. Looks like you've got an excuse to bring a sword to a gunfight, MacLeod."

There were muzzle flashes ahead. Luckily, revenants were terrible shots, but they were shooting a lot. Bullets smashed into my grill. One headlight went out. Honeybear's window cracked. Sam leaned out the window and started shooting like crazy, only from their reactions, he was actually hitting them.

Rather than stop in the open and get pinned down, I drove right through the revenants. The first one got clipped and flew off into the weeds. The next went right under the bumper and I could feel it crunch under the tires and undercarriage. I hoped that one didn't break my oil pan.

I hit the brakes and slid in sideways behind the van. A girl had been dragged from the back. A man dressed in black was wrestling her around, trying to use her as a human shield. Two more armed men came running out from behind the van.

Sam was out of Honeybear before it had even stopped moving.

In a flash he raised the CAR, fired two shots, then shifted over and fired two more. Both gunmen fell. He must have run dry, because he immediately dropped the carbine and drew his pistol. The last cultist put a knife to the girl's throat and began screaming his demands just as Sam put a .45 through the bridge of his nose. No hesitation.

They'd gone down so fast the dust from Honeybear hadn't even caught up to us yet. The girl was still standing in the headlights, stunned, the kidnapper's blood all over her nightgown.

The last two humans had climbed into the tractor trailer. It began rumbling off. Were they seriously trying to escape in that thing? Yes, they were. It began to rumble towards us. I realized that among other things it could crush Honeybear like a tin can. I needed to stop that truck *fast*.

A badly broken revenant came limping up as I got out, so I took it down with two swipes of Mo No Ken, then reached into the back seat and took out one of the LAWs. I extended the tube and aimed it at the truck's grill.

"Shit!" Sam realized what I was doing, grabbed the girl, and pulled her behind the van so she wouldn't get hit with shrapnel.

The rocket exploded and shredded the front of the truck. The engine began to burn as it came to a stop.

None of the dead had been Thornton. Madam Courtney's warrior loas were rejoicing tonight, but this didn't feel complete yet. Alpha and omega. I knew I still had something I needed to do.

The truck was partially engulfed in flames when I got the door open and pulled the driver out. He had been hammered by the explosion, intestines spilling out of his enormous fat gut.

I didn't bother with kindness. Not for the likes of him. I tossed him out of the truck onto the ground. The passenger was a girl—dead as she was going to get short of the roasting her body was about to endure. I recognized her. Sherri Harvey. Fifteen. Probably seventeen now. One of the sleepover party from Pueblo, who Madam Courtney had declared lost to the darkness. Son of a bitch.

I jumped down to the ground and looked down at my only brother.

"Well, hello, Thornton. Long time no see."

"I need a hospital," Thornton gasped. He was trying to fit his intestines back in his gut.

"Seriously?" I said. "You have to know the penalty for what you've been doing. And that it has nothing in the way of appeal. I'm going to get *paid* for killing you and your girlfriend. So I gotta ask you, bro. What the *fuck*? Even for you, stealing little girls is low. And you're about the lowest sack of shit I know."

"Chad?" Thornton said.

I realized he hadn't even recognized me.

"Yeah, Thornton, it's Chad. Now, again. What the *fuck*? Kidnapping virgins? Why?"

"Fuck you, you little bitch," Thornton shouted. "Get me a doctor! You have to help me! I'm your brother!"

"Oh, wrong answer."

The fire from the destroyed engine was basically contained under the body of the truck. I reached down, grabbed a fistful of his intestines and pitched them in the fire.

Thornton had been my nightmare growing up. So abusive I still carried the physical scars much less the emotional ones. Despite that, if I didn't need the information I wouldn't have done it. But later I had to admit to my father confessor it felt good to get the bastard back. I had to say a lot of rosaries. Not for doing it, but for it feeling *good*.

Thornton started screaming. There are nerve endings in intestines.

I pulled the intestines out of the fire like reeling in a line. "Want me to do that *again*? Answer me!"

"*You're* why! It was *you*!"

"That makes no sense at all!"

"Remember Debby Southfield?"

"Who?" I asked, confused.

"Debby *Southfield*. My prom date."

"Oh..." That had come out of left field. "Cute brunette? Kinda chubby?"

He was getting weak from blood loss, going into shock. "She spent the whole time at the house talking to *you*! And the whole rest of the night talking about how *cool* you were. You were four years younger than I was but every time a girl came around it was all about Chad! Chad! Chad! 'Chad's so dreamy.' 'Thornton, your brother is really cute.' You got all the girls, you little fucker! I had to work for it! You just smiled and they all came running! Why do you think I fucking hate them so much!"

What the fuck?

"That's... That's... You blame *me* for kidnapping girls, young girls, killing their families, human fucking sacrifice!" I shouted. "How much for virgins, Thornton? And what did you do with the girls who weren't virgins? Rape them?"

"Of course," Thornton said as if *any* of this made sense. "And sacrifice them. Non-virgin sacrifices work for most things. Sell them to vamps. Twenty thousand for a virgin. Five thousand for a non-virgin. Even I wasn't willing to rape the virgins for that much cash."

"Twenty thousand dollars for a virgin?" I said. "That's a lot of money."

"Any idea how hard it is to find a virgin these days?" Thornton said.

Then he died.

And surprisingly enough didn't rise. I took his head off just to be on the safe side.

While I'd been interrogating my psychotic scumbag brother, Sam had checked the trailer and discovered a couple more girls tied up inside, kidnapped hitchhikers Thornton had found on the way. He got them out before the whole thing burned down.

After we'd hacked up the revenants and tossed the still-moving pieces into the truck fire, Sam joined me back at Honeybear.

"So I take it that pork-cracklin'-looking fat-ass was your brother?"

I didn't really want to talk about it. "Yeah."

"Seems kinda messed up. Funny though, all that long-ass drive here and you never once mentioned to me we might be chasing your own blood relative."

"Does it matter?"

"Beats me." Sam shrugged. "My brothers are pretty cool. I can't really see any of them taking up necromancy as a hobby. Well, maybe Scott. But he joined the Coast Guard, so he's a little *touched*."

"You don't seem surprised it was my brother."

"That weird red-headed kid . . . Milo, I think it is. He gave me a heads-up who might be behind this. He wanted me to keep an eye on you. I think he was worried you'd go off the deep end batshit revenge crazy and 'damage your immortal soul' or some such."

"That was nice of him to worry," I said. "What are you going to tell Milo?"

"Eh, I'll say it went great. All you did was yank out his guts like a garden hose. Seems like a rational, proportionate response to me . . . Uh . . . But you did kill your own brother. You want to talk about it?"

"Not at all."

"Good. I really ain't the guy to talk to about feelings and shit, so how about we finish cleaning up this mess, find the nearest bar, and get stinking drunk?"

Sam Haven was going to make a great Monster Hunter.

Oh, boy, was this a lot of excitement in a small town. Especially when we explained, politely, to the nice sheriff's deputy that we had to burn the headless bodies that were still flopping around. He kept shooting them but they wouldn't stop flopping! They just won't stop moving! How can they keep moving? Given that the house was filled with kerosene and the family was outside in their nightgowns trying to explain the unexplainable . . .

Then there was the explosion of the LAW to account for.

And did I mention the burning truck? Which got more spectacular when it got to the fuel tanks and I'm really glad we got the girls out first.

Oh, *boy*, this was a *lot* of excitement in a small town.

I cut through some of the Gordian knots and walked into the house to use the phone. I pulled out my little black book of numbers and ignored MCB.

"Go," the sleepy male voice said.

You had better have a damned good reason or balls of steel to call an FBI agent at home in the middle of the night.

"Hey, Special Agent Grant. This is Chad Gardenier from MHI. Remember me? I solved your case. Six human perpetrators dead. Various undead perps deader as soon as we can convince the local authorities to let us burn the bodies. Wights and revenants just keep moving until you burn them. Oh, by the way, you're welcome."

"I heard you raised hell with a certain subcommittee that doesn't exist," Don said, no longer half asleep.

"For good reason," I said. "MCB totally screwed the pooch on this one. Which is why I'm calling you guys first. Can I go get the local yokel deputy and have him talk to you? I think the only reason he hasn't drawn down on us is we're better armed."

Don sighed. "Put him on."

CHAPTER 10

After we got back from Oklahoma, I requested another meeting with the Select Committee. No answer. Too bad. I wanted to rub their faces in my succeeding where the MCB had failed.

For a little while life returned to "normal."

A few days later I was back in the team room when Sam Haven fielded a call from the SIU.

"Giant pissed-off crocodile..." he said in a confused tone, looking at the note.

"In the 17th Street Canal," I finished, sighing. "Bring a Barrett and some LAWs just in case."

Why sobeks always chose the 17th Street Canal was one of those mysteries of life. They turned up every few months and were major pains in the ass. I hadn't dealt with one since the new breed MCB had arrived and was sooo looking forward to it.

We didn't know where they came from, how they got here, what they were doing here, or why a few times a year one tried to wander down the 17th Street Canal, but as per usual, the bipedal-Egyptian-crocodile-god thing had gotten itself stuck on the main pumping station and was trying to climb the levee. Their bipedal form made it hard for them to do anything, really. They weren't pathetic, by any stretch of the imagination. They were seriously dangerous up close or if they got into the neighborhoods, but they fricking *always* got stuck at the pumping station.

When we arrived at the pumping station on Lake Avenue, there were some bystanders in the area watching the latest in New Orleans hoodoo. There weren't very many because it was late and the rain was keeping most people indoors. MCB was trying to chase off the witnesses, and Agent Robinson was in a heated discussion with an old woman up on the railroad tracks. It was clear that MCB was trying to get the crowd to disperse but short of opening fire on them that was unlikely to happen. And SIU was being passive-aggressive about helping them out.

"Afternoon, Agent Robinson," I said, sauntering up.

"You *will* go back to your home," Robinson snarled at the old lady. "Or I will place you under arrest!"

"This is a free country, young man!" She shook her umbrella at him. "And I will go wherever I damned well please! Are you going to arrest all of us?"

"From what I've seen, they're more likely to just machine-gun the civilians and be done with it," Sam muttered to me.

"Lieutenant Wade," Robinson shouted. "Place this woman under arrest!"

"What do I charge her with, Agent?" Wade said in a slow, somewhat dumb-sounding, Cajun drawl. Local law enforcement missed Special Agent Castro's brand of leadership as much as I did. "I really need a solid charge, Agent. The DOJ is all over our ass lately for all sorts of violations of civil rights. I mean there's a whole task force—"

"We *are* the DOJ! Just do it!"

"Well, I'd really like to see that in writing..."

I interrupted the shouting fest and addressed the old lady. "Mrs. Thevenet. How are you doing today?"

"These G-men don't have no respect," she said with a sniff. "Act as if you can pretend voodoo don't exist in New Orleans! Sell that to the tourists, young man!"

"New brooms," I said, shrugging. "You know they lost all their good people at Mardi Gras."

"That is classified!" Robinson shrieked.

"He'll figure out how it works sooner or later," I said, ignoring him. "Right now, we really need to just play along. Figure you can get these people to sort of wander away? Nothing new here to see, anyway."

"Well, if they're going to do something, they should be finding out who keeps sending this hoodoo down here," Mrs. Thevenet said angrily. "This is the fifth time in a year and a half!"

"I told you to place her under arrest!"

"And I said I'd need something in writing," Wade said, crossing her arms. "Me and my department ain't gonna get sued 'cause *you're* all hot and bothered."

"I totally agree, ma'am," I said. "But in the meantime, do me a favor, okay? Try to get people to clear the area. Right now, we've gotta get started on clearing this up."

"I'll do it this once as a favor, young man," Mrs. Thevenet said. "But I'm definitely going to call Congressman Bouvrier. I pay my taxes!"

"Any communication about this incident is a violation of federal law!" Robinson snapped. "If you so much as pick up the phone to call your congressman, I will, I guarantee you, arrest you. And you will spend the rest of your natural life in prison."

She was so old that probably wasn't that much of a threat. "You ain't from around here, are you?" Mrs. Thevenet said, walking away. But she started chivvying her people to clear the area.

"Just an FYI, Agent Robinson, Congressman Bouvrier is the second most senior majority member of the Select Committee. And her third cousin. She grew up with the congressman's mother. Might want to reconsider that threat."

"Just stay *out* of this, Gardenier! And you can just go back to your shack! *We're* going to clear this incident!"

"Excuse me? Since when does MCB clear incidents?"

"Orders of Special Agent Campbell. We're taking responsibility for all yellow-level threats from now on. You cowboys make too much of a scene when you deal with something like this!"

"Well," I said thoughtfully. "Since we are read in, mind if we stay and watch?"

"Feel free," Robinson said. "We'll show you how a professional deals with this sort of thing."

"Oh, this is gonna be fun," I said as we walked back to my car.

"That agent is the easily agitated sort, ain't he? Now I'm wondering if he meant *cowboys* as a personal insult." Sam thumped his knuckles against his ridiculous rodeo champion belt buckle. "I'm wounded." He went to retrieve his gear bag.

"First off, no point to the armor. With a sobek, if you're

close enough for the gear to matter, it don't matter. Thing will rip right through it or kill you by impact with its tail. So you get all hot for nothing."

"So how do you kill it?"

"We've done it enough times we've got a system. There's a kill spot on the back of the head that's about a foot across," I said, holding my hands up a foot wide. "You shoot it through there, with something big, at a certain angle. Angle's important, too. What you do is get waaaay back and shoot it there. If you hit it at the wrong angle, or miss the spot, or hit it anywhere else on the body, it just pisses it off. If you hit it near the spot or at the wrong angle, you can cause it to thrash. As you can see, it's already damaging the levee. Enough levee damage and New Orleans floods. So getting it right the first time is sort of important."

"Only that jittery rabbit-ass agent won't let us. Boy really needs to switch to decaf before he strokes out."

"We make too much noise or something," I said, disgusted. "So they get to kill it."

"Isn't that sort of stealing our PUFF money?" Sam asked.

"I'm just hoping they get the shot right."

The crowd had been duly shuffled off by SIU, NOPD, and Mrs. Thevenet, and now the agent who'd been trailing Robinson was up on the railroad bridge with some sort of super-duper sniper rifle. The thing looked as if it had some sort of suppressor on the end. So, you know, they could pretend they *weren't* shooting a fifty-foot bipedal crocodile.

The real problem, though . . .

"No, no, no, no," I muttered.

"What's wrong?" Sam asked.

We were standing under the shade of a live oak, watching the proceedings, arms crossed.

"I'm pretty sure that's a .308," I said. "Something along the lines."

"It is," Sam said. "That's an Accuracy International. It might be chambered in .300 Win Mag. Good rifle."

"Whatever. Very much the wrong caliber. There's no such thing as too large with a sobek. There *is* such a thing as too small. Fifty-caliber's the way to go with one. *Too* small if anything. And I'm pretty sure they're going to fire at—"

The sniper took the shot as I was saying that and the round hit the kill spot. But it was at the wrong angle, or maybe just didn't penetrate enough, and the sobek began to thrash and bellow, tearing at the bank of the levee.

The local supervisor for Army Corps of Engineers ran onto the train bridge and started haranguing Agent Robinson as the sniper fired again. Having previously dealt with the guy, I knew he was understandably protective of his levee. Because much of New Orleans was below the water line and if the levee ever broke, most of the city would be flooded a story deep. He really *liked* to keep water out of the city. What he did *not* like was sobeks tearing up his dams. He was really definite on that subject. Which was what MCB was giving him.

This time the round bounced off the armored skull and the sobek got even angrier. It spun around in place looking for what was hurting it and decided that it must have something to do with the train bridge. Giant jaws clamped on one of the trestles and it tried to death roll.

The MCB sniper leaned over, rapidly working the bolt, and kept firing, bullets bouncing every which way. And from the looks of things, the bridge was probably going to have to be temporarily closed and surveyed to assess the damage. Assuming the pissed-off crocodilian didn't pull it down.

I'd never seen someone as red in the face as the Corps guy. And from Robinson's attitude, he was giving a senior member of the Army Corps of Engineers the MCB "if you don't shut up I'll arrest you" line.

That was going to go over just dandy. MCB might think it was powerful but you didn't comprehend powerful until you dealt with the Army Corps of Engineers.

"I've seen enough," I said, shaking my head. "Let's roll back to the team shack. I do *not* want to be here when this incident finally gets cleared and MCB is looking for someone to blame."

We were about halfway back to headquarters when the phone rang.

"Gardenier," I said.

"Who the hell did you call, Gardenier?" the voice on the other end snarled.

"No one. Lately. Who may I ask is calling?"

"This is Special Agent Campbell. So you're *not* responsible for calls from the Army Corps of Engineers and half the Select Committee?"

"Nope. We rolled to the sobek. Robinson told us you guys were handling it. We watched the beginning of said handling, then left. Didn't need to call anyone. Your guys did all the work."

"Turn around, go back, kill the sobek," Campbell said as calmly as he could manage.

"No."

"*What?*" Campbell shouted.

"The sobek is currently pissed off, agitated and very dangerous. It has been repeatedly wounded by your agents. MCB took responsibility for it, so *you* kill it. You want some advice on that, I can give it. But I already called Franklin and MHI is *not* going to be blamed for another Class Five incident."

I got a *click* for my troubles.

"I hear those things are worth a really nice PUFF," Sam pointed out.

"There'll be another one in a few months. And they really would have used this to make us look bad. Campbell is a manipulative conniving bastard and his report would make us out to be 'incompetent' or at least 'very indiscreet.' There's no clean way to kill that sobek now that it's enraged."

We were nearly back to the shack when the phone rang again.

"Gardenier," I said as politely as I could. I figured it was Campbell again or someone else yelling at me.

"Chad! Congressman Bouvrier! How are you, young man?"

"Fine, sir, fine," I said, sliding smoothly into Southern mode. "And how is Bambi?"

"Curvy and beautiful as always." Nobody could ever remember the names of the various paramours and trophy wives of the seventy-year-old congressman so he insisted everyone just call them Bambi. Saves time. "Are you taking another sabbatical, son?"

"I earned the one after Mardi Gras, but if you're referring to the sobek, no. Just not taking that one."

"Is there a reason?" the congressman asked.

"MCB took responsibility for clearing it, sir. They are taking all large incidents from now on according to the agent on site. I wouldn't wish to steal their thunder."

"They bungled it," the congressman said. "Mrs. Thevenet was

watching the whole thing. I'm not sure if you heard but they missed the shot. It's now out of the canal and rampaging through her neighborhood. She is rather unhappy. And since there is now a fifty-foot crocodile wandering through New Orleans, I can't think of anyone who *is* happy."

I hit the brakes, did a U-turn and hit the siren and lights.

"On it, Congressman. Mrs. Thevenet's on the west side of the canal?"

"Yes, she is," Congressman Bouvrier said. "I take it you're on your way back?"

"Congressman, I really need a favor," I said.

"If it involves getting MCB off your back, consider it done. When I'm done with this new special agent, his hide won't be missing a single spot that hasn't been scored."

"There is no way, if the sobek is out, we're going to be able to do it quietly. This is heavy-weapons time and no joke. Campbell has to be made fully aware of that. Through the chain of command. He won't take it from you. And what we're going to have to do at this point will piss him off royally."

"I understand, son. I'll make the calls."

"We really need to get together again sometime soon, Congressman," I said. "Dinner at my place?"

"You set a fine table, Chad," Congressman Bouvrier said. "Why don't you have Remi call my people, look at the schedule?"

"Will do," I said, weaving through traffic. I made a left turn through a red light and hit my horn at someone who didn't know what a purple flashing light meant. "Sort of need to hang up at this point, Congressman."

"Understood. Good talking to you, Chad."

"Sam," I snapped, handing over the phone. "Call the office. Tell Franklin we need everybody. Full call out. Boots and saddles and every heavy weapon we've got!"

By the time we got back, the sobek was two blocks up Lake Avenue. Looking down the long boulevard, it was one continuous scene of flipped cars, torn-down power lines and crushed homes.

The crocodile was wandering from side to side, wreaking havoc in a more or less chaotic fashion but steadily heading southward on the road. It had always seemed that the sobeks had a destination in mind but none had previously made it past the pumping station. This one, though, was determined to get to wherever it was going and seemed equally determined to do as much damage as it could on the way.

We'd stopped at the intersection of Lake and Bordeaux and it was about a block up, just short of Narcissus. NOPD was trying to clear the area but people were being people. Gawking, fleeing, some of them in cars, some of them on foot. One guy was out in his front yard with what looked like an elephant gun shooting at the thing. Which was just pissing it off more.

"I'll entertain suggestions here," Sam said.

"We're pretty well fucked," I said, getting out of the car. "Crocodilians can soak up an unimaginable amount of damage before they die. That goes for just about every kind. You can shoot them in the body all day long. They'll slowly bleed to death but not fast enough. The only really good way to kill them is hit them in their remarkably small brain. Which takes an angle you can't get from the ground and especially from in front."

I'd opened up the trunk and reached inside. "Time to read it the LAW," I said, tossing him one of the rocket launchers. "Which is going to, at most, slow it down."

"Two LAWs is only going to *slow it down*?" Sam said.

"Fingers crossed."

We both hit the sobek in the abdomen with the rocket launchers. This caused some of its guts to spill out on the road and knocked it down.

"Hell yeah!" Sam yelled in a satisfied tone.

Then the damned thing started struggling back to its feet.

"Back in the car. Get on the phone. Ask Franklin when he's going to get here and how many heavy weapons he's got."

The crocodilian was not particularly smart, but it could put *very big rocket signature* together with *very big hurt* and count to two. So it was now concentrated on catching Honeybear. Which was fine by me. I wasn't going to let it catch me, and chasing us, it wasn't doing excessive secondary damage. The question was where to lead it to.

My first preference would be back into the canal. They'd always had a hard time getting out. Their bipedal form was bad for climbing, and there was less damage they could do to people in there. Problem being, there was a fence along the canal and no bridges in this area. If I went over to the canal we'd probably end up trapped up against it. That would be bad.

Lake Avenue did not continue forever. It ended at Metairie Road which was a fairly major cross street. There was a gas station at the corner. I vaguely considered luring it into the gas station then blowing up the pumps. Two problems. First, pumps don't really blow up like they do in movies. Second, this was already a big enough incident and whoever was currently on their ass, MCB would flip the fuck out.

There was no place to lure it, no place to corral it that didn't involve more loss of life or a much larger presence. Except the Metairie Bridge. That was a bigger incident but discreet had gone out the window when the fucking MCB sniper missed the fucking shot.

Sam was still talking to Franklin on the mobile phone. "Tell him to park on the Metairie Bridge, east side."

To get it into a kill zone we needed to get it to follow us. I looked in the rearview mirror. The sobek was tiring and didn't seem to want to chase us anymore. There was a large apartment complex at the corner of Lake and Bordeaux and I didn't want it getting stuck in there.

"Lean out and shoot that thing again."

"You're serious," Sam said. But he leaned back out the window and started shooting it with his CAR-15 popgun. The sobek didn't seem to care.

"We need something it will notice." I stopped the car and got out.

"It's sort of meandering this way still," Sam pointed out.

"SEALs," I said. "Sheesh. Quit whining. Help me get Bertha out."

We got the Barrett .50 caliber unpacked, the trunk closed, and the weapon in the front seat before the sobek caught up. Just. As I backed up, fast, it leaned over and clomped its jaws shut on where the car had been. But it also dropped on its face, so it took a bit for it to get back up. And it was pissed again. Then it tripped on some entrails and sprawled. I stopped to let it get up.

"Keep shooting it," I said as I honked the horn and flashed the high beams at it. "Make sure it knows it's us. And I'm going to take the next turn."

"Uh-huh," Sam said, taking the time to stuff some orange foam earplugs in. The Barrett is a huge, long, heavy, and generally unwieldy gun. Sam was a strong guy, but I suppose I couldn't expect him to just hang Bertha out the window like with his carbine, but it still pissed me off when he turned around in his seat, levered Bertha about, and smashed out my back window with the muzzle.

"Hey! I just got Honeybear out of the shop!"

"Now who's whining?" Sam said as he lined up the shot.

Realizing that the ejection port was right next to my head, I hurried and got my muffs off the dashboard and pulled them on. Sam fired. A big shell casing spun past my face. The muzzle brake tore up my upholstery. Stuffing flew into the air. Poor Honeybear.

But that got its attention. The sobek was back up and following us.

I drove slow enough the sobek could keep up. The big mobile phone started ringing, so I answered.

"Chad? It's Franklin."

"We're sticking and moving on this thing getting it to chase us and ignore everything else."

"Good. We're—" As Franklin said that, Sam let go with another round of .50 right next to my head.

"What?" I yelled. The sound was deafening. And my ears were already ringing from the LAWs.

"We're at the bridge!"

"I'm leading it back towards the canal. Going over to Orpheum, then I'm going to turn east on Metairie. I'm hoping it will jump in around there and just head uptown that way. We might be able to get a shot in on it if it's down in the canal. Tell NOPD and SIU to close Metairie! Get set up on Metairie protecting the crossing if you can. We'll try to drive it into the water there."

"We've got the LAWs and the Ma Deuce," Franklin shouted his answer. He could tell I was mostly deaf from the fire. "The MCB is going to shit a brick."

"We don't get this shut down quick we're going to have hundreds of civilian casualties," I yelled as Sam fired again. Check the mirror. Still following us. "This is their abortion. We're just trying to fix it!"

The sobek, fortunately, was not particularly fast in normal circumstances and was having a lot of trouble with the spilled intestines. By the time I got off the phone we were just to the intersection of Grenadine and Orpheum. Orpheum paralleled the canal and had a high iron fence to keep people from falling or climbing in. The sobek could negotiate it easily but I suspected it wasn't going to head straight for the water.

And it didn't. It just kept following us as I made a slow turn south on Orpheum.

"You got any more ammo for this?" Sam said.

"There's more mags in the trunk. We'll can stop again, get out, and get the rounds."

"Just because you can ride next to the edge of the cliff don't mean you should, Chad."

"What?"

"I'll just space them out more. Anything that'll soak up two LAWs like it wasn't even hit has my full admiration."

"They're also tasty. Make a fine jambalaya."

"I so don't want to know how you know that," Sam said.

"We used to have a Cajun sniper. Cajuns will eat *anything*."

When we got to Metairie Road it had been blocked off by NOPD and Sheriff's Office. Good thing it was late at night because otherwise it would have caused one hell of a traffic jam. The Metairie Road bridge was the only way to cross the canal for a mile on either side.

Franklin and most of the rest of the team were in the middle of the road on the far side of the bridge setting up the M2 .50 caliber machine gun, generally called a "Ma Deuce." The team van was parked to one side, more or less blocking the side street that paralleled the canal on the east side, back open.

I was pretty sure the Ma Deuce was, for once, spitting in the wind. You could pepper a sobek all day long with .50 cal and get nowhere. But they also had six light antitank weapons laid out.

I pulled up next to the machine gun on the same side as the team van and got out. Metairie Road curved at the bridge and I looked at the sightlines.

Franklin was shouting orders. "If we don't force that thing to go in the water, we're going to have to hoof it." The sobek made the turn onto Metairie. "Damn. That is bigger and uglier than expected."

I went over, picked up one of the LAWs and moved to the other side of the road to keep the backblast from interfering with the team.

The sobek was about halfway across the bridge. Franklin lit

it up with the M2. We started hitting it with the LAWs. Each round from the rocket launchers knocked it down. But then it got up again. Down. Up. Down. Up.

If we'd been able to hit it from the rear, they might have had some effect—if we could hit it on the back of the head as it was swaying along in its ungainly walk. From the front, we were just tearing it up more but not really stopping it. Knocking it down and slowing it was the best we could do.

By the time we were out of LAWs, everybody switched to small arms. The sobek had taken a lot of damage at that point. It had been hit by eight weapons designed to take out light armored vehicles, the shots from the MCB sniper, and all the .50 that Sam had peppered it with. Speaking of which, Sam had gotten more ammo from the trunk and was adding to the carnage firing Bertha off-handed.

The sobek finally decided it had had enough. The water to the side was inviting. It clumped over to the side and more or less fell off the bridge.

"Bertha," I said, holding out my hand.

Sam didn't want to give her up but he handed her over.

I ran onto the bridge and spotted the sobek. It wasn't moving much, but I could tell that was because it was sort of resting up. Not dead or even really dying quick. The amount of damage we'd done to it would kill it. Eventually. But it could be hours. I considered the angles and decided I was at a decent spot for a kill shot. I rested Bertha across a railing. I'd have preferred being about thirty feet up or that the sobek's head was thirty feet closer. Or that it would...

The sobek struggled to its feet—again. It was ignoring us, clearly planning on continuing on to whatever its destination had been. But as it got to its feet, for just a moment the angle was juuust right for a...

I didn't even realize the sear had released until the *boom*. And the sobek dropped deader than a doornail. It didn't even thrash once. One shot, one kill, baby. Oorah for Marine marksmanship.

"*That* is how you are *supposed* to kill a sobek." I looked over at Sam. "The one shot, one kill thing. Not the shooting up half the city part."

"Well, it took a while," Sam said, "but nice shot."

"Thanks."

✧   ✧   ✧

"Was it really necessary to use *six* rocket launchers?" Special Agent Campbell fumed.

"It was eight." I was packing up Bertha and didn't even bother turning around.

"*Eight*?" Campbell was furious. "Are you completely insane or are you a moron? Why the hell were you shooting it with rocket launchers when you *yourself* said they didn't work!"

"Because it was all we had." I was weary, getting rained on, and getting tired of having to replace car windows. "Sobek stopped. Situation fixed. Scene cleared. Anything else, Special Agent?"

"Get out of my sight."

"Have a nice day," I said and left.

CHAPTER 11

"This is a pretty good ritual," Sam Haven said, leaning back in the seat of Honeybear and looking out over Lake Pontchartrain.

I have a ritual for the full moon. I've talked about it before. I clean up myself and my gear. I go to confession, take communion, then I have a really good meal with some really good wine.

In this case, I'd taken Sam with me to K-Paul's, Chef Paul Prudhomme's world-famous hole-in-the-wall restaurant. We'd been in gear, pretty much fully rigged out, so Paul was kind enough to let us sneak in the back and eat at the chef's table in the kitchen. Hot as hell, food was delicious. There were better places in New Orleans than K-Paul's in my opinion, but Sam enjoyed it. Sort of. He didn't want to admit that he wasn't into "foreign muck," but Prudhomme had gotten him over most of that by telling his backstory. Because Paul came from a tougher background than Sam.

"According to the Catholic faith I am now good to go for reentry to heaven," I said. "Touch of some minor venal sins like checking out hot girls and some would say gluttony. But otherwise, I'm pretty good to go."

I hadn't taken Sam along with me to church. I wasn't as close to him as Milo. But he knew about it. "So the number fifty-seven, that's like a religious thing with you or something?"

"It's a recurring sign. When I died I was told to be on the lookout for the number fifty-seven. I've found it's symbolic. It's shown up in some damn weird places."

"Sounds like nonsense, but that was a really good meal," Sam said, picking shrimp etouffee out of his teeth with a toothpick.

"Based on experience with New Orleans' full moons, always possible to be my last," I said. "Full moons have been heating up almost back to normal. Fewer loup-garou since Earl took care of the assholes who were creating all the new ones. One good thing he did before he fucked us."

"Earl's a good leader. You should get off his case. How was he supposed to know you guys would get attacked by an army of crayfish? On the scale of likely events that's got to be somewhere to the left of getting anally violated by Gumby."

"It's New Orleans. Weird shit happens." Then we got our first call of the night, and it was right next door. "Speaking of which..."

We only had to drive for a minute before we heard the screaming through the open window. There was a twenty-something girl running as fast as she could in high heels. And behind her was...

"That a grinder?" Sam asked, looking at the thing on the shore.

"Fricking moon's not even *up*, dammit!" I snarled, getting out of the car.

I'd even noticed the girl earlier as she'd walked by. She'd been with some redneck in a ball cap set on sideways. Pretty hot brunette, she was basically Points with more chest and a few years off of her. The boyfriend appeared to be missing. Based on the human leg hanging out of the monster's... mouth? Boyfriend was in its gullet.

"I don't think that's a grinder," I said, heading to the trunk. The whatever-it-was looked more like a mobile pile of seaweed. Similar to a grinder in size and shape, but not the same. Just another monster. "You see any grinder teeth?"

"No," Sam said thoughtfully. "We made flash cards in newbie training, but I don't know what the fuck that is. I think it's dissolving that guy with something."

"When in doubt, blow it up and burn it."

"Help! Help! Oh, God, help me!"

"Working on it," I said as the girl came running up to Honeybear. The thing was squishing itself along behind her, but it didn't seem particularly fast. In classic horror movie style it had probably slithered up while they were making out.

"Please, my boyfriend!" she was out of breath.

"Working on it," I said, finally finding the right satchel charge. "And, miss, I'm sorry to tell you this, but I don't think he's going to make it." And what I was about to do to stop that thing would make sure of it. "Just let me do this, okay?"

"What are you going to do?" she and Sam asked more or less in unison.

I just walked over towards the thing swinging the claymore bag in my hand. When I got to within about thirty yards of it, the thing seemed to sense my presence. It was definitely using some sort of enzyme on the girl's boyfriend. The leg had stopped thrashing and I could see a yellowish slime burning up part of the exposed leg.

"Miss," Sam warned, "you're gonna want to duck."

The monster seemed to be composed of some sort of seaweed. I'd been told that some seaweed was algae and not a weed at all. It came from the sea and was some sort of weed so...seaweed. I left the rest to marine biologists. I pulled the fuse on the incendiary satchel charge and tossed it on the monster. It stuck. The thing reacted by heading for me, faster than before.

I wasn't going to run toward Sam and the girl, so I headed across the street instead, fast as I could go in armor. Two reasons. One, I didn't want to get dissolved. Sounded like a nasty way to go. Two, I didn't want to get burned by my own satchel charge when it detonated. A really nasty way to go.

Unfortunately, we were down the end of Breakwater Drive. Depending on how long it lasted I was going to hit the water going that way. So I angled a bit to the right as I hit the road and broke into a sprint on the solid pavement. I could hear the thing slithering along behind me, a wet *schlup, schlup, schlup*.

Then there was a *pop* followed by a *fizzzzz* and a squeal from the seaweed monster.

"Pop, pop, fizz, fizz," I sang, turning around to face the thing. "Oh, what a relief it is..."

The satchel charge was a mixture of a white phosphorus grenade for trigger, a couple of pounds of thermite, and some plastic film cans filled with jellied kerosene for longer lasting burning. Milo had made it.

The monster was very wet and thus didn't burn very well. But the nasty charge was so hot it just kind of melted right through its body and burned a hole in the asphalt, sticking the whole

thing in place. It wasn't going anywhere. Just flopping spasti-
cally, curling up around the fire and sort of banshee wailing in
a weird, high, piping tone.

"Want me to bring over the flamethrower?" Sam yelled.

"Nah," I said as the thing finally settled down and was good
seaweed. "Think that's got it."

To answer the professional question: Muldjewangk. Although
it was one of a half dozen creatures with the same name. FUCCN
was 57862-4 in this case. PUFF, twenty grand.

To answer the *obvious* question: the young lady was so excited
to meet a top-secret Navy SEAL who was also a member of
Hoodoo Squad that she quickly forgot her masticated boyfriend.
We nearly had a little war over that. Hitting on girls at incidents
was *my* standard way of finding dates. I didn't need some redneck pinniped sticking his ball-balancing nose in where it didn't
belong. On the other hand, we had a lot of incidents and a lot
of girls to chat up. Honestly, picking up girls in New Orleans
was sort of like ... clubbing baby seals.

When we had time.

"I understand that we need to get this under control," Agent
Robinson told us. "But we also need you to be *discreet*. Do you
even understand the meaning of the word?"

This time Decay and I had been dispatched to cover a shambler
outbreak in Metairie Cemetery. Problem being, the outbreak was
daytime, Metairie was right off I-10, which was ground level at
that point and since it was the middle of the day, the interstate
would be busy. Fortunately, as far as we knew *at that time*, the
outbreak was on the back side of the cemetery and away from
the interstate. And Metairie had fences so they shouldn't get out.

"We'll do the best we can considering we're going to be
shooting zombies in broad daylight in a very large cemetery. I
promise discretion to the point of not using a rocket launcher
because it's generally pointless with shamblers. Do we have a
positive location of the outbreak?"

"According to the caretaker it's over by Iris Avenue." Lieutenant Hale was another promoted sergeant in SIU. The good part
about working SIU was the promotions tended to be fast. The
bad part was that it was like getting promoted in World War II,
because you were stepping into a dead man's shoes.

"Perimeter shut down?"

"Sort of," Hale said.

"Define 'sort of.'"

Hale frowned. "Ask the G-man."

"The outbreak is in a remote part of the cemetery," Robinson declared. "I saw no reason to surround the place with police cars. That just causes more people to notice."

"Agent, in this town, you try for subtle, it's going to bite you in the ass. So I'd *suggest* you put cars on every entrance, put them along the fences, and have some on patrol."

"Clearly you *don't* understand the meaning of discreet. Let me do my job and you do yours, Hunter."

"I was trying to help," I said, opening up Honeybear's door.

"Where are you going?" Robinson demanded.

The MCB agent was really confusing poor Decay. "Into the cemetery?"

"In a *car*? What part of discreet was *unclear*?"

"You keep using that word," Decay said, climbing in the passenger seat. "I do not think it means what you think it means."

"We're sure as hell not going to *walk* all over that fucker. It's *huge*. And in the car we can break contact among other things. And, you know, not get *bit*? Also, from the point of view of any witnesses, it's a lot better to have a car driving in a cemetery, normal, than having two guys rigged up like commandoes walking all over it, Abbie-normal. So let us do our job and you go do yours, Agent!"

"Finding all of these again is going to take all day," Decay said as he shot another shambler in the head.

We were right by the Confederate monument circle, out of the car and dealing with a couple zombies that seemed to be headed in the general direction of Pontchartrain Expressway.

"Not our problem as long as we get tissue samples. That asshole Robinson can worry about it."

"Yeah, yeah," Decay said, walking over to cut off the right ears.

I looked over my shoulder as I heard the blurt of a siren. Hale was driving up, sort of fast for a cemetery, and had hit it to get my attention. Hale pulled up next to me. "We got real problems now."

"Which are?"

"Some shamblers got out the main east gate."

"That's right by the Pontchartrain off-ramp." I blanched. "Don't tell me..."

"Trucker just jackknifed when he hit a zombie on the interstate. There's more wandering around the pileup. Traffic's backing up to Metairie. And only one side's backed up so all them tourists is driving right by a bunch of undead wandering around I-10."

"There's a time for discreet and a time to shut this the fuck down."

The tractor trailer was parked across two lanes, shutting down traffic all by its lonesome. Problem being, the trucker had gotten out to check on the "person" he'd hit and been swarmed.

Zombies aren't precise. Unless they are being directed by a necromancer, they just do their thing. They search for the living to feed on. They're mostly attracted by sound, and anything that indicates a living human presence.

Like tourists honking horns at the "people" who had wandered onto the interstate. You can't always get a good look from a car and while the people in the front, who had come screeching to a stop to avoid the truck wreck could see there was something seriously weird going on, all the other assholes behind them were honking their horns. Some of the zombies were heading up between the stopped cars, towards the honking. Others were trying to break into the cars. People were trying to drive through them and panicking. Just as we arrived a station wagon filled with a family plowed into the tractor trailer.

Most of I-10 was either elevated or lined by a low concrete wall. Opposite the east entrance to Metairie Cemetery there was an off-ramp from I-10 to Pontchartrain Boulevard. It was this off-ramp the zombies had used to get onto the interstate. Another was down on the off-ramp having been hit by a car which, probably driven by a local, had then sped off. Then a following car had stopped to help the "injured" person in the road. And that driver, female, had also been attacked. So that car was blocking the off-ramp. Not to mention the zombies still feasting on her warm corpse.

I rolled Honeybear up to the stopped car. "You got plenty of rounds?" I asked.

"Loaded up," Decay said.

"Let's do this."

I rolled out of my door, hefted my Uzi and went to work. I hit the head of the driver as we passed.

I held my hand up to a car that was rolling forward, covered in zombies who were trying to get to the passengers inside. Again, another tourist family. I made eye contact with the male driver and just held my hand up like a traffic cop for him to stop. Then I pointed at his kids and put my left hand over my eyes. He and his wife got the message and turned around to cover their kids' eyes.

Then we shot every zombie off that car in a couple of seconds, single taps to the head.

"Hey!" I yelled through the rolled-up window. "I know you want to get your family to safety but I need you to stay right here, blocking traffic! You'll be okay!"

"You're nuts!" the guy screamed. "They're eating people!"

"Just stay here!" I hoped he'd listen. We needed traffic stopped.

Decay had trotted over to the group around the wrecked station wagon. One had gotten through the cracked front window and to at least one of the parents in the front seat. He was clearing the ones around the car when I yanked open the back door and climbed in.

"Hi, folks," I said, leaning over the front seat and shooting the female zombie in the head. The dad, driver again, was still alive. She'd been ripping at his carotid artery and he didn't have much time left. The wife and mother, presumably, had climbed into the back seat to escape the undead and the kids had pushed even further back, up into the piled luggage in the cargo area.

"Medical is on the way," I said, pulling out a bandage and putting it on the man's neck. "I need you to apply pressure to this, ma'am. Now don't go anywhere and just stay in the car. You're going to be okay. We've got this."

To make sure they didn't leave, I took out the keys, then shot two of their tires. It sounds cruel but I'd already seen the bite mark on the mom's arm. She needed to not leave town. And the kids were shortly going to be orphans.

It took a few minutes to clear the scene of walking dead. When we were done, the interstate was littered with bodies and still jammed up. Which was how it was going to have to stay until MCB had the bodies cleared and the scene under control. Including rounding up all the witnesses and bitten.

I didn't like their job but I agreed with it. Pity the converse wasn't true.

I'd leave it to the Feds to shoot the bitten in the head. There was probably more than that one mother and father. That was what MCB was for. Hopefully, Robinson would have the decency to do it at the hospital and away from the kids.

As we walked away from the scene, I heard the bark of a 10mm. I didn't even look. I could tell by the screams and the direction it had come from the station wagon.

So much for decency.

There had not been another kifo eruption for weeks. I tried using the rune of Onesh I had picked up in Britain, hoping that it would point me toward evil sort of like Madam Courtney's crystal charm. Only it did not work as advertised. It spent most of the time hanging from Honeybear's mirror, doing basically nothing.

Until one day I was driving back from a call out with Decay and he noticed the rune had started to pull unnaturally, almost like it was magnetized. Since it hadn't worked at all so far, there had to be a kifo worm really near.

The area was pretty standard New Orleans neighborhood. Narrow houses that went back much further than you'd expect. Some of them were barely ten feet wide and half a block deep. Some were brightly painted, others plain. All had bars on their windows. Fairly well kept up. Working class rather than ghetto. 424 South Clark was a duplex. Narrow, story and a half, white. There was a garage, apparently, on the bottom floor with living quarters on the top. The garage and upper were split.

"Cover story?" Decay asked as we got out.

"Depends on if they're locals or not." I was trying to play the new MCB's game as much as possible but if they recognized us as Hoodoo Squad I'd just run that gambit.

The woman who answered the door was Hispanic, in her thirties and had apparently been sleeping from the look of it. We'd had to knock quite a long time to get her up.

"No buy!" She had a thick accent. There was an inner door and an outer barred and screened door. She'd opened the inner but clearly wasn't opening the outer. "Go 'way!"

"Madam, we're checking out a report of some trapped methane

gas in the area," I said in Spanish. "We just need to do some tests in your garage."

"What kind of tests?" she asked suspiciously.

"Methane gas is naturally produced by decay. It can build up in enclosed lower areas and lead to spontaneous fires and even explosions."

"Who you with?" she asked.

"The EPA," I said.

Decay was wearing his usual cargo pants and boots and the scalp lock and piercings were sort of obvious. "You don't look like EPA."

"We're contractors, ma'am."

"I'm calling the police." She started closing the door.

"Good. Ask for the Sheriff's Special Investigations Unit." I pulled out an MHI card. "Tell them I had this. They can explain everything."

She looked at the card and blanched. "This is magic stuff."

"The way things are working these days, I can neither confirm nor deny. But we have readings on something either in your house or your neighbor's."

"I let you in the downstairs," she said, still suspicious. "But not upstairs."

"That's fine."

When she let us in, I saw there was an Astra .25 dangling in her hand. "You try anything, I shoot you."

"I think she's immune to your charms, Chad," Decay said, grinning.

"How long have you lived in New Orleans and have you ever encountered anything weird? Weirder than normal that is."

"Yes. I work at the hospital. Nurse's aide. I know about the magic. This town is cursed."

Then there was no use lying. "Get out the rune, Decay."

Decay pulled it out and followed the swing towards the back of the garage. Behind the single-car garage was a section of rooms and hallways. Most of it was filled with various buildup of residents. Papers, toys, old bicycles. Whoever owned the rental clearly had never moved anything out that was left behind, just moved it to the ground floor.

We followed the swinging amulet back into a cluttered room and found one of the fungal symbols under a pile of old newspapers.

"Oh shit," Decay muttered.

"Don't touch it! We need to back out of here fast."

It was the largest one I'd seen. I was pretty sure the only reason it had never triggered was the area was deserted and the residents stuck to the upper floor. One kid down here playing around and there'd have been another kifo outbreak.

When we were back in the sunlight I took a deep breath. "Ma'am. Get everyone out of the house. Is there anyone next door this time of day?"

"No, and I'm the only one home."

"We need to evacuate the neighborhood. *Don't* go back in that house. Not for *anything*."

"You sure it's a kifo?" Agent Robinson asked. "There hasn't been an emergence here."

"Same symbol," I replied.

After I had alerted Franklin and the team, we had done as directed and brought in the MCB. Campbell had dispatched Robinson, whose career was more or less at nadir after having overseen a Class One event which turned into a Class Four. I wasn't privy to the internal discussions but I was pretty sure that letting a handful of slow zombies out of a fenced-in cemetery to close down a busy freeway wasn't well regarded in MCB circles.

As the first agent on scene, Robinson was being even more twitchy and hypersensitive than usual. "And you used a rune of Onesh? A likely story. MCB has tried that. The rune doesn't *work* in New Orleans. All it does is swing around in circles!"

"My theory is if there's a mava beneath the city, it's putting out jamming signals like mad. But at the same time, all the effects, including kifo worms, are putting out other jamming signals. The reason the rune swings in every direction is there's stuff all over the damned place. So you need to get close. We drove right past it, and that symbol is by far the biggest one we've seen. Probably the only reason we picked it up."

"I can't afford any more debacles. Before I allow any actions I need to see this so-called symbol with my own eyes first," Agent Robinson insisted.

"Okay," I said. "But be careful as hell. Don't touch it."

"I know what I'm doing, Gardenier!"

✧   ✧   ✧

"You're a witness," I said, pointing at Lieutenant Bechard from SIU. The sounds from the interior of the house had finally died down. "I *told* him to be careful!"

"This worm is a zit ready to pop, Special Agent," I told Campbell. "I *warned* Agent Robinson to be careful with it."

Robinson had never exited the house.

"I was present, sir," Lieutenant Bechard agreed. "Agent Robinson was... dismissive of Mr. Gardenier's warning."

When the rest of the MCB had shown up, Campbell had ordered the police to evacuate the entire neighborhood. They'd gone with a build-up of methane gas again. Freaking methane gas. It was *everywhere*!

"Damn it, Robinson..." Campbell was looking a little ragged. The news was reporting that all the deaths related to the cemetery breakout had been caused by a multicar pileup, but the local MCB must have been scrambling to track down and intimidate into silence any passerby who had seen the undead or our clearance thereof. And now it looked like his right-hand man had just gotten eaten by a kifo worm. "He should have known better. *You* should have known better."

"How was I supposed to stop him? You guys don't listen to me!"

"Why would we? Even though our director is too stupid to see it, I still think you're corrupt and covering for a cult."

Luckily for Special Agent Campbell, that was when Franklin walked up and interrupted us. "I'm sorry for your loss. I think what's been going on with it is it's been growing for a long time without any actual food input. It's been down there in that basement waiting for something to come along; sadly, that was your man."

Campbell was seething and searching for someone to blame. "Have *you* looked at this thing?" Campbell asked Lieutenant Bechard.

"Special Agent," he spit out some dip. "You can shoot me in the head if'n you want, but I ain't goin' in that fuckin' house. Not after what I heard."

"I'm not even real comfortable about bringing in the bomb pig. I'd guess that the bigger the symbol, the bigger the worm. And that was one damned big symbol."

"I hate this town," Campbell said.

"Embrace the suck," I said. "You going to let us do our jobs or not?"

"Just get rid of this thing," Campbell said. "And . . . see if you can recover Agent Robinson's body."

Franklin and I exchanged a glance. We both knew that Robinson was being digested in the belly of the mava paṇauvaā. But we decided not to push things. "We'll check."

"If this thing comes out, don't fucking hesitate with the napalm," my words muffled by the visor of the silver suit.

We had never used a decoy bomb pig on this fresh of an eruption. The worm could still be right beneath the surface. The plan was to get the pig in position with cover from two flamethrowers. Decay was on one and Sam Haven on the other. Jon Glenn and I would drag the pig.

"Got it," Sam said. "Looking forward to burning your ass."

"The good news is we have an eruption point. We'll set the pig down near that and then get the fuck out."

"I've done this before," Glenn had helped Milo with the heavy lifting for a few of those. "Let's just do it."

We found the hole right near where we'd found the symbol. Before, it had been a little section of hallway and two small storage closets. Both of the closets were gone now. The walls were in splinters and the built-up crap that had been stuffed in them was scattered everywhere. The worm had even broken out the walls between the two sides of the duplex. The other side was just as trashed.

"Let's just stop right here," I said to Glenn as we reached the destroyed area. "It should be close enough." We still had to set the wires and prep it. The detonators and safeties were on the outside of the pig up under its belly. The wires were coiled by them and held on with tape, ready to be set. I grabbed one as Glenn grabbed another and stretched them out.

As we were doing that, there was a rumble from under the ground and in a flash the kifo worm was just *there*.

I didn't hesitate. I pulled the safety on the fuse, turned and yelled: *"Run!"*

I was still holding the wire in my hand. As I bolted, it triggered the fuse.

Glenn, unfortunately, had looked at the worm. I don't know

if he'd never looked at one before when they were killing them or if it was the incredible size of the thing. He'd fought hoodoo on his own for years but it had been "normal" stuff. Zombies. Weak vampires. A werewolf. The sort of shit you see in movies. He'd done it right, he'd done it smart.

He'd never seen anything like the kifo worm. And, unfortunately, he reacted like most people do the first time they see anything supernatural. He froze.

Pro-tip: There is a time to save your buddy and a time to save yourself. Knowing the difference between the two is important. And accepting that sometimes you leave people behind is also important. I'm not *justifying* letting Glenn die there. I'm explaining. Jon Glenn outmassed me by about a hundred and fifty pounds. I could not pick him up and carry him out with any sort of speed. If I'd even hesitated long enough to grab his arm and pull him, the worm would have gotten us both.

I repeat, there's a time to be a hero and a time to run like hell. If you don't learn that, you won't last long in this business.

As it was, the only reason the worm didn't catch me was Sam Haven. He didn't hesitate either. He filled the hall with fire.

The worm scooped up the frozen Glenn and our "offering" and disappeared back into its hole to avoid the napalm.

"Shit," I said, running through a house which was now thoroughly on fire. "Shit, shit, shit..."

"Wasn't anything you could do, man," Haven said, patting at the flames.

"I know that." We were leaving behind little droplets of napalm and getting the house even more thoroughly involved. But I still have to live with it.

"Honest to God, we were *trying* for discreet," I said, holding up my badly burned glove in a Scout's salute.

"I only count three of you," Campbell said.

"Thing erupted while we were setting the trap. Glenn froze. Sorry, but we didn't see any sign of your agents."

About then there was another serious rumble from underground and the burning house more or less exploded. The kifo worm was massive. It reared up through the roof, hissing and whistling in agony.

They'd brought up a fire truck and were rigging hoses to

get the house fire under control. At the sight of the kifo worm, most of the firefighters froze in horror. The smarter of them ran like hell.

Despite being covered in napalm, out in sunlight and with a hundred pounds of thermite burning in its gut, the kifo worm was only mortally wounded. And seriously pissed. It grabbed one of the frozen firefighters with a pseudopod and pulled him into its mass, absorbing the body in a flash. Sam and Decay weren't exactly slow, though. They ran forward and started covering it in napalm, driving it back onto the burning house.

There was exactly nothing the rest of us could do. I just watched the thing being consumed by the flames. The smoke was still pouring out of the hole as it crumbled to ash.

The kifo was dead, but both of the flanking homes were now seriously on fire and all the firefighters were gone.

"Well, boys, looks like it's up to us to put out the fire!" Franklin shouted as he headed for the fire truck. It wasn't our job, but our team leader wasn't the type to just stand around while people's houses burned down.

"Anybody know how to run one of these things?" When I looked around, Special Agent Campbell had fled. "Embrace the suck."

CHAPTER 12

So now we get to one of the most important episodes in my life as a Hunter. The reason I sued MCB. And won. It was a rainy Tuesday. Calls had been slow. There hadn't been a kifo eruption in the weeks since we lost Glenn. So we were hanging around the team shack when lo and behold two of my favorite people in the world showed up: Myers and Franks.

I'd been helping Franklin with paperwork when I got called back to the team room.

"Agent Myers," I said, nodding in greeting. Being former MHI, the junior agent wasn't very popular around here. "Traitor" was one of the nicer things my coworkers called him. He may have been a duplicitous jackass, but he had been a good Hunter, and he'd stepped up at Mardi Gras when the MCB had lost all their senior leadership. I just nodded at Franks and wondered why these two were back in town. "Good afternoon."

"We need to ask you some questions, Gardenier," Myers said. "You're coming with us."

"I won't be interrogated without the presence of counsel."

"You don't have the right to counsel in supernatural investigations."

"I do if such counsel is read in on the supernatural," I said, as calmly as I could. "And in this town, throw a rock and you find a lawyer who knows about the supernatural."

"Franks," Myers said. "Bring him."

Now, Franks just did not care. He would drag me by the hair if he felt like it.

"What's this about?" Franklin asked. Half the team was up and ready to pounce. The new guys didn't know Franks. Bad move. Franks would fight the whole office and probably enjoy it.

"Down, boys. I'm going peacefully. You want to cuff me?" I turned around and put my hands behind my back. "I'll be fine, guys. Let it go."

"Hell I will," Sam growled.

"None of your concern, Haven." Myers said. "Just stay out of this."

"Last time I heard those same exact words out of an MCB agent's cock holster, you cowards massacred a cruise ship full of civilians."

"Get the hell out of our way if you know what's good for you. Franks, cuff him."

"Call Mr. Lambert, will you, Franklin?" I asked as Franks put on the cuffs. I won't say Franks and I were friends but we had fought side by side. I think I even saved his life at Mardi Gras, but that did not matter with Franks. Those cuffs bit to the bone. I'm not sure he even knew how to put them on lightly.

"You call *anyone*, the MCB will throw you in prison," Myers snapped on the way out.

I hoped Franklin would call his bluff.

They took me outside and Franks put me in the back of the car with a shove. Myers dropped a bag over my head.

"Is that strictly necessary?" I knew the sound was muffled but it was a reasonable question. The answer was a hard blow on the side of my head. Okay, they were playing by those rules. This would be interesting.

I probably should have been scared. The classic black helicopter boys were whisking me away to places unknown to interrogate me. I was probably going to be beaten up. There was a fair chance I'd get shot in the head. Also a fair chance I'd see the inside of a federal prison. I wasn't sure what they were pissed about, could be any number of things, but I wasn't going to let it get to me.

Prison would suck, but I really don't fear the one thing most people fear most: Death. It's not that I'm suicidal, but I long to die. I've been to heaven. It was a nice place. I'm looking forward to going back. Duty really is heavier than mountains and death really is lighter than a feather for me. I was sent back for one unknown mission. One moment when I have to achieve perfection as a Monster Hunter. Then I die. At a guess, painfully. I don't know when that will be but I'm okay with it whenever it comes. I simply don't fear it.

So all this was just another frustrating episode in a world full of frustration. I'd said I was an addict about Monster Hunting. But, frankly, if it wasn't for the whole mission-from-God thing, I'd probably find *some* way to give it up. *This* sort of shit was just getting on my nerves. I was halfway tempted to *try* to get them to kill me. Franks wouldn't mind. Franks really did not have the emotional parts to mind.

I had been expecting them to take me to some out-of-the-way spot to interrogate. But instead they took me straight to the Franklin Federal Building at Lafayette Square. I could tell even through the bag over my head. Church Street to Girod and into the underground parking lot. I recognized the bumps on Church which seriously needed resurfacing. God knows, I'd been there enough meeting with MCB back in the good ole days when Castro was in charge. I missed him.

When the car stopped I was as helpful getting out as I could be. It didn't matter. Franks just manhandled me out of the car and nobody can manhandle someone like Franks. Then it was more or less being carried by one arm through a series of corridors. Elevator down. One, two, three levels. The MCB interrogation and holding area. Turn left, turn right, one...two...three...ten paces. Interrogation room four.

Hard steel seat. If the bag was off, the room would be a light salmon. Facing one of the de rigueur reflecting windows. Table, bolted to the ground. Two chairs, both steel. Not so heavy as to be a useful weapon.

And sure enough, the hood came off.

"Given my current relationship with the committee, you'd better have some serious probable cause for this, Dwayne."

Only Myers and Franks had been joined by Special Agent Campbell. Of course, Myers was still a junior agent. Grabbing a Hunter off the street was over his pay grade.

"Nice try. This has been cleared," Campbell said, sitting down across from me. "I know you're involved with the Dark Masters and I know you killed your brother just to shut him up so he couldn't implicate you in the ring. I requested assistance to clear this up once and for all, so Washington dispatched Agent Franks. And believe me, when Agent Franks assists in an interrogation, the truth always comes out. And now you're going to answer some questions."

"Gardenier, Oliver," I said. "156-25-7819. Monster Hunter."

"That's the way it's going to be?" Myers asked.

"Absent counsel, yes."

"You know you don't get counsel here," Campbell said. "We're the only ones who know where you are."

"We're in the federal building. MCB detention and interrogation. Room Four."

"Nice guess. Where's the rest of the cells?"

"Ten paces that way." I gestured with my chin. "Turn left. Five paces. Three cells on the right, two on the left."

"You know what I mean!" Campbell nodded at Franks.

I'd been hit quite a few times. I'd been shot a couple more. Getting hit by Franks was more like being shot. I ended up on the floor, shaking my head. I'd lost at least one tooth. And I can safely say he'd pulled his punch.

"That was an *honest* answer. You *asked* where the cells were. They're around the fucking *corner!*"

"He's correct," Franks stated helpfully.

"The *Dark Masters'* cells," Campbell snarled. "Where are the *rest* of the Dark Master cells, Gardenier?"

"I have no *clue.* I'm not part of the ring and never have been."

"Really, Chad?" Myers said. "We get the reading that you're involved, you go snooping about it around the world. Then you *conveniently* find your brother's cell and take out the only lead we had. Nice way to tie up loose ends. Just stopping the kidnappings is not going to save you from prison."

"That was months ago!"

"Government may move like a glacier," Campbell said. "But whatever ends up in front of a glacier is crushed eventually. Because of your relationship with some committee members, the director was hesitant to take extreme measures, but now your time has come."

"That wasn't my fault. *I'm innocent!* I was *never part of the ring!* But you're *never* going to believe that, are you? So now we're *definitely* on the only-in-the-presence-of-counsel thing. Time to break out the pliers, Franks."

"Won't need them," he said simply.

"It's good to be in the hands of a pro—" And then Franks hit me again.

It took a long time and it wasn't pleasant. Since you're reading this, I didn't die and I'm not writing these memoirs from prison. I did end up in the hospital, however. The chart was fairly extensive.

Dislocated shoulder. Broken left wrist. Broken right forearm. Contusions over eighty percent of my torso. Two broken ribs. Internal bleeding. Skull fractures. Broken right occiput. Broken nose. Four missing teeth. Six broken fingers. Seven fingernails ripped off. It was *more* painful than it sounds.

The problem with interrogating someone under the assumption that they know something they don't is that they cannot tell you what you want to hear. Campbell—who hated me anyway—was convinced I knew about more cells. If I even hinted I agreed, I was going to a secret prison forever. There would be no trial or anything like that. It would simply happen.

Later I found out that Campbell had been really close with Agent Robinson, mentor and protégé, and he blamed me personally for Robinson getting eaten by the mava. There hadn't been any more Dark Masters kidnappings after Thornton's death, so the MCB director had been ready to believe my testimony before the committee. At least until Campbell used Robinson's death to sell the story that I was still a menace, hence his insistence of bringing in Franks for a *special interrogation.*

I didn't crack. After the beating started I didn't even wisecrack, believe it or not. I just took it and kept reciting my name and social. Oh, and I didn't *hesitate* to scream. A lot.

I don't know when they actually stopped. I was drifting in and out. Something about a subdural cerebral hematoma. Give Franks his due, he knew how to not *quite* kill someone.

I do remember it was actually Franks who called it.

"All we want is the truth."

"Truth," I muttered through busted lips. I'd spent most of the time on the floor and was starting to like it there. "Truth. Gardenier, Oliver..."

"Franks..." Myers sounded tired and unhappy. As the unfortunate bastard picked to be Franks partner, he'd been sent all the way from Washington for this, and he'd come to the realization that I was telling the truth.

"He knows nothing," Franks finally declared.

"I'll be the judge of that!" Campbell replied. "But I think we'll give Gardenier some time to contemplate—"

"I'm bored," Franks said. "We're done."

I passed out. Wasn't the first time, but this time they didn't wake me up again.

The rest of it was hazy. I'd been in the Marine bombing in Beirut and it was like that. Light and dark. Voices...

"...too extensive to treat here...!"

Muttered something, sharp...

"...probably have thought of that before you *beat* someone to death..."

Good. I was going to die. Sorry, God, tried to do the right thing...

I didn't die. I *wanted* to die. Especially when I woke up in the hospital room with Franks staring at me.

I could only open one eye. I just looked at him. He looked back.

I'm not sure what Franks is. I'm pretty certain he's not entirely human. He has none of the emotions of charity or mercy or conscience that make us human and I've seen him take a fatal head wound and just keep fighting like it was nothing. But what he does have is an absolute sense of duty. He wouldn't be upset killing a building full of orphans if there was a real need to do so. Say they were all vampires or had been bitten by loup-garou or zombies or pick a reason to wipe out a nest of orphans. He'd shoot every little tot in the head, wring their necks like chickens, whatever, and go have dinner. Wouldn't bother him.

But he knew, and I knew, that this mission had been flawed from the outset. He was sure now that I had nothing to do with the Dark Masters. He knew that Campbell had acted unprofessionally, emotionally, so wound up in his anger that he'd lost all objectivity. And that he, Franks, had wasted his valuable time beating me half to death for no good reason.

So I just looked at him and he looked back. I would say it was a staring contest but I actually passed back out after a while. So I guess he won.

"Mr. Gardenier?" a voice said.

This time there was no Franks. There *was* a Myers.

"Gardenier, Oliver..." I said. I tried to remember my social and couldn't. *Damn*, I'd been hit hard.

"Mr. Gardenier?" the voice said again. "I am Samuel Koltts, your legal counsel."

I turned my head, wincing in pain. There was another person in the room. Short, spare, very nice suit. Not MCB. Not with that suit. That was a three-thousand-dollar suit. Nice tie.

Myers was really there and just as clearly unhappy which suited me fine. Ugly suit.

"Lambert?" I asked.

"Yes," Koltts said. "Mr. Lambert sent me to represent you in this matter."

Albert Aristide Lambert was the senior named partner of Lambert, Klein, Masson and Kempf, one of New Orleans' most prestigious law firms. The Lamberts were old ooold money and power. My *gentleman*, Remi, had worked for them previously and I'd retained them shortly after joining Hoodoo Squad. There were always minor legal matters to clear up with Monster Hunting and most of Lambert, Klein, Masson and Kempf's better attorneys were read in on hoodoo. In New Orleans they had to be. Koltts was a new one, though. Him I didn't know.

"No questions 'til fully recovered," I muttered.

"That is *not* going to fly," Myers said.

"Agent Myers," Koltts said, smiling thinly. "I am aware of the broad brief given to Monster Control Bureau as well as the rationale thereof. And I also have a read-in federal judge who thinks your bureau should be shut down. You may feel free to continue to dig the very deep hole you are currently in. Or you can accept that no questions will be presented to my client until such time as he has recovered, by *my* definition, and I have had time to fully counsel him on this matter. As you were just *informed* by federal injunction. Is there some part of *injunction* you don't understand, Agent, or should I write it down in very small words for you?"

It took six weeks for me to recover to a physical condition where I could do much. It took a week for me to get discharged, go home, and have a long coherent conversation with my attorney. It took three weeks for Lambert, Klein, Masson and Kempf to open up a can of whoop ass on the MCB like they'd rarely known.

Despite what Special Agent Campbell thought, despite what Agent Myers thought, it turned out it was possible to sue the *ever-living crap* out of the MCB. And all of them. Personally. Mr. Lambert was puzzled that I did not want to include Franks. My rationale was that Franks was essentially a non-self-directing weapon. It would be like suing my Uzi.

The judge did require Franks to give a top-secret deposition to my attorneys at one point. I was *pretty* sure Franks wouldn't kill them. He was used to asking questions, not being forced to answer them. I wasn't present, but it was recorded and I watched the tape several times, with the sound off, just to watch his expression. And, yes, Franks does have facial expressions. They range from slightly annoyed to very annoyed.

It was a basic necessity that there were a few federal judges read in on the supernatural. I had no idea what most of their cases involved. Many of these judges, while recognizing the importance of the First Reason, were also fairly uncomfortable with the MCB's often draconian actions. Torturing a suspect and justifying it by a reading crossed *several* lines. MCB was basically just another government agency, which meant they could get in trouble for breaking the law, same as everybody else. It was just that they were so shrouded in mystery and lies that it seldom happened. Normally, suits against the MCB were tossed for *national security* reasons, but this time they wound up with an angry judge.

About the time my lawyers opened up the can of whoop-ass, MCB tried to retaliate. They turned up all sorts of nasty stuff about the law firm, the Lamberts, my attorney. The fact that Mr. Lambert had a mistress was trotted out to Mrs. Lambert who apparently replied that of *course* he had a mistress, so did *she*! Mr. Koltts turned out to be gay. This is New Orleans. Your point? They tried bribery, but the lawsuit was pure gold from the law firm's end, so that just led to *another* federal suit.

What MCB mostly learned was that trying to corrupt a New Orleans legal firm was like trying to fight a rainstorm with a fire hose. Had Agent Castro still been alive he could have told them that. Because of the secretive nature of their job, the MCB wasn't used to being sued, and screwed up every step of the way. Accountability was an indecipherable mystery to them. The Lamberts could smell a *very* juicy suit. It was like panning for gold in a virgin stream. Every overturned rock was pure litigation gold.

Here's how we calculated damages. I was earning huge PUFF fighting monsters. MCB had beaten me practically to death, was trying to get me canned as an MHI employee, and was generally interfering in my ability to earn income. And, oh yeah, violated the *shit* out of my rights. I couldn't get them arrested for that but I could make them pay through the nose. How much was I out? Not just for the six weeks of recuperation. Their harassment was liable to cost me my income in perpetuity. I should last until I'm eighty with any normal job. Figure out how much the lost income was over that time. Then multiply that times some number, maybe five, for pain and emotional suffering.

One hundred million dollars was less than the total but it was a nice round number. And I don't care how big your secret black ops budget is, that's real money. Then there were legal fees, which were legally permissible to be tripled. Good lawyers cost a lot of money.

As long as the suit was ongoing, by order of our judge, I could not be deposed, questioned or otherwise contacted or harassed by Monster Control Bureau regarding pretty much *anything*. Oh, and MCB had, naturally, had all my permits revoked. Which led to another lawsuit thrown on the pile. Unfortunately that made it impossible to do my job.

The suit could potentially take years, absent MCB offering a settlement I would accept. And MCB had no clue how to negotiate a settlement. Their invariable MO was demonize, vilify, destroy. Negotiate was not in that list.

The Shacklefords loved that I was causing the government discomfort, but my presence was making life complicated for them. I couldn't work, so I took a leave of absence. I packed up and went to England to attend Oxford. And, yes, it took a year before the MCB settled. An interesting year and fruitful in many ways, but I still missed hunting.

CHAPTER 13

Before I talk about my time in England, I'll finish my story about the lawsuit. While I was away, it got so bad the judge overseeing the suit threatened to pass an injunction against *any* action by MCB, shut them down entirely until they could be thoroughly vetted. Now that did get into national security issues, and I'm sure somebody at MCB started contemplating the pros and cons of murdering federal judges. Luckily someone at Department of Justice got the MCB to see reason and settle. That was shortly after Franks was deposed and, being Franks, answered all the questions posed to him *frankly*. Lots of silences, lots of muttered "Classified" until it was explained in very small words that in *this* deposition there was no such thing. Then he talked. Frankly.

And the judge hit the roof and DOJ very quietly went into panic mode.

"We are not going to pay Mr. Gardenier a hundred million dollars."

The attorney representing MCB was not from MCB. They didn't have *anyone* trained to negotiate a settlement involving violation of constitutional rights. Chris Welch was a standard DOJ attorney who was read in. The sort that *usually* handled excessive-force and violation-of-constitutional-rights suits.

I had just flown back to the US, and was in a DC conference room sitting across from Myers, who was looking furious. Good. Beat me half to death, will you? I'll beat *you* to death with *lawyers*. Everybody *knows* that's *worse*. Even though Campbell had been the senior agent calling the shots, and the only reason Myers had been there at all was because he was Franks' current gopher, secretary, and caddy, they had left the junior agent to answer for the MCB during our negotiation.

"The exact number from our calculations is one hundred million, one hundred fifty-six thousand, *four hundred twenty-eight* dollars," Koltts said. It was me and my attorney on one side of the table, Myers and his on the other. "That would cover his loss of income from Monster Hunting as well as pain and emotional suffering penalties, and deprivation of rights penalties based upon projected income, as well as his extensive medical bills from the torture."

"Which is, clearly, out of the question," Welch said. "Just off the top, the wage calculation is based upon an eighty-five-year life span and retirement at sixty-five. Actuarially, Mr. Gardenier's maximum life span is closer to forty-five. The pain and emotional suffering penalties are based upon avoiding *Monster Hunting* which is in and of itself *filled* with pain and emotional suffering."

Got me there, I thought.

"The pain and emotional suffering in this case is based upon deliberate *torture* by members of federal law enforcement in violation of his Fifth Amendment rights," Koltts said evenly, "as duly attested and sworn by Agent Franks—no first name, no middle initial—but who *did* give a *very* accurate, indeed blow-by-blow, testimony as to the nature of his actions at the behest of Special Agent Campbell who was in turn directed to do so by the director of the Monster Control Bureau, Director Harold Wagner. The fact that no one even *tried* to lie about any of the things that were done sort of says it all, don't you think?"

"I object to the repeated use of the term 'torture,'" Welch replied. "Hostile interrogation is the correct term."

"Torture: The action or practice of inflicting severe pain on someone as a punishment or to force them to do or say something," Koltts recited the dictionary definition. "In the case of my client, it is reasonable to describe the actions of your agents as both."

"You really don't get it, do you?" Myers was supposed to sit there quietly, but he was getting really angry. "We're trying to save lives! We protect the whole God-damned world!"

"What is there to protect, Agent, if *this* is what you consider perfectly acceptable?"

"You think *this* is bad?" Myers snarled. "Do you have any clue what would happen with a breakthrough of the Great Old Ones? Or the Fey get back in control?"

"I've heard those arguments *repeatedly*, Agent. Would you like to explain the part where protecting the world from those issues required my client be taken to a dim basement and beaten to the point he required extensive surgery? Please, Agent. Inform *all* of us what *exactly* you were going to find out from my client that would prevent a breakthrough of the Great Old Ones! Prevent the Final Battle! That would permit you to absolutely ensure that the Fey, who lost power to humans in *prehistory*, will not resume hunting us as animals! Please, Agent, present your logic! I would personally *love* to hear it!"

I held up a hand. "Dwayne. Franks said it. You heard it. I told you I had no involvement in the Dark Masters' operation. If I had, I would have told you because, well, I was *really* tired of being beaten. You weren't listening. On a not exactly digressing note, if you're torturing someone for information, *not listening* is probably the stupidest thing you could possibly do! Campbell got frustrated at being in charge of out-of-control New Orleans and losing a friend and took it out on *me*. That's all that happened, Dwayne. You all, serially, got frustrated and angry at stuff I had *nothing* to do with and found someone to hurt. And you can blame me. You can blame God. You can blame your boss.

"But mostly, Dwayne, you can blame yourself. You can blame normal human emotions and too much power and too much frustration. The reason I didn't include Franks in this was that he only does what he's told. He doesn't let his emotions cloud his judgment as you do. You beat me to close to *death* because you were frustrated and you felt like you *could*. And you know it. And you sort of hate yourself for it. And you might even have already learned your lesson.

"But the MCB hasn't learned the lesson," I finished, looking at the DOJ attorney. "Are you familiar with the Stanford studies, Mr. Welch?"

"Yes. I am. I'm surprised you are." The attorney didn't look happy.

"Are MCB agents taught about the Stanford Studies, Agent Myers?" I asked.

"The exact nature of our training is—"

"No," Welch said. "I checked. They are not."

"I was about to say *classified*," Myers snapped.

"This suit isn't just about *you*, Dwayne. Quit taking everything personal. It's about the MCB and how it works and why it really needs serious oversight and better training in due process."

"What are the Stanford Studies?" Koltts asked.

"Well, there are a bunch—it's Stanford after all—but in this case, the ones that are important are the studies of human power dynamics. Attorney Welch?"

"Are you planning on including these in the suit?" Welch asked.

"Do I say yes, no?" I asked Koltts.

"Are they germane?"

"Extremely."

"Then definitely," Koltts said. "Why?"

"A psychologist at Stanford randomly selected groups of sixty students. Twenty were made *guards*, randomly, and forty were made *prisoners*. The guards were then given more or less unrestrained power over the prisoners. The premise was that the more intelligent and thoughtful a group, the more they would tend to use reason and persuasion versus force as a power dynamic. The primary study was about rehabilitation versus incarceration. Now, keep in mind, we're talking Stanford students. Highly intelligent. Very liberal. Very open-minded. What would you guess the results were?"

"They used reason and persuasion?" Koltts said.

"Attorney Welch? Would you care to tell my counsel, not to mention Agent Myers, the results?"

"They went flat nuts," Welch said.

"Nice way to sugarcoat it."

"I've dealt with numerous excessive-force complaints in my time at DOJ. That's my specialty. Both defending excessive-force suits and investigating them. So, I am extremely familiar with the Stanford Studies. To expand on they went flat nuts: given unrestrained power over the prisoner group, the guards turned into animals in short order. They became extremely and excessively sadistic within days or weeks. They beat and tortured the prisoners. Played games with them. Did everything within their power to make their lives a living hell."

"We don't *do* that!" Myers snapped.

"Care to look at my hospital report?"

"We do what we have to do!"

I stopped and growled and shook my head. I'd tried *so* hard to control my temper but it was getting out of hand. "Because you're all pissed off at *Earl*, you beat *me*, you pissant son of a bitch!" I shouted.

"You cannot *speak* to me that way," Myers ground out.

"Or *what*? You'll beat me to death? I'm back in shape, there's no Franks to protect you and I'm no longer in *handcuffs*. Bring it."

"And I think we need to all calm down," Attorney Welch said calmly. "Agent Myers, you *especially* need to understand that these proceedings are *not* an absolute power dynamic. Nor, Mr. Gardenier, are they on your side. These are negotiations."

I was suddenly very tired. "Then let's negotiate."

None of this changed a thing. MCB continued to use the First Reason to promote power-mad ogres like Myers to higher and higher positions. I could see the day when they'd convince the committee that Hunting should only be done by *proper officials*. And then there'd really be no one to watch the watchmen. And not long after that, folks, MCB would start to forget their First Reason and it would become more and more about the power alone.

I've seen it in the current administration. They like the power of the MCB. It's nicely unconstrained from the Constitution they abhor. They can use the threat of Outworld Entities for any sort of evil. And I've *yet* to see—several times promoted since my beatdown—nowadays Supervisory Special Agent Dwayne Myers realize how dangerous that is.

Which is why, yeah, I'm *deeply* involved in politics and will stay that way to the day I die.

"Here's my negotiation. All my legal bills, plus all my medical bills, plus *lots* of dollars in cash, definitely two commas but doesn't have to be a hundred million. But the rest of that one hundred million: suspended judgment, any further similar incident and it kicks in automatically. Any investigation that does not have *strong* probable cause and it kicks in automatically. Any arrest for any reason that does not have *strong* probable cause and it kicks in automatically. You'd better be able to *prove* in a court of law that I'm guilty of something before you so much as open my *mail*—and, yes, I've noticed you've been opening all my mail—or it kicks in automatically."

"That's never going to fly," Dwayne sneered.

"Any federal agency which is influenced by MCB to deny me normal and proper procedures and it kicks in automatically. That means, by the way, I want *all* my licenses back, like, *immediately* or quicker. And you had better drop any investigation into my doings unless you've got something better than a bad spell casting. Absent something along those lines with a really light trigger and a *strong* kick, extremely broad and very *serious* penalties, hurts so bad it's noticed at the *highest* levels, see you in court."

Myers just threw his hands up in the air in frustration.

"Mr. Welch, you want to explain to the agent why you *don't* want to go to court? Especially when my attorney puts *Franks* up on the witness stand and he's sworn to tell the truth, the whole truth and nothing but the truth? We all know he won't do anything else once he opens that clam called a mouth. Now, I'm tired and pissed at the fucking country I've nearly given my life for *several* times. So let's get this over with."

To make a long story short: they settled.

I got four million dollars and change. My attorneys got about six.

When the brief on the settlement was presented to His Honor that the US Government would be on the hook for seventy million dollars if the MCB didn't get off my ass and stay off it, he looked at the US Attorney, scratched out the "70" and scribbled in "100." Then signed it with a flourish.

I never mentioned it, but I'd met the federal judge overseeing the case before. At a dinner party. During Mardi Gras. Last year. When I came flying through the party chasing a vampire right before I had to battle killer mantis shrimp.

I think he probably should have recused himself but it wasn't like we were even properly introduced.

And I was back in the Monster Hunting business.

BOOK TWO

City of the Dead

CHAPTER 14

For the year while the suit was ongoing, I was out of the loop on Monster Hunting. Hoodoo Squad lost another Hunter while I was gone, medically retired. Norbert left as well but not for those reasons. You see, he had all the usual demons of having grown up in the ghetto and had a hard time getting away from them. That's a long way of saying that with PUFF money rolling in, he got seriously into drugs. Started with painkillers after a major injury and those were his stock for a while, to the point where it got noticeable, then heroin to feed the opiate jones and cocaine to pick him up for hunting.

Then he got busted distributing and that was that. He got a last check and please don't bother to reapply.

Drugs are one of those things nobody really talks about in hunting but they probably take out as many Hunters as vampires. You get beat up and are on the injured list for a while and the nice doctor gives you lots of painkillers to reduce the hurt. And boy, yeah, they feel good. And, yeah, they are addictive as shit. I was never really drawn to them. They're nice when I hurt but I like the way my brain works and don't like it being fuzzy. But the physical addiction was something I had to learn to manage. I'd just wean myself off them. Some guys couldn't do that. Some guys get addicted to tranquilizers to try to deal with the fear. And the last thing you want when you're hunting is some guy who's going "Whoa, dude, chill out. Vampires is no big thing!"

Norbert was one of those who couldn't kick the habit. Timmy in Seattle had the same problem although that wasn't why he quit.

Me, the only thing I'm addicted to is hunting and the whole time the suit was ongoing that was a nonstarter. Fortunately, I didn't need the money. I had savings and investments, and despite the cost of the house and Remi, pretty good savings.

New Orleans was relatively calm. There had been no more kifo eruptions. So even though there was a giant monster hidden somewhere beneath the city, it was being quiet. Maybe Glenn and Agent Robinson had been good enough sacrifices to last a while, or maybe it had gotten tired of having all its pseudopods burned off and had gone back to sleep. Franklin assured me he'd call if there were any new developments, and in the meantime MHI would keep trying to figure out how to track down the mava.

Because of the mutual "do not contact" orders, for the first time in a long time I had MCB off my ass. Which felt good, but left me with too much time on my hands.

So I mostly closed the house and moved. To Oxford. And I brought Remi.

It wasn't to hunt monsters, though. I had other addictions I could feed in the meantime. Growing up, I'd been careful to get straight C's my entire school career because I hated my mother who was an academic. I'd also refused to properly play the violin, which she'd insisted I study from about the age of five. Problem being, I was both a natural academic and a natural musician. I loved both. I had to be *very* stubborn to throw both over. I don't know how many times I was in the middle of a beautiful concerto when I realized my mom had come home and had to switch to horrible squeaks and squeals to cover up.

Now I had time, I could indulge in both. So I moved to England at least part of the time.

Part of the time because of taxes. If you live in England full time, even as an American citizen, you're responsible for a good bit of an English tax burden. And English taxes are insane. I don't know how anyone gets anything done there. Given my current issues with government in general, and lack of income other than return on investments, I wasn't big about paying taxes. If MCB really did cut me off from Monster Hunting permanently, assuming they let me live and didn't gin up some fake charges to put me in prison, I was probably going to find a tax haven to settle down. Or maybe take my skills overseas.

MI4 had never had an issue with me beyond what the MCB had given them, so I was free to enter England again. Oxford was glad to have me and my tuition money back. The house I rented was nice. Nice enough at a certain level I wished I could just settle there. Two-story brick townhome. One of the nicer ones in the Oxford area. Beautiful back yard. You really can't grow grass anywhere else the way you can grow it in England. Okay, Seattle and Portland, but for the same reason: lots of rain.

My day for the first few months was pretty routine. I'd get up predawn, stretch, work out, go for a run. Then after some katas, generally in the back yard, I'd head in to the university. It was a lot like being back in Seattle. I missed the Monster Hunting but was more than happy to have a chance to just get back to studying them.

I really love Oxford. The food sucks but there's an energy and it's always possible to get into a good intelligent conversation. At least if you can avoid politics, which I tried to do assiduously. And there's more information about monsters, if you know where to look, than any other place on earth. I suppose MCB and MI4 might have more. But not much.

Oh, and there's another great thing about Oxford. Girls. Damn the girls are cute. English women seem to really go downhill at a certain point—I think it's English food that does it—but in their twenties they're very nice. And extremely open-minded in many cases.

I showed up slightly late in the term, still pretty banged up from the beatdown by Franks. My main faculty advisor for the master's was Dr. Madrigal Henderson. Dr. Maggie was in her sixties, former VHI member and knew, I swear to God, just about everything there was about any monster they had ever encountered. Since my reference was Rigby, Dr. Maggie's old boss at VHI, I had no issues getting in.

She taught the master's level discussion on "Incorporeal Entities and mythological beings." The class was small. Fifteen people started, ten finished. There were no tests. It was just part of what you needed for a master's in mythology from Oxford. If you couldn't cut the mustard, that became clear in your orals.

Oxford had been the preeminent center for studying the

162 *Larry Correia & John Ringo*

supernatural since at least the thirteenth century. Getting into those *particular* programs required personal introductions or references from people in the know. Basically they had to be read in somehow before they could even apply. It is a very small, very elite group of students. It turned out I was the only professional Hunter in the class.

I walked in early and sat towards the back. I didn't want to kick anyone out of a seat. There were two people in the room when I walked in, male and female. Slowly, more students trickled in. A few looked a bit worse for wear from carousing. One of them looked at me puzzled—I was clearly in his seat—then took another. Dr. Henderson walked in shortly before class was supposed to begin and started without preamble.

"We have an addition to the class as most of you might have noticed." Dr. Henderson was a short woman, in her sixties, but looked as if she still pumped lots of iron on a daily basis. "Mr. Gardenier is from America. He is working toward a doctorate in linguistics. For those of you who have studied the American Sasquatch, you might recognize the name as the author of the current dictionary as well as North American Gnoll and its relationship to Teutonic Gnoll. Mr. Gardenier?"

"Pleasure to meet you all. Since first names are usually acceptable at Oxford, please call me Chad."

"We continue with the discussion of the sociology of the Montserrat jumbees..."

I hadn't even known there was such a thing as sociology for ghosts. Or that one way to get ghosts to leave an area was to help them fulfill whatever need kept them bound to this plane. MHI rarely worked with ghosts since you couldn't get a PUFF on one. There were specialty courses in *just* incorporeal creatures. There were guest lectures by people as diverse as Malay witch doctors and British supernatural coroners. There was so much information thrown at you at Oxford on monsters it was like being in a rainstorm.

I loved every minute of it.

Most of the class was focused on the academic side. When the word got around that I was a Hunter, some of them were less than thrilled. Even though most Oxford grads had no problem with eradication, there was still an undertone of "these are fascinating creatures, mankind shouldn't be hell-bent on wiping them all out."

✧   ✧   ✧

There was a regular gathering at the Harcourt Arms in Jericho. It was away from the student roistering areas and the tourists so you could have a conversation about monsters without throwing too many people off. I liked it because it was about as traditional as you got and when the weather was good, rarely, you could sit out back in the beer garden. This day the weather was good. Cold, but after two and a half years in New Orleans, cold felt good.

"There are fewer and fewer monsters to be found around the world," Guillermo Knight said. "Should we really be killing them all off?"

"Is that a devil's advocate position?" I asked, taking a sip of ale. The other nice thing about the Harcourt Arms was they stayed to traditional ales and had a fair selection. The interior ran to dark wood and big fireplaces and traditional English beer and food. I liked all of that except the "food" part. Fortunately, I'd brought Remi and he'd brought ingredients.

"No." Knight was tall with a distinctly academic sort of look. Always head-in-the-clouds sort. Nice guy, smart, but I don't think he'd ever had a tough day in his life. "I'm no monster lover like those profs at Cambridge, but humans are extinguishing thousands of species a day. Is it really necessary to make the supernatural extinct as well?"

"I'm the new guy." I really didn't want to get into it. "Anyone?"

"The passenger pigeon didn't rip people's throats out," Melanie Williams said.

I'd already had my eye on Melanie. Short, blonde, fairly good-looking. But I'd also noticed various twitch reactions. I'd dealt with too many survivor females with so many trip wires you were constantly walking through a minefield.

"Tigers rip people's throats out and would you have all of them disappear?" Knight replied.

"Tigers don't reproduce off of the human population," Johnson Kearney said. Johnson was short, dark-haired, and half-Irish with all the hotness the land of Eire tended to breed. He'd never had a monster encounter but he was hell-bent on removing every last stain from God's Earth. "Vampires have five billion people and increasing to feed on and grow their own population."

"Trust me. They're hardly endangered," I said.

"What about the yeti?" Knight asked.

"Yeti forms aren't PUFF-applicable where I'm from. They're

being wiped out by reduction in habitat and poaching. And if a Hunter team finds poachers of yeti or sasquatch? Well, there's more than one reason we always carry a shovel."

"Are you saying sometimes Monster Hunters kill humans?" Knight asked, aghast.

I thought about my brother dying from a disembowelment. My face must have given away the answer.

"Oh..."

"I've killed necromancers, and once blew my best friend's head off to keep him from slowly dying of spider toxin. Killing humans? I don't lose sleep. But as to your primary contention: There probably *are* some supernatural entities which are endangered. I could even see putting certain types in zoos. But I flat guarantee you there's a gnome close enough I could hit it from here with a rock. The supernatural is anything but endangered. It has *always* lived in constant contact with humans, and humans are anything but endangered. Specific *species* may be endangered. The supernatural is anything but."

"There are fewer Fey," Knight argued.

"Because they're extremely dangerous. The only reason they're not at open war with us is that they know they'll lose. Then they really *would* be extinct. I know MCB wants to extinguish them. And there are even more Fey *creatures* than you'd think. Most keep a low profile, especially the ones who belong to courts."

"There aren't any Fey courts left in the world!" Knight snapped.

"Where the hell did you get that?" I asked. "I know of one. Hell, I've bound one."

"You bound a Fey court?"

"Eh." I shrugged. "I'm pretty good with a violin. I made a contract with a Fey queen and a Fey princess."

"That I have a hard time believing," Knight said.

"I'm not going to call a fucking Fey princess just to prove it. Besides, the one princess I know is a total ditz."

"You know a fairy princess?" Kearney said.

"Princess Ashain Vohola Sasasha Shallala. Total airhead. Mostly. She's a pretty shrewd businesswoman as it turns out. She—I am not joking—invented Valley Speak. Like totally. Runs a club in Seattle now. Has a small court of hangers-on Fey and a larger court of hangers-on humans. I don't think the humans know she's Fey."

"You're serious," Knight said.

"Like, totally..." Damn it. Just *thinking* about Shallala and I end up using Valspeak. "Fey magic is, like, totally pernicious. And 'til you've seen a royal one without their glamour you don't know for ugly. There ain't no ugly like Fey-ugly. Take it back, Old One ugly is uglier than Fey-ugly but only just."

"And next he'll be telling us he's met a Great Old One," Knight said caustically.

"Never met a 'great' one. Those can destroy your sanity just by proximity, but we've got a constant problem with something they created and left beneath New Orleans. It's this big underground entity that sprouts up pseudopods, like gray-green shoggoths. Really nasty. One of the things I'm trying to do while I'm here is figure out a way to find the actual creature."

"Maybe we can help. What is it called?" Melanie asked.

"*Mava paṇauvaā*, but that just means 'worm mother' in Gujarati." I gave the other students the rundown of what I knew. "And, Guillermo, these things seriously *need* to be endangered."

"I'm not sure I'd argue for the continuance of an Old One entity," Knight admitted. "Certainly not a major one. You are a Hunter; shouldn't you be back there dealing with it?"

"The rest of the company is looking for it. I've currently got some legal issues back home. I'm letting my lawyers handle it. Until the MCB settles my lawsuit, I'm stuck."

"Can anyone win a suit with the US Monster Control Bureau?" Kearney asked. "Aren't they more or less untouchable?"

"So far. In the meantime, I like it here. I was rather frowned upon at one point by MI4. Since then, they went to the bother of looking into the whole thing, and now it's MCB who has frosty relations with them. I'm not a fair-haired boy to MI4 but they're not on my ass. However, on the original discussion... I don't personally believe, from my own experience and from knowledge of the field in general, that the supernatural is in any way endangered. Is humanity as a whole endangered by it? Will it wipe us out? A Great Old One breaks through? Yes. The Fey are probably a nonthreat in terms of extinction of the human race, as long as we keep them in check and the same goes for all the supernatural. If we don't control epidemiological monsters like vampires, loup-garou and zombies, then we're going to find ourselves in a full-up apocalypse. And from a purely human perspective, keeping them in check to protect human life is important. Which I'd really like to get back to doing."

"I can hear it in your voice," Melanie said. "You enjoy it, don't you?"

"Enjoy is probably the wrong word. I'm on a mission from God. Literally. I'm addicted to it. Not to the money, although the money is good, but to the mission. There ain't nothin' like standing on the dead body of some massive monster you've just killed. The feeling can't really be described."

"Do you think you'll be able to go back?" Kearney asked.

"Depends on how the suit winds up," I said. "In the meantime, being able to append 'Doctor' to my name helps with persuading politicians who have never seen a monster that I know what I'm talking about. And if I can't? Have you heard any of the rumors from Eastern Europe? There's always a need for Hunters somewhere."

CHAPTER 15

I was sort of surprised, mid-term, when I was put in as a substitute instructor in Introduction to Mythology. This freshman course was three days a week and designed for anyone who wanted an elective—it was not aimed at the read-in. It was one of Professor Henderson's classes. I was one of three teacher's assistants but after my first week, Professor Henderson just gave me the lecture notes and had me conduct. For Oxford, it was one of the easier electives. I mean, the main reading was stuff like *Bulfinch's Mythology* and Campbell's *The Hero with a Thousand Faces* and Frazer's *The Golden Bough*. This wasn't anything, in my opinion, related to Monster Hunting.

I was wrong. It is absolutely true that you learn more from teaching a class than from taking one. It was even fun. I'd give the lecture, based on the assigned reading, ask some questions, then take questions and answers. The students were all bright, most of them were not much younger than I was, and while there were plenty of dullards who were just taking an elective to fill a requirement, most were interested in mythology. I eventually was able to pick out a few who'd had supernatural encounters. There were, also, a few who would just believe in anything.

The really funny part, for me, was the two days spent on "sexual entities in mythology." That ranged from Zeus, one screwing motherfucker of a god, to things like Orang Minyak.

As someone with actual experience, I discussed it, but I tried not to say too much.

"Zoovnuj Txeeg Txivneej." I wrote the phonetic spelling on the board then adding the Hmong. "The Vietnamese Forest Man. Similar enough in many respects to the original satyr, They're about three feet tall. Purple skin. Pot-bellied. Batlike face with a pig's snout and tusks. They were referred to as 'Big Dick Nine' by American forces who en— by American forces in Vietnam who were aware of the myth. They're rapey little bastards."

This occasioned a certain amount of laughter from the class. I'd drawn a cartoon while I was talking. I thought it was a pretty accurate representation.

After the laughter died down a young woman near the back held up her hand. "How would you know that?"

"Well..." I couldn't say that I had met one who wouldn't take no for an answer while it was trying to break into a young woman's home, and killed it with a grenade. "I've studied the field extensively."

"I don't find that funny at all," she snapped. "And I'd ask that you keep the ribaldness down."

There was one of two reasons she didn't find them funny. One was she was a feminist, the other was that she was a victim, or at least knew one.

"They're not funny, actually," I said. "Where loup-garou is a predator of flesh, the various sexual supernatural entities are predators of innocence. They feast, then leave their victims, by and large, alive and shattered. There's a valid argument as to which is worse. The flip side is that if you really pay attention to the horrors in the world, you can either laugh or cry. And the oceans are made of the salt of human tears. In my case, I laugh. Human laughter, human music, human ingenuity in all of the stories we study have been the weapons by which humans have overcome the powers of the supernatural. I would add that in some cases heavy weapons are useful as well."

"I still don't find them funny," the young woman said.

You should see one one time, I thought. It was pretty clear it was "feminist," not victim.

"So how do you kill one?" one of the male students asked.

"It's a myth," I said quickly. "Obviously you can't kill a myth. But from the myths, they're pretty much invulnerable to most weapons but are vulnerable to fire. I'd generally suggest filling them full of rounds 'til they've stopped moving, then tossing a thermite grenade on them . . . if you're writing a fiction novel or something."

"Writing a story" was generally what I used when someone asked a direct question that indicated they knew about the supernatural. That guy seemed to know about the supernatural or, given the number of English Literature majors in the class, was planning on writing a book.

"However. Please, for reality's sake, ensure that your character works with others and has some training. I hate books and movies where people think they can hunt supernatural entities on their own with very little training or equipment. Nobody in a single vampire movie, zombie movie or other horror movie I've seen who survived probably would have. Or at best they would have survived through sheer luck or someone else saving them. If you are planning on using this class to write a story, please ensure your monster hunter characters are properly trained, competent, armed and prepared. And we move on to incubi . . ."

The portion where we discussed werewolves and similar mythology, lycanthropy in general . . . it was sort of tough for me to stay away from reality. MI4 wasn't quite as jumpy as MCB, but I didn't want to get kicked out of the country again.

"Lycanthropes in human form are widely described as having very short tempers. When they lose their temper, like the Incredible Hulk, they change into full were-form. This can take some time for new lycanthropes, a couple of minutes is the general description, down to less than a minute for experienced werewolves. All of them must change at the full moon."

"The textbook says that is a relatively new popular conception which does not match historical—"

"They're wrong . . . Next question."

"Is there any given reason why?" Briscoe asked.

I was starting to pick out the ones who were knowledgeable of the reality of the supernatural. Miss "I don't think they're funny" was a militant feminist like my mother. The kid who kept asking pointed questions, Leonard Briscoe—I got the feeling he knew this stuff was real. His questions were too directed.

"From what I've gleaned from reading the myths, the moon exerts some type of force which is detectable by the lycanthrope.

They literally can hear it or feel it. Some werewolves...excuse me, people *claiming* to be werewolves, have said it is a humming noise that's always there, but gets stronger with the lunar cycle. When the hum reaches full peak, they're unable to withstand the pressure to change. What it is or where it comes from remains a mystery."

"Mr. Gardenier?"

It was a young woman. She hadn't asked many questions but they'd all been...pointed.

"Miss Heard?" I didn't remember the names of most of the students—too many and why bother?—but I remembered hers.

"Is there any way other than silver to kill a werewolf?" she asked quietly.

"The myths describe pure silver as the most useful weapon. Has to be pure. Can't be silver nitrate. At least according to the myths. In addition, if you put enough damage on them, they die. Cutting off their heads also works...According to myths. Obviously."

"And silver works in all myths, worldwide?" Briscoe asked. "What about pre-metal tribes? Do they have similar myths?"

"No silver means beheading. Lots and lots of damage. Pretty much the most common method. Oh, and fire, of course."

"What about enough bullets?" Briscoe asked.

"More like enough rocket launchers," I said, grinning. "You can shoot them full of holes with a fifty-caliber, and they just keep on regenerating. According to the myths. If you...I mean, *your character* doesn't have access to silver, you could have them run the lycanthrope over repeatedly with a steamroller. It would be a bit like a Wile E. Coyote cartoon. I'm pretty sure they wouldn't regenerate from that."

"They have an incredible sense of smell. How do you keep them from finding you?" Miss Heard asked.

That was an oddly specific question. "Wolfsbane is the traditional answer. All the supernatural entities with supernatural senses are equally vulnerable to something that affects those senses. If you're writing a modern novel, you can use modern materials. Take your average werewolf. Wolfsbane will throw them off the scent. I've never tried it, but I've been told that pepper spray and tear gas really do a number on werewolves because they are so sensitive...theoretically. They also have sensitive hearing. I don't know what a very strong stereo might do to them, but I suspect they don't really like heavy metal," I added with a smile. Based on Earl, they really hate it. "Any more questions?"

"There are times you sound like you're not actually talking about myths."

The questioner was one of the cuter girls in the class. I'd decided not to hit on girls in the class but she was a very cute little buxom redhead named Beverly that had me rethinking that. "Ginger," as the Brits put it.

"I've studied this stuff a lot," I said, grinning deprecatingly. "Alas, it's sometimes a bit too easy to believe it's real when you delve into it enough. But I'm well grounded in the area. They're just myths, miss. No more. And we're out of time."

I was packing up after class when Miss Heard walked up. I knew she had been wanting to ask questions after class for a while but was just too shy. So I kept focused on gathering my papers to keep from startling her.

"Ran into a werewolf?" I asked quietly, when most of the class had left the room. There was enough noise to cover the question.

"I'm not sure I..." she said fearfully, backing away.

"The term is 'read in.' If you've had experience with the supernatural, there's things you can talk about with other people who have. *And* things you can't. That's from a vampire claw." I touched the scar on the side of my face.

"Are you with Van Helsing?" she asked, eyes wide. "I thought they were only English."

"I'm here because I'm friends with some of them." The class was mostly out but the sound was dying down. "That's how I got into Oxford in the first place. But, no, I'm on sabbatical from MHI."

"MHI?"

The rooms were designed to carry sound and when she said that, it carried. Briscoe's head snapped around and he looked back with a tight expression. I shrugged at him and leaned over.

"Can't talk here. Come by during office hours. We'll talk."

Later that day I saw Briscoe as he was walking through one of the quads and waved him over.

"MI4?" I asked quietly.

"Not sure what you're asking." Briscoe kept his face tight.

"I was wondering. You seem to have a clue, but you don't have the twitch reaction of someone who's been a victim like Miss Heard. You look military. Since I'm currently in decent graces with MI4—so I don't think you've been sent to shadow me—why the silver question? I know you know the other answers."

"More or less testing you." Briscoe shrugged. "Your reputation precedes you. Both good and bad. But much of it is..."

"Too impossible to believe? No kidding. I sometimes wonder how I survived some of the stuff. Or why."

"So..." Briscoe frowned. "The Forest Man. I was actually interested in that one. We sometimes get them here among immigrant communities. Personal experience, I take it."

"More or less how I described it," I said. "Shot full of forty-five and dropped thermite on it. The entire incident was more ludicrous than scary. The thing was just...silly."

"You took it on solo?"

"The first year in New Orleans *most* of the hunts were solo," I said darkly. "It was a bad year. Lots of casualties. We were seriously outnumbered but fortunately not outgunned or outsmarted. If part of the reputation is I've done stupid things solo, that's why. So you're not keeping an eye on me. Can I ask why *are* you here?"

"I was recruited to BSS Special Action Squad out of the Regiment," When someone in this country said "The Regiment" *that* way, they meant 22nd Regiment. Special Air Service. Special Action was the Brit equivalent of SRT. "But I was a sergeant. No college. After my initial tour they suggested I get a degree, work towards becoming a regular agent. So here I am."

I looked around the quad. "Has to be a bit of a change."

"For you as well," Briscoe said.

"It's tough," I said. "But until the suit is finished, one way or the other, I can't hunt in the US. I'm not currently interested in going over to one of the foreign companies. And I like academics. Also, honestly, I need the break."

"I can understand that...given that you're the American with the biggest PUFF earnings of the last three years."

"Really?" I thought about it for a moment then frowned. "I wonder if that's part of why MCB's been so on my ass? That means I've had more encounters than anyone else. It makes sense they might suspect I'm arranging them."

"I can neither confirm nor deny," Briscoe said.

"I'm not one of the bad guys. What's the term? A hare that runs with the hounds? I know it happens. Not me. I just eat, live and breathe hunting monsters. And have ended up in places and times when there's a lot of them and not many Hunters."

Briscoe contemplated me for a bit, then shrugged as well. "I'll take that on a bit of faith. *A bit.* You don't seem like the necromancer type."

"You met that many necromancers?"

"Enough. The ones I really don't trust are the ones who are deep into the mystical, even on our side. Necessary, but..."

That made me think about Ray. Where I was becoming a walking encyclopedia of monsters, he was a walking encyclopedia of hoodoo. But Ray is as trustworthy as God. "Care to discuss it over a pint some time?"

"Sure. But I know you Marine types. No holding hands."

"As long as you promise no PLFs off the bar," I said. "I know you parachute types."

"Well," Briscoe said, thinking about it, "I don't know if I can *promise*..."

"It's open," I said to the knock. I had an office. It was a broom closet of an office but I had an office.

Karissa Heard was a short mousy brunette who I was pretty sure was socially averse even before whatever happened to her. I was grading papers when she showed up. It was definitely the worst part of being a TA, but it was part of the job. And better than filling out PUFF paperwork.

"I must say, I love your accent," Karissa said, coming in and sitting down.

"What accent?"

"Your New Orleans accent."

"I don't have a New Orleans accent." I was confused. "Do I?"

"It is quite pronounced."

"Think yer hearin's that, dawlin'," I said, then paused and listened to what I'd just said. "Ah-ight, may have a point. Been by couple years. Where y'at?"

"Excuse me?"

"'Where y'at?' is a, yes, New Orleans shorthand, meaning not your physical location but your psychological state." I made sure I was using something resembling the Queen's English. "What happened? I'm assuming you had a werewolf encounter. How are you coping with the experience? Where y'at? Start with what happened."

"My father turned into one," Karissa said. "Just out of the blue. It was..."

"Horrible." I nodded. "The sudden realization that someone you know and love and trust has become a monster."

"You know about all this?" Karissa said. "Really?"

I gave her the short version: "I've killed a bunch of them."

"How?"

"Silver bullets in most cases, a few with a sword." I rolled my chair back and pulled up my shirt, exposing the scars on my abdomen and chest. "That's not *just* loup-garou, but quite a bit of it is loup-garou. So since you now have someone you can talk to about it...talk." I leaned back and just waited.

"It didn't sink in at first," Karissa said. "My mum..."

"You ran and survived; your mum didn't?" I asked.

"Yes." Karissa frowned. "There was an old coal store in the basement. Heavy iron. I used to hide in it when I played hide and seek with my cousins. I ran and hid. Mum...didn't."

"How old were you?"

"Nine."

"That's rough."

"You are a master of understatement, Mr. Gardenier."

I passed her a tissue. "When I first got into this, I had a very good friend, Jesse. We hunted together for nearly a year. Monsters, girls, fun, what have you. We were like brothers. Then he was bitten by a giant spider. He faced weeks of agony as the poison slowly ate his flesh away, starting with his belly where he was bitten, or someone could give him grace. I blew my best friend's brains all over my lap. I've died, gone to heaven, and been sent back, been the only survivor of my team, seen a bunch of my friends go to the Green Lands. The sole redeeming feature of the knowledge of the supernatural is the equal and equivalent knowledge that life is everlasting. That your parents are, unquestionably, in a better place. That, absent using the knowledge you gain to go to the Dark, you will see them someday."

"That doesn't bring them back," Karissa said. "That doesn't make up for all the time we lost. That doesn't..."

"Doesn't bring them back," I said. "Don't. If that's what you're taking these courses for, don't try it. Not as ghosts, not as revenants. That's one of those go/no-go lines. Both legally and morally."

She nodded. "Of course."

"You could never talk about what happened. Did you?"

Karissa looked down again. "I ended up in an institution."

"Did they manage to convince you werewolves didn't exist?"

"Nearly. When I got out, I got sort of obsessive about studying the supernatural. That's when I started to really wonder. There was so much about it and it was all so similar."

"Gotta love how we manage to file all that away as 'myth,'" I said drily.

"I don't understand why they don't make it public!" Karissa said angrily. "I spent years in institutions being told that my father had just gone mad! They slandered my father's memory and my own life! For what?"

"I was beaten to within an inch of my life by agents of my own government for what they felt was a good cause. Their First Reason I agree with. I rather disagree with the beating. The answer to 'why,' you'll have to be cleared for and take master's-level courses. That lays it out. You have to know and understand what is really out there, much worse than mere lycanthropes. Was it necessary for them to make your life such a nightmare? I personally think governments should set up institutions specifically for survivors who have a hard time coping with the sudden reality of the horror. Places where the mantra is 'yes, the horror exists but the secrecy is necessary.'"

"Is it?" Karissa asked angrily. "Is it really necessary?"

"Have you ever looked at the death rate from violence in New Orleans?"

"Not really," Karissa said, puzzled. "I understand the whole of the United States is, sorry, very filled with violence. Especially gun violence."

"Heh." I shook my head. "Gotta love how the supernatural cover-ups feed right into the gun-grabbers' hands. At least two thirds of the reported violent deaths in New Orleans are due to the supernatural. Your story is repeated every month in New Orleans, in a city far smaller in population than the London metropolitan area."

"That is . . ." she said, frowning. "I'm not sure what that has to do with my experiences."

"Besides the fact that I've had this conversation many times?" I said. "Actually, not as many as I'd like. Most people in that situation do not survive. All those murders and suicides you read about? A lot of them are from the supernatural. One of the reasons it is so out of control in New Orleans is the *knowledge* that it exists. But the death rate in New Orleans is nothing compared to what could happen if MI4 and the ever-be-damned MCB didn't squash the truth."

"I'd rather fight it," Karissa said. "I think."

"If you have any question about whether you want to fight it, you don't want to. Don't take this the wrong way. You're a very nice young lady. Nice and Monster Hunting are generally contraindicated."

"You're a nice fellow," Karissa said, smiling.

"Not even close. You, on the other hand, are a very nice young lady. Kind, generous and, face it, just a tad bookish as opposed to 'me kill monsters good.' Smart as well. And there is a need for that in this industry. So if you would like to help, that's my suggestion. Learn first. Find a specialty within the field, work to back up the fighters. We need people like you."

"Really?"

"Really. Bottom line: I'd suggest the best place for you to contribute would be in the support end. That's not a gender thing; I've known some great Hunters who are women."

"I could do that," Karissa said, brightening.

"I know a fellow named Rigby. I'll mention your name to him. I'm sure he'll be in touch."

"That will be fine," she stood up. "Thank you. And thank you for . . ."

"Listening?"

"I don't care what you say. You're a nice person. And I'm glad there are people like you in the world."

"You know Briscoe?" I asked. "The fellow who was asking such pointed questions about how to kill werewolves?"

"I don't know him personally, but yes."

"Probably a guy to get to know," I said.

"Why?"

I thought about that for a moment, then shrugged. "Can't

really get into it. Just...someone you can trust. I know that's hard to manage, but chat him up some time."

"I'll think about it."

If you're wondering, they got married two years ago. I wasn't able to get free to attend the wedding, but I sent a nice gift, a silver dagger, and wished them well. Marriage works for some people in this business, not me.

Beverly the Ginger on the other hand...

Sigh.

Beverly wasn't read in. Beverly had never had an encounter. What she was really into was vampire and erotic entities' myth roleplay. Score.

I am such a dog.

CHAPTER 16

Couple months into the second term at Oxford I got a visit from MI4.

"Is sir in?" Remi asked.

It was winter in England. Most people hate English winters. After two years in New Orleans, I loved the rain and the cold. But it wasn't weather to leave people on the doorstep. On the other hand...

"Depends on who is calling upon sir," I said, turning over some notes I'd found regarding the second Dutch expedition to destroy the Indonesian mava. They were internal memos of the Dutch colonial administration. I had to wonder how Oxford came up with them. I'd also had to learn Dutch but, eh, Dutch, Deutsch, whatever.

"They would not vouchsafe their identities, sir, but I would tend to surmise members of Her Majesty's government," Remi replied. "Some version of MCB would be most likely, sir."

"MI4," I said with a sigh. "Please tell me they made it as far as the parlor and are not on the stoop."

"I rather considered sending them to the servant's entrance, sir." He'd had to nurse me back to health after the beatdown and wasn't favoring government entities at the moment.

"Show them in, Remi. We're playing nice with these assholes."

"Mr. Gardenier," the lead officer said, shaking my hand. "Senior Officer Gordon and Officer Frye, MI4."

Senior Officer Gordon was short and stocky with thinning hair and a multiply-broken nose. His suit was rumpled and he was wearing a trench coat that reminded me vaguely of that Columbo character on TV. He looked more like one of those long-term London street bobbies who'd somehow wandered into being a detective and had the confused look you'd expect.

I was going to be watching him very carefully. You didn't become a "senior officer" of MI4, equivalent to an MCB special agent, if you were dumb.

Frye was Briscoe with a few years on him. Medium height, brown eyes, shaved head, very wide shoulders, Popeye forearms. Clearly some sort of Brit special operations background.

I shook his hand too and gestured to matching wing-backed chairs.

"Nice place," Frye said, looking around.

The small mansion had come complete with decorations.

"Rental. Not as nice as my one in New Orleans. You know that. To what do I owe the pleasure of a visit by England's Finest?"

"I hear you're an expert on Gnoll," Gordon said.

"I've written a dictionary on North American Gnoll," I said, shrugging. "The expert is probably Dr. Witherspoon-Bunders. But..."

"He's retired," Gordon said. "We need a Gnoll expert who's still capable of fieldwork."

"Why?"

"There are various immigrant Fey groups turning up in England," Frye said. "Mostly refugees from Eastern Europe. We don't have language with all of them. In some cases even our contacts in the same species don't have language in common with some of them."

"Stuff's coming in from the hills hasn't been seen in a thousand years," Gordon said, growling. "It's worse on the Continent but we've got our fair share."

"Something's hunting gnolls in Manchester," Frye said. "Normally we don't bother with...supernatural internal disputes. But it's spilling over to humans."

"Killing them or eating them?"

"Killing them," Gordon said. "What would eat a gnoll?"

"Don't ask a master's candidate at Oxford a question like that," I said, smiling. "Giant spiders come to mind. I take it you've autopsied the humans. Cause of death?"

"Unknown," Frye said. "Best our doctors can say is heart failure. No wounds, no toxins, soul was not stripped. No clear indicators of death magic. You're aware that there is a spiritual mark left from something like, say, a voodoo doll?"

"I work in New Orleans," I said drily. "Normally."

"All of them just . . . died from natural causes. Same apparent cause of death in the gnolls. However, given the fact that one of the dead was a healthy twenty-three-year-old and there have been three sewer workers who died, all in the same four-block area, either it's some sort of disease that's spreading from the gnolls to humans or it's the same supernatural entity.

"While some of the gnolls are Brit gnolls, ones we can communicate with, they don't know what the entity is. They can't even detect it. But they know, somehow, that another group knows what it is. That group, unfortunately, doesn't have a common language and is very . . . clannish. We're not even sure where they came from. They also have an ongoing territorial dispute with the local gnolls. The locals suspect they brought down this curse on them. We need to determine if that is the case and what the nature of the entity is. To do that, we need to talk to them, which we cannot do."

"So you're asking me to get the foreign gnolls to confess to murder," I said. "I take it you'll have the usual sort of response to that: Kill them all; God will know his own."

"We just need to get the killings stopped," Frye said. "And they need to know that there are rules about that sort of thing here. If some of them need to die to get that across, some of them need to die. But we need to find out what is causing the deaths."

"So you'd like me to go up to Manchester and try to figure out their language, talk to them and find out what they know about this killing 'thing,'" I said.

"He's not as dumb as he looks," Gordon said.

"Neither are you," I said. "What you're probably looking at is an incorporeal, given the cause of death. Some sort of wraith. I can see several potential issues to this mission. The first that springs to mind is whether you're going to believe me if I say that it's not the fault of the foreign gnolls. It's possible it's something that followed them here or they're completely unconnected. Simple coincidence. As you noted, you've had various 'ferenners' coming over from the East. This could be part of that. The second that springs to mind is that I'm sure as hell not going on an op unarmed. And you Brits get all weanie about people being armed. The third is that assuming an incorporeal, we're not only going to have to find out what it is, but how to destroy it. The gnolls may not know that. They're not particularly into the occult per se. They don't even have shamans."

"From last to first," Frye said, nodding. "Find out what it is and we'll figure out how to destroy it. As to the second, we'll send in a support team to cover you."

"Nice knowing you gentlemen," I said, standing up. "Remi will get your coats."

"Look, you..." Gordon growled.

"Two issues," I said. "First, gnolls under the best of circumstance are skittish. If they're being hunted, they're going to be even more skittish. One person is the best choice to make contact under those conditions. Second, the best way to protect a person is for them to protect themselves. Okay, more: I don't know the backup team, and I am probably the least trusting person you've ever met. I'd need assurance that they'll do their job if the shit hits the fan, and assurance that they're competent to do it, and you can't give me that. I'm not knocking your people, but I have a different view of what 'competent' means and even competence has different meanings. Are they going to follow my fire/no-fire order? You'll notice I haven't thrown in 'how am I getting paid for this?' I'm going to be armed for my own protection, I'm going to be either solo or with at most one other person at my back or you'll need to find another linguist. As to my fee, I'll accept standard rates for this sort of thing. Much less than I usually get paid, I'll add. But the *conditions* are firm. I *will* be prepped for battle. Or find another linguist."

"It is illegal to arm a foreign national for this sort of thing," Frye said placatingly.

"It is illegal under British law to do more than half the sort of things that are your daily bread and butter," I said, sitting down. "Ditto US law for the MCB. Strawman argument. Gentlemen, I'm not going to go all cowboy on your turf. I don't know what sort of exaggerations you've been getting from MCB, but I am, generally, discreet, and when I am not, I have a damned good reason. So let's work something out. Or find another linguist."

"Wait," Gordon said, holding up a hand to Frye. "We'll work

something out. As to the believability: you do know what we do for a living, right? This job is like the Mad Hatter's bloody tea party. You have to believe ten impossible things before breakfast. So . . . we'll arrange to get your toys. But only for this op. No wandering Oxford dressed for a bloody op."

"Agreed," I said.

"Find out what's killing people," Gordon said. "We'll detach Briscoe for your backup. He's a good lad and steady. Give him some field experience in something other than monster killing. Find out what it is. We'll probably know how to dispatch it and Bob's your uncle."

"Sure," I said, grinning. "It's always that easy."

The next bit was making contact with the gnolls and learning their language. I wrote the details of how to do that already in the first memoir. So I'll gloss over most of it. Because the enemy was more interesting.

Turned out the gnolls were from deep inside the Soviet Union. Their language was a gnollish variant of Permian. Not the geologic record, the tribal group. The Permian tribes are an offshoot of the Finnish-Ugric lingual group which is also called "Uralic." In the human languages, there are about two hundred phonemes shared between several tribal languages, Finnish-Ugric-Permian and some with Samoyedic.

Before going to visit them I'd boned up on every known variant of Gnoll in Dr. Witherspoon-Bunders' seminal *Gnoll Dialects of the World*. The man had to have had no sense of smell to collect all the variants he collected. But he had missed a few. Despite claiming that it was "a complete collection of all gnollish dialects with etymological tree," he'd missed pretty much every type of Gnoll I'd ever dealt with. Really it should have been entitled "Gnoll dialects of England, France, Germany, and Scandinavia with a bit of rudimentary Finnish picked up thirdhand." That is *not* everywhere that gnolls are found.

Fortunately, the Finnish section had some similarity and from there I was able to build enough of a basis to communicate. Took about a week.

The Permian gnoll tribe mostly hung out around Hulme Park, and Briscoe and I had many a fine adventure suiting up and clambering down into the sewers in the area. From time to time I'd have a lorry of garbage collected to make friends and get some intelligent—for gnolls—conversation. Finally I had the thing pieced together, and we arranged to meet up with Gordon and Frye again.

"Right," I said, taking a pull on my beer. "Item the first. Not the fault of these gnolls. At least not directly."

The nice thing about working with the English is unless you're forced to go "downtown," you can pretty much figure the meeting will be in a pub. The British, bless their tyrannical hearts, even have a pub in every police station. Right in there. No need to go out to get hammered. It's better than Germany that way.

"So they say," Gordon said.

"As I mentioned, trust and belief," I said. "According to them, their tribe was cursed by a Baba Yaga a long time ago. Don't ask me how long a long time is. They don't have a calendar. In the time of their forefathers, before any living gnoll in the tribe. Gnoll average age is about two hundred, so long time. Best I got. The curse was to be haunted by some sort of specter. They leave gifts for it to keep it away. There's probably been a certain amount of pilfering of food, drink and tobacco in the area as well. I've passed on the proper propitiation to the other gnolls so they're not going to get killed anymore. But you're either going to have to get the sewer workers to leave out some Guinness and Prince Albert along with their sandwiches or we've got to get rid of it."

"What's it called?" Frye asked. "We're fairly good at this sort of pest control."

"You're joking right?" I said. "It's called *ub!tah po hahfack!* All that means is 'evil night spirit.' It's a previous *unknown dialect* of Gnoll, Officer Frye! There probably is a name for it. It is probably a recognized spirit. We might be able to figure it out. But just knowing what the gnolls call it isn't much use. And it is definitely incorporeal. But that's about as much as I could get. There's not a lot of terms in their language for boogiemen."

"I hate this sort of crap," Gordon said.

"Tell me about it," I said, sighing.

"This is a Finnish-Ugric linguistic group, yes?" Briscoe said.

"Yes," I said, shrugging. "Gnoll variant but yes."

"Then will their 'boogiemen' be Finnish-Ugric as well?" Briscoe asked.

"Possibly," I said, frowning. "There's only one battle cry at this point, gentlemen."

"To the Unseen Library!" Briscoe said.

"A para who enjoys research," I said, shaking my head. "Will wonders never cease."

"A Marine who can read," Briscoe replied. "Will wonders never cease..."

"I had to talk the librarian into letting me leave with this," Briscoe said, slamming a heavy tome onto my desk. "Is it me, or does he look *just* like an orangutan?"

"He looks just like an orangutan," I said, still grading papers. "Balding red hair, long arms, flat face. Where y'at?"

"What?" Briscoe said.

"What do you have for me?" There were times I still missed New Orleans.

I'd more or less deputized him as my... deputy. Research assistant maybe. I had papers to grade. That sort of thing was what undergrads, and junior MI4 officers, were for.

"*Piru*," he said.

"You're welcome," I said, then frowned. "You weren't saying thank you?"

"No," Briscoe said.

"It's 'thank you' in a rather obscure Indian language," I said. "Also a type of evil night spirit of Slavic derivation."

"And the master is beaten," Briscoe said. "Uralic, not Slavic. Or it was originally Uralic and got transferred to Slavic according to this."

I picked up the book and looked at the title page. "*Spirits, Myths, Heroes and Devils of the Finno-Uralic Tribes*. So that's saying *piru*—which I'd sort of put aside as being Slavic, not Uralic—is Uralic?"

"According to this," Briscoe said, grinning.

"So how do you banish it?" I asked. "Does it say?"

"Uh..." Briscoe said, then frowned. "No. Do you know?"

"No," I said. "We haven't covered Slavic or Uralic in incorporeal creatures. And I don't usually get into them since they're not PUFF-applicable. Guess you've got more research coming your way."

"Drat," Briscoe said, picking up the book.

I went back to grading papers. Bloody essays. *Everything* at Oxford was bloody essays and of course the TAs had to grade them. And, no, the students were no better at writing them than American students. I was running out of red pens.

"I've found a book which is said to have various spells and incantations for dispelling Slavic and Uralic spirits," Briscoe said, dropping a book on my desk again. It was another weighty tome.

"So how do we dispel it?" I asked. "You could have just done notes."

"I don't do runes," Briscoe said. "It seems that the Germans were having trouble with Slavic and Uralic supernatural entities going *way* back. This was written in the eleven hundreds in Germany but it simply transcribed the Elder Futhark runes for the spells assuming that anyone who was reading it also read Elder Futhark."

"Go down to the linguistics department," I said with a sigh. "Ask Professor Furnbauer for his Elder Futhark dictionary with my kind thanks. I'll need to bone up."

"Oh, you have got to be fucking kidding me..." I said as I finished the translation. Maybe I was wrong? I'd have to get a second opinion. Was Professor Furnbauer read in?

He was. And the translation was right. Bloody hell. This was going to be complicated. And my orals were coming up. On the other hand, the book was interesting and this was shaping up to be a great paper. I was considering translating the whole thing since it had dozens of wards, traps, dispellations, and charms I'd never run across anywhere else. Publish or perish had serious meaning in our job.

Two days later I grabbed Briscoe as he was leaving class.

"Go down to the geology department," I said. "Ask them about some sort of crystal or stone that changes color between 'firelight and sunlight.' One color in sunlight, different color in firelight. Only found in the Ural Mountains."

"If so, it'll be bloody hard to get our hands on," Briscoe said.

"Worse, we'll need one the size of 'the last joint of a tall man's thumb,'" I said. "Just find out what it is."

✧   ✧   ✧

"You're not going to like this," Briscoe said.

"I'm not liking anything about this," I said. "I'm not liking having to depend for information on eleventh century alchemists, gnolls whose language I think I'm translating right and an undergrad para who has enough trouble with English much less any other language."

"Thanks for the vote of confidence," Briscoe said.

"What am I not going to like?" I asked.

"Alexandrite," Briscoe said. "Extremely rare, color-change variant of chrysoberyl. Changes color from green in sunlight to red-purple in artificial light. Named after Tzar Alexander the Second. Only mined in a few areas, the Northern Urals, Sri Lanka, and Brazil."

"We'll need the Urals one to be sure," I said, frowning. "Bit of a trick what with that being the Soviet Union. And a good, clear, pure-quality one."

"More of a trick than you think," Briscoe said. "The Russian deposits were the finest in the world. 'Were' being the important word. They were all mined out in the 1950s. 'Of the size of a large man's thumb' is about ten carats. I asked Professor Shelley how much that would cost and he said, 'Oh, about a hundred.'"

"Hundred dollars?" I asked.

"Hundred *thousand*," Briscoe said. "Pounds."

"Not my problem," I said, grinning. "That's on MI4."

"You're bloody insane," Gordon said. "A hundred thousand pounds?" He patted his pockets for a moment. "Here, let me just *pull it out of my arse*, why don't I?"

"The night creature is a piru," I said. "Or at least a Uralic version of the piru. It's found in Slavic folklore as well. Previously, and I've checked with Dr. Henderson, there was no known way to dispel or entrap one. According to the book Briscoe turned up, there is a way using a Ural alexandrite and a spell. The fact that they're rare is unsurprising given that piru are really nasty spirits. As I said, Dr. Henderson had no answer to how to dispel or kill them. Generally you do what the gnolls are doing which is propitiate them. But if you want to dispel it, you're going to need a big alexandrite. And it will be destroyed in the spell so you won't even be able to sell it afterwards."

"Bloody hell, there goes my budget," Gordon said. "We've got the area blocked off for now. I'll have to get back to you. That really is a bit of a budget item for us at the moment."

"Feel free," I said. "I've got exams coming up."

"That do?" Gordon said, setting a large reddish-purple gem on my desk.

I'd done well on my orals. Now all I had to do was pass the written portion and turn in my thesis and I'd have my second master's.

"Pretty," I said. The stone was deeply colored, cut in an oval and just beautiful. "Hate to ruin it."

I pulled out a loupe and checked to be sure. I'd followed up on pretty much everything Briscoe had brought to me and there was a way to check if it was a Russian stone.

"Bit of a budget line item," I dropped it in a pocket.

"I had to call in a favor," Gordon growled.

"Favor from whom, might I ask?"

"MI6," Gordon said. "Let's just say it didn't come out of my budget. Or theirs. I had to get authorization but it came pretty quick. Seems this beastie has gotten out of the sewers. Two people were found dead from natural causes in the area in the last few days. Both were in the prime of their lives. And MI6 had to burn a cell. So this had better work."

"I tried out some of the White incantations from the book," I said. "They worked well enough. Only one way to find out. And if it doesn't, you won't have my ass to chew, if you know what I mean."

"When can you get started?" Gordon said.

I had exams all week. If I missed one there went my master's. And I really needed to bone up before each of them. Not to mention sleep.

Death is lighter than a feather. And I could sleep when I was dead.

"Tonight."

"You don't really need to be here," I said.

The capture and destruction of a piru takes more than just an alexandrite. First, the piru must be attracted and fed. They liked expensive food, drink, and drugs. Yes, drugs. Tobacco will do but opium has much the same effect on them as on humans for some reason. We were banking on heroin for that. You could find it on various street corners in Manchester, and it wasn't like we were in danger of getting arrested. On the other hand, MI4 could just get it out of an evidence locker, which they had.

We were doing the rite in an alleyway off of the Sanctuary, which I thought rather ironic in the circumstances. It was where the now three people had died of "natural causes," one each night.

You bring them in by burning tobacco and alcohol, then set up a little tableau with the various comestibles laid out. Checking the police reports, all three of the dead had been smokers, if young enough that it shouldn't have caused their deaths, and all three had been drinking. So they'd "called" the piru but hadn't offered to share. Die, humans, die. Handy tip: always be unselfish if you're being tracked by a wraith. If one shows up when you're smoking and drinking, offer them a fag and a shot. Or else.

"Rather want to see what we've been chasing," Briscoe said.

We laid out a brass tray with some shots of rum, a prime cut of lamb, and a small brazier on it. Then we lit the rum and dropped pipe tobacco on the coals in the brazier.

We were right by a storm drain and it took about fifteen minutes for the piru to appear, following the scent of burning alcohol and tobacco. It was just a darker shadow amongst the shadows, a tenebrous fog rising from the storm grating.

The piru floated closer. It was difficult to see in the moonlit darkness even with the help of the streetlights. It moved from shadow to shadow. We'd placed the tray in shadow, knowing it would avoid any sort of light. It was generally bipedal; I'm fairly sure it wasn't anything derived from human, though. You get a certain feeling around human ghosts and this was definitely unearthly.

The wraith floated to the tray and into the smoke from the tobacco and the burning essence of the rum. It was clear it was feeding in some way. Maybe it just liked the aroma. But it also made contact with the lamb. I'd gotten a tissue sample and I intended to check the differences between the original and the sacrificed. It was pretty sure that the people who had "died of natural causes" had died of some sort of loss of something. Phosphate, calcium, something. It would be easier to find between the two versions of lamb.

Since we were properly propitiating it, we weren't in any

danger at this point so I took notes as carefully as I could. I knew there was no way to photograph it but I wish I could have.

The rum had burned out so Briscoe lit another shot. Give the guy credit, para or not he wasn't fazed by an otherworldly spirit being.

Once the piru was feasting I opened up the nickel bag of heroin and dropped that on the brazier.

The result wasn't immediate. The thing wasn't moving real fast as it was but it slowly... slowed until it was simply hanging there in the smoke from the fire like a black sheet on a clothesline.

I got out my cheat sheet and the irreplaceable gem. I laid the gem on the tray, in contact with some of its tendrils of shadow, and began to read.

The toughest part of the whole thing had been finding the proper pronunciation for some of the Uralic and Germanic in the incantation. Dean Carruthers had put me in contact with a traditional Uralic speaker and that had helped. Some of the words were close enough to tribal Tibetan I had to wonder if there was a racial connection.

I began the incantation, calling upon the owl spirit and the moon spirit and the spirit of the gem to bind and entrap this creature of darkness. Three repetitions and I could see it starting to sink into the stone. It also was starting to move so I gestured at the second heroin packet and Briscoe tossed it in. Good little wizard's apprentice.

It took nine repetitions of the incantation but finally the piru sank into the stone completely.

I picked the stone up with a pair of tongs and winced.

"Let's hope this works," I said and dropped it into the brazier.

Nothing happened at first but then a sound started to emit from the stone. It was so high-pitched at first it wasn't even audible but dogs started barking in all the flats nearby. Then it was in the audible range, for me at least, and I started to get the whole *banshee cry* thing. Horrible sound, eerie and painful to the ears despite being surprisingly quiet. A bit like what a hamster would sound like if it was being slowing burned to death. At least a bizarre space hamster.

Finally, with one last tortured wail, the priceless gem shattered amongst the charcoal bricks and it was done.

"Did we get it?" Briscoe asked.

"Only way to know is if nobody dies tonight," I said. "Let's pack up. We've both got exams in the morning."

Nobody died that night nor in the subsequent weeks. A guy died of a heart attack three weeks afterwards in the area but he was a risk case, so all good.

The lamb samples were subsequently bent, folded and mutilated by MI4's labs. There was a significant difference in the levels of isoleucine, an amino acid, between the two samples. Notably less in the one that the piru had touched. So apparently, besides liking to get high, pirus steal isoleucine. The pathologist who gave the report started to explain about isoleucine and I asked him not to. I've got enough stuff stuffed in my head. I'll leave that to the medical professionals. Bottom line, not enough will kill you.

I later went back and translated the book of incantations and traps for various Slavic and Siberian entities as well as adding quite a few others from Europe and Eurasia. The three-book set: *Identification of, Protections Against,* and *Traps for Supernatural Entities of the Slavic, Siberian, Balkans and Eurasian Spirit Tribes* by Dr. Oliver Chadwick Gardenier, PhD (CrLing), is available from Oxford University Press. If you have the clearance. There's a complete copy in the MHI library as well.

Now to explain why I added all that to my memoirs besides as a commercial plug:

My *teacher* hat is on at this point, so bear with me with the pro-tip. One reason for this long explanation of tracking down one minor entity is this is stuff you're going to have to learn at some point. You can't always depend on someone else to do your research for you. I don't mean you have to learn Proto-Uralic. But you do need to learn the Dewey Decimal System.

It's also about teaching. I could have taken the time to go look all this stuff up myself. But part of why Briscoe was at Oxford was to learn how to do the research. So I *delegated.* And that, too, is part of your job once you get past "me dumb grunt." He learned how to find some very obscure stuff in the sometimes baroque library system. For that matter, he found the tome that had exactly the right information. I might not have. Why? I knew where to look, he didn't. Sometimes sending out the person who doesn't know the "right" answer is the right answer. Sometimes it's not. But until that day, we didn't have an answer to piru. We found it because Briscoe went and looked in what was basically the wrong place.

Most of this particular memoir, for one reason or another, has been about the *background* of hunting. Everyone likes the big fight scenes. But hunting is about *more*. Learn the more.

For God's sake, at least learn Latin and crack a book once in a while. Don't just expect me or Milo or Ray or whoever is the equivalent in your day and age to do all the work.

CHAPTER 17

In summer, Oxford doesn't shut down completely but it does shut down mostly. The lawsuit was still wending its way through court and I was still persona non grata in US hunting. So I took a few trips to work toward my doctorate. There was no new information about the potential mava paṇauvaā beneath New Orleans. I'd done all the research I could at Oxford. It was time to sally forth.

I started in the US, specifically in the Everglades. There was a known group of swamp-apes in the Everglades and nobody knew how to communicate with them. Time to change that.

As I drove through the endless mass of sawgrass on an airboat, I noted that I really should have done this in winter. Summer in England is a charm. Summer in South Florida was killing me. I was back in the heat and hating every moment of it.

My guide was an old Seminole who spoke barely passable English. I'd book-studied Seminole in preparation and he spent most of the ride yelling corrections to my accent. Finally we reached the cluster of hummocks where the swamp-apes were reported to have been sighted. He dropped me off, fast, and took off. He clearly thought I was an idiot for going anywhere near them.

Florida swamp-apes are not pacific herbalists like the sasquatch. They were omnivorous and were known to have attacked, and rumored to have eaten, humans. But I wasn't worried about being eaten by swamp-apes. They were going to have to fight the mosquitoes.

193

I found a clearing to set up camp, sprayed on some more OFF!, laid out the tasty viands I'd brought to propitiate the hostile cryptids, sprayed on some more OFF!, inflated the boat I was going to use to get from one hummock to the other, sprayed on some more OFF!, drank some water, cursed the heat, sprayed on some more OFF! and finally just got in my tent, despite it being—if anything—hotter inside, and sprayed insect killer all over to kill the mosquitoes that followed me in.

Then I shot a spider so big I swear to God it should have been PUFF-applicable. Christ, I hate the tropics and subtropics. Those idiots who think exploring jungles are fun are fucking nuts.

I had a mantra, though, to keep up my spirits. Doctorate. Doctorate. Doctorate. Doctorate.

The fuckers attacked in the middle of the night.

The first inkling I had was when my tent collapsed. Then the hooting started and I was punched through the tent material so hard I was sure I was fighting trolls.

"*Guh! Guh!*" I yelled, hoping that some Sasquatch remained in their language. Other than that I just balled up and took it. "Guh! Guh! Oomph! Oomph!" (Friend, friend, good good.) Then I tried some Louisiana Swamp-Ape since they were closer. "Yut! Yut!"

Whatever was pounding me stopped attacking.

"Yooo?" it said in a querying tone.

"Yooo?" I said back. "Oomph?"

There was a rustle and they were gone.

It took a few weeks for me to finally make real contact. Weeks of moving from hummock to hummock, swatting insects, avoiding alligators and rattlesnakes and giant spiders. In a couple of cases, actually PUFF-applicable giant spiders.

They were smaller tribes, I'm pretty sure fairly inbred, smaller in stature, meaner and much devolved from the noble sasquatch. The language was much devolved as well. Forget phonemes, there were barely two hundred words in the language and sixteen related to mosquitoes. For one thing, they were a primary food source as well as a scourge. The swamp-apes picked them off of each other and ate them as they were foraging.

And aggressive? Jesus. They make chimpanzees look tame. I figured out the beta posture pretty quick and spent most of my time learning their language at arm's length. Territorial as hell.

The family groups even got into it frequently and viciously. Fortunately, they weren't quite as strong as chimps and I eventually got a reputation as someone who could hit back. Hard. Not quite the way you're supposed to do crypto-anthropology, but after watching one family group rip an alligator to pieces for lunch, I wasn't taking any chances.

I spent most of June among those fucking monsters and it was the worst June of my life. I can understand them being off the PUFF table but it's a near run thing. Doesn't really matter. Between inbreeding and habitat loss, they're pretty much going to be extinct in short order. I'm not going to sweat it.

I flew back to England, wrote up my notes and then headed to Canada.

Why Canada? There were, and are, Laurentian yeti. Shorter, darker and squatter than sasquatch, they are frequently mistaken for brown bears. They're also more aggressive, similar to swamp-apes. But at this point I had pretty good contact techniques and was able to make contact more smoothly than in Florida.

The bugs were nearly as bad as Florida's but at least it was cooler. In fact, one night it snowed. Blessed relief.

The language was even more removed from Sasquatch than Swamp-Ape, yet richer. Many more nouns, some fairly complex verbs, several adjectives that were more related to Inuit, with whom they must have made contact in the past. They even had cursing which neither other group had developed. Three of their curses, though, had an etymology that escaped me until I was on my way out and the Quebecois guide dropped a heavy pack on his foot. Ah. Etymology accepted.

June in Florida. July in the Laurentians (better than Florida). Now it was off to Nepal where I hoped to make contact with true yeti.

I didn't climb Everest, but I went there to see where Sir Edmund Hillary and Shaman Tenzing Norgay defeated the Goar-ahli Snow Demon. Why did they climb Everest? "Because *it* was there." The snow demon, that is. It had been using Everest as a safe redoubt only going lower to steal children to eat.

I did make contact with the yeti. They were even more shy than the sasquatch but I had Hillary's book to fall back on and I was really just verifying the data. Most of it held out. I think either Nepalese yeti were less developed than Tibetan or he'd exaggerated a bit. They weren't nearly as insightful as he'd described. I'd put them as less developed than Laurentian. But most of his information held true and at least the dictionary was more or less on.

I got a full plate back tattoo in Katmandu from an old man whose family had been doing tattoos back to prehistory. All freehand, no predrawing, all hammered. Absolutely beautiful depiction of the Wheel. He was also a shaman and the tattoo was supposed to be a ward against scryings. If it actually worked, maybe the MCB wouldn't be able to make up any more bullshit readings about me.

The yeti wasn't the only thing that brought me to Tibet. While I was there I tried to track down more original scrolls with information about the mava. I did not have many contacts there, but Rigby had given me directions to a few obscure mountain monasteries.

There were a few things there of use. Most of the description of the mava was, as noted, extremely euphemistic and the sheer horror of the sight of the thing translated clearly despite being second- or thirdhand and in Tibetan. And much of it I initially took to be so euphemistic as to be useless. "Of a multitude of that which is used in the airiest places." I mean, what the hell does something like *that* mean?

But one phrase kept cropping up, "Of like unto the crown of the Most Perfect." Crown could mean many things. It could mean brow, top of the head, since the lamas of that period shaved their heads presumably bald, it could also mean the hat they wore, it could mean what most people take as a crown. I had no idea.

My lucky break came in an unexpected form. While I was studying at the monastery, a monk arrived and presented me with a note and a summons. Somehow Father Pema in Crestone, Colorado, had known I would end up here eventually, and sent a letter of introduction ahead. It must have been a good letter, because I was invited to meet with an expert who *never* spoke with Westerners.

I took all my notes with me to Nepal to meet with a lama in exile. The lamas of Tibet had been the lords and priests of that land from time immemorial. They were worshipped nearly as gods but by and large maintained an ascetic lifestyle that would make most homeless in the US throw up their hands in anger.

Lama Kotokai had once been the abbot of a monastery housing a thousand monks and libraries with even more thousands of scrolls, some so ancient they were as fragile as snowflakes. Now he lived in a thin-walled, drafty hovel on the poorest edge of Katmandu where he ministered to the flock there, dispensing wisdom and medicinal healing and blessings.

And he was probably *more* content.

It was Lama Kotokai who figured out the hidden meanings in my notes.

"This crown refers to the hat of the Most Perfect of the period," he told me, nodding over my copy of a copy of a copy of the original text. "They were made in the shape of the shell of a sea creature. These shells were very prized by the people of that time for they came from far away and were quite rare. 'That which is found of the airiest places' is ropes, such as are used on bridges. These are the airy places."

Okay, so, covered in ropes. Tentacles? Probably. But the rest?

"With humility." I bowed. "There are many shells of sea creatures, Most Holy One."

"This was a sort of clam." He pulled out a sheet of paper and sketched on it with a stick from the fire. "There. This was the form of the body of the mother of serpents according to these writings of the apprentice of the Most Perfect."

I looked at the thing and blinked. It made no sense.

Every indication I'd had was that the body of the mava paṇauvaā was amorphous like its pseudopods. But this was, indeed, a clam. Sort of. Sort of a cross between a clam and a snail.

A clam with *tentacles*? Did those even exist? Wait. What was I thinking? If this was a creation of the Old Ones, it wasn't even from this *dimension*.

"I must ask, with humility. Does this indicate that the body was hard? I had been under the impression, perhaps mistaken, that it was quite soft."

"Hard," Lama Kotokai said. "Very hard. Like rock. Such is known of the Sacrifice of the Most Perfect Thubten. Their covering is like armor. If you have such in your land, they must be expelled most quickly. They settle in and cause great havoc to all around. They summon the worst of the guras, mavas and srul.

It is said that they are but the *young* of Those Who Are Not Named. Those Who Are Not Named spread their seeds among the worlds. When the time is right, when the stars align, some hatch and, like the butterfly or the locust, go through stages of change. In time, when the changes are complete, they become one of Those of the Darkest Stars."

Those Who Are Not Named covered a lot of entities. Tibetans. If it's bad, we don't talk about it. But Those of the Darkest Stars. I had to think about that one for a second. I'd heard it somewhere before. No, I'd *read* it somewhere before. I'd read a lot of stuff.

It wasn't in English...Tibetan...No. Nepali?

Sabaibhandā'adhyārō tārāharu?

That's the Nepalese term for Old Ones. Great Old Ones. *Great Cthulhu sleeps* Great Old Ones! End of the world, do not pass Go, Extinction Level Event Great Old Ones!

Oh, shit.

It wasn't a servant. It wasn't some mindless creation. The fucking thing was a *larval Old One*? Here? On Earth? Specifically under *my house*?

Oh, shit.

I wanted to scream at the top of my lungs but you didn't do that around a lama. I just thanked him and left a large donation for the poor.

Oh, shit.

There went my property values.

There wasn't much in the way of fine hotels in Katmandu in the late eighties. I was in a fleabag with a couple of single beds, a rusty sink, barely functioning toilet and a black and white TV. I went back to it to think and turned on the TV for background noise.

So...did MCB *know* what a mava really was? Generally MCB knew more than they let on. Only if they knew there was a baby Great Old One they'd probably be doing "underground nuclear testing" beneath New Orleans. In this case, I might have made myself the greatest living expert on mava in the world. I probably knew more than MCB at this point.

The problem was, I was on MCB's shit list. They might or might not believe me. All I really had to go on was the words of some old fucker in a saffron robe. I was not on MI4's shit list, though. They owed me for taking out that piru. They'd probably believe me. But it wasn't like the thing was under Manchester: it was under New Orleans.

I needed more proof. Hell, I wasn't sure if I was panicking. I was having a hard time believing there was a larval Great Old One under New Orleans. Did being larval mean it was only an "Old One" and not a "Great Old One"? How did you get the honorific "Great" when you were an Old One? Size? Territory? How fast it melts your brain? Just how long do they remain "larval"? And what happens when they hatch?

I was pretty sure I knew the answer to *that* one.

More interesting question: How long do they remain larval and how long had it been cooking? These things were a complete mystery. It was assumed they could live for millions of years. Their larval stage could be a long time, like millennia or even aeons. "That is not dead which can eternal lie and with strange aeons even death may die." Lovecraft must have had some sort of line to the pure quill.

Was it ready to hatch? What sort of sign would there be? Or did we have until the sun went cold to worry?

I wasn't really watching the TV, it was just on for noise. There was only one channel that occasionally had on English programs and it announced it was changing to a "blockbuster" movie.

Blockbuster. It was some horrid B-grade SF flick from the 1950s called...

It: The Terror from Beyond Space!

I got up and changed the channel. In my current state of controlled terror, this I did not need.

Wow. Apparently the Nepalese are *really* into 1950s horror flicks. *The Monster That Challenged the World*...

Is about a mollusklike monster which lives under the Salton Sea in California and is released due to nuclear weapons testing or an earthquake or something.

I was about halfway through the two-hour run. I did some math and figured that I'd tuned in with fifty-seven minutes to go. The Nepalese host who did comedy skits during the commercial breaks said the movie was from 1957.

When the guy I was assuming was Saint Peter had sent me back to the world of living, he'd told me to watch for signs. And specifically my sign was the number fifty-seven.

"Okay, God," I said, looking up. "Got it. Giant mollusk creature. Bad thing. Do something."

I called the airport and booked the next flight out. Time to head back to the States and see if I could scrounge up some proof that didn't involve signs from the Almighty.

The in-flight movie?

On the flight from New Delhi to London: *Alien*.

Flight Number? Indian Airlines Flight 257.

On the flight from London to Atlanta: *The Blob*.

Flight Number? You guessed it: 1157.

On the way out of the airport in New Orleans there was a homeless guy standing there with a sign: THE END IS COMING.

"But do you have a specific date?" I asked him as I got in the car. Remi had previously redeployed to New Orleans and picked me up.

"Sir?"

"You don't want to know."

Once is coincidence, twice is happenstance, three times is "Okay, God, I've *got it*! You can turn down the volume."

"Things are worse here than I thought, Remi. I'm really thinking about moving."

"Out of New Orleans, sir?"

"I'm not good with this continent. If I could find another planet, we'd be moving that far."

CHAPTER 18

There was a lot of catching up to do. I couldn't get a long distance call to work from Nepal, but I had called Ray from New Delhi. Upon briefing him about the mava possibly being a baby Old One, he'd hit the roof. What had just been a regional problem was now an all hands on deck, priority-one, company freak-out.

My meeting with the DOJ lawyer and Myers was covered previously. Why didn't I bring up the possible Old One under New Orleans? Because I didn't have any proof and it wasn't part of the agenda. If I could find something, anything solid, I'd... I wasn't sure what I was going to do. MCB needed to know. On the other hand, I could easily see them nuking the hell out of New Orleans. I'm not sure what cover they'd use for that but I really didn't want to see my house nuked.

On the other hand, Old One. Larval admittedly. We needed intelligence and proof. Since the MCB hadn't signed the settlement papers yet, I couldn't engage in "Monster Hunting." But for "research" I was the man for the job.

LaGrange Seismic was a small company housed in a warehouse in Elmwood. They were the first ones in the phone book I'd been able to get an appointment with, simple as that. I'd just told them I was a prospective customer.

The receptionist was a middle-aged lady with bottle-blonde hair and otherwise indistinguishable. "Chad Gardenier. I have an appointment with Mr. Smith."

"Of course, Mr. Gardener," the lady said. "If you could wait just a moment while I call him?"

Gardenier, I thought. I might hate my name but I hated even more when people couldn't pronounce it. Smith was medium height, brown hair and beard, heavy-set.

"Mr. Gardener," he said, shaking my hand.

"Gardenier. Not a big issue. Where can we talk?"

The meeting room was small, musty and smelled of paper, ink and dirt. Not "dirty" dirt, but the kind of smell you get in construction trailers and civil engineering companies. It was from all the dirt shaking that goes on and people coming in covered in the stuff. There were piles of rolled up paper in every corner. I was pretty sure I had picked the right place.

"My company is interested in the potential that there might be a large anomalous...object beneath New Orleans." I chose my words carefully. Now that we knew the mava had a super hard shell with a gooey center, we had a potential way to locate it. Ray had been kicking himself for not thinking of this avenue of investigation sooner. "The exact nature of why is proprietary. This object will be approximately one hundred and twenty meters in length and composed of...stone? I'm aware that is a very generalized term to geologists, but..."

"You meant the Frandsen Anomaly?"

"I'm not sure. What is the Frandsen Anomaly?"

"It's a big cell more or less under Bourbon Street," Smith said. "It was discovered back in the late sixties when modern seismic was really starting to kick in. There was a paper done on it in the early seventies and it even made minor news. I don't know if that's what you're looking for, because it is a little bigger."

"How much bigger?"

"Not a lot in geological terms...About double that. It's closer to two hundred meters."

"Oh..." That couldn't be good. That was way bigger than what the PUFF adjuster assumed the last one had been. "What sort of work has already been done? At this point I'm willing to pay you for your time just for a briefing."

"Not really my specialty." Smith leaned back, folded his hands over his stomach, and furrowed his brow. "It's a large carbonaceous meteor that seems to have landed more or less intact probably during the Pleistocene era based on its depth. It's mostly known because of the issues it causes."

"Issues? Like odd acoustics or something?"

"The guy who did most of the work on it was Neil Frandsen. He was one of my professors at LSU. But...I really like the guy, but he sort of went crackers towards the end."

"Crackers?"

"He insisted it was a UFO." Smith grimaced. "Again, really thought he was a great guy but..."

"Crackers. Yeah. What set him off?"

"This was after I was out of college and I was just getting started on this gig. So I wasn't directly keeping up at the time. As I got it, some seismographers found this anomaly and Professor Frandsen got a grant to check it out. When they drilled it, they got back some samples that indicated some sort of proto-life indicators. Later they figured out it was contamination. But Professor Frandsen went off about it. Started saying it was proof of extraterrestrial life, which admittedly would be a big deal. That was what made it a minor news story at the time. Then he started into it was a UFO and the end of the world was coming."

"Did he report that to the government?"

"Would you believe it if you were government?" Smith said, grinning. Then he stopped. Apparently I wasn't as poker-faced as I'd hoped. "Why are you interested in it again?"

"Proprietary. Is Professor Frandsen still at LSU?"

"No. He resigned. Asked, just did it—I've heard both stories."

"Any idea where I can find him?"

"Nope."

"Okay," I said, standing up. "Not sure what your minimum billing is but time is money. How much?"

Neil Frandsen, PhD (GeoPh), did not reside in Louisiana anymore, thank you for your inquiry, according to the secretary for the Dean of Geology at LSU. No, we don't know where he resides presently. Will there be anything else?

I tracked down his old colleagues. They were one and all saddened by his "sudden change in demeanor." Some of his less enthusiastic colleagues were more on the order of "he was always an arrogant ass and he just finally cracked." One of them at least had a forwarding address.

He'd moved to Canada. Northern Canada. *Really* Northern Canada, up by the Arctic Circle Northern Canada. Ever heard of Yellowknife? No, me neither, not before then. Of course, the fact that it was the capital of the Northern Territories means real geography buffs know where it is and probably most Canadian school kids know for all of a day so they can pass the test. But regular people? Not so much.

How do you get in touch with him? You either write him a letter or go visit in person. And don't expect a friendly reception.

It was September by then. I was supposed to be back at Oxford. I'd written a tersely worded telex to Dr. Henderson telling her I was going to have to extend my "sabbatical" due to real-world issues. Now I was going to northern Canada to interview a crazy professor. Gotta love my job.

Yellowknife was a fair-sized town, mostly 'cause it was, you know, a capital. Decent if small airport. Fucking weather was the pits. It was September and there was already a blizzard on the way. Why the hell would anyone exile themselves to a place like this? Oh, yeah, "The End Is Coming!" Like you'd be safe up here.

Frandsen lived in a cabin off of the Frontier Trail about ten miles outside of Yellowknife. There was a large sign on the driveway—DO NOT ENTER! THIS MEANS YOU!—along with a heavy metal gate. The driveway went around a rock outcrop to the distantly visible cabin.

"Friendly fellow," I said, paying the taxi driver. It wasn't a yellow cab by any means. When I'd asked if there was a taxi that could take me out to the guy's house, the nice Inuit young lady at the ticket counter had called a cousin who picked me up in a rattletrap pickup.

"I'll stick around," Aviqming said. "You probably won't be long. He doesn't take too kindly to visitors."

"'Shoots them' doesn't take too kindly or tells them to get the hell out?"

"Generally tells them to get the hell out. Shooting's mostly for the bears and moose. Don't pet the moose."

"A moose once bit my sister."

"Heard it," Aviqming said. "I've got a better one. A moose once killed my cousin. Seriously. Avoid the moose."

"Will do." I headed down the driveway.

The area was low scrub and dwarf coniferous trees with

multiple outcroppings of rock. The driveway more or less wandered between the outcroppings. I could see why a geologist would like the area. Why anybody else would live here was the question. The trees and scrub had been deliberately cleared in a large area around the cabin. As I walked down the driveway, a rifle poked out of an upstairs window.

"Go away! I don't want any!"

I slowly held my hands up over my head. No sudden moves. There might be moose.

"Professor Neil Frandsen?"

"Nobody here by that name!" the man shouted back. *"Go away!"*

"I'm here to discuss the anomaly! I need to know what you know about it!"

The response was a bullet that hit off to my side. Pro-tip: You don't shoot in front of someone. The ricochet is liable to hit them. Frandsen apparently knew this pro-tip.

"Would it help if I told you I believe you're right and I need to know what you know so I can do something about it?"

"Or you're here to shut me up!"

"Can we discuss it without shooting?"

"You got any guns, drop 'em!"

I squatted down and started disarming myself.

"Who's with you?"

I was getting tired of all the shouting. "Just the guy who drove me from the airport! I swear, I'm on your side! I'm one of the good guys!"

It took a while. I could vaguely see the outline of presumably Frandsen moving around checking the surroundings. There's paranoid and there's "Lunatic Fringe." I was going to have to handle this carefully.

"Go tell Aviqming to drive back," Frandsen yelled from the front porch. "I'll radio when he needs to pick you up. Might not be long."

Former Professor Neil Frandsen was short and burly with iron-gray beard and hair and bright, intelligent, but suspicious blue eyes. He had a rifle trained on my chest as I sat down in the offered chair.

The interior of the cabin was cluttered with books and charts. Homey, clearly a single man's domain, but well organized. The charts seemed to mostly be geological data of the surrounding region.

"I go by Robert Heinlein's adage that you should always give a man ten words before you kill him," Frandsen said. "You've got ten words."

I thought about that. "It is a dangerous creature that has to be killed."

"Repeating what *I* said isn't going to save your life." Frandsen pointed the rifle at my head.

"Do you know what it is? I do."

"I know what I think it is," Frandsen said. "But whenever I've told people what I think it is they call me crazy. And I've had plenty of people who write books for and about crazy people try to get me to open up. Figure you're one of them."

"I don't write books about crazy stuff...Okay, I do write, but it's academic. My job is to kill monsters. Simple as that. You were in New Orleans. Ever hear of Hoodoo Squad?"

"No." Frandsen frowned. "But maybe it wasn't called that then. You're a Monster Hunter?"

"Yes. And the anomaly is what's called an Old One. Very bad juju. Which is why I need to know everything you learned about it. If it hatches, the whole world's in for a very bad time."

"Why the hell do you think I'm up here?" Frandsen finally laid the rifle across his lap. "Prove you're a Monster Hunter and not one of those UFO book writers."

"I'll have to take off my coat." I pulled off the layers I was wearing and showed him my scars. I started pointing them out. "Loup-garou. Vampire. Ghoul. That weird one is from some sort of shadow demon...Do I look like a writer?"

"This thing...You can't kill it." Frandsen set his rifle aside, and got up to get a bottle of Wild Turkey. "It's something from beyond time."

"They've been killed before. It's generally called a mava paṇauvaā, Gujarati for 'worm mother.' I believe it is the larval form for an extremely deadly alien species."

"No kidding. Which is why I'm up here," Frandsen said. "Once I figured out that thing was alive, and I couldn't get anyone to listen, I headed for the most out-of-the-way area I could move to. This plat is about as stable geologically as you're going to find in the world. I figured that if that thing started moving there'd be all sorts of crises. And one of them was bound to be geological. And sociological. Up here there's too few people to be a problem."

He might have thought that sounded bad, but it was actually a remarkably optimistic take on what would happen. Old Ones meant blood, fire, madness, and then lights out.

"Did you call the government when you figured it out?"

"Of course I did!" Frandsen said angrily. "The minute I put two and two together. They blew me off!"

"You got the wrong department." This could have been handled well before my time. Thanks, God. "Let me start at the beginning…" I gave him the standard MHI "the supernatural is real but there are people who can do something about it" talk. After that, and a lot of Wild Turkey, he was ready to talk freely.

"When we found the anomaly on seismic surveys, it really wasn't looked at as a big thing. How a big cell of rock got dropped under New Orleans was a puzzler, though. Do you understand New Orleans geology?"

"There's oil under it?"

"Some," Frandsen said. "New Orleans and the surrounding area, most of the delta region for that matter, is composed of Pleistocene-era loess. There's thirty thousand feet of loess silt under New Orleans before you get to Cretaceous limestone bedrock."

"Loess is…sorry, 'dirt' formed from the glaciers grinding rocks and releasing it as dust, right?"

"Get you a C in my class," Frandsen said grumpily. "Close enough. That 'dirt' as you say—soil would be a better term—got washed down by the river that's more or less where the Mississippi is over thousands of years during the Pleistocene."

"Pleistocene. Mammoths. Ice Age."

"Which is when you got continental glaciers," Frandsen said. "And most loess formation. That was when most of the Mississippi delta built up. There's more recent, within the last few thousand years, surface geology. But under *that* is pretty much undifferentiated silt going down twenty to thirty thousand feet. So when we found a gigantic cell of what looked like rock three thousand feet down, it was a sort of 'Hmmm, that's interesting' moment."

"Generally the best time in science."

"Not this time. I wished I'd never gotten involved." Frandsen took another drink. "Best hypothesis was an asteroid that somehow came down more or less intact. Bottom line, we got some grants and drilled down to it."

He took another drink.

"You gotta understand, core tapping at those depths was sort of in its infancy. We were mostly getting ground-up bits of whatever the hell it was made from. The drill guys kept wearing out heads. What we were getting wasn't making any sense, either. When we hit the hard stuff, it seemed to be organic. So we sent it to the biology lab..." Frandsen paused and seemed really reluctant to continue.

"And?"

"Dr. Catherine Ramos was in charge of analyzing the organic materials. I really liked Catherine. I'd never really dealt with her until we found organics in the anomaly. But working with her was a real charm. We sort of had a thing. Then she started to...change."

"Get a bit crazy?" I asked.

"Bit?" Frandsen snorted. "By then we'd penetrated the shell. And it was definitely a shell. Carapace. Something. We got up this weird liquid. Gray-green. Just came gushing out of the mud from the pumps. Smelled...horrible."

"Like dead cattle bloating in the road mixed with some sort of horrible chemical spill."

"So you've smelled it. Ever seen a world-class biologist try to analyze it?"

"No."

"Catherine was grounded, sane, totally rational," the former professor said. "Two days after she got the sample, she was in a nut house. Been there ever since. One of her grad students committed suicide. The rest quit. Drillers got sick. Quit. One of them killed another guy with a wrench over nothing. I was feeling the effects. Anybody who touched those samples went nuts. That's when I realized we'd struck not gold but pure evil. I shut down the drill and pulled out. I stopped researching geology and started researching theology. That's when I realized we'd struck something that had been biding its time from before time."

"And in 'strange aeons even death may die,'" I quoted.

"Exactly," Frandsen said. "But when I tried to tell people..."

"They thought you were nuts. Doomsayer prophets tend to get dismissed. One of the issues I'm going to face. I'm sort of surprised, though, that it didn't come to the attention of the right authorities."

"Well, if there are right authorities, they certainly screwed this one up. I've managed to keep up with it. Some of my real friends still send me reports. I know they do it just to humor their crazy friend, but they do humor me. The thing hasn't really moved. Slight upward movement but no real acceleration. Though at the current rate, it will surface in five hundred years or so."

"Unless it hatches," I said. "But like you said, dawn-of-time stuff. It could hatch in five hundred years. Or five minutes. Or five million. Really don't know. But it is, yes, just as bad as you think it is. Worse." I thought about it for a few moments. Dr. Frandsen gave me the time. "I need you to come back."

"No way in hell," Frandsen replied. "I'm quite comfortable where I'm at, thank you."

"You're the expert. The only expert. You want the world to end or you want to do something about it?"

"I'm prepared." Frandsen shrugged. "If people wanted to do something about it they should have listened when I was telling them back in the seventies."

"You're bitter. I get that. You just got ignored and ridiculed. I recently got beat most of the way to death by federal agents. I'm going to have to go back to *those same people*, the ones who put me in the fucking hospital, and tell them that they're wrong. Again. That what's down there isn't just some scavenger creature but a full-on Old One. The thing they fear the most, and that I found it when they couldn't. That they missed it. And I'm going to do that, one way or another. I'm going to convince them. Because if I don't, world ends.

"And there is no 'prepared,'" I added. "Get over that naïve notion. This thing breaks out, there's nowhere on earth to hide. You can't just hide up here. Not for long."

"I'm old," Frandsen said. "You said yourself it could break out in five minutes or five thousand years. I'll take my chances. Here. Not in New Orleans. Screw you."

"Fine. Can I at least get your data? We're going to have to replicate your drill. You can at least give me what I need to do that."

Frandsen thought about that for a bit then shrugged. "That you can have. For what good it will do you. You're going to expose the drillers to this stuff, you know. Again. It's evil."

"Ultimate evil," I said. "Which is exactly why we have to kill it."

CHAPTER 19

On the way home I had a layover in my old stomping grounds of Seattle.

It was tempting to just go to Saury and get some good sushi, but there was one other avenue of investigation into the mava that I had not pursued yet.

The night club was in a bad part of town. It was an ugly brick building with no signage. There was a big metal door, and when you knocked on it, the bouncer looked at you through a slit. The vision slit was about a foot and a half higher than I was tall, which would be your first clue this wasn't a normal club.

I knocked and got eyes.

"What's password?" The bouncer had a very deep voice.

"Party, party all night long," I said, trying not to sigh. "Party little Princess 'til the break of dawn. Shake your little groove thing, yeah, yeah, yeah. Shake your little groove thing, Princess Shallala."

"You gots do dance too. Princess says you gots do the dance when you says the password!"

"I'll slip you twenty bucks if I can skip the dance part." There weren't any witnesses, but I had my pride. "Just tell Shallala I did it."

"Deal."

I stuck the money through the hole and the door opened. The bouncer was a troll. Trolls make good bouncers. As tough as my friend Decay is, he had nothing on this guy. Shifty bastards though. He'd probably spend that twenty on porn.

At night there would be human customers and human employees

212 Larry Correia & John Ringo

and the Fey servants would hide, and Shallala would put on a glamour and mingle. But during the day, there were no humans inside. There was movement in the shadows, but any Fey creatures who were here must have smelled that I was a Hunter and were hiding.

"Princess in her dressing room." The troll pointed.

I knocked on that door and she yelled for me to come in. She was at a table, in front of a mirror, putting makeup on.

Shallala wasn't using glamour.

"Aaagh!" I yelled, turning my face away. "For God's sake, Shallala! Glamour or something!"

Royal Fey weren't beautiful, to humans, in their natural form. Quite the opposite. Their actual form was utterly alien. Truly "different" in a horrible and terrifying way. I had no question they were from another dimension or planet. Whatever they were, the Fey weren't saying.

"Like, you humans look just as bad to *us*!" Shallala said, but when I turned back she was glamoured. "I'm all, like, 'grody' all day surrounded by monkeys, you know. Gross!"

And this was why I had not bothered to see if the Fey knew anything. If there was a Fey out there who wasn't insane or an asshole, I had not met them yet.

"Like, what *now*, Chadwick? I'm getting ready to go out!"

I was apparently looking into her vanity mirror. She was now illusioned as a naked and beautiful blonde human female. Yeah. Right. Once you see Fey-ugly, it's one of those things makes you wish there was a brain scrub. She might look like a supermodel now, but I could still only see the Fey.

"We've got a situation."

"Again?" Shallala said. "You had a situation here before. I, like, totally had to save the day for you."

"This is a bit different," I said. "Are you aware that Old Ones leave larva behind on planets?"

"*Shushukanala*," Shallala said, shrugging and continuing to put on makeup. I don't know why she felt the need. The glamour covered it. "Gag me with a spoon, human. Like, *everybody* knows that. How dumb face can you be? They're more like big stupid eggs. The eggs are asleep, like *forever* since they're totally immortal, until, like, wakey wakey, and then boom! I just ate your stupid planet, losers."

"What causes them to 'wakey wakey'?"

"Usually by, like, food being around and, like, people being dumb butts and using Old One magic. Like necromancy and stuff. Depends on how much, like, food and worshippers are around," Shallala said, shrugging and continuing to trowel on makeup. "Blood sacrifices. Whatever."

"What if they had, like, a totally very-into-magic entire city over them?" I asked. Shit, fucking insidious Fey magic! "With, like, lots of food and plenty of worshippers?"

"Not long, then. We were, like, totally killing them before you humans stole fire. Fey courts always kill them as soon as we find them. 'Cause they're, like, totally grody and if they get to adult they're, like, *impossible* to kill. Like, you got to totally kill them when they're young, or sucks to be you! Wait..." She stopped putting on makeup and actually looked at me, suspiciously. "Like, how come you're asking?"

"There's, like, one under New Orleans."

"*What?*" she screamed, her glamour suddenly dropping. Fey-ugly again and clearly upset. The makeup goop was clear on the gigantic Fey bug-eyes and it was...wrong. "No way! How big is it?"

"It's, like, about two hundred meters long. Is that bad?"

"How *big* is that? What's that in *real* words? The metric system is lame! *Tell* me it's little. Like the size of a car."

"I don't know in your terms." Did Fey use the inch pattern? Never checked that at Oxford. "But more like the size of a high school football stadium. Including the bleachers."

"There's never been one on earth even close to that big! How did you stupid humies let one grow that big? That's like practically *adult*!" She screamed again, starting to put her makeup away. She still hadn't reglamoured. I think she was panicking. "Do you know what one of those *does* when it grows up? I've got to go. Nice planet you had here. Now we're going to have to find a new one! That's, like, what we *get* for letting you stupid primates try to run things!"

This thing scared the crap out of a Fey princess who could probably level an SRT without breaking a sweat.

"Don't worry. We're going to handle it...What are you doing?"

"Looking for my suitcase! I've, like, gotta pack!"

"We could use your help. There's a clause in the contract—"

"Stick the contract up your big dumb butt! Try an' enforce it after your planet blows up!"

She had the troll escort me out.

✧   ✧   ✧

Frandsen had a lot of stuff. Shitloads of stuff. Charts. Plats. Pages that were just columns of numbers. Early computer print-outs. I hoped somebody would understand it, I sure as hell didn't.

The next question was what to do with it. This wasn't MHI level; this was MCB, but I wasn't even sure SRT could handle it. The last time a mava was attacked it wiped out a sepoy regiment. Before that, it was five thousand crack Chinese soldiers. What did the MCB do in situations like that, call the DOD? We were going to need some serious firepower. Air strikes. Napalm. If it hatched, Katy Bar the Door.

We had to at least inform MCB. Seriously inform them as in formally and full up. Write a report, submit it to DC. I'd just cost them millions of dollars, so why would they believe evidence I'd gathered from a discredited crackpot? That was going to go over like a lead balloon.

It was a long flight back. I pored over what I could understand of all the geology gobbledygook and considered how to kill the thing, preferably without digging up the Superdome. Pump holy water in through the drill? Could you do that?

I have a real hard time admitting when I'm in over my head, but as soon as I landed, I had to swallow my pride and call Earl Harbinger for help.

Ray Shackleford was the one who made MHI's case concerning the danger posed by the mava directly to MCB Director Wagner. Even though I was the one who had done most of the research, I stayed in New Orleans. As far as Ray's presentation went, that Hunter who had just sued them for millions of dollars didn't exist. Chad who? Sorry, Director, don't know the guy. He sounds like an asshole.

Unfortunately, Special Agent Campbell also attended the meeting. His position was that there had not been a kifo outbreak all summer. In fact, the last time one had been seen had been when Agent Robinson had lost his life. MCB New Orleans' official stance was that the creature had probably gone back to sleep, the idea that it was actually a larval Old One was laughably absurd, and any operation sufficient to destroy it would pose too much risk of exposure.

We'd done our homework and come up with a plan that would allow us to bring a maximum amount of firepower with a minimal number of witnesses. We simply needed MCB's permission, oh . . . and the whole Marine Corps waiting nearby, in case things got out of hand, would be nice. That was a hard sell.

Trying to convince them that the real reason New Orleans was such a supernatural hotspot was because of this entity's true nature, and thus worth the risk to attack it directly, was a harder sell.

In the end Campbell wanted to pass the buck. He was more worried about the very real chance of witnesses than the tiny off-chance that the mava was a world ender waiting to bloom. New Orleans had been relatively quiet for months, the Select Committee was off his back, and Director Wagner wanted to keep it that way. They would conduct their own investigation into the threat . . . Of course, under the new oversight rules that investigation might take "quite some time."

Of course, Ray wanted to know what "quite some time" meant.

Sadly, since their recent lawsuit, the MCB was revamping their policy and procedures concerning nonimmediate supernatural threat assessments. Once the new policies were in place, *then* they would investigate this matter accordingly. If things heated up before then, the MCB would "reassess the situation." In other words it was, "permission denied. Thank you very much, Mr. Shackleford. You can show yourself out."

Hoodoo Squad and Team Happy Face had been waiting around the team shack for word from Ray. After he called, everybody who had gotten their hopes up that the MCB would do the right thing for once was pissed.

Earl waited for the anger to die down before making an announcement.

"As long as that thing is down there, innocent folks are gonna keep on dying. Fuck the MCB. There's too much at stake. We're gonna put this town right once and for all, even if we have to do it ourselves."

"Are you saying what I think you're saying?" I asked.

"I am. We've made a plan. Now we've got a lot to do to get it ready. Let's get to work."

CHAPTER 20

All we had to do was put together a big mission, build a team, gather resources, prep a battle space, and do it without the MCB catching wind of it and shutting us down.

First step was finding another geologist. Preferably one who was read in, or at least wouldn't just assume we were crazy. That turned out to be a very short list, as in none. Luckily, Neil Frandsen had an attack of conscience. He never said what made him change his mind, but he decided not to sit it out at the ass end of Canada after all. He flew down from Yellowknife, called the number on the business card I had left him from a payphone, and asked to have somebody come pick him up from the airport.

"Can you show us where we can get a drill into it?" I asked. I had grabbed Ray and we were standing around a map of the city.

"Drilling to it will be fairly simple. Drilling through it is the tough part."

"Can you pump stuff down to it?" Ray asked.

"That's more or less how drilling works," Frandsen said, smiling slightly. "As you drill you pump in what is called 'mud.' It's a mixture of various stuff, mostly water and concrete. The concrete hardens the walls of the drill bore so they don't collapse on you and the water keeps the drill head cooled. The remaining water brings up whatever you're drilling through. Filter that out and reuse the water. What do you intend to pump in? Poison?"

"Something like that. Do we have to drill straight down to it?"

"No," Frandsen said. "Otherwise we'd have to drill in through the Superdome."

"I could probably arrange that," I said thoughtfully. And it wouldn't be the worst place to have a knock-down drag-out. Separated from the surrounding area by parking lots and fences. Better than Bourbon Street. Speaking of knock-down drag-out: Harry would probably want to put it on pay-per-view. Probably not the best idea.

"There's no ports. You have to have access to the actual ground. Otherwise, you have to drill through the foundations. No matter how much access you have, they're not going to let you drill through the footings of the Superdome."

"We don't know how quiet it's going to get when we hit it, though. From the historical records, these things tend to react violently."

"The place to do it is a warehouse, then," the geologist said. "You can drill in sideways from one of those. You're still going to have to cut through the floor but that's easy. There are even some that have already been used for that in the New Orleans area. People get upset when they see drill rigs in their backyard, so you hide them in a warehouse. Common."

"Know if there's a big warehouse in the area that's not being used at the moment?" Ray asked me.

"I don't. But I'll call my real estate lady."

I met with Madam Courtney in order to buy a warehouse. She ended up having a vision.

"Oh, this is terrible. Terrible! The work is not done! The loas had their revenge, but only part of their revenge! Alpha and omega, beginning to end. Only your brother's foulness leaving the world was not the end at all, merely a prelude."

"What?" I was sitting in her office holding a page of industrial real estate listings. She had been sitting behind her desk when "the spirits came upon her." "Can't be, Madam Courtney. It's over. He's dead."

"Nay, it was the Dark Masters who first caused the beast beneath to stir. It was they who accidentally woke its hunger and brought this curse upon the city. You ended them, but you did not end that which they woke!" She pounded her desk for emphasis. "Your work is not done! The true end is before us!"

"Hold on . . ." The local kifo eruptions had only been going on for a few years as far as we knew. The old vampire I'd met at Mardi Gras had made the outside meddling sound like a relatively new phenomenon. Thornton hadn't been selling virgin sacrifices for that long, so the timeline fit. "Are you saying that unbeknownst to my evil idiot brother, something his cult did caused the mava to activate?"

"It is so. It was some of their dark rites and spells that the beast felt and reached out for. Fates entwined. You were there at the beginning; now you must be there at the end. Trust in the loas."

"Sure. Got it."

"Very well. You will bring justice with a flaming sword . . . Now let us speak of this property the loas have picked out for you. It has a lot of square footage, is very private, and an excellent value."

"So what are the effects going to be?" Captain Rivette asked.

With MCB sitting this one out, any official response was going to be up to local authorities. If there was one thing Captain Rivette didn't like besides being around hoodoo, it was taking responsibility for an event. On the other hand, it was clear to SIU that this thing needed to be dealt with. Earl and I paid them a visit.

"We don't know, exactly," I admitted. "The only records of previous battles with them are ancient and incomplete. It's going to react and it's going to raise 'servants.' We're pretty sure that's undead. Could be other Old One entities if there are any in the area. Like shoggoths."

"They're bad, right?" Lieutenant Hale said.

"Giant black man-eating blobs," Earl said. "They don't like fire; burns them right up. I've fought them before. Just don't let them latch on, because they'll tear you to pieces in seconds. The latching-on part is tough though, on account of it sprouting tentacles at will."

"Oh . . ."

"The other problem will be the kifo worms. They're what we used to call 'the basement boogie.'" As I said that, most of the cops and deputies blanched. Most of them had not seen one but were familiar with their handiwork. "We anticipate they'll be attacking at our location but they might break out anywhere that they're already present."

"They don't like sunlight, though," Lieutenant Bechard pointed out. "But you're planning on breaking through at night?"

"If it goes like the historical record, this is going to be bigger than Mardi Gras," I said, shrugging.

"You really want thousands of people caught up in this?" Earl said. "We're planning on initiating around zero three hundred. Most of the street people will have even packed it in by then."

"You're worried about witnesses?"

"No. I'm worried about collateral damage, which is why, that night you NOLA boys are gonna make up an excuse to evacuate the whole neighborhood around that warehouse for us."

Frandsen had assumed we would be pumping poison down to the mava. In a way he was right.

The lamas who had helped interpret the ancient records had all agreed that the mystic unguents of the Most Perfect would have been merely a carrier for the power of the Great Lotus, which could be anything imbued with sufficient faith in goodness, light, and purity. Those things were anathema to the Old Ones. Father Pema had suggested holy water.

Lots of holy water. Like tanker trucks full of it.

Pro-tip: Hunters often use blessed items. Most creatures you'd consider "unholy" have adverse reactions to them, sometimes violent ones. But it isn't an easy way out. We've seen over and over that religious items are only as strong as the person using them. If their faith wavers it's basically useless.

So if you think you're fighting on the side of the angels, you'd better really believe it or else. End pro-tip.

Hunters come from a wide variety of faiths, so theological arguments can get heated, but this religious stuff works if you believe in it hard enough; but that even if you are inclined that way, it still takes a lot of juice to actually channel the power of God. Blessing a little basin of water? No problem. Blessing thousands of gallons to use as a weapon against an otherworldly being during a battle that could potentially rage for days? Big problem.

Unholy evils always try to get in your head and find weaknesses. Everyone on this mission would come under psychic assault. They'd need spiritual help to survive. So all of us began discreetly calling upon our respective clergy to see who would be willing to help. Franklin had made friends with a local reverend who had dealt with quite a few supernatural problems, real solid, salt-of-the-Earth man. Milo called in some of his Mormon friends. Even though it weirded out the Christians, I invited Madam Courtney and some of her associates to join in. This was, after all, her town.

In the end we had several flavors of Christianity, some Buddhists, Hindus, and hoodoo (White side obviously) to drive off the seed of evil. 'Cause the Saints Come Marching In.

To represent the Catholic Church, I had told my local father confessor and asked for his help, but Earl told me I hadn't needed to. He had made a call because he knew "some Catholic guys."

A few days later "some Catholic guys" showed up at the team shack. From the way they looked, I suspected Earl's call had been long distance direct to Rome. There were a few priests, and several extremely physically fit men with Swiss accents and military haircuts. There were records in Oxford originating from the Vatican's Blessed Order of St. Hubert the Protector, one of the oldest Monster Hunting organizations in the world. I suspected that these priests were from their "Secret Guard," an order which supposedly no longer existed.

Earl introduced me to the senior priests. "This is Father Madruga and Father Ferguson. Fathers, this is Chad. We call him Iron Hand. Most of what we know about this thing is from his research."

"Nice to meet you." Madruga was Hispanic, and Ferguson was a redhead nearly as muscular as the Swiss Guard. We shook hands. "I'm glad His Holiness sent you."

"Oh, it's not like that," Ferguson said.

"We are simple priests, merely here to provide whatever aid we can," Madruga said. He was in his fifties, short, fit and stocky, broad-shouldered with black hair and eyes, and some serious facial scars that looked to be from fire. One eye was milky white and clearly blind. "Nothing more than simple priests."

"Sure." There was another man with them, not a priest, but not one of the Swiss Guard either, who I won't give much description of for reasons which will become obvious shortly. "Who is he?"

"That is Fedele," Father Madruga said. "When Mr. Harbinger told us what you are potentially dealing with, we asked for him to assist us. He is something of an expert in the field."

Fedele nodded in greeting. "Hello."

"I didn't know you were Catholic, Earl."

"I ain't. I just like working with professionals. These boys are all right."

"They seem kind of secretive. Fitting. Since 'secret' is in the name of their order."

"We do not know what order you speak of," Madruga said. The priests did not seem comfortable with that getting out. "It would be best not to share such speculation, my son."

"This way, Fathers," Earl said. "We'll go over the plans."

They walked away, but Fedele lingered for a moment.

"So, Mr. Iron Hand. I believe we have a mutual friend."

"Who?"

"A nice old fisherman who calls himself Pete." Fedele smiled. "You will certainly be going back to see him again before I do. When you get there, please tell him hello for me."

Okay. This guy was legit. "I'll tell Pete hi."

"Thank you." The holy warrior began walking after the priests, then paused. "Another favor I must ask. When you write your memoirs, please refrain from writing any specifics about me, or record anything noteworthy you may see me do during the upcoming conflict. The 'secret' part of the name is a matter of doctrinal pride."

"I'll do that."

I kept that promise, but pro-tip, if you ever meet a combat exorcist dispatched by the Vatican, just stay out of his way.

"Most of the drilling should be pretty standard," I said, pointing to the schematic. "It's the last part we have to worry about."

Getting the right drill crew had been tough. You couldn't put out an ad for drillers that had experience with hoodoo. It had taken various calls to contacts. Brad from my old team in Seattle was from Oklahoma and knew a couple of good-ole boys that had experience drilling *and* the supernatural. Ray had some that he knew had experience with the supernatural but who chose to not join the cause. Earl knew a couple more.

When we told everyone more or less what we'd be doing, they'd all jacked up their hourly. A lot. And every single roughneck had showed up armed to the teeth.

"The mava is about three thousand feet down. From the previous record the exterior is extremely hard. They went through three drill bits drilling through a bare four meters of shell."

"They get what it was?" Daniel Scott asked. He was a weathered tough guy, who had spent most of his life on offshore oil rigs. "That's some tough shell."

"We're dealing with stuff that doesn't really abide by the laws of physics as we understand them," Ray explained. "This is beyond anything any of you have dealt with. It's not really amenable to normal analysis. It doesn't make sense to a material scientist because it's not really of this universe. It's really bad for one's sanity, too."

"Going crazy when you study them too hard is just one problem," I continued. "Upon piercing the shell, you start getting the ichor from this thing. It pretty much drove the last drill crew nuts. Since we're not sure what mechanism that works by, when we get to the shell, we're going to have to suit up."

"And we have to communicate," Ray added. "A lot. If you're feeling the effects, you're going to have to back away. We'll be pumping holy water in to destroy it. If that doesn't work, we'll drop back and punt. I'm not losing the drill crew the way they lost the last one."

"Explain 'lose,'" Al Gordon demanded. The drill team leader was one of Brad's contacts and had the same cowboy look going as Sam Haven, except he was shorter and heavy-set.

"Some of them went nuts. Others ran. One of them killed two others with a shovel. Stuff like that," I explained. "This is full-on horror movie stuff. If you're feeling weird, just back off and see Father Ferguson, Reverend Hawkins, or the religious authority of your choice. We'll have plenty to choose from. Praying over this stuff actually works if you've got enough faith. If you start feeling consumed with uncontrollable murderous rage, take a break."

"That's how Al normally is," Daniel said. "So how will we tell?" The drill crew had a laugh.

"How long for the stuff you're using to kill it?"

"We don't even know if we *can* kill it, Al. It's our best guess. It's got the volume of the inside of a high school football stadium. If we have to pump it entirely full of holy water? We'll be here for weeks and probably have to reset to drill it at multiple points."

"Assuming MHI can afford that..." Al muttered.

"We'll run out of lives before my family runs out of money," Ray said. "We'll switch people out as we need to. When we hit the shell, we'll start pumping the holy water. Hopefully that should reduce some of the effects. And when we punch through and it hits the internals, we're expecting a large-scale response."

"Despite that, we need to keep drilling 'til we're deep in the interior," I continued. "We've got no clue about anatomy but our best bet is to pump that bitch full of holy water."

Ray was assessing the crew while we briefed them, looking for any signs of weakness. These men were tough, but they weren't trained Hunters. "Men, I can't accentuate this enough, but we're facing true evil, like nothing you've ever imagined. I can't predict how, but it will attack you—body, mind, and spirit."

"Yeah," Gordon said, looking around and shifting a bit in his chair. "We didn't ask for enough money on this one."

"Shit," Daniel said, shaking his head. "I don't want to lose my soul to the devil."

"This thing, if it breaks out, is the end of the world," I said seriously. "Full-up Revelations time. Do not pass go, do not collect two hundred dollars. Go right to the apocalypse. Killing it before it hatches is the only way to ensure the safety of the world."

"If you've got a problem with any of this, walk away now," Ray warned. "There's no shame in knowing when to call it."

None of the drillers left.

"Last point," I said. "We won't be repumping the mud. It's going to be diluted ten to one with holy water then dumped."

"You check with EPA on that one?" Gordon asked.

"We got permits for dumping the *mud*," I said, shrugging. "We can't exactly say it's going to be mixed with the ichor of an unclean *thing* that has ravaged the human soul since the beginning of time and is just waiting to break free so that it can lay waste to all life on earth. But if you'd like to submit the paperwork..."

"Nah," Gordon said, grinning. "I'm good."

The smells and sights were too familiar. The smell of dead things and vomit and shit and chemicals not meant to exist on this planet. The horrible mucous on every wall, covering the colorful if crude drawings of houses and dogs and horses and kittens. The gold stars and decals of Disney characters.

This time the mava had hit a kindergarten classroom. Several children and a teacher had vanished, screaming.

Decay and I were the first on scene. "This didn't have to happen, man."

He was right. With our limited resources, it was taking weeks for MHI to set up a mission the MCB could have set up in days, if not hours.

"We gotta find the symbol here," I said, looking around the destroyed classroom.

The floor was tile. I groaned at the thought of having to pull it all up looking for the fungus symbol.

The room beyond was a small storage room where the teacher kept all her special materials away from the students. There was a rolling cupboard in the corner filled with pencils, construction paper and crayons.

Pushing it aside we found the loathsome fungus symbol underneath.

"*Now* it's time to get the pig," I said, gritting my teeth.

An hour later the classroom was on fire, another pseudopod was burnt, and Special Agent Campbell was waiting for us in the parking lot. I was still trying to avoid MCB agents as much as possible, but Decay about lost his mind and had to be held back by a couple of other Hunters from punching Campbell out.

"Kids, Campbell!" Decay shouted. "It got little kids! How about MCB *reassesses the situation* now!"

The senior MCB agent had nothing to say in reply.

CHAPTER 21

The warehouse was very large and crowded.

In the center was the drill rig. I'd seen drill rigs around, who hasn't, in the news and TV shows and even just driving through Oklahoma, Louisiana and Texas. They were big scaffold-looking things reaching up to the sky. Everybody knew that was what drill rigs looked like.

This wasn't that drill rig. The rig was laid sideways on a trailer. They'd just driven it into the warehouse that way. The pipe, called a string, was held at an angle of about ten degrees and went into an already cut hole in the thick floor of the warehouse. The rig was laid in about fifty feet from the south wall and the full string and entry stretched halfway across the four-hundred-foot-long warehouse.

To both sides we had installed giant water tanks. They looked like aboveground swimming pools and even had ladders to climb in. Usually these would refill from the "mud" pumped out by the drill. But holy water needed "pure" water. So the diluted mud was being dumped into a storm drain and, at least in part illegally, then dumped into the nearby Mississippi. What would happen when the mava goop started being pumped out was anyone's guess. Hopefully just a fish kill. A repeat of Mardi Gras or worse would be unpleasant.

North of the tanks were six fire trucks manned by volunteers from the New Orleans Fire Department. There hadn't been a lot of takers on this one. NOFD liked hoodoo about as much as NOPD. But they'd previously lost some men to a kifo worm, so we'd managed to get enough volunteers.

There were lines from the trucks leading up to the roof of the warehouse as well as more inside. We were planning on throwing around a lot of fire. Having a way to put it out was a good idea. NOFD was willing to run the trucks, which was a specialized job. They weren't willing to run the lines. The lines were going to be in harm's way of hoodoo. Couldn't say I blamed them.

In addition to the big tanks, the fire trucks, the drill rig and its peripheral equipment, there was *our* equipment. MHI had brought in every piece of lethal hardware in its inventory. We'd had to build in an ammo bunker for all the ammo. There were tanks of prepared napalm to refill the flamethrowers and Hunters to run it up to the flamethrower teams. Prestocked ammo supplies and preloaded magazines. Cases and cases of grenades, LAWs, RPGs, and Carl Gustavs. We'd put in extra orders for all the firepower we were planning on throwing. If this *wasn't* a mava, we were going to lose a lot of money on this deal.

If it was, then the lowest estimate we'd gotten from the PUFF adjustor was astronomical. Even with all the costs of the operation, we'd make bank.

Our building was part of a regular block of identical prefab concrete warehouses. Each was four hundred feet long, a hundred and fifty feet wide, with a broad boulevard between them running north and south and narrower streets, still big enough to take two tractor trailers, running east-west. The doors were heavily reinforced to prevent burglary and the only windows were near the high roofs. Counting the thick precast concrete walls, they were virtually impregnable.

But virtually wasn't good enough. Milo had been given a construction crew, the company checkbook, and told to make this place into a fortress. We still didn't know what the mava was going to throw at us, but Milo had reinforced everything just in case. The already thick floors had been built up with rebar-reinforced concrete everywhere but our drill hole. It would take kifo worms a while to batter their way through that.

We'd set up double-height Jersey wall blockades on the broad boulevards, angled to push anything that couldn't climb them into the narrower streets. That was where we'd also set up most of our firepower. The premise was that any attackers would be pushed into the kill zone. The kill zone was littered with claymores and other explosives. It was going to get hot in there. We'd ensured that the other warehouses didn't have anything that would detonate from the heat and the concrete walls were pretty resistant.

The walls were high enough that even a shoggoth would need some time to slither over them, and they were back-stopped by more stacked Jersey walls to prevent pressure pushing them over. Hopefully, they'd hold.

But the mava would probably summon some ghouls, wights, vampires, what have you. They could climb right over the things. They could climb the walls of the freaking warehouse. Vampires and wights could climb the *other* warehouses and make the jump across the narrower sections.

Earl promised that he had some special secret weapon which would take care of any undead, but we'd see.

At six points up along the "long" sides of the warehouse we had belt-fed guns mounted. Two M2 .50 caliber Ma Deuces and four M-60 Pigs in .308. They were going to be putting plunging fire onto anything that got onto the boulevards. Two of the M2s were mounted at each end of the building and could swivel to cover the narrow "streets." If the claymores, napalm bombs and other explosives didn't do the trick, Ma Deuce was the gift that just kept giving.

Getting in and out of the warehouse was the tough part. We'd seriously bunkered up. The fastest way out was from the roof. Which was why LifeLift was also on standby. We *were* going to take casualties and would be carrying them out by helicopter.

Nearly every MHI employee in the country was here. I saw people I had not seen since training. Either the MCB did not know what we were up to, or if some figured it out they were smart enough not to alert their superiors. We hadn't been shut down yet. Everything was ready.

Earl got on the warehouse intercom.

"Start the drill."

For hours the priests had taken turns blessing the water. We needed the holy water not only for the drill mud but for mixing with the "stuff" coming out of the drill. We'd already noticed effects just from the mava's shell. Get near the discharge and you were *immediately* assaulted by the presence of evil. How the last drill crew had managed was the real question—it probably hadn't been as bad when the creature was asleep. This was bad, but the mava's internal essence was supposed to be worse. Of course, we were mixing it with holy water which was unquestionably dropping the "pure evil" level. When it was fully diluted, you didn't get any "feel" off of it at all. Just the initial stuff coming out of the hole.

"Father Coglin," I said, walking over to my old confessor who was standing by the edge of one of the tanks. "Bit easier with help?"

"Do you know who that is?" Father Coglin asked quietly, gesturing with his chin at Father Madruga.

"That priest?" I said. "He's one of the people my boss called—Father Madruga."

"*Monsignor* Madruga. He's Cuban," Father Coglin said. "He was a priest when Castro took over. He had a way out but stayed behind to minister to his flock. He was horribly tortured by Castro's people but refused to renounce his faith. Led an underground railroad to get people out until there was a definite kill order sent down against him. His junior priests and the surviving nuns had to more or less drag him to the boat. He literally had to be tied up to keep from returning. The scars are from where some of Castro's torturers tossed gas in his face and set it on fire."

"Jesus." It's worth noting that humans can be as bad as the things Hunters fight.

"Watch your tongue, Chad," Father Coglin said. "Only in places and times where one is truly tested can you be sure of a person's faith. For the rest it's just words, to be believed or not. Only God knows the human heart. Monsignor Madruga is what every priest should aspire to be. As strong in faith as any human being on earth. *Assured* of sainthood. Except he's apparently disappeared from the face of the Earth for the last few years and no one has known where he's been."

"Ah," I said, nodding. "In that case, very glad he's here."

"Time to suit up." Earl radioed. "They're through the shell and in the mava's guts."

We'd been told that it would be about several minutes before anything that they were drilling through reached the surface. So they had time to suit up before the mava gunk reached the drill site.

"Now we find out if this is what we think it is," I said. "See you when we're done, Father."

"God will prevail this night, Chad," Father Coglin said, making the sign of the cross. "Have faith."

I headed for the drill rig. Since this was my brilliant idea, I was in charge of the crew and the Hunters around the hole. I wanted to be close when we broke through the shell to see just how bad this stuff was. And be in the circuit when we figured out what the Tibetans meant by "servants."

"We're through," Frandsen said. Our geologist was all duded-up in a silver suit. "And we're getting some really weird effects already. Stuff that wasn't in the last drill."

"Define weird," I said.

"Drill head is in soft material but heating up way more than it should," Al Gordon said. "And we're getting spurious movement. Like there's something hitting the string from the side."

He pointed at the pipe that was the drill "string" and you could see it was jumping like something was hitting it.

"Is it going to break?" I asked.

"Don't know. A thousand holes and I've never seen anything like that. Could crimp, yeah. But so far it's holding. Just weird. Not sure what's causing it. Could be something in the material we're drilling has movement. Could be something in between."

"What the hell?" one of the drillers yelled. "We got *foam* coming out!"

The mud, a mixture of various nontoxic chemicals, bentonite, and holy water, was now foaming. It smelled like...

"Kifo worm! Get your respirators on!" I shouted. Then I got on my radio. "This is Iron Hand at the drill. That's kifo juice coming up. I can smell it. Incoming kifo!"

"It's not going to be able to fit through the bore, is it?" Al asked.

"Hell if I know." The borehole was about fourteen inches in diameter. The string took up six inches of that more or less in the middle. I wasn't sure a kifo could get up the whole borehole much less past the string.

"We can't keep it on track," Frandsen said, looking at his readouts. "We're getting a lot of anomalous movement. Something, and I'd say it's your kifo worm, is banging the hell out of the string. Couple of hits. Stops. Couple more. From what I'm reading, it looks like they're getting closer."

"It's sending up a pseudopod to find out who's hurting it. Can you tell how far away?"

"Hang on," Al said, starting to strip out of his suit.

"Careful," I said. The stuff was foaming up even more when

it hit the holy water being mixed into it, and giving off horrible smelling steam. The holy water was literally *burning* when it came in contact with evil. That explained the heat at the drill head. "Don't touch the foam."

"Ain't gonna." The upper part of Al's silver suit was around his waist. He backed up onto the string and held up a hand to keep the driller from pushing forward. The string was still spinning but he put his hand on the string, carefully, and felt it. "Couple thousand feet at least. I can feel the impacts. They're not hard. More like occasional soft pushes. I'd say you're right. It's trying to follow the string back to here. So what're you gonna do about it? We can't keep drilling if you're shooting around my hole."

I keyed my radio. "Boss, this is Hand. Kifo worm is working its way up the string to find the source of the attack. Two thousand feet and closing. May be a partial breakthrough at the string."

"Got that," Old Man Shackleford radioed back. Oh yeah. I said almost everybody had turned out for this. MHI had brought in the big guns. "So far there ain't no reports of activity outside. Teams Two and Four, peel off and reinforce on the hole."

The Hunters confirmed. If that kifo showed itself, it was in for a surprise.

"I can perhaps help," a voice said over my shoulder.

It was another of the priests from the Secret Guard—Father Ferguson.

"The pseudopod will have to push its bulk up through the bore while being burned by holy water. Given the effect we are already seeing, I don't see it doing so. However, if I am wrong, I can probably hold it at the bore opening."

"With what, Father?" Gordon asked as he put his suit back on.

"The power of faith, young man," Father Ferguson said. "This creature is ultimate evil. It burns from the mere touch of holy water. It cannot face the full holy power of God."

"Well, Father, as you say." Gordon hefted a .45-70 lever action. "You use the power of God. I'll just shoot it, if you don't mind."

"As long as you pay mind to ricochets," Father Ferguson said, smiling faintly. "I'm averse to friendly fire."

"And I think we got mava juice," I said, turning my face away with my hand over my nose.

The ... stuff coming out of the borehole was now beyond foul. If the holy water had had any effect on it, the power had been spent in the long lift from the depths. Generally a gray-green to black, it was coming out in vile-smelling chunks and you could *feel* the evil coming off it in waves. I shook my head as my mind was assaulted by unclean images. It was like it was reaching into my brain and pulling out every sin I'd ever committed or thought about committing. If this was the remnant, post-cleansing essence of an Old One, I could see why a breakthrough would be bad on toast. Forget the "servants," the zombies and wights and ghouls and vampires that would be called to it and wreak havoc in its unholy Name. Every human being in the range of its effect would act out every evil fantasy they'd ever had to the best of their ability. Total chaos would reign in *seconds*.

"That is quite unpleasant," Father Ferguson said, apparently unperturbed.

I looked over at Al who was looking at the weapon in his hand.

"Al," I said, as calmly as I could. "Just put it down."

I didn't know who he had enough of a problem with to want to kill. But I'd found myself fingering my silver-loaded .45 and contemplating that Earl, who I still blamed for the loss of my last team, was nearby and possibly wouldn't see it coming. I knew what was going on, though. I'd faced something similar with a vampire one time. I knew how to fight it. It was hitting Gordon bad, though. The silver suits and respirators were useless against this stuff.

"Shit, shit, shit..." the driller was saying.

"Give me the weapon, Mr. Gordon," Father Ferguson said calmly. He laid his hand on Al's shoulder and placed the other hand on the weapon. "Don't let this power take you. You are a good person, Mr. Gordon. This thing's power is not greater than God's. Feel the power of God upon you, Mr. Gordon. Feel the sin fall from your mind."

Gordon blinked at that and slowly handed the priest the .45-70.

"That's better," Father Ferguson said, setting the rifle on the desk. "We are here on behalf of God, against which no evil can prevail. All of you! Fight the evil! Push it from your hearts and trust in God!"

This thing had to be put to bed permanently. Forget "strange aeons" and shit. It had to die now. That was the one dark part of me that I was willing to let loose at that moment. The sheer desire to rend this evil thing to permanent, unquestionable death.

The main thing that I noticed, immediately, was that the open tank where additional holy water was being admixed with the foul ichor from the borehole was boiling with power and foaming up. It was about to overflow.

I ran over and grabbed one of the spare pipe sections and put it across the top, just like putting a wooden spoon on a pot that was boiling over. The mess settled down but I wasn't sure we were getting all the "evil" out of it. The outflow was still nasty as shit. And the smell...

I finally just went over to the side and retched. I wasn't the only one.

"We need to increase the ratio of holy water being mixed, Mr. Gordon," Father Ferguson said. "Can we do that?"

"Yes," Gordon said, still holding his head. "Yes, we can. Dan, increase the pump rate on the mix water. Triple it."

"Got it." Dan was just as clearly feeling the effects from the stuff but he started adjusting dials.

"I would recommend holding the drill for now," Father Ferguson said. "Just let the holy water pump into the body of the beast. When we start to get less horror coming up, then push downward. Do that over and over again to clear out one section. Then perhaps adjust the drilling or withdraw and drill another portion."

"You've done this before?" I asked the mysterious priest.

"Nothing even close. Call it divine inspiration."

"Sounds like a plan, Father," Gordon said, then made a face. "Father...sorry about that back there."

"Everyone holds some sin in their heart, son." Father Ferguson patted him on his silver shoulder. "Everyone. It is like fear in combat. Everyone has some. It is what you do about it that matters. After this battle we'll talk. But for now, we do battle against one of the worst evils mankind has ever seen in its history. That gets you some solid points with the Almighty."

"Where are we with the worm?" I asked.

"Stop the spin. Just hold in place and pump mud." Al put his hand back on the string and felt it for a second. "I can feel it moving up. Different now. I think now that there's more 'bad' in the mud and less 'good' it can just run right up the bore."

I put my hand on the string and felt what he was talking about. The string was mostly still on our end, slight vibration from the idling drill rig, but you could feel a bumping against it. How he could tell how far I had no idea. There was an art to it.

"Can you switch to pure water, no admix, in the mud?" I asked.

"It'll tend to break down the walls of the bore," Gordon said. "Which, come to think of it, would be good. Dan! Cut the mix on the mud. Pure holy water!"

All the mud, now pure holy water, came out at the bottom of the drill at the bit. The new mix had to first go down thousands of feet then back up. I keyed my radio.

"Sam, Milo, get down here on the drill rig," I radioed. "We have a situation." Then I switched frequencies. "Boss, this is Hand at the rig. The mava mix was overwhelming the holy water. We've stopped progressing the drill and are just flowing holy water to it. Be about thirty minutes until that has effect and we see what that does. The stuff coming up is almost pure mava essence. The mud isn't burning the kifo worm anymore and it's coming straight up the bore. We may have a kifo outbreak here shortly. Called down my backup. Copy all that."

"Copy, Hand," Ray III said, not over the radio but from right over my shoulder. "That stuff isn't half horrible, is it? Kinda *claws* at your mind."

I should have known the old man would show up right wherever the trouble was. If he was having any issues with whatever was clawing at *his* mind, it wasn't obvious. I suddenly had to wonder what sort of sins lay in the heart of MHI's CEO.

"I'm starting to think Earl needs to stay as far away from this as possible," I said carefully.

"Good point, young man." The Boss touched his radio. "Earl. Do not approach the drill site. Say again, do not come near the drill site."

"Feeling it from clear up here," Earl replied. He was on the roof with the gun teams waiting for the "servants" to show up. We'd expected some mental effects, but nothing like this. "Wondered what that was. I'm heading for the far end of the warehouse."

"Father Madruga could possibly assist him," Father Ferguson said. "If he is having troubles..."

The Boss and I looked at each other at that one. "With respect, Father, probably not," he said carefully. "Earl has...particular issues in regards to rage."

"Ah..." Father Ferguson thought about that for a moment.

"Yes, I was briefed. A most unfortunate curse, and one of the rare wills able to constrain it. Will he be able to maintain control... given the circumstances?"

"I've never seen him lose it, Father," I said.

"I have," the Boss said sadly.

"Harbinger will be under a particularly harsh assault," Father Ferguson said. Gordon had gone off to adjust something else on the rig so no one else was close enough to hear him over the machinery. "If he is driven to change because of the influence of this evil—"

"If Earl is taken over by this foulness, I will take appropriate action myself. It's my duty, my responsibility." Boss Shackleford thought about that for a long time. Then he said something that came as a complete surprise to me. "He's my father."

I'd never seen that particular expression on the old man's face. I could swear to God he was damned near crying. I put it down to the effect of that evil goop. Only thing that could have been causing it. That and I'd just noticed this fucking warehouse was dusty as hell.

What the fuck was it like growing up with a father who was... Earl? Because they kind of looked the same, I'd kind of always figured Earl was the Boss's illegitimate son. I'd had that completely backwards. The PUFF adjuster had used "Shackleford" as one of Earl's names. How old *was* Earl when he got to being... Earl? Come to think of it, how old was Earl? The Boss had to be in his sixties and Earl couldn't have been... normal when he'd... How old *was* Earl?

"We got anything from SIU yet?" was what I asked, because there were questions you don't ask. Especially not at a time like that.

"Not so far," Boss said, the unburned half of his face hardening. "I'd guess this thing's going to start the party when that worm gets up here and finds out where 'here' is."

"What the fuck is...?" Sam Haven said as he and Milo arrived. They both had their hands over their noses and mouths and Sam seemed to be having some issues as well. His hands kept gripping the M-203 he was carrying. Hard.

"That's the mava juice."

Sam and I had both opted for M-203s. Most of what we expected to fight wasn't susceptible to silver and the 5.56 worked well enough at zombie shots. For that matter it would tend to slow down some vamps as well as wights and ghouls if you got a head shot. Last, the 40mm grenade worked on *everything*. Milo was rocking a flamethrower and sidearms. He clearly didn't like the smell coming from the hole but if the mystical effects were bugging him, Milo didn't let it show. He still seemed as perpetually cheerful as ever.

"Don't allow the evil to touch you, son," Father Ferguson said, laying his hand on Sam's arm. "It tries to find your sins, those you have committed and those you have contemplated, to use those against you. Fight it. Find God."

"I'm trying, Father," Sam said, working the tobacco in his cheek. He spit to the side and shook his head. "Ain't gonna let no boogieman bring up nothing I've fought most of my life."

"How are you doing, my son?" Father Ferguson asked Milo.

"I'm good. My sins aren't comparatively interesting in this crowd."

"You are strong in faith," Father Ferguson replied, smiling. "It pours off you like the evil from this monstrosity."

"I just pray a lot," Milo said humbly.

"And he refuses to do anything bad, like, ever," I said, grinning. "Most boring friend I've got."

We had about a dozen Hunters gathered around the rig. I put my hand on the string again and shook my head. Now *I* could tell it was close.

"This is it. Any suggestions?"

"Fire?" Milo said, holding up the nozzle to his flamethrower.

"That's your answer to everything!"

"Don't damage the equipment. The mud comes back out and is pumped to that tank," Gordon said, muffled by the silver suit. "Your napalm is going to burn the sh..." He glanced at the priest. "Sugar out of all that."

"I should be able to hold it, here," Father Ferguson insisted.

"Not disagreeing with you, Padre. But a backup plan is always useful," the Boss said.

"If you bless the tank on that fire truck, we'll get one of the fire hoses." Sam suggested. "Kill the worm with more holy water. Direct application."

"I like it," the Boss said.

"I get the nozzle, you get the hose," I said as we unrolled one of the fire hoses. The NOFD guys had not been happy to hear one of the kifo worms was headed up the bore. They'd turn on the pump for us, but they weren't going anywhere near the hole that was spewing mind-altering evil.

"Hell with that," Sam said. "It was my idea!"

"You're the new guy. You get the hose."

"You can't even handle one of those things," Sam protested. "They whip around like nobody's business. You're scrawny! You're going to get picked up and thrown around the room."

"Not if you're doing your job on the hose," I said.

"Exactly."

"Fire it up!" I yelled. I had the gate mostly closed on the nozzle. But we'd want pressure right away if we needed it.

The hose started to writhe as the water pressed forward and, as instructed, I had enough of an opening for the air to come out. There wasn't much since the hose was flat but it came out with a nasty shriek; then we had water. I closed the nozzle all the way.

"This thing tries to get away from you," Sam said, holding on tight. "You'd better hope I don't lose my grip."

"Always said SEALs were wimps," I said.

"You did not go there! You pick the one time we're getting murderous thoughts blasted right into our brains to piss me off. Just tempt me to kick your ass, why don't you?"

"You're the one complaining about something the most-*junior* firemen can figure out," I pointed out.

"It's here," Father Ferguson shouted.

The kifo worm erupted through the borehole in a mass of eyes and teeth and pustulant pseudopods. The drillers ran screaming. They weren't really doing anything at the moment, anyway.

It was having to press its bulk around the mass of the string and up through the narrow bore. So it was much smaller than normal. And it was causing the muck from the mava to squirt everywhere, which was vile. Some of it splashed on me and the wave of evil thoughts got worse.

I started to open up the valve but Father Ferguson just stepped forward, fearlessly.

"Begone, spawn of evil!" he shouted, holding his cross out. "This place is sealed against you!"

The kifo worm shrieked in agony and sucked back down the bore and out of sight.

There were a bunch of Hunters ready to attack, but we really didn't want to accidentally damage the equipment. "Kifo worm really didn't like the padre," I radioed. "It's back in the hole. Hold your fire."

Gordon overcame his fear, went back, put his hand on the string, and shook it. "I don't feel anything!" he shouted.

"Stand back, everyone," I said.

I put the valve on spray and hosed down the entire area. Wherever the blessed water hit the mava ichor, the two reacted like a couple of combustible chemicals.

In the process I got myself and Sam nice and wet. The "burn" from the holy water hitting the mava juice didn't even feel like burning. More of a tingling sensation. The unholy thoughts it caused faded a bit. They didn't go away entirely but I'm no saint.

CHAPTER 22

The drill team kept working. Get a little deeper into the mava's guts, then pump it full of holy water. Once the foulness died off, repeat. Between the priests taking turns at the hole and liberal applications of holy water, the kifo worm had not been able to come up the borehole.

Except this was going to be a war of attrition, and the larval Old One was desperately trying to defend itself.

I was up on the roof, taking a mandated break from the mava's evil aura. The evil thoughts got better the further away you got from the hole. I was standing near Earl when we got the radio call from the police.

"Every single dead thing in New Orleans is headed for your position, *cher*," Juliette told us. "You've got road-kill snake zombies headed your way. I've got calls coming in from all over the city. Graveyards are waking up. According to the officers on scene, every tomb is either smashed open or rocking," the dispatcher radioed. "They're not attacking anyone, just headed your way. I don't know what deity you pissed off, honey, but it is seriously pissed!"

"Roger, Dispatch. Thank you for that. Tell your officers do not engage. I repeat, do not engage. Keep civilians out of the way and let the undead pass," Earl radioed back, then turned to me. "See? We told them we were better off breaking through in the middle of the night while most folks were safe in their homes."

He sounded remarkably calm, considering the news that potentially thousands of undead had just been summoned to kill us.

"MHI teams, stand by. SIU, come in."

"SIU here," Rivette replied. "Confirm dispatch. We've got all sorts of things approaching our perimeter."

That meant some of the undead had reached the surrounding blocks that local law enforcement had evacuated for us.

"Do not resist, SIU. Get out of the way and let them pass. We're ready for them."

"Roger, MHI," Rivette radioed. "Good luck."

"Fortune favors the prepared," Ray III said over the radio. That old man was so hard that he had stayed by the drill the whole time, unfazed. "MHI teams. This is it. We have been the thin line between the darkness and the light for danged near a hundred years and we ain't ending here. We're about to put the fear of God into these undead sons of bitches! When we're done, New Orleans is going to be the most peaceful place on Earth! Now cowboy up, kill the monsters and get paid."

"We got incoming," Earl radioed as the old man finished. "Looks like wights or vamps. Moving fast on the first quadrant. Scattered. Looks like about twenty."

I could not make out what he was pointing at, but someone at that corner did, and opened up with a Ma Deuce.

"Time for our secret weapon. I hope the fucking thing works." Earl turned around and shouted toward the middle of the roof. "Ray, how's it going?"

Ray had been working on something here at the warehouse for weeks. The Shacklefords wouldn't say a word about what it was. Apparently it was complicated, so Ray had asked for Milo's help, but not mine. Which was a little insulting.

"It uses a complex system of mathematical calculations based on the geometry of ley line intersections. If I'm off in the archaic system of coordinates by much at all, a priceless magical artifact will be irreparably lost forever. *So how do you think it's going?*"

"Which is why we never move the stupid thing out of Cazador," Earl muttered so that only I could hear him. "Great, Ray! Now hurry and wrap it up. We've got incoming."

"Damned confusing magic rock." Ray swore a bunch more as he went back to working on something inside a big steel safe that had been bolted to the roof. "No pressure or anything!"

"Earl, what is that thing?"

"One of Isaac Newton's ward stones."

"Fuck..." I'd read about those at Oxford. Hell, the only reason there was a library at Oxford was that Isaac Newton had built one of these things to save England from a Great Old One. They were considered one of the rarest, most valuable, most powerful alchemical inventions of all time, creating a field that violently expelled necromantic energy. "You have a *ward stone?*"

"Yeah. Just the one. I stole it from Adolf Hitler."

"Okay, how fucking old are you? Never mind. A ward stone? You're risking a ward stone here? That's got to be worth *billions* of dollars. You could buy a *Nimitz*-class aircraft carrier with one of those. I read they are fragile and sensitive. They wear out! There aren't hardly any of them left and our best scientists can't recreate them. The smallest screw-up and it's done."

"Yep..." Earl paused to light a cigarette. "I'm aware. We've got it dialed in for Cazador safely, but I only risk moving it for special occasions, because anytime we move it could be the last. But I figured this party qualified."

"That's a hell of a risk."

"Remember how you were all pissed off at me, because I didn't give a shit about your team, and I didn't give a shit about your town? Truth is, I had no way of knowing what was gonna happen to Mardi Gras. I made a call. I sent Hunters where I thought they would be needed most. I guessed wrong. People died. My people died. Innocent people died. When you're a leader, it's all balancing risks against costs, and sometimes life comes along and kicks over the scale. You needed somebody to blame, and that's fine. I've had a long damned time losing a lot of good men to get used to it."

"Earl—"

"Don't care, Hand. But don't ever fucking question my commitment to my hunters again. And if you're ever tempted, just remember I brought the *Mona Lisa* to a knife fight for you."

Dr. Henderson would have shit bricks. Hell, the entire faculty of Oxford would have shit so many bricks you could build a house. But I was more warrior scholar than just scholar.

"Will it actually kill undead like they say?"

"I think we're good!" Ray shouted.

"Just enjoy the show." Earl grinned.

✧   ✧   ✧

For the next twenty minutes I watched undead pop like firecrackers.

Shamblers kept on coming. When they crossed the invisible border they just exploded. Other shamblers would see that happen, but they were too stupid to process the danger and they'd just blunder on until it was their turn to explode too.

The smarter undead, like ghouls and wights, they'd see one explode, and then the rest would hold back. Waiting. Every now and then those would start screeching, like they were whipped into a frenzy, and they'd rush forward to die. A quick check on the radio confirmed that the frenzies coincided with the drill moving forward, deeper into the body of the mava. It was driving them to attack us.

We were killing so many undead that, even if we failed to eradicate the larval Old One, the city would be quieter just from the lack of corpses to animate.

But the mava was getting desperate. We got a panicked radio call from Frandsen. His readings suggested that there was a lot of activity beneath us, as in possibly dozens of kifo worms digging their way toward us.

"Problem is we don't know if the ward stone will kill the pseudopods." Ray IV had joined us at the edge of the roof to watch the fireworks display. "It destroys undead, but when we've seen it used on typical servants of the Old Ones, it just hurts and drives them off."

"I've got a feeling these will be so motivated they'll push through the pain," I said.

Then we got another call from the police.

"Bad news, *cher*." Juliette said. "We don't know what to make of it, but figured I'd warn you. One of them worms broke into the morgue. Doc Wohlrab said it grabbed all the corpses right off the hooks. He said he could see the bodies getting sucked into the ground like they were going down a straw. Then the worm just disappeared. Then a minute later got a call from a patrol car said the same thing, only the worm came up through the road and gobbled up a bunch of shamblers that were headed your way."

"Thanks for that, SIU," Earl said. "Any idea what that means?"

"Maybe it's eating them for energy," Ray IV said. "The kifo must be able to sense the necromantic energy and it's reaching out to them...or something. That sounds weird as hell."

"I have no idea what it's doing. And that scares me." It was time for me to get back to the rig.

You could hear the Ma Deuce open up overhead. And here I was holding a freaking fire hose.

"Quad two," Franklin radioed. "Fast movers on the south flanking roof incoming. I've got at least ten bodies on this worm."

It hadn't taken long for us to figure out why the mava had suddenly started absorbing every dead body it could get its grubby pseudopods on. Regular undead blew up when they tried to cross the ward stone's boundaries. Kifo worms began to burn, but it took a while for them to break apart. But wrap a body in kifo slime, attach it to the worm with a nasty tentacle like an umbilical cord, and that zombie suddenly had staying power.

Not to mention they were suddenly a whole lot faster, stronger, and they could come flying at you like a yo-yo on the end of a string.

Kifo worms had started erupting through the asphalt all around our warehouse. They hadn't made it through our heavily reinforced floor yet, but it felt like a constant low-level earthquake in here, and there were cracks appearing.

There was a massive thundering against the walls at that moment and one section of what I'd thought was impregnable precast concrete disintegrated as another kifo worm broke through.

"Oh, no, you don't," I said, turning and opening up with holy water.

As the water hit, the worm was covered in burning foam, but slime-coated undead launched themselves at us.

An NOFD firefighter was lifted into the air, screaming. A slime-covered wight tried to grab one of the exorcists and recoiled as he lifted his cross and shouted in Latin. More worms were breaking through the walls and squirting undead at us. They were freaking everywhere. They were *all* attacking *at once*.

No wonder the Chinese lost five thousand men.

But they didn't have a fire truck full of holy water.

I let the hose blast, playing the nozzle back and forth across one long wall of the warehouse. The spray would only reach so far so I started working my way down the wall, blasting worm after hideous worm. Like napalm, it stuck, causing a reaction that was even nastier than their normal. Chunks of the worms were burning off from the foam. Ghostly blobs of dissolving flesh were everywhere.

But it wasn't enough. More were still breaking through. We were getting hit from so many places at once that I couldn't keep up with all the warnings on my radio.

The real problem was the NOFD guys. One team of them had gotten a hose into action and were attacking the worms. The rest were running around like chickens with their heads cut off, trying to find a way to escape. And there wasn't one, because we were inside a building that we'd turned into a sealed bunker.

While some of us were spraying the worms, other Hunters were shooting. Only the corpses covered in slimy tentacles were extra hard to kill. You could head-shoot a zombie all day and do nothing, since it was now basically the mava's puppet.

"Screw the walls! We need to back up to the drill." Sam was still on the hose behind me. "That's what we need to protect."

"These things will figure out we've got people on the roof. Want to bet they can't punch through?"

"Earl will handle it! Only chance we've got to kill this thing is the drill." He began backing up. "We protect the drill and the drillers!"

"Roger," I said, backing up with him.

A kifo worm came in from off-vector and I couldn't get the hose around fast enough. Then a stream of fire hit it.

"Holy water ain't the only thing they're afraid of!" Milo shouted as the kifo worm backed away, covered in napalm. The thrashing tossed burning jellied gasoline everywhere. I had to spray the stuff that caught. We had a lot of flammables in the building.

"Boss," Sam said, keying his radio. "Get the firemen to pull their trucks toward the drill rig."

"On it," Ray III radioed back. "Bullets ain't doing shit. All MHI on the ground floor. Grab hoses as teams. Fight these things with holy water! Milo, that means you. Quit spraying fire all over the place!"

The old man had been badly burned in Seattle, ruining half his face and one of his hands. He'd had a lot less liking for flamethrowers since then. And we had a more or less continuous stream of holy water as long as the pumps kept running. The various priests and assembled clergy were now *in* the tanks of holy water, blessing them and covering each other with the power of God as the kifo worms approached.

The worms, though, had a hard time getting to them. Being

burned by the power of God and Isaac Newton, they didn't have as much structural integrity and could only lift so far in the air. They were mostly crawling along the ground. And the entire area around the tanks was, at this point, covered in holy foam. Not to mention it probably had a "bad" radius, from their POV, that went out a ways.

"You!" Sam yelled as one of the firefighters ran past. "Get in the tank! It's holy water! They can't get you there!"

The guy, of course, totally ignored him and ran straight past one of the worms. A pseudopod flicked out and wrapped him up.

"Shit," Sam snarled.

I was playing the hose back and forth trying to keep them off of us, off the drillers, off the rig. It wasn't working.

Other teams were running hoses too. As a kifo approached, I found myself covered in foam.

"Watch where you're pointing that!"

"They won't touch you if you're covered," the Boss yelled from behind us. "Spray everybody who's not in the tanks!"

Well, most of the NOFD had either gotten in the tanks or were dead. Some of the drillers had been taken as well. That left…

I turned around and sprayed the old man and Milo right in the face.

"You're welcome," I yelled, then my feet slid out from under me.

It was both horrific and humorous. The foam was slippery as hell and it was getting everywhere. The kifo worms were starting to withdraw from the walls because it *was* everywhere. They couldn't lift themselves out of it and it was eating away at their blasphemous tissues, burning them with holy essence.

What was happening outside the warehouse was, arguably, worse than what was happening inside. New Orleans had been collecting more and more undead over the years, drawn by the field effect of the larval Old One. We'd killed them as fast as we found them, but it turned out there were lots of things we'd never known were in the New Orleans area. Those are not dead which sleeping lie and many of them had been gathering awaiting the arrival of their dark master.

Now they were all surfacing, shielded in slime, tethered to a baby dark god, and attacking the warehouse.

At a certain point it gets down to statistics. When MCB finally showed up, along with the National Guard, the Army, and every single other group that had somewhat been read in on the supernatural or could be trusted to keep their mouths shut, a count was made of everything that was now "fully" dead in the area of the warehouse. In many cases that involved counting limbs, dividing by four, and rounding up.

Undead were flooding in from all over the region and ignoring anything to get to the warehouse. Ghouls were running full tilt down I-10, wights were being hit by cars, getting back up and running away. Then there were all the rest. We didn't get too many vamps, and the ones we did were young, so apparently the mava didn't have the strength to enslave the strong willed. Yet. Keep in mind it was basically a baby.

They didn't all turn up at once or we'd never have stood a chance. But the firefight outside while we were fighting the kifo worms was getting pretty intense.

The truly fun part was that it wasn't just human undead. Try slime-covered zombified *cats* for size. They might have been road kill. They might have been previously buried pets. We never checked. And bats. And raccoons, possums. Dogs. Dog zombies!

What we hadn't noticed while we'd been spraying worms, was that we were getting fucking overrun.

We went from water, to fire, to guns and grenades. When they closed to hand-to-hand range, Mo No Ken slid out of its sheath. I quickly discovered that if I slashed through the tentacles shielding the undead, the ward stone would take care of the rest. I got hit with a lot of fragments and goo from exploding shamblers.

As they got closer, Sam had switched to bashing things with his 203 until he broke the plastic stock off over a wight's head. Looking around, he picked up Al Gordon's abandoned .45-70 lever action rifle and started in with that.

"This thing rocks," he said, crushing the skull of a ghoul dog.

"Yeah," I said, taking off a shambler's head. "As a gun it makes a great *club*!"

Milo's flamethrower was out. I picked up the quiescent fire hose. Then I noticed there was no pressure. "I need holy water!"

"One of them must have figured out how it worked," the Boss shouted. "Pump's dead."

We were in dire straights, deep shit, and doomed. The interior of the warehouse was ankle-deep flooded with once holy water, mava juice, the foam that resulted when they mixed, blood, guts, limbs and assorted body parts, floating kifo chunks, and sinking brass.

At the beginning of this memoir, I already wrote about those last few moments. Again, it sucked. I was about to go tell Saint Pete hello like I'd promised that weird exorcist I would. Oh yeah, and him...I keep my promises, won't write about how I saw him take down a kifo worm with nothing but a sword, but to reiterate: don't mess with a mystical holy warrior.

That's when a flaming portal opened in the floor, the Fey showed up, and everything got even weirder.

The Wild Hunt was terrible to behold. Armed with spears crackling with purple energy they were lightly armored and their Fey visages could be seen with the naked eye. Under the sodium lights of the warehouse, they were even worse to see than the other times I'd had to deal with them. They were massive, seven feet tall, gut-wrenchingly horrible to look at, their armor in all the colors of the rainbow. Their multilegged mounts were more like narrow beetles or spiders than real horses.

The Hunt tore into the undead with fury. Their spears tore into the mass of undead, blasting them with fairie fire. The blasts were more powerful than the 40mm rounds we'd been using. Zombies were blown apart. The dying kifo worms virtually disintegrated.

They slammed into the mass of undead, slaughtering them mercilessly and pressing them back to holes in the walls.

Suddenly a series of blasts came in on our position and I hit the deck as undead were blasted into constituent particles around me. My ears were ringing and I could barely see.

When I looked up, it was at one being I'd hoped to never see again in my life: Queen Keerla Rathiain Penelo Shalana.

A few years back I'd bound her and her court in a Harper's Challenge and then by a very in-depth and complicated contract. Fey had very long memories and they did *not* like to be bound.

"Truce?" I said from the foam-covered floor.

"Why do you think I'm here, you idiot?" she said, holding her hand out. Thank God she was in glamour in her usual business suit. Because there is ugly, and then there is "Fey-ugly."

From the look on the remaining half of Boss Shackleford's face, he wasn't sure to throw the grenade in his good hand at the Fey or not. They were scary as all get-out, but they hadn't attacked us, and the drill rig was once again clear of undead. "Friendlies?"

"Yes, sir! Hopefully. These are the ones I...met in Seattle."

"Very well then." He got on his radio. "Hey, Earl, if you see some weird Fey goings-on, don't shoot at them. They're Hand's acquaintances from Seattle."

"Okay," I said, struggling to get off the slippery floor. The Queen did not offer her hand. "Now I know I'm hallucinating. This is a dream as I'm dying, right?"

"I am here to keep an Old One from gaining a foothold in a world I occasionally happen to enjoy. I have other things to do than bandy words with an idiot," she said. "I'll leave that to my equally idiotic daughter."

And she vanished.

"Still hallucinating?" I said as Shallala strolled up to me. Thankfully, she was also in human form, with bib overalls with really big hair. She was wearing rubber Wellingtons which were faintly steaming from the touch of the holy foam on the floor.

"Grody. Any way you could, like, quit pointing that thing at me?" the fairy princess asked Father Ferguson, who was keeping his cross extended between them. "The White God is, like, totally judgy and bossy."

Father Ferguson lowered his cross slightly and looked at me. "Friends of yours?" he asked, with "that" tone. The "if you have friends like these we need to talk" tone.

"Sort of?" I said carefully. "Shallala...Uh, hi? Thought you were leaving the planet?"

"I called Mom after you left and, like, told her I totally *needed* to leave," Shallala said. "But she said, like, hell no or whatever, I was all, like 'bound' or something, so she, like, called up our court's Wild Hunt."

It wasn't a battle. It was a massacre. I realized then why the MCB was so terrified of Fey. I'd never really gotten it until that moment. My only previous experience was with binding them. Doing that made them seem weak. They're anything *but*.

Shallala might be a dingbat with a short attention span but she was a *scary* dingbat.

CHAPTER 23

I was up on the hammered battlements of the warehouse sur-
veying the damage. The battle was over. The streets were littered
with corpses and body parts—most of them scorched beyond
recognition. MHI had expended ammunition by the ton. It was
going to be a bitch to clean up.

It was apparent when the mava finally bit the dust. Kifo worms
were getting fewer and fewer but they were still trying to nose in
hours later. Then one by one they just collapsed and turned into
foul-smelling mush. The mud was coming up clean. Relatively
clean. There was still tons of dead larval Old One down there,
but now we were rinsing it out like a cyst. The evil bombard-
ment was gone. The goo was just goo. The sun was rising on a
new and improved, Old-One-free New Orleans.

Queen Shalana suddenly appeared before me.

The other Hunters on the roof didn't even seem to notice.
They were too tired. And she looked normal. The scary Fey had
long since disappeared. Only a few of us humans had interacted
with them at all.

"I'd apologize for arriving so late to the battle but I do not
apologize to humans."

"Better late than never," I said. "Despite our somewhat hostile
history, may I ask why?"

"The Old Ones are as much a threat to *us* as humans. We
were battling them before you apes first began chiseling your

251

252 *Larry Correia & John Ringo*

history onto stone tablets. Kill an Old One and the whole universe rejoices. It is always better to kill them while they are larvae. When my daughter told me of your warning, I summoned the Hunt. Then I had to ask for permission to intervene."

"Permission?"

"I have known your king for many years," Shalana said, smiling. "Since he was a mere actor in pictures. He was good. I like his films. Better than the trash they make these days."

She looked up, and a moment later I heard the sound of helicopters.

"His minions, on the other hand, were less than thrilled by their orders. I must go. There may be issues when they arrive. Their pet monster hates our kind and vice versa. By the way, according to my new agreement with your king, our previous contract has been nullified. My daughter's court is free to leave Seattle."

"I'm sure they will miss her."

She turned and looked at me with vertically pupilled purple eyes. "I hope we never encounter each other again, Bard, because unless it is for such a cause, be assured I will rip your soul from your body and torture it for a thousand years."

"Got it," I said. "Still have to say 'Thanks.'"

And she was gone.

"...if you think you can get away with causing a Class *Five* event *and* allying with the *Fey*, you are *wrong!*" Director Wagner himself had turned up.

"Well, my boys briefed you in on this, asshole, and you did diddly squat!" Boss Shackleford wasn't about to back down to no MCB borocrat asshole.

The MCB had shown up too late to participate in anything other than cleanup and cover-up. Franks was looking more pissed than usual. Probably because there wasn't anything left to kill. And he hated politics.

"Director Wagner," I said, nodding. "I take it you're planning on rounding us all up and putting us in docket for...alliance with the *Fey* was it?"

"You just butt out of this, Gardenier," Wagner said. He was normally considered very diplomatic and capable of lying right to your face with ease. Not at the moment.

"You might want to talk to the President about that first, unless you want the arrest warrant you serve on Camp David to be a surprise."

"*What?*" Wagner said.

Now that I'd said that, I sure hoped the Queen hadn't been yanking my chain.

"You had your chance to end a threat, Wagner, and you chickened out." The Boss shook his hook hand at the MCB director disapprovingly. "See that giant pile of body parts over yonder? That's all PUFF-applicable. Those big old chunks of translucent blubber floating by? PUFF-applicable. The slug god we're still dredging up? PUFF-applicable. And when New Orleans' outbreak rate drops like a stone next quarter? Stats don't lie, and the Select Committee loves it some stats. You cross my company right now you're cutting your own throat, and you know it!"

"Especially when it comes out there were MCB just sitting at the Marine base nearby waiting to see how it shook out, so they could swoop in at the last minute to blame us if it all went wrong." It was just a wild guess on my part, but from his reaction, I was right.

"How dare you!" Wagner said, grinding his teeth. "I'll have you—"

"Ah, ah, ah," I said, raising a finger and speaking very fast. "A hundred million dollars out of MCB's budget if you or Franks so much as lift a finger without probable cause."

Old Man Shackleford snorted at that one.

"And as for your assertion that we were allied with the Fey," I continued. "Where *is* your probable cause? *I* don't see any Fey here. If any just showed up on their own, what were we supposed to do about it? We were kind of busy. I'm sure that the good holy men present here will be hard pressed to say that *they* saw any Fey. How could you *suggest* any such *thing*, Director? All I see is an alliance of many different faiths—proof that America's constitutional guarantee of freedom of religion is working—allied to destroy an unholy and ancient evil your organization has been unable to find, much less battle, for what was it?"

"A really long time," the Boss answered. "And one of those witnesses you'll need to testify is the geologist who tried to warn you about the existence of this monster twenty years ago. Too bad y'all ignored him. That will make your bureau look brilliant."

"You do not want to go there with me," Wagner ground out.

"Going to have me beaten half to death?" I asked.

"Or possibly try to pull our charter?" the Boss said. "Look, Director, after this little debacle, I'll be amazed if you have a job. You might not have realized just how bad this was going to get, but you deliberately left it to the local authorities, and they used us. And it turned into, well, *this*. I've had about enough of your empty threats, and I'm too damned old to take a beating, so either start to arresting or get the hell out of my way."

For once, Wagner was speechless.

"That's right. It has dawned upon you just how badly you have done. You'd better cover your ass, boy, because it is about to start raining fire. Today, we're the heroes, and you're just the cleanup crew. So hop to it."

In case you're wondering: backhoes. Lots of backhoes. It was like moving a massive earth mound. Upside was in New Orleans you could easily find some grading contractors who were on MCB's list of people who were "read in."

The scariest thing about the whole cleanup was that we found out MCB has portable incinerators. I want to think that that's just because some bureaucrat was forward thinking and foresaw that there might be a huge undead outbreak someday. But the fact that the United States government has massive portable incinerators for bodies scares the shit out of me to this day.

The surviving drillers didn't have any problems with mava juice. There was a holy man or woman standing behind every one of them, praying over them and keeping the power of the mava back.

I hadn't wanted to get stuck with clean-up duty. I would have rather done like most of MHI, which was still in town, and been hunting straggler undead, who'd gotten animated by the mava but who hadn't made it here in time to get destroyed. But sadly, the Boss had taken a liking to me, and I had been drafted as his gopher. When Raymond Shackleford the Third declares you his assistant, you say "Thank You Sir May I Fetch You Another Coffee." I spent days working and sleeping in the mostly destroyed warehouse.

Third day after the battle, Special Agent Showalter showed up. Make that newly minted "Acting Director Showalter." He had been the first MCB agent I ever met and just as dickish as they tended to be. On the other hand, he took a slightly different tack than Wagner. Or at least played the game that way.

"It's New Orleans," Showalter said after shaking the old man's remaining hand. "No issues. People know *something* happened. From what I've gotten, you could hear the gunfire and explosions at the Marine base across the river. Then there were all the people who saw the undead making their way through the town. And the undead that are still roaming around in cemeteries shows *something* major happened. We'll put the truth in the *Truth Teller* and be done with it."

"We truly did everything we could to avoid witnesses or civilian casualties, Director." It was remarkable how much more diplomatic and polite the Boss was when he was dealing with an agent who was not yet proven to be a coward or an idiot.

"The safest thing would have been to not pick the fight at all, but I've already been informed by the committee such hypothetical might-have-beens are off the table. So, for all the efforts you took to keep this from public view, thank you. The timing, the warehouse, arranging the evacuation—that is all appreciated. Such consideration makes our job so much easier."

"You have no idea how rare those words are comin' from a man in your position."

We'd already gotten the word that Special Agent Campbell had had to be committed. The stress had finally gotten to him and he'd had a complete nervous breakdown. I had Remi send flowers.

"So no problems with our charter?" Ray III asked dubiously.

"The biggest problem is going to be the PUFF paperwork," Showalter said. "Who gets what credit? We've got streaks of terminated undead that seem to have occurred from air-drop napalm strikes. Assuming that was you," he added drily.

"Might have had some help." He wasn't about to admit to having our temporary allies lobbing magical faerie fire. "I won't go so far as to say *heavenly* help like all these fine religious folks."

"'The enemy of my enemy is my friend' only goes so far," Showalter said. "But in this case, if you happened to have had some help from entities which are normally PUFF-applicable, no harm no foul. Again, it got the job done and we *didn't*. A point that several very senior people made to me when I was appointed interim director. As to the friendly enemies? Everybody in this business has odd contacts." He looked at me as he said that.

"I know people," I said, trying to look innocent.

"In this case, I'd say that was a good thing," Showalter said. "In *this* case."

"I said I know people. Nothing about them *liking* me. There's some people, for values of people, I hope I *never* see again. Because they've explained to me what they're going to do to me and it isn't pretty."

"On the PUFF," Showalter said. "We're going to give MHI eighty percent of what's in the immediate area. The remaining twenty percent goes to a series of Swiss bank accounts I was handed by the President. I'm sure that's another Iran-Contra thing and going to shadowy black ops and not to beings we normally shoot on sight. You okay with that?"

"Sounds fair," Ray III said. "I'll just assume it's going to the guys flying the planes that dropped all that there napalm."

By that time MCB had pretty much taken over. They'd relieved the drillers and firemen along with an admonition not to talk. We gave all of them a huge bonus. Military guys who knew their way around a drill rig and fire pumps took over. Gordon and his surviving people left happily.

We'd been told that even with the mava dead all the "goop" would have to be pumped out and "rendered," that is mixed with holy water to remove the evil before it got dumped. That was left up to the local priests, because Father Madruga and his entourage had disappeared without even saying goodbye.

Madam Courtney and her people performed a big ceremony after the MCB bulldozed the warehouse. It was supposed to remove any curses and drive off any lingering evil spirits. Plus, she promised that it would increase the property's resale value.

She told me that the loas said now the circle was complete. Alpha and omega. What one brother had caused, the other had fixed. A curse had been broken.

I stuck around long enough to watch the last of the kifo worm mush get scraped up and dumped in an incinerator, then gratefully packed up and went home. I was looking forward to the hot tub.

✧　　　✧　　　✧

"Is sir in?" Remi asked.

Sir was definitely in lately. In the six weeks since the mava bit the dust, there had been no more than the occasional supernatural event. Outbreaks were down across the whole region. If we hadn't just made the biggest bank in PUFF history on the mava and the rest of the battle, MHI would be looking at a very bad quarter and so would I.

As it was, I was actually in the hot tub, alone for the first time in days, perusing tropical islands. I was thinking of buying one. The real cost wasn't the island, it was the upkeep. I had that covered as well.

The PUFF on a larval Old One was so record-setting, that Treasury was having to pay us in *installments*. The PUFF was so high that even though we had spent millions of dollars on construction, armament (Ray IV alone had fired over fifty LAWs and RPGs during the battle), and subcontractors (Al Gordon's team could all retire as millionaires and I think Neil Frandsen used his "consulting fee" to buy most of Yellowknife) there was still a huge profit left over.

I was given primary status since I was the one who'd tracked down the mava and gotten most of the plan into place.

I could afford an island.

It appeared my political problems were a thing of the past. Committee members were returning my calls again. The new interim MCB director wasn't being an asshole. I was so popular with the committee I could probably have sex with a Fey on the Capitol steps and get away with it. Not that I'd ever stick my dick in one of those. There were tentacles and stuff.

"Is it work?" I asked.

"It is," Remi said. "They vouchsafe that there is ..."

"You'd think with this town settled down that we'd be *done* with sobek," I said, looking through the scope at the fifty-foot bipedal crocodilian. I had him square in my sights but I hesitated. "Mr. Johnston?"

"What are you waiting for?" the Army engineer asked, furious.

"Any way you can think of to let it over the pumping station that *won't* damage things?"

"You nuts?" Sam Haven said. "You saw what that thing did the *last* time! I like Honeybear and all but I really don't want to have another low-speed, super-alligator chase across the city again."

"Crocodile," I corrected Sam, as I got up from out of the prone. "Look, these things magically appear every so often. I'm tired of them. I thought it must have something to do with the mava and they'd just go away, but obviously not. They *always* follow the same path. We'll get a helo and track it. If it gets out of the canal and threatens anything, I'll pop it. But I want to know where the damned thing is *going*. Maybe then we can get them to stop."

We had to get a crane while the thing continued to do damage to the levee. But Mr. Johnston agreed with the basic logic and we got it done.

Once down in the canal it stayed there. We'd arranged a Corps Huey instead of borrowing Mr. Aristide Lambert's Jet Ranger, and we trailed it down the canal.

It passed the Metairie Bridge without incident then just continued down the canal.

We'd arranged for SIU to block roads but people were coming out to watch the fifty-foot crocodile walk down the canal. And it just kept going. It wasn't bothering anyone if it wasn't bothered. People were taking pictures. It was New Orleans. MCB would just do a story in the *Truth Teller* and some badly retouched photos in the *Weekly World News*, and it would just be another "impossible" story out of New Orleans. Like the flying saucer that caused a zombie outbreak until it was destroyed by a meteor that was probably thrown by another alien race it was fighting. Possible alien fugitives were possibly on the loose in the New Orleans area, and people should be careful around cemeteries until they were all tracked down.

Aliens were the MCB's answer to everything now.

Then again: Fey.

The sobek wandered down past the New Orleans Country Club where golfers were gathering at the fence to watch it pass. Palmetto Street started paralleling the canal around there and you could tell the locals from the out-of-towners. The not-locals were taking one look and then driving away as fast as they could. The locals were getting out and watching. I saw one guy who must have been out grocery shopping toss a big chunk of meat to it. The sobek caught it in midair and seemed to nod as if to say "Thanks for the snack."

New Orleans. New York had Broadway. New Orleans had street theater and there wasn't much better street theater than a fifty-foot crocodile. I was waiting for the second line to start.

It continued south, crawling under bridges and under Airline Highway. I think some not-locals spotted it off the highway. But it wasn't bothering anyone. MCB's problem.

There were news choppers up by that time following it. They'd never be able to release the tape but they were, by God, going to get *that* shot. There was an FBI chopper up in New Orleans Parish. All of them were staying well back from us. MHI had this. They had to be wondering when we were going to take the shot—but would wonders never cease—they weren't interfering.

Just past Airline Highway it started looking like it was trying to find a way out. It kept scrabbling at the sides to the northeast. There was a small building and an open area that looked like a ball field. The building looked like a school or a daycare or something. Fortunately, there weren't any kids on the playground.

"Call SIU," I said over the intercom. "Tell them to get a car down there and make *damned sure* all those kids are inside. If it threatens the school, I'll take it, but I want to see where the damned thing is going."

"If it gets out, it could get up to the highway," Sam pointed out.

"I'll stop it if it does. Open up the doors."

The Huey had sliding doors. I mounted the Barrett and leaned in, following the croc in my scope. This would be easier than shooting frogs off the Superdome.

"Pilot, I need to be about a hundred feet lower for the right angle," I said over the intercom.

"We really need to be that close?" the pilot asked. He clearly wasn't happy being in the same state.

"You can back up from it, but I need a twenty-seven-degree entry angle on its head."

"Got it," the pilot said. "Can somebody check port to see if I'm running into anything?"

"Got it," Sam called. "Clear port and back on port."

"Clear starboard back," I said, looking over. I didn't want to hit a power line.

I tuned out the calls as the sobek, convinced it couldn't get out by the highway, headed further down the canal. SIU and state troopers had closed Palmetto for a couple of blocks down and were holding back traffic in the area. No innocents were in sight of the croc.

It finally managed to scramble out at the corner of the field where Monroe Street terminated at Palmetto. It made its way across Palmetto, which was elevated, down onto Monroe. Monroe was closed for a couple of blocks back but I wasn't going to let it get far. There was a major highway in threat, the school or whatever, houses. I wasn't going to let this one go on a rampage like the other.

The croc instead headed into the field, stopped, dropped onto its belly and started digging.

It dug for about fifteen minutes as we watched, pulling up the dirt with its stubby forelimbs and tossing it back with its back limbs.

It finally got to whatever it was it was looking for and stood up. It had what looked *exactly* like a pirate chest clutched in its claws.

Then it vanished.

One second there was a fifty-foot-tall bipedal crocodilian standing by a hole in the ground. The next moment there was a hole in the ground and some big-ass paw prints.

We never did figure out what the hell was in the chest. I've searched every record I could find. The closest I ever came to it was a vague reference to Jean Lafitte's treasure and something he found that he'd hidden because of the hoodoo.

But that was the last time a sobek was ever seen in New Orleans.

I missed another big PUFF bounty but it's not about the PUFF. It's about keeping people safe. New Orleans was never threatened by another sobek, and I call that a win.

EPILOGUE

About a month later Sam Haven and I got called to Cazador. I was ready to go. New Orleans is a great town when you're hunting monsters. Even if not. The aura of Hoodoo Squad was still on, probably more since we'd apparently ended the true danger of hoodoo. We were treated like kings. Plenty of fish in the New Orleans sea and they practically jumped in your boat. The food was good.

But it was also hot. Steamy hot. And I was getting as bored as I'd been at Sandals. There was less activity than *Seattle* in my day. Maybe a minor call-out once a week. It was a far cry from our wild, nonstop, full-moon monster fests. Oh, there are still monsters in New Orleans—don't let your guard down—but the ones that remain are far more interested in keeping their heads down.

Ray wouldn't say why the call but I had my own sources. Eastern Europe was heating up. Bad. An entire town had been wiped out by what amounted to a lycanthrope army.

"We're forming a team to head to Eastern Europe," Boss Shackleford told us, looking around the conference room.

I knew all the people in it.

Sam Haven, former SEAL and all around badass.

Milo Anderson, hippy goofy vicious monster killer.

Susan Shackleford, the baddest bitch in the valley, now freed enough from mommy duties to go earn some of that delicious PUFF money again.

Raymond Shackleford the Fourth, brilliant scion of a Monster Hunting family.

Earl Harbinger, the meanest and unquestionably toughest monster killer in the business.

And then there was me. Iron Hand. The top PUFF recipient in recent history *before* I was instrumental in killing an Old One.

"The place is getting overrun with vamps and werewolves and every other kind of boggle. NATO's formed a new group, the Organization for Supernatural Security Cooperation in Europe. US/Western-country PUFF bonuses and it's a virgin playing field."

Some of those Eastern European girls had been turning up in the strip clubs in New Orleans. If they all looked pretty much the same, I was on this like stink on a mava.

"Who's up for it?"

"Cowboy up," Sam said.

"Kill monsters," Milo chimed in.

"Get paid," Susan said.

"It's get *laid*, Susan," I said. "Get *laid*."

Milo just shook his head while the rest of the group laughed.

We were MHI's top Hunters. The monsters had better run at our very names. Eastern Europe was never going to be the same.

And neither was Monster Hunter International. Because we weren't all coming home.

AFTERWORD
by Earl Harbinger

Chad started to talk about our mission to Eastern Europe, but there was no sign of that record anywhere in the archives. I don't think he ever got the chance to write it.

That was the job where we lost Susan and everything changed. Her disappearance pushed Ray down a dark path that eventually ended in an event that ruined our company and cost ninety-seven Hunters their lives.

Including Oliver Chadwick Gardenier, the Iron Hand. Rest in peace, you magnificent bastard.

Milo brought these memoirs to me, saying I'd be the best one to finish the story.

I'm not sure that's the case. Me and Chad didn't always see eye to eye. But Milo is a persistent one, and when he gets an idea in his head, he doesn't ever let up. Milo was just a kid back in those days, and he still thinks of Chad like an older brother. If I didn't write this, Milo would bug me for the rest of his life. Which would be short. So here goes.

When I first met Chad Gardenier, he struck me as one of those know-it-alls who I figured would wash out of training. Sure, he was talented, smart, and a hard worker, but there are plenty of tough guys and smart guys who get killed in this business because they don't have the sense when to shut up and listen. Why would they need to? They were born knowing everything.

Chad had that too-clever-for-his-own-good trait in spades. If we don't catch those in time and get them straightened out or weeded out, the question isn't whether they'll get messed up or killed out in the world, but rather how many members of their team will get hurt in the process.

I wasn't much impressed to start. My background is straightforward, country, get shit done, and don't put on airs about it. Chad was too damned froo-froo for me. He was always dressing up. Tailored everything. These were the eighties. It was all about flash. He barely even mentioned things like the fancy dinner parties he'd hold at his place in New Orleans.

I'm a beer and steak kind of guy. Chad was caviar, raw fish, and then arguing over the quality of the wine list with the sommelier for thirty minutes. I don't even know if he liked wine, or if he just wanted everybody else at dinner to be impressed how much he knew about it.

But I'm getting ahead of myself. First impressions. He didn't strike me as a man who could go the distance. As much as Chad despised his parents, he'd grown up with snooty academics, so when given any opportunity to try and show off how smart he was, he'd take it. Boy couldn't help himself. He was that way from his newbie class, and it never really changed his entire career. Hell, on the night he died he was still lecturing party guests about some esoteric something or other so everyone would know how clever he was, like how he was the only guy in the world who had ever learned Yeti sign language or some shit.

Yet he'd been a Marine, and that inclined me to like him. We've hired a ton over the years. They tend to do pretty damned good as Hunters. He worked hard, and got to give him credit, the boy had a mind like a steel trap. In those days he was one of our sharpest, when it came to the supernatural probably as tuned in as Ray IV or Marty Hood. I suppose it says a lot about Chad's actual character about how he turned out in comparison to either of them.

Seattle: I hoped working for the Nelsons would help temper him. Maybe even teach him some wisdom and humility to go with those smarts. But instead he ended up almost getting our company in a war with the fucking yakuza of all things, and then made a bargain with a Fey court.

Every time I got a report, I was either tempted to fire his ass, or impressed that he'd pulled off some crazy stunt, and sometimes both simultaneously. The Nelsons loved him like a son. Still do to this day. Those two can't help but psychoanalyze everybody they meet. To them, Chad was a product of his environment. A genius overachiever, raised by an evil mother, a dirtbag father, and an abusive brother, who hid his smarts out of spite. Once he was free of them, and able to do what he wanted, of course he desired recognition from his peers. The Nelsons like to say all of us are the sum of our experiences.

I once asked the Nelsons how to fix him. They said there was no *fixing* people, there was just providing some guidance when possible, hoping for the best, and enjoying the adventure. That's not the kind of employee evaluation that fills a leader with joy. There's usually a fine line between cocky and confident. Chad didn't have a line. Only it ain't bragging if you can do it on demand.

He got the job done. He always got the job done.

Then New Orleans. I tell you, Hoodoo Squad saw some shit. They had more action in less time than just about any other team in MHI's history. Pipe hitters and party animals, those boys did *work*.

I hated New Orleans. I despised that town. It's pretty quiet now, thanks to the sacrifices of Hoodoo Squad, but for several years back in the eighties it was a constant thorn in our side. Anything that could go wrong, did.

I knew Chad blamed me for what happened to his team on Mardi Gras. He hated my guts for it. That's okay. Sometimes a man just needs someone to blame so he can get back to work.

Yet again, through all that blood and chaos, Chad still got the job done.

As many of you are aware, a couple years ago I got into a fight with the demon Rok'hasna'wrath, devourer of souls, reaper of worlds, and a bunch of other self-appointed titles that asshole wouldn't shut up about. Many of my memories were damaged or lost. I'm still trying to put some things back together. That said, I've still got enough left to know that Chad's versions of events sometimes diverge significantly from the way I remember them happening.

But, the whole bit about being blown to hell in Beirut, and being sent back to life, supposedly by Saint Peter, until he could fulfill some important mission from God? I didn't buy that the first time I heard it from him. Believe me, for the kind of men who end up in this line of work that sort of belief ain't particularly odd. There's plenty of tough sons a bitches who think they're destined for something great, until life busts them in the chops, and they either die badly, or get over their foolish notions.

Except I saw how Chad went out... So I believe it now.

You chose the right man for the job, Pete.

That Eastern European mission he started writing about at the end was a hard one. The thing about Monster Hunting—sometimes you do everything right, and people still die, while other times you do everything wrong, get lucky, and live. That time we did everything right. I put together the best team. We worked hard. We fought smart. We picked fights we could win and avoided the ones where we were at a disadvantage. We still got the rug pulled out from under us and it ruined everything.

By that time I can't say that I liked Chad, but I trusted him with my life. He still rubbed me the wrong way, yet I knew he was one of the best Hunters I had. The man could solve problems, and he could fight. He also could annoy the hell out of me, and cause more trouble than he was worth. Between him and Sam picking up on half the female population of every town and village we rolled through, or him and Milo annoying me with some crazy scheme, or him and Ray rocking the political boat agitating to get a Communist dictator overthrown, I can't say if he made my life easier or harder.

I've never written about how we lost Susan. I don't really want to. Someday, maybe. Chad didn't get to it here, and I'm a little glad for that.

In brief, we got outplayed. It wasn't until years later that I learned just how badly we'd been tricked back then. At the end of a battle, part of our team had broken off to chase down a weak and wounded vampire. I'd been with Sam and Milo. The pursuit had been Ray, Susan, and Chad's call. Only they ended up blowing up a castle, and Susan disappeared in the chaos.

It was like she'd vanished. We searched the wreckage for days, and after we'd given up hope that she was alive, we dragged the river, and explored miles of forest and catacombs. We searched for weeks and came up with nothing. Even I couldn't find her... and I'm decent at tracking.

The logical assumption was that her body had been eaten by one of the ghoul packs that infested the area. Those things consume bodies so thoroughly, that it's like they're scrubbed from the face of the earth, bones and all, leaving not a trace.

I'd never seen a man break as hard as Ray did then. We weren't finished there, but Ray was. He sank into a place so black that eventually it nearly doomed us all.

We had all loved Susan, and I know that Chad held himself to blame. He was never quite the same after that.

But he still got the rest of that job done. That's kind of the thing about Iron Hand. Some of us loved him, and some of us hated him, but when you needed a puzzle figured out, or you really needed something killed, he was the man to point at it.

Which was why the night of the Christmas Party, when it was do or die, just one chance to get it right, and I had to send somebody to do something that meant almost certain death, I picked Chad.

After Europe, most of us got back to work. Chad went up to the New York team. Manhattan in the nineties had a lot of monster activity. Part of that big "crime cleanup" was actually the city instituting some new Hunter-friendly policies that allowed us to be a little more proactive. He was one of my best troubleshooters... and trouble causers. It usually worked out.

It went pretty much how you expected. Manhattan had all that fancy culture Chad prided himself on appreciating, plenty of snooty politicians and professors to wow, and about a million single ladies. Chad got a penthouse and decorated it like he was a Japanese Hugh Hefner. He dragged along his poor butler Remi too. Now, that there was a dignified fella. I don't know how he put up with it.

One day Remi told me Chad went from having a different woman on his arm for every event, to just the same one, over and over. Apparently he'd finally found a woman he couldn't drive off. Well, stranger things have happened.

Chad damaged his sword in New York. The man was distraught. I didn't get it. I never understood any of that mystical bushido nonsense. I appreciate quality weapons as much as the next Hunter, but when I buy knives I always order some spares, because you're going to lose or break them. They're just steel tools.

Not for him. Chad was all into that soul-of-the-sword mystique, and he'd talk your ear off about it. I think the idea of having to retire Mo No Ken hit him like the death of a teammate.

The last time I talked to Chad on the phone was to give him what I thought at the time was good news. Ray went nuts when Susan died, simple as that. All his friends had been worried about him ever since—Milo especially. I know Chad had visited a few times over the intervening years, trying to get through to Ray, to bring him out of his funk. He'd always left frustrated.

But the reason I called was to tell Chad that it looked like Ray was finally shaking off his depression. Chad had been on that mission, he deserved the update. Ray was getting out, even working again. He even wanted to put together something big to celebrate the company's one hundredth birthday. I thought it sounded like a waste of time, but everybody else thought it was a great idea, especially Ray and Susan's kids.

It was going to be the biggest celebration in company history, I told him. Everybody was invited. I figured Chad would appreciate it because this sort of thing was right up his alley.

MHI was going to throw a Christmas party.

Everybody had a real nice time, up until when the killing started.

I had spent a lot of money. Big crowd, Hunters brought spouses and dates. All our retirees had been invited too. We rented this resort place on the Gulf that Ray had picked out. He told me that him and Susan had visited there, and it had been real nice. He lied right to my face and I didn't know any better. He'd never been there. He wanted that spot because it was on sacred land, a conflux of power, something that a crazy person would pick out as the ideal spot for a ritual.

Even the band knew who they were playing for, what we did for a living, and the kinds of things we did it to. The caterers and bartenders were all people who were in the know. They brought in food and booze by the truckload.

This was when MHI was at its largest, so even with all the Hunters busy working a job, we still had a few hundred people show up. Lots of old friends reunited, buddies who'd fought together, experienced folks who hadn't seen each other since training, and a bunch of newbies trying to fit in and sound tough. I knew them all, and thinking about the ones we lost there still hurts.

But this memoir is about one in particular.

Obviously, Chad arrived fashionably late, in a tux, with what I first thought was a supermodel on his arm, and I shit you not, wearing his fucking samurai sword. I supposed it was his fashion accessory and conversation starter. Why the hell not? It was a Monster Hunter party. Have fun.

I made some polite conversation with Chad. Small talk I guess they'd call it. We still weren't what anyone would call friends. But when I got close I got a better take on his girlfriend. The nose knows. Me and her needed to have a word, so I gave her a knowing look, and then went to have a smoke. A minute later she excused herself, ditched her boyfriend, and came outside to talk with me alone. Even the parking lot had a good view of the ocean.

"I'm kind of surprised, seeing one of your kind show your pretty face here," I told her.

"I've earned my PUFF exemption."

"You got your tag on you?"

"I'll show you mine if you show me yours."

"Lady, there's a couple hundred Hunters here who'd cap you for the bounty, then go back to drinking without a second thought."

"They could try, but it wouldn't be necessary." Then she showed me her silver PUFF-exemption tag. From the number etched on it, I guessed the issue date would have been around 1945 or so. "I did my time."

"Does Chad know what you really are?"

"No. I'd rather keep it that way. I love him."

I was starting to like this one. "Just don't break his heart."

"I don't think any woman could."

"We both know you ain't no ordinary woman."

The party went on for hours, everybody having a good old time.

Many of you know this story. A few of you who read this were probably there.

There was a commotion on the dance floor. I was across the hall, but I saw that it was Ray, up to something. When I heard him speak it was so loud that my first thought was that he'd gotten a microphone, and maybe he was going to make an announcement or something. Only he was staggering around, unnatural, and the words weren't right. He was speaking some weird language.

In these memoirs, when Chad writes about all those languages he knew, that was no bullshit. He really had the gift of tongues. When Ray started speaking, I saw Chad leap up and look in that direction, with a look on his face like *what the hell did you say?* That's probably because he was the only man there who recognized the ancient words.

"Somebody stop him!" But by the time Chad shouted that, it was too late.

Later on we found out the spell was supposed to bring Susan back from the dead. I don't know what Ray thought would happen, like after he made a blood pact circle in the middle of a dance floor in front of the whole company, she'd rise up through it like some glowing angel and everybody would cheer. Except poor delusional Ray had been conned, suckered by a necromancer who'd been playing the long game. That wasn't what that spell did at all.

The circle beneath Ray's feet vanished and he dropped right through into nothing. There was a crack of thunder and a rush of air. The closest people on the dance floor got swept off their feet. And then it was like thousands of claws clicking, and monsters came pouring out of the hole. It was so fast, and there was so many, the dance floor erupted like a volcano, only instead of lava . . . bodies.

We've fought these things a couple times since, but this was our first encounter. They're sort of man-shaped, but mostly buglike, with shells like crabs, claws and teeth that can shred a man to the bone in a flash. They're colorful bastards, bright orange, and red, purples. Too many eyes, too many joints, all so damned alien that the sight of them shakes even the hardest Hunter in battle.

And a horde of them came swarming out.

This was sudden violence. We weren't ready to fight, nobody was geared up, most of us were drunk, and then out of nowhere we were waist-deep in unexpected razor-sharp insect monsters, tearing us to pieces.

It only took a heartbeat or two, but God bless MHI, we reacted.

Guns came out. Tables were flipped for cover. Wounded and innocents were dragged out of the way. And my people went to town.

The hole just kept pumping out monsters like a chest wound leaking blood. I was killing things and shouting orders in between. Hunters ran for their cars and came back with heavier weapons. Those barely made a dent. All around, our people were dying.

Of all the memories that son of a bitch, Rocky, could rip from my mind, oh why did he have to leave this one so perfectly clear?

Before I say something about how Chad died, there's one brief shining moment that shows exactly how that man lived.

Ray the Younger got ripped limb from limb. His sister Julie, just a young woman then, she jumped in swinging a table leg, clubbing down monsters, refusing to abandon her dead brother's side, screaming like a berserker. The Shackleford kids had turned out to support their dad, and he'd condemned them to hell. Julie was surrounded. She was going to die and I couldn't get there in time. But thank God, Iron Hand did.

When the Shackleford kids were little, they'd taken a liking to him, and he was so protective of them they had even called him Uncle Chad. Well, he earned that title that night. He'd already run his pistol dry. Most of us had by then. But he'd pulled out that damaged sword and gone in swinging, throwing himself right into the middle of the demons and hacking through shells and into arms and legs. He shoved Julie away from her brother and steered her out of there, cutting down monsters the whole way.

To this day, I've never really talked to Julie much about that night. I don't know if she even knows it was Uncle Chad who saved her life.

By a miracle, we got organized. We held that ground, that dance floor turned into a killing field. We established choke points, locked down the halls, and then had to deal with monsters clawing their way through the floors and ceiling. I can't say how we knew, instinct maybe, just being human in the face of something so *not*, but however we got it, all of us had the understanding that there was no retreat. It was hold now or lose forever.

We found out why when *something* pushed against the rift.

The floor lifted like a bubble. A different reality mingled with our own. I can't really explain what it was we saw through that hole. The thing beneath New Orleans had been one of their babies. This was a father. Of those of us who lived, some who saw through to the other side quit, a couple went crazy and wound up at Appleton. Yet that thing, that God-awful cursed thing, unless we did something, it was coming through.

Only for a brief instant, across a room full of demons, I saw that Ray Shackleford was still inside the rift. Ray was the key. He'd started this. My only hope was that pulling him out would end it.

Many of you know the story that I somehow made it into the

gate, and into the other dimension, grabbed Ray, dragged him out, and that closed it.

This is about the somehow.

Problem being, I couldn't get through. There was just too much distance and too many demons between us. I needed to get to the other side before it was too late. I needed somebody to punch through, to create a gap I could use. But looking at that wall of claws and spines, whoever I sent was as good as dead.

I spotted Chad, holding back monsters with a bent sword. His girlfriend was hiding behind him, wounded, with a spine piercing her side, but she'd be fine. It's tough to put down her kind.

I walked up and said, "Iron Hand. Make me a hole."

He understood. When hell had come to town, when there wasn't anyone else we could depend upon, I knew he was the one person who could and would make that hole. Without fear. Without hesitation. Even Milo or Sam might have hesitated.

Not Iron Hand.

With that damaged katana, he stopped trying to hold the line, and like the Marine he was to the core, he charged the enemy. He knew he was going to die, horribly, painfully. He didn't let that worry him. He laid into those demons like there was no tomorrow, hacking them down faster than they could kill him.

He got cut, stabbed, bit, but he just kept going. I'm wondering now, at the end, with the blood loss and the poison and the pain...during that did he realize and know that this was what he had been sent back to the world of the living for?

It was his perfect warrior moment. Maybe there was something to all that soul-of-the-sword stuff of his after all.

Chad kept cutting and moving. It was just the two of us in a sea of monsters. I followed in his wake, smashing down anything that got close, until the portal was near enough for me to make my move. We had to climb over piles of corpses. A claw ripped out one of Chad's eyes. Another sliced through his abdomen and spilled his guts, but Chad still kept fighting. He was covered in blood, human red and demonic orange. He lost a hand, but kept using his sword with the other. Then Mo No Ken broke over the head of a demon. In a flash, they were all over him, biting and tearing.

And Chad turned to me as the monsters sliced his flesh to ribbons and tore him into to pieces...and he smiled.

Because he was on the way back to his precious Green Lands.

So as Chad traveled to one world, I leapt through the gate into another.

I will never write of the horrors I saw on the other side.

There was still a whole lot of killing to do. While it seemed like an eternity to me there, only a minute or two passed on Earth. When I came out of the hole, carrying Ray, the spell was broken. The gate slammed shut behind us. The room returned to normal, except now it was torn apart, covered in bodies, and the resort was burning down around us.

If you are reading this, you know the rest. We evacuated. MCB rolled in and dropped the hammer on us. The place burned for days with an unnatural hellfire, but if we hadn't stopped that breach, it would be the whole world burning.

One last thing I remember, as I was there on the beach, counting bodies to the rising sun, I noticed the address on the front gate of the resort for the first time.

57 Gulf View.

Like I said before, good call, Saint Pete.

Iron Hand was one of the toughest Hunters it has ever been my honor to have known. Oliver Chadwick Gardenier would go in against overwhelming odds, the nastiest, toughest, scariest supernatural creatures on the face of the planet and rip them a new asshole.

Iron Hand died a hero to the core.

And his daughter is pretty badass, too.

Earl Harbinger
Monster Hunter International
Cazador, Alabama